THE LONG KILL

Reginald Hill

CHIVERS PRESS
BATH

First published 1986
by
Methuen
under the author's pseudonym Patrick Ruell
This Large Print edition published by
Chivers Press
by arrangement with
HarperCollins Publishers
2000

ISBN 0 7540 2203 X

British Library Cataloguing in Publication Data available

Printed and bound in Great Britain by
REDWOOD BOOKS, Trowbridge, Wiltshire

I was a fell destroyer . . .
. . . and when the deed was done
I heard among the solitary hills
Low breathings coming after me
Of undistinguishable motion, steps
Almost as silent as the turf they trod.

CHAPTER ONE

Jaysmith was a firm advocate of the cerebral approach.

He always shot at the head.

The head he was shooting at this bright autumn morning was a noble one even when viewed through an Adjustable Ranging Telescope at 1,250 metres. An aureole of near-white hair surrounded a tanned leathery face in which the crinkles of humour seemed at least to equal the furrows of care. It was the head of an ageing man, seventy at a guess, who must surely now be reckoning that he was going to be allowed to slip naturally from life in the fullness of his years. Another minute would teach him the error of such confidence, and also the error of whatever lust for power, pleasure, or political change, had put him at the end of Jaysmith's rifle.

Still, there were worse ways to die than suddenly, in your garden, looking across the peaceful fields of St-John's-in-the-Vale to the swell of the eastern fells, drinking a cup of coffee and feeling the warmth of a September sun on your November skin.

The old man lit another Caporal. He was practically a chain smoker. This, thought Jaysmith, was the last link in his chain. He began to make his final checks.

He had worked out five possible lines of fire on the os 1:25,000 sheet before leaving London. Two of them he had discarded on his first slow drive along the valley the previous Sunday. Two more had failed his strict on-the-ground examination. The last was the longest, but that didn't bother him. He preferred the long kill, the longer the better. And with his equipment, his meticulous preparation and, above all, his accuracy, distance had never posed any difficulty. That was why he was the best.

He had till Sunday morning to make the target. It was only Thursday now, but there was no reason to delay. In fact, with the weather so perfect there was every reason to go ahead. He stretched his muscles systematically and began to quarter the ground below him with his Zeiss binoculars.

He was squatting on a lichened rock in a steep gill cutting down a rocky outcrop which his map told him was called Wanthwaite Crags. Eight hundred feet above him was the fell summit called Clough Head. Fears that the fine weather would crowd it with walkers had proved unfounded. It was clearly not a fashionable top. He had checked all possible approaches from the east, south and north before descending. The only signs of life had been the nodding head of a grazing sheep and the slow flap of a raven's wings. Now he looked westward. A car moved slowly along the valley road. A tractor buzzed purposefully across a stubble field half a mile away. Nothing else. In any case, even in this stillness the Sionics Noise Suppressor on his M21 would scatter the sound of his shot untraceably.

He drew in a long deep breath and let it out slowly. St John's Beck winding through the valley below was a ribbon of glass. The trees in the garden of the house called Naddle Foot were still as a painting. The moment was perfect.

He squeezed the trigger.

2

The bullet missed. It passed close enough to the old man's ear for him to flap his Caporal at a buzzing fly. Then it buried itself deep in the rich earth of the upper level of the tiered garden.

Jaysmith sat utterly still. There were many possible explanations. A gust of wind along the channel of the beck; a slight change of atmospheric pressure; an imperfection in the bullet; at this range any one of these could translate itself into several inches at journey's end.

Yes, there were many possible explanations. But only one cause.

Gently he massaged his temples and blinked his right eye rapidly a couple of times. It focused perfectly on the M21 as he began to dismantle it with practised ease. But perfect focusing for a job he could have done in pitch blackness was not enough. There was a weakness there. He had suspected it two targets ago when he had shot the Austrian. And last time out he had been almost certain. It had been a perfect shot in the eyes of the world. Only Jaysmith knew that as he squeezed the trigger, the Chinaman had raised his teacup and bowed his head into the path of the bullet.

Two weeks ago he had paid a Harley Street optician an exorbitant fee to put a clinical label on it. It was not a condition which could be in the least detrimental to any normal activity, the man had assured him. He should have retired then, at once, without thought. But this target had already come up, unusually soon after the Chinaman, and marked ultra-urgent. Something had made him reluctant to refuse it. Loyalty to Jacob, perhaps. Or professional pride. *Professional pride!* Amateurish stupidity was what Jacob would call it.

3

He packed the sections of the dismantled rifle in the internal pouches of his specially constructed rucksack. Now he was just a fellwalker again. With athletic ease he climbed up the steep gully to the top of the crags. Here he paused and glanced back across the valley. Without the A.R.T. the house was just a dark red monopoly token set on green baize. The reprieved man in the garden was completely invisible. He didn't even know his name. Jacob never provided more than was necessary for a target. In this case it had been a head-and-shoulders photograph of the man, the OS sheet NY 32 with the house called Naddle Foot ringed in red, and a deadline.

Plus of course an order for twenty-five thousand pounds paid into his Zurich account.

That would have to be returned. A pity; but there was plenty left for his retirement.

Retirement! At forty-three. Statistically he had just become another unit in the unemployment figures.

The thought amused him and he let out a snort of spontaneous laughter that would have surprised the few people who knew him at the middle distance which was as close as he ever permitted. But there was no one here to take notice except the grazing sheep and the indifferent raven.

His long economical stride took him swiftly across the sun-blanched grass of the shallow saddle between Clough Head and Calfhow Pike. Now he followed the tumbling path of a long beck, a strange exhilaration making him take the descent faster than was really safe, and by the time he reached the old coach road which runs from St-John's-in-the-Vale across to the next valley of

4

Matterdale, he was panting as much from this inexplicable excitement as the exertion. Slowing to a more sedate but still deceptively fast pace, he moved eastwards along the old coach road to where he'd left his BMW parked outside the village of Dockray.

Even at his rapid pace, and mostly downhill, it was still over an hour since he had aborted the target. Normally he preferred more rapid access to his car, but in this case his best protection after the event had been to blend into the landscape as an ordinary walker. Now there was no event to be after. For all that it was still with some relief that he dropped the rucksack into the hidden compartment beneath a false panel in the BMW's boot. An identical rucksack containing conventional walking gear lay in the boot. These isolated country areas were full of sharp eyes. And ears too.

He had a phone call to make and he decided to make it from the nearby village instead of waiting till he got back to his hotel. Security apart, he felt eager to get it over with. It was the first admission of failure he had ever made. The best that could be said for him was that he had made his error with time to spare and he had not alerted the target. But it was not just his sense of responsibility which urged him to haste. He was suddenly afraid that if he waited till he got back to the hotel, he might put off the moment even further. And that after a bottle of wine and a good meal, he might persuade himself it had been a trick of the wind after all.

He went into the public phone box and dialled a London number. A woman's voice answered, bright and breezy.

5

'Hello there! Enid here. Jacob and I are out just now but we'll be back soon. Leave your message after the tone and we'll be in touch as soon as ever we can. 'Bye!'

He waited then said, 'Jaysmith. Tell Jacob I can't make the deal. There'll be a refund, of course.'

He contemplated adding, 'Less expenses,' but dismissed the idea as a small, unnecessary meanness. Let the parting be complete and painless.

Gently he replaced the receiver and stepped out into the golden September air. He drew in a long deep breath and let it out slowly. It tasted marvellous. For the first time in twenty years he felt totally relaxed and free.

CHAPTER TWO

The dangers of Jaysmith's new sense of relaxation became apparent when he entered the hotel bar for a pre-dinner drink that evening.

'Evening, Mr Hutton. Any luck today?' called Philip Parker, the Crag Hotel's owner-manager, and it took Jaysmith a moment that could have been significant to a practised observer to react to the name.

Pseudonyms and cover stories might now be totally irrelevant but they could not just be shed at will. At the Crag he was William Hutton, businessman; and in conversation with Parker he had let it slip that, as well as the fellwalking, he was on the lookout for a house or cottage to purchase. It was those sharp country eyes again; he wanted an

6

excuse to be seen anywhere, walking or driving, during his stay.

'No,' he said, slipping onto a bar stool and accepting the dry sherry which Parker poured him. 'No luck at all. But I enjoyed my walk.'

'Oh good. The weather's marvellous, isn't it? Excuse me.'

Parker went off to the side hatch of the bar where one of the girls from the dining room was waiting with a drinks order. Parker's quietly efficient wife, Doris, looked after the kitchen and dining room, while he exuded bonhomie in the bar and at reception. He was a rotund, breezy man in his early fifties, a redundant sales executive who'd sunk his severance money into the small hotel five years earlier and, as he was willing to explain to anyone willing to listen, had not yet seen any cause to regret it. In fact his enthusiasm for the Lake District was so evangelical that Jaysmith had soon regretted the intended subtlety of his cover story. From the start, Parker had taken an embarrassingly close interest in his alleged house-hunting and now, the dining room order dealt with, he returned to the topic.

'So no luck then,' he said.

'No,' said Jaysmith. 'The market seems pretty dead. In fact, with the weekend coming up, I think I've exhausted all the possibilities, so I'll check out tomorrow.'

Parker looked so taken aback that Jaysmith felt constrained to add, 'I'll pay for tomorrow night, of course.'

He had booked in till Saturday. If he'd made his target he'd have stayed the full week in order not to excite comment, but now there was no point.

7

'Oh no, it's not that,' said Parker, slightly indignant. 'It's just that I heard today that there's likely to be just the house you're looking for coming on the market in the next couple of days. It's called Rigg Cottage and it's just outside the village, up the bank on the road towards Loughrigg. It belongs to an old lady called Miss Wilson who's finding the long haul up the hill more and more difficult. Also it's really too big for her with the garden and all. So she's thinking of moving down into the village. There's an old cottage become vacant. Semi-detached and her best friend occupies the next-door cottage. Actually the vacant one belonged to Miss Craik, another old friend, who died a couple of weeks back and the family had always promised to give Miss Wilson first refusal.'

He paused for breath and Jaysmith regarded him quizzically.

'Your channels of information must be first-rate, Mr Parker,' he said with hint of mockery.

Parker grinned and glanced conspiratorially towards the dining room. Lowering his voice he said, 'To tell the truth, it's Doris who told me all this. She's quite chummy with Mrs Blacklock, the old lady in the other semi, and she passed it on, in strict confidence, of course. Like I'm doing to you.'

'Of course,' said Jaysmith.

'Which is why there's nothing to be done till Miss Wilson makes up her mind. But when she does, if I know her, she'll want everything settled in five minutes which is why it's a pity you'll not be on the spot.'

'Yes, isn't it?' said Jaysmith, exuding regret as he moved fully into his William Hutton role. 'A real

8

pity.'

At dinner, he ordered a full bottle of Chablis instead of his usual half and settled to a mellow contemplation of the limitless joys of retirement.

O what a world of profit and delight . . . the words drifted into his mind and he sought their source. It wasn't altogether apt. They were from Marlow's *Dr Faustus* whose world of profit and delight had been purchased by selling his soul. Or perhaps the words were too apt. He pushed that thought away and concentrated on working out why he should know the quotation. Oriental Languages had been his subject, not English literature, but now he recalled that he'd once acted in the play at university; or rather not himself, but that incredibly, hazily distant young man whose name was now as vague as all those he had since inscribed on hotel registers in his career as Jaysmith. And he hadn't been Faustus either. An ostler, that's what he'd been. A grasping gull made a fool of by magic.

Shaking the memory away, he returned to the future. He could go anywhere, do anything. Tomorrow, back to his London flat. Next, the Continent. Italy to start with; a villa in Tuscany till autumn died. Then on to the Med, Greece, North Africa, always south, keeping abreast of the retreating sun.

The prospect filled him with surprisingly little enthusiasm. It was odd, like looking at a beautiful, naked and available woman without feeling excited.

'Everything all right, Mr Hutton?' said Parker, doing his end-of-dinner mine-host round.

'Fine,' said Jaysmith. 'Sit down and have a drop of Chablis.'

'That's kind.'

He filled a glass for the hotel owner and emptied the remaining drops into his own. He realized with amused interest another effect of his new relaxed state. A couple of sherries and the best part of a bottle of wine had left him feeling slightly drunk.

'Tell me,' he said. 'When you were made redundant, did you know at once what you wanted to do?'

'Far from it, old boy,' replied Parker, delighted to be invited to explore a favourite topic. 'Best thing that ever happened to me, I see it now. But at the time, I was simply shattered.'

'And you'd never thought of living up here and running a hotel?'

'Never.'

'So what happened?'

'I more or less sat with my head in my hands for three or four weeks, then one morning I got up and knew what I was going to do.'

'You knew that you were going to buy a hotel in the Lake District?'

'Not exactly. But I knew I was never going to work for anyone but myself again. I was absolutely certain about that!'

Jaysmith felt let down. Hoping for some sort of dramatic revelation, instead he was hearing about a conventional revolt against the boss-servant relationship.

Nevertheless the idea of taking time to adjust, of letting things ripen at their own speed, was not without its appeal. But where to let the ripening process take place? Not London, that was certain. Whatever residual pressures might remain from his old life were centred on London.

The answer was absurdly obvious but he did not reach it by any kind of open-cast logic. Instead, after a couple of soporific brandies in the bar, he heard himself saying to Parker, 'I've been thinking. There's really no desperate need for me to be off in the morning. In fact, if that old lady's not going to make up her mind for a few days, I can easily hang on into next week, if my room's going to be vacant, that is.'

Parker smiled with triumphant delight.

'We'll be glad to have you,' he said fulsomely.

Jaysmith did not return the smile. Faintly surprised, he was still trying to work out whose voice he had just heard speaking. It wasn't Jaysmith's, certainly. And it hadn't even sounded like William Hutton's.

No, it had been both more familiar and more distant, like the voice of a dead loved one conjured up by a medium at a seance. And then it came to him that in some odd, ghostly fashion, the voice he had heard belonged to that naively hopeful, irretrievably remote young man who had once played the foolish ostler in *Dr Faustus*.

CHAPTER THREE

Summer was dying like a lady this year. Leaves flushed gently from olive to ochre with no savage assault of gale to rip them down; bracken singed at the edges and heather burned purple with no landscape-blackening downpour to dampen the glow. The locals assured Jaysmith, not without nostalgic pride, that it was not always thus.

11

Jaysmith took their word for it. Though he had presented William Hutton as a long-time lover of the Lake District, his only real previous acquaintance had been as a small boy on a day trip to Windermere with his mother and stepfather, who had stared indifferently at the mountains and lake, explored the souvenir shops, eaten ice cream and fish and chips, and left him in the coach with a packet of crisps at each of the many pub-stops on the sixty-mile journey back to Blackburn in Lancashire.

His mother had died when he was fifteen. His stepfather, to do him credit, had supported him through the loss and the next couple of years at school till he got the exam results needed to take him to university. But first had come National Service. After basic training he had been posted to Hong Kong. He went home on embarkation leave, and the night before his departure his stepfather had told him apologetically but firmly that his stepbrother, four years his senior, was getting married and coming to live in the family home. His wife-to-be was pregnant. The strains this would put on the limited accommodation made it sensible for him to think from now on of making arrangements to look after himself.

He had never been back to Blackburn since that day.

His first taste of the East had brought balm to his pain. From the very moment its first rich warm exotic scents came drifting over the sea, he was fascinated. He had been planning to read French and German at university, but within a couple of months of reaching Hong Kong, he was writing to ask if he could transfer courses to the School of

Oriental Languages. The facility with which he learned Chinese made him a highly valued member of his unit, but it was another talent which the Army spotted and nurtured that won him all those privileges and comforts a regiment bestows on those that bring it honour. He turned out to be a natural marksman capable of winning trophies at the highest level, and thus rapidly promoted to sergeant, well out of the way of any parades, fatigues or guard duties which might dull his eye.

For his part, he enjoyed his unsuspected excellence, and even let his enjoyment spill over into civilian life, becoming a prominent member of his university shooting team. But he never dreamt that this was a talent with any commercial value. It had taken fate at its most unpredictably tragic to nudge him onto that path.

And now it had taken a fractional weakening of the right eye to nudge him off it.

For the next three days he put past and future out of his mind and set out to turn his pretended intimacy with the fells into fact. A need to be fit and the demands of his job had taken him into some of the roughest terrain in the world. He was expert both practically and with maps. But hitherto his expertise had been focused on one thing only— the job in hand. Landscape to him was considered solely in terms of best approach, best hide, best line of fire, best escape. Here in the Lake District for the first time in two decades he went exploring simply in search of delight. He did not have far to seek. Eschewing guide books in his desire for personal discovery, he spent the days in long high walks, armed only with map and compass. Any feeling of condescension for this somewhat narrow area of rather lowly mountains soon disappeared. The physical demands were great; he never had to look far for the exhilaration of danger; and whether he was standing windblown on the bald head of Gable with the stark wildness of Wasdale stretching below, or descending from the gentle swell of Silver Howe in the gathering dusk towards the sun-gilt shield of Grasmere which at the end of a long day felt very like home, he was ravished by the sheer beauty of it all.

Small the Lake District might be, but three days' exploration was scarcely enough to scratch the surface of its great variety and when Parker greeted him on Sunday evening with the excited news, 'She's made up her mind! Miss Wilson. She's definitely going. I can arrange for you to see Rigg Cottage tomorrow!' Jaysmith felt surprisingly put out.

He had what looked like a perfectly splendid walk mapped out for Monday and it was most irritating to be forced to postpone it for what was now an unnecessary piece of role-playing.

Doris Parker who was standing alongside her husband sensed his hesitation. She was a pleasant, calm, down-to-earth woman who was used to coping with her husband's enthusiasms.

'Don't take any notice of Philip's hard sell, Mr Hutton,' she said. 'There's no need to look at Rigg Cottage unless and until you want to. I only heard at church tonight that Miss Wilson is definitely selling.'

'But the whole point is for Mr Hutton to get in quick before it comes on the open market,' protested Parker.

'It might be worthwhile,' conceded his wife.

'She'll certainly not be happy about paying an agent's commission. But it's up to Mr Hutton if he wants to see it, dear.'

Her broad-set grey eyes fixed speculatively on Jaysmith and he smiled at her and said, 'Of course I'd like to, if you can arrange it. I'm really very grateful.'

Triumphantly Parker went to the telephone and returned a few minutes later with the news that eleven o'clock the following morning would suit Miss Wilson very well.

Jaysmith nodded his agreement. He'd have preferred to get the tedious business out of the way even sooner, but at least he would have the whole afternoon for the mountains. In any case, he could stay as long as he liked. The mountains weren't going anywhere without him!

*   *   *

The next morning he used his unexpected post-breakfast period of non-activity to read the newspapers in detail. There was no reference to any violent death in St-John's-in-the-Vale and there had been nothing on the local TV and radio news either. Presumably Jacob had not been able to make new arrangements before the deadline elapsed. That would not please him.

He put the thought out of his mind and drove up the winding road out of the village to keep his appointment.

Miss Wilson was curiously almost exactly as he had pictured her. Anything between seventy and ninety, she had snow-white hair and clear blue eyes in a cider-apple face. But any impression of gentle

15

cosiness was soon dissipated. She carried her five feet three inches as straight as a guardsman, albeit with some help from a stick, and when she spoke it was in a clipped, brusque, no-nonsense tone.

'I'd not be moving from here if it wasn't for this leg,' she informed him sternly, as if he had hinted suspicion of some less creditable motive. 'Now the place is getting too big for me, the garden's taking over, and the hill's too steep. Not that I can't climb it, but it takes me twice as long as it once did, and me mind's back here already doing me jobs while me body's still halfway up the bank, and there's nowt so ageing as always letting your mind race on ahead of itself.'

Politely Jaysmith agreed, which seemed to surprise her, not because she anticipated disagreement but because she could see no need for a mere man to affirm that she spoke plain truth.

She proved remarkably unsentimental about Rigg Cottage and talked about it as if it were already settled that he would buy.

'The sitting room fire smokes in an east wind,' she said. 'I've been meaning to get it fixed these thirty years. That'll be your job now.'

She sounded almost gleeful.

It occurred to Jaysmith that this was a house whose faults could be freely pointed out because its more than compensatory attractions advertised themselves. Built of grey-green Lakeland slate, it stood foursquare to the east, as simple and appealing as a child's drawing. The sloping garden which overlooked the lake was full of shrubs, mainly rhododendrons and azaleas whose blossom in June, Miss Wilson proudly and poetically assured him, burned like a bonfire. Now, however,

16

the colours of autumn were beginning to glow, with Michaelmas daisies challenging the turning leaves to match their rich orange, while mountain ash and pyracantha were pearled with red berries which the blackbirds would soon devour.

It also occurred to him that if he really were looking for a house in the Lake District, this might very well be the kind of house he was looking for.

A thought stirred in his mind.

Why not?

He dismissed it instantly. It was once again the voice of that forgotten young man who played the ostler twenty-odd years ago. Jaysmith, however, knew the dangers of sentiment and impulse. It was one thing to decide on the spur of the moment to treat himself to an extra week in the Lake District, quite another to invest a large sum of money and, by implication, a large piece of his life here.

William Hutton, holiday-maker and property-seeker, would have to speak soon. Miss Wilson had shown him the outside first, as if reluctant to miss any moment of this glorious autumn morning. Now they moved indoors, and all was exactly as it should be, the right old furniture in rooms of the right dimensions, with just enough of light coming through the leaded windows and just enough of heat coming from the small fire in the huge grate.

'Old bones need a fire almost all the year round,' she said, seeing his glance. 'That's what we started with, that's what we end with.'

Curiously he had no difficulty in understanding this enigmatic statement. Man's move away from the beast was emblematized by a group crouching around a fire. And Jaysmith had felt the need of that fire in many a long cold hour spent in patient, motionless waiting.

The door bell rang. Miss Wilson left him and returned a moment later with another woman whom, with that tendency to instant mini-biography he had already noted in denizens of the area, she introduced as her niece, Annie Wilson, a widow, who lived out Keswick way, just back from her holidays and come for lunch.

Jaysmith was presented in similar terms with all of William Hutton's known and assumed background and purposes spelt out. He guessed that Parker had been rigorously cross-examined.

The newcomer shook his hand. He put her age as early-to mid-thirties. She had a long, narrow, not unpleasantly vulpine face, with a sallow complexion, watchful brown eyes and thin nose, slightly upturned, giving the impression that her nostrils were flared to catch the scent of danger. She was dressed in gloomy autumn colours, dark brown slacks and a russet shirt, with her long brown hair pulled back severely from her brow and held back with a casually knotted red ribbon. Her body was lean and rangy and she moved with athletic ease.

Jaysmith felt she regarded him with considerable suspicion. Its cause soon emerged.

'You're selling Rigg Cottage!' she exclaimed to her aunt.

'That's right. I've talked about it often enough.'

'I know, but it's so sudden. Didn't you discuss it with anyone? With pappy or Granddad Wilson?'

'No I didn't,' said Miss Wilson tartly. 'As you well know, else your father would have told you when you got back and James would have told you when you were staying with him. I've always made up me own mind and always will, so there's an end to it. Now tell me about you and young Jimmy. When's he coming to see me? I thought he might come with you today.'

Annie Wilson laughed and suddenly a decade was wiped off her face. Jaysmith watched, fascinated by the transformation.

'He started back at school today, auntie. He'll be round next Sunday as usual, I promise you.'

'Just see he is,' grumbled the old lady. 'He could have been here yesterday if you'd got back earlier. It's not right leaving it till the day before school starts. Too much of a rush.'

'Granddad Wilson wanted us to stay as long as possible,' said the young woman. 'He doesn't see much of Jimmy.'

'Then he should get himself up here more often,' retorted Miss Wilson. 'The wedding, the christening and the funeral, that's been about the strength of it these past few years.'

Annie Wilson's face lost its animation and the ten years came back with whatever was causing the pain visible in the depths of her eyes.

'Jimmy bought you a present in London,' she said abruptly. 'He asked me to give it to you.'

She handed over a packet in gaily coloured wrapping paper.

Miss Wilson said, 'I'll look at it later. I've got to show Mr Hutton upstairs yet.'

'I'll show him,' offered the younger woman. 'You sit down and open your present.'

For a second the old woman looked doubtful, then she agreed. Jaysmith guessed that despite her independence, she might value her niece's opinion of him as a prospective buyer, and he guessed also

19

that Annie Wilson wanted a chance to check him out for herself.

He played William Hutton to the best of his ability as she showed him round the bedrooms, enthusing over the view from the main bedroom window. It looked out over the valley, across the lake to Town End with the great swell of Seat Sandal looming behind.

'Yes it's hard to beat anywhere in the world,' she said. 'Have you set your heart on Grasmere, Mr Hutton, or will anywhere in the Lakes do?'

He almost admitted that his knowledge of the area was limited to what he'd been able to garner in the past three days, but this would have sounded very strange from William Hutton, prospective resident and eager house-hunter.

'I love it all,' he said expansively. 'But Grasmere best of all.'

'And you walk, of course?'

He gestured towards the eastern heights.

'It's the only way to get up there, isn't it?'

She nodded, and suddenly thirsty for more of her approval, he went on, 'I wouldn't like to count the happy hours and the glorious miles I've passed on the tops.'

Which was quite true, he told himself ironically. The reward for his boast was to make her laugh and shed those years once more.

'You're as keen as that, are you?' she said, gently mocking his grandiloquence. 'You'll be telling me you're Wainwright next.'

He didn't know if he succeeded in not registering his shock. Wainwright was a cover name he'd used on the Austrian job. How the hell did this woman know . . . ? Then it came to him that, of course, she didn't. The name had some significance he didn't grasp, that was all.

He smiled and said lightly, 'Just plain William Hutton. Is this the last bedroom?'

She nodded, her face losing its rejuvenating lines of laughter and settling to the stillness of a mountain tarn, momentarily disturbed by a breeze. He wondered if she'd noticed something odd in his reaction after all. But when she opened the bedroom door and motioned him in, something about her stillness focused his attention on the room itself. It was small with a single bed and a south-facing casement window with a copper beech almost rubbing against the glass. On the walls hung several photographs of what he saw were early climbing groups, young men, often moustachioed and bearded, garlanded with ropes and wearing broad-rimmed hats and long laced-up boots, standing with the rigid insouciance required by early cameramen. The background hills were unmistakable. Even his limited acquaintance enabled him to recognize the neanderthal brow of Scafell and the broad, nippled swell of Scafell Pike. The pictures apart, there was no sense of the personality of the occupier of this room, or indeed any signs of recent occupation. But twenty years of nervous living had honed his sensitivity to atmosphere and suddenly he heard himself saying, 'Your aunt brought up your husband, didn't she?'

She looked at him in amazement and said, 'Why? What has she said?'

'Nothing,' he assured her. 'She said nothing. I just got the feeling that once this had been his room, that's all.'

Now there was anger alongside the surprise and

21

all her initial distrust was back in her eyes.

'What are you, Mr Hutton?' she demanded. 'Some kind of policeman keeping his hand in on holiday?'

'I'm sorry,' he said. 'I didn't mean to be offensive. I just . . .'

But she was walking away.

'That's all up here, Mr Hutton,' she said coldly. 'We'd better get back downstairs to my aunt. She'll be wanting to get lunch ready. I hope you're as quick with decisions as deductions.'

He was very angry with himself. The remark had just slipped out and Jaysmith was not accustomed to anything but complete self-control.

Miss Wilson was holding a small pot replica of Big Ben in her lap.

'Tell Jimmy it's very nice, dear,' she said. 'Now, Mr Hutton, what do you think?'

He hesitated. When he'd arrived, he'd had it all worked out. *A delightful house, but not quite what I was looking for.* But now this formula would cut him off from Miss Wilson and her niece for ever. That was something he discovered he didn't want to do, at least not without a chance for further thought.

He said, 'Would it be possible to come back this afternoon? It's hard to take everything in at a single viewing. You can often get mistaken impressions at a single encounter, can't you?'

He glanced at Annie Wilson as he spoke, but got nothing in return.

Miss Wilson regarded him thoughtfully, then turned to her niece.

'Well, I daresay we can put up with you trampling round again, can't we, Annie? But give

22

us time to enjoy our lunch. Three o'clock, let's say.'

'Fine,' said Jaysmith. 'Three o'clock.'

The old lady showed him out, Annie Wilson having disappeared with a perfunctory farewell into the kitchen.

'One thing,' said Miss Wilson on the doorstep. 'You've not asked me price, young man. It may be too high for you.'

He rather liked her directness. It also occurred to him that he would rather like her good opinion.

He said, 'If you really think of me as a young man, Miss Wilson, then I'll be happy to accept any estimate of the house's value based on the same principle.'

A sunbeam of amusement warmed the old face. Then she closed the door. There was a little red Fiat in the drive, presumably belonging to Annie Wilson. Carefully he backed the BMW past it and drove down the hill to the Crag Hotel.

CHAPTER FOUR

Jaysmith ate a snack lunch in the hotel bar and told the openly curious Parker that he had liked Rigg Cottage, but needed a second look.

'Quite right, old boy,' said Parker. 'Never rush into these things. On the other hand, don't hang about either. There is a tide and all that.'

'You're probably right,' said Jaysmith, finishing his beer. 'By the way, who is Wainwright?'

'Wainwright? You mean the walking chappie?'

'Probably.'

Parker was regarding him with considerable

23

surprise.

'How odd,' he said.

'Odd?'

'That someone as keen on the Lakes as you hasn't heard of Wainwright! He's the author of probably the best-known series of walkers' guides ever written. You must be pulling my leg, Mr Hutton. Every second person you meet on the fells is clutching the relevant volume of Wainwright!'

'Of course, I know the books you mean,' lied Jaysmith. 'Me, I've always managed very well with the OS maps.'

He left the hotel a few minutes later and strolled through the sun-hazed village to a bookshop he had noticed on a corner. There he found shelves packed full of the Wainwright guide books. He bought Book Three, entitled *The Central Fells* which included much of the terrain around Grasmere. A glance through it explained its popularity: detailed routes, pleasing illustrations, lively text; there was possibly something here even for the man who lived by map and compass.

It was after two-thirty. Slipping the book into his pocket, he set out to walk up the hill to Rigg Cottage. It was a good distance and a steepish incline and he found himself admiring the old lady for having stayed on so long.

At the house he was relieved to see the little Fiat still in place, but there was no sign of Annie Wilson as Miss Wilson showed him round the ground floor once again.

'Has your niece gone?' he asked casually.

'No, she's out in the garden.'

'You mentioned a boy, Jimmy. Are there any other children?'

24

'You've got sharp ears and a long nose, young man,' said Miss Wilson reprovingly.

'If I'm going to become an inhabitant, I need to adapt to local customs,' smiled Jaysmith.

His impudence paid off.

'No, just the one,' said the old lady abruptly. 'They'd been married barely seven years when Edward died. It was just before Christmas last year.'

Nine months and still grieving. Grief could last forever unless life wrenched you out of its course. And even then you could not be certain if you were really living or just escaping.

'You look around upstairs by yourself,' instructed Miss Wilson. 'I don't bother with the stairs unless I have to.'

He spotted the younger woman from the window of the room with the mountaineering pictures. She was reclining in a deck chair at the bottom of the garden with her feet up on an ornamental wall, her eyes closed against the slanting sun. He stood for a while, watching, till she shifted slightly. Suddenly fearful she might glance up and see him at this particular window, he turned away and went downstairs.

'Well?' said Miss Wilson. 'What do you reckon?'

'We haven't talked about a price,' delayed Jaysmith.

'I thought you said you'd leave that to me,' she replied, her lips crinkling. 'Well here's what the agent reckoned he'd advertise it for if I put it with him, which I'm going to do tomorrow if it's not sold today.'

She mentioned a figure. It was hefty, but, from the little bit of expertise Jaysmith had had to gather

25

to keep up his end in conversations with Phil Parker, it seemed reasonable.

Miss Wilson added, 'But for the pleasure of not paying an agent's fee and not having hordes of strangers and more than a few nosey local devils tramping around the place, I'd knock a thousand off that, Mr Hutton.'

He scratched his chin and whistled softly.

'That's very generous of you,' he said. 'Very generous.'

He hoped that Annie Wilson would materialize at some point to show a protective interest in her aunt. But he saw now that the old lady would not take kindly to being protected and that the niece would remain determinedly absent till negotiations were concluded.

And if the conclusion were no sale, he would be politely shown the door and his chance would have been missed.

His chance for what? He wasn't quite sure, but Parker's words rang in his ears . . . *there is a tide in the affairs of men . . .*

He said, 'On the other hand, I rather feel that for a cash sale, no property chain to worry about, no pressure to complete, or delay when you are ready either, all this guaranteed, you might come down a little lower.'

'How much lower did you have in mind, Mr Hutton?'

'Oh, another couple of thousand, I'd have thought.'

She looked outraged but he also saw behind the outrage what he had already guessed at—the haggler's spirit burning bright.

They went at it hard for another fifteen minutes.

'I'll need to go out and talk to Annie,' she said at one point.

She was gone a couple of minutes only. Shortly after she returned they settled for a reduction of the agent's price by fifteen hundred pounds.

She offered her hand. He took it. Her grip was firm and warm.

'That's settled then. You'll have a drink. Come into the garden.'

He followed her out. Another deck chair had appeared alongside Annie's.

'It'll be whisky to seal a bargain,' said Miss Wilson, returning to the house. 'Sit down.'

She went back inside. Annie opened her eyes.

'You've bought it then,' she said neutrally.

'It is irresistible,' he said.

'Did you knock her down?'

'Only as far as she had decided to go. Probably not as far as that,' he said ruefully. 'I think she was very gentle with me. If she'd really tried her hardest, I suspect I'd have been *raising* her price. She's rather formidable, isn't she?'

He had struck the right note. She smiled at him now and nodded.

'When she came out to see you just now, what did she say?' he asked.

'Nothing,' she said. 'She just came out, got that deck chair you're sitting on from the shed and set it up, then she went back inside. Why?'

'She told me she was coming to consult with you,' he said.

Slowly she began to laugh and he laughed with her. It felt like a long time since there had been such a moment of shared pleasure in his life.

'You two sound very jolly, I must say,' said Miss

27

Wilson, returning with a tray on which stood a decanter and three glasses.

Jaysmith struggled to his feet to offer her the deck chair but she said, 'No, I find them things too awkward for me nowadays. I'll sit on the wall here if you'll shift your feet.'

Obediently Annie removed her feet from the ornamental wall and her aunt sat down.

'Take your jacket off, man, and enjoy the sun,' exhorted the old lady.

Obedient in his turn, Jaysmith removed his jacket. As he draped it over the back of the deck chair, the Wainwright guide fell out of his pocket. Quickly he picked it up and replaced it, wondering if Annie Wilson's expression of amusement only existed in his mind.

He stayed for half an hour, deftly fielding questions about his background. At the end of this time the younger woman said, 'I really must be off now, Aunt Muriel. I promised I'd pick Jimmy up from school.'

'You'll spoil him.'

'First day back. After this, it's the bus and a nice healthy walk. I'll bring him round this weekend.'

'Make sure you do.'

Jaysmith rose too.

'You can get in touch with me at the hotel when your solicitor's ready,' he told Miss Wilson.

'You're staying on then?'

'A few more days.'

He was wondering how to keep contact with Annie Wilson when she said, 'Like a lift down into the village, Mr Hutton? I can't see your car.'

'No. I walked up this afternoon.'

'Spoken like a real enthusiast. Of course, if you

want to walk back . . .'

'No. Uphill was enough. Downhill's often much harder.'

'There speaks an expert.'

He folded himself into the tiny car, leaving the two women to take their farewells. A moment of panic hit him as he waited.

What am I doing? he asked himself. I've promised to buy a house just so that I can talk a little longer with a woman I've only just met who may turn out to be dull as ditchwater, or reckon that I'm even duller!

But the panic vanished like morning mist when she climbed into the driver's seat.

They hardly spoke on the short descent into Grasmere. She dropped him at his hotel. To invite her in for tea or a drink was manifestly absurd when he knew she was going to pick up her son.

He held the car door open and said, 'Thank you.'

'A pleasure,' she said, putting the car into gear.

'Look,' he said, 'I'd like to see you again.'

'If you're coming to live up here, I daresay we'll bump into each other,' she said with a smile.

'No. I mean sooner. What about tomorrow? Lunch, say.'

She stopped smiling and studied him closely.

'I don't often eat lunch,' she said. 'Except when I go to auntie's. Otherwise I just grab a snack.'

'Me too,' he said. 'So why don't we eat our snacks together?'

She thought for a moment then nodded gravely.

'All right. Why not? Half past twelve suit you?'

'Fine. But where? What's the best place round here? You're the local. You name it.'

'Best place?' she echoed, letting in the clutch

29

and beginning to move gently away. 'Well, one of my favourites is the *Lion and the Lamb*. Let's meet there, shall we? Twelve-thirty prompt. 'Bye!'

She smiled at him, her face suddenly alive with humour and mischief, and then she was gone.

That night before dinner Jaysmith studied the Cumbrian telephone directory in the bar. There were only two *Lion and Lambs* listed. One was in Gosforth which a glance at his map told him was about fifteen miles to the west as the crow flew but a long drive along high, narrow winding roads as the car went. The other was in Wigton, thirty odd miles north and almost at Carlisle. Neither was what he would call local.

'Can I help?' enquired Parker who'd been observing his search from the bar.

'It's nothing really,' said Jaysmith. 'I just made a casual arrangement to meet a friend in a pub locally and I can't remember its name. I thought it was the *Lion and the Lamb*, but I see there's nothing nearer than Gosforth.'

'I don't know a pub of that name round here,' said Parker. 'What about you, dear?'

His wife had just come into the bar to get some drinks. She shook her head when the problem was explained and said, 'No, there's only one *Lion and Lamb* round here that I know of.'

After she'd gone, Jaysmith said casually, 'What did she mean?'

Parker gave him the same look of surprise he'd shown at his ignorance of Wainwright.

'Up there, of course,' he said.

He pointed at the window. Evening was well advanced but there was still light enough in the sky to provide a foil for the massive outlines of the

30

nearer fells. One in particular seemed to loom over the hotel.

'Helm Crag,' said Parker. 'Home of Grasmere's tutelary deities.'

'Of course. I'm sorry, my mind was too much on pubs,' smiled Jaysmith, not having the faintest idea what was being said to him.

Later in his bedroom he made sense of it by looking up Helm Crag in his newly purchased guide book. He found it described as possibly the best-known hill in the country because of the rock formation on the summit whose silhouette was said to resemble a lion couchant and a lamb. The *Lion and the Lamb*!

He cursed himself mildly. Such ignorance displayed a week ago when he was still planning the kill would have been a real error of security. It would have been too large a task for the police to interrogate every hotelier and guest house proprietor in the Lakes, but there would certainly have been media exhortations for them to report any oddities in their recent guests. Parker was just the man to volunteer his services.

But now it didn't matter. He enjoyed the feeling of perfect relaxation once more. It didn't matter!

Except, of course, for the fact that Annie Wilson might have been testing him.

He examined the proposition and quickly dismissed it. As a test it was pointless. He must have been the only person within fifty miles who didn't know what the Lion and the Lamb was. Such ignorance was scarcely credible and all too easily remediable.

So, no test. Just an invitation to a picnic.

He switched off the light and his thoughts

31

simultaneously. It was a trick of mental discipline he had developed over twenty years. Usually he could fall to sleep within a minute. Tonight for some reason it took just a little longer but the sleep when it came was as dark and undisturbed as ever.

CHAPTER FIVE

The ascent of Helm Crag was a delight; not much over a thousand feet but full of interest and beauties. He had set off in plenty of time and it was not much after noon when he reached the summit.

He removed his rucksack and laid it on the ground at the foot of the group of rocks which he presumed gave the fell its nickname. But that was not the only interesting formation; the whole of the summit ridge was strewn with shattered slabs and broken boulders among which he wandered for a while, musing on that sense of peace underpinned with menace which mountains always gave him.

When he returned to his rucksack, it was gone.

'Over here,' called Annie Wilson.

He looked around. She was sitting in a well-sheltered declivity looking westward. His rucksack lay at her feet with hers.

'You move fast,' she said approvingly. 'I was barely five minutes behind you when you started climbing, but you must have gained ten on the way up.'

'I never saw you,' he said frowning.

'Move like the old brown fox, that's me,' she said.

He sat down beside her. The old brown fox; he

32

recalled his first sense, quickly modified, of a certain foxiness in her features; still, the description fitted well enough, except for the *old*. Dressed today in a heather-mixture shirt and dark green slacks which clung a little closer than walking trousers really ought to, she reclined among the rocks like a creature of them rather than a visitor to them. Her long black hair hung free today and there were some small green lichens in it picked up from the boulder behind her. The brown eyes in that narrow intelligent face had instantly registered his appraisal so he made no real attempt to conceal it.

'Will I do?' she asked.

'You fit the occasion perfectly,' he said. 'And me?'

She looked him up and down, her eyes lingering on his well-worn but beautifully maintained boots. Custom-made many years ago, they were a perfect fit, light and supple, with great reserves of strength, and with the lace lugs, like the lace tags themselves and all metal parts on all of his equipment, veneered a non-reflective brown.

'You don't stint yourself do you?' she said touching the leather.

'If a thing's worth doing, it's worth doing best,' he said lightly. 'I've brought tongue sandwiches and a piece of salmon quiche. What about you?'

'Apple, cheese, and a bramble pie,' she said.

'We complement each other perfectly. Do you mind drinking Chablis out of a cardboard cup?'

'As long as it doesn't come out of a cardboard box first,' she said.

They began to eat. Conversation flowed easily, but shallowly too. She refused to let him penetrate

33

far into her personal life, and as he was by need as well as nature reticent about his own background, he could hardly suggest a fair exchange.

'When shall you move into Rigg Cottage?' she asked.

'That depends.'

'On what?'

On what happens between me and you, he thought but did not say. It was not that he was afraid to say it; simply that he was not yet ready. Her response might be indignation, but he did not think so. If it were, it would be on her aunt's behalf, not her own. More baffling would be the simple question, 'What do you want to happen between us?'

The truth was, he didn't know. He was attracted to her, but this might simply be a symptom of reaction to his decision to retire. He felt relaxed, able to enjoy himself, and the first attractive woman to come along was *ipso facto* in the right place at the right time. He was surely too old for love at first sight. He had even begun to think he was getting a little too old for lust at first sight. Indeed, this did not feel like mere lust, though desire was moving languorously through his veins as she brushed pastry crumbs from her swelling shirt and stretched her long slim legs.

'On business,' he said vaguely.

'What precisely is your business, Mr Hutton?' she asked rather sharply, as if provoked by his vagueness.

'To tell the truth it's almost non-existent,' he said. 'I ran a little management consultancy firm, almost a one-man show, but the recession's been too much. I've sold out to a competitor while

34

there's still something to sell out. So now, like thousands of my fellow citizens, I'm drifting into early retirement. Just a few loose ends to tie up, that's all.'

'None of these loose ends could affect your purchase of Rigg Cottage?' she asked, suddenly alert.

'No,' he said. 'I've been making some sound investments against this day for years. The sale is secure, believe me.'

She said, 'At the moment it's only as secure as your handshake, isn't it? I don't mean to be offensive.'

'Don't you?' he said, slightly piqued, a feeling he knew he had no entitlement to, since, if she had given him the brush-off yesterday, he might already have reneged on the deal. 'It takes two to shake hands, you know. And tell me this; if someone turned up today, cash in hand, with a better offer, how would you advise your aunt to react?'

She frowned a little, then smiled.

'Even your brief acquaintance with Aunt Muriel must have taught you she'd feel no need to ask for advice from me,' she said.

He said, 'They don't by any chance let women become Jesuits nowadays, do they?'

She smiled again and turning away from him said, 'I spy with my little eye something beginning with H.'

He let his gaze drift to the horizon.

'Harrison Stickle,' he said promptly.

'Good,' she said. 'Your turn.'

'B,' he said.

'Bow Fell,' she replied.

'You know you can't see Bow Fell from here,' he

chided. 'The Langdales get in the way.'

'So they do,' she said innocently. 'I give up then.'

'Blea Rigg. There.'

He pointed.

'So it is,' she said. 'Well done.'

'I pass the test then?'

'Do you? My marking scheme is, to say the least, eccentric.'

'But it was a test?'

'A tiny one,' she smiled. 'When I saw that brand-new Wainwright fall out of your pocket, I did wonder if you mightn't be shooting a line with all that great fellwalker stuff.'

He complimented himself on having studied both his Wainwright and his os map carefully for a good hour that morning. But perhaps it was time for a bit of truth to get himself a rest from those searching eyes.

'You're right to some extent, I'm afraid,' he said. 'I *was* trying to project a good image. To be honest, my Lakeland walking was all done when I was a mere lad. So any expertise I've got's a bit dated.'

'Those boots don't look like they've been in the coal hole for twenty years. Or do you use them to garden in?'

'No. They've been around a bit.'

'Where, for instance?'

'Oh, here and there. Alps, Andes, Pyrenees, very low down in the Himalayas, rather higher in the Harz. Yes, here and there, you could say.'

She looked at him darkly.

'Well, that's me put in my place, isn't it?' she said. 'And finally, overcome by age, you've returned to these undemanding hillocks, is that it?'

'Don't be silly,' he said easily. 'One thing I

36

learned early was that any hilly terrain that takes you more than half a mile off a road in uncertain weather deserves great respect.'

'What a wise man you are, Mr Hutton. Though I'm glad to say the weather doesn't look at all uncertain at the moment.'

'No it doesn't,' he agreed looking out across the sun-gilt landscape. Was it only a week since he had greeted the forecast of a settled spell of fine autumn weather with a coldly professional gratitude that it would bring the target out into his garden and make the long kill possible? He turned his gaze onto the woman. For the moment her company was like this late reburgeoning of summer. How long it would last, how far it might take him, were not yet questions to be asked. For the moment her presence was to be enjoyed like the autumn sunshine without threat or complication.

'What shall we do this afternoon?' he said.

'I'm sorry?'

'I thought we might go on to Calf Crag then back to Grasmere down Far Easedale.'

She sat upright and said, 'Whoa, Mr Hutton! Our appointment was for lunch, not a day's outing. I've got things to do this afternoon. I ought to be on my way back down now.'

He must have looked disappointed for she smiled faintly and added, 'You mustn't take things for granted, Mr Hutton, not with me anyway. I have a tendency to the pedantic. I expect people to mean what they say and I prefer them to say what they mean. You should have been more precise in your proposal.'

'And if I had been?'

'Then very probably I would have come with you. It's not every day a little Lake District mouse has the chance to scurry in the wake of a Himalayan Yeti!'

She started packing the lunch debris into her rucksack. He followed suit, saying, 'Then let me be precise about two things. One: would you please stop calling me Mr Hutton? Two: will you spend tomorrow, or as much of it as you can, walking with me?'

'What shall I call you?' she said.

'Jay,' he said after a fractional hesitation. He should have been prepared, indeed he had thought he was. *William* was out of the question. *Hutton* he had conditioned himself to respond to, but he would probably walk right past anyone addressing him as *William* or *Bill*. His real name belonged with the old years; he might yet come full circle and touch them again but for the moment the gulf was too deep, too wide. Which left Jay, the closest familiarity he permitted those few who came close to being friends. But he didn't like giving it to this woman, didn't like the cold breath of his previous life it brought into their relationship. Hence the hesitation.

'Jay? Why Jay?'

'My middle initial,' he said easily. 'It was used at school to differentiate me from another William Hutton, and it stuck.'

'All right. Jay.' She tried it doubtfully.

'And I'll call you Annie if that's all right.'

'No!'

She was very emphatic.

'Anya,' she said. 'My name's Anya. Too outlandish for good Cumbrian folk like Aunt

38

Muriel, but Anya's my name.'

She spoke lightly but Jaysmith caught a hint of something deeply felt. Perhaps her husband, being presumably good Cumbrian folk too, had called her Annie and she didn't like to hear the name on another man's lips.

'All right, Anya,' he said. 'Yes, it suits you better. Annie is too . . .'

'What?' she challenged him.

'Buxom,' he said.

They laughed together.

As they began the descent, Jaysmith reminded her, 'You haven't answered my second very specific request.'

'I was thinking about it. To tell the truth I could do with a good walk after a week in London. But I couldn't start till, say, ten AM and I must be down again by half past three.'

'Five and a half hours,' he mused. 'Let's say . . . what? Eighteen to twenty miles?'

She looked at him in horror then saw the amused twist of his lips.

'Thank heaven you're joking,' she said. 'I was wondering what kind of mountain goat I'd fallen in with! Two miles an hour is quite rapid enough for me, thank you very much. I like to be able to stop and admire the view from time to time. Perhaps I'd better pick the route.'

'Accepted,' he said.

'What? No macho resistance at all?'

'When I was a young man faced with the choice between scouting for boys or being guided by girls, I knew which side my bread was buttered on,' he replied.

'Yes,' she said thoughtfully. 'That's the

39

impression I get of you, Jay. A man who knows which side his bread is buttered on.'

* * *

In the Crag Hotel, Jaysmith had been very noncommital about his encounter with Miss Wilson, partly because of his own ambivalence of feeling but also because he reckoned the old lady was entitled to be her own gossip in Grasmere. But that night Parker greeted him with a broad smile, outstretched hand and hearty congratulations on his purchase of Rigg Cottage.

'So the news is out?' he said.

'Out? Trumpeted abroad, old chap! Everyone in the village knows. And they're all dying of curiosity about you.'

Even with allowance made for Parker's hyperbole, this news did not please Jaysmith. After a professional lifetime of not drawing attention to himself, even this very mild and local limelight was distressing. A half bottle of champagne appeared on his table at dinner with Parker's compliments.

He said to Doris Parker who had delivered it, 'Really, I should be paying you a commission.'

She smiled in her placid down-to-earth way and said, 'Bring a few friends in for dinner occasionally and that will do nicely. You'd rather just have your Chablis, I suspect?'

He nodded.

She said, 'I'll take this off your bill,' and went away with the champagne.

After dinner, in the bar, Parker showed a strong tendency to act as his mentor in the minutiae of Grasmere life so he escaped to the lounge and watched television for a while. The news was the usual mishmash of political piffle, royal baby rumours, sporting highlights and bloody violence. There'd been an attempt on the life of the Turkish Ambassador in Paris, a botched-up job by some idiot with a Skorpion machine-pistol leaping out from behind a potted palm and spraying the vestibule of the hotel where the Ambassador was lunching. A doorman was killed, an American tourist seriously injured, and the assassin himself cut down by a hail of security men's bullets which also killed a lift attendant. The dead and the injured were all filmed in glorious technicolour.

Jaysmith's disgust must have shown. The female half of an elderly couple, the only other viewers, said, 'It's horrifying, isn't it? Quite, quite horrifying.'

He nodded his agreement, but did not explain that his disgust was merely at the sight of the carnage caused by amateurs. Was he himself an amateur now? No, only if he started killing people without getting paid for it and that wasn't likely! Even then, he would still proceed in a professional way. That was what he was, a retired professional. Fully retired now. He had sent a coded telex to his Swiss bank instructing them how to pay back the last unearned fee. Jacob would not be pleased, but his displeasure would be professional not personal. He would have to find a new man to do the job, if the job still had to be done. He would not miss Jaysmith; there would be no farewell speech, no commemorative gold watch.

It was only to Jaysmith himself that his retirement was of any real moment. It was a slightly disturbing thought.

41

He watched the weather forecast. The Indian summer was to go on a little longer.

He said goodnight to the elderly couple and went to bed.

CHAPTER SIX

That night he dreamt, and the dream brought him awake. It was the first broken night he had had in more years than he could remember.

He dreamt of Jacob, or rather of Jacob's voice. Jacob's face he could hardly recall, except for something faintly simian about it, like one of the great apes looking with weary wisdom out of its cage at the shrill fools beyond the bars who imagined they were free. It was many years since he had seen the face, but the voice was still fresh in his ears: dry, nasal, with its irritating habit of tagging interrogative phrases onto the end of statements, like little hooks to draw the hearer in.

In his dream he picked up the phone expecting to hear Enid. Over the years one young Enid had replaced another as his route through to Jacob. What became of the old Enids? he sometimes wondered, but was never tempted to ask. In his relationship with his employer as with his targets, distance suited him best. With women too. Until now.

Instead of Enid's voice, Jacob had come instantly on the line. He spoke without emotion, without emphasis.

'You're Jaysmith,' he said. 'I invented you, didn't I? You're Jaysmith now and for ever, aren't you?

There's nothing else for you. You're Jaysmith, Jaysmith, Jaysmith . . .'

Suddenly with the voice still in his ear he had been back in the gill on Wanthwaite Crags. Across the valley he could see the red roof of Naddle Foot. He brought his rifle up to his eye and the terraced garden leapt into close focus. The white metal chair was there and in it a sleeping figure. He traversed the weapon and adjusted the sight till the silvery head filled the circle, quartered by the hairline cross. Now the sleeper woke and slowly raised his head. But when the face was fully turned to the sun, Jaysmith saw to his horror that it was not the old man after all, but the woman he had just met, Anya Wilson. She smiled straight at the gun, though she could not possibly see it, and his finger continued to tighten on the trigger . . .

With a huge effort of will he forced himself awake. If anything the waking was worse than the dreaming. It was four o'clock. He rose and poured himself a drink and sat by the window looking out into the night. *It had all been a dream:* that was the childhood formula which put such things right; but now fully awake he knew that this dream was true.

He was Jaysmith. He should have been back in London days ago, packing his belongings, easing himself into one of the alternative lives he had prepared over the years. Where could it end, this lunacy of pretending to buy a house and running around after this child, Annie or Anya or whatever she liked to call herself? She was at least fifteen years his junior, recently widowed and not yet emerged from that unthinkable pain. Suppose he did worm his way into her affections? It would be as bad almost as making her a target with his rifle.

43

His room faced east. After a while the false dawn began to push forward the great range of fells which runs from Fairfield to Helvellyn. He felt their advance, hard and menacing; it seemed that if he sat there long enough they would rumble inexorably onward to crush the hotel and the village and all its unwitting inmates. There was strength as well as terror in the thought. It confirmed his own certainties, silenced his own debates. In the morning he would rise early and pay his bill and leave, and that would be an end to Mr William Hutton and probably the beginning of a good half-century of speculation for the trivial gossips of this unimportant crease in the coat-tail of the universe.

He went back to bed, the future resolved, and slept deep.

When he awoke it was a quarter to ten.

'Oh Christ!' he swore, touched by a new terror in which the great threat was that she would not wait for him at their rendezvous point. So potent was this that he forewent both breakfast and shaving in his rush to get there.

She looked at him with considerable disapproval.

'The good burghers of Grasmere will expect a much better turnout from the new inmate of Rigg Cottage,' she said.

'I came out in a hurry,' he said. 'I had a bad night.'

'And how did the night feel, I wonder?'

He glowered at her and the mockery faded from her eyes and she murmured almost to herself, 'Are we always so bad-tempered in the morning, I wonder?'

44

He got a grip of himself and smiled ruefully and said, 'I'm sorry. As for what I'm usually like in the morning, I don't know. It's been a long time since there was anyone to tell me.'

'Anyone who dared, you mean?'

'Or cared. And really, I did have a bad night.'

He got in the car beside her. She had arranged to pick him up at the edge of the village on the road leading up to Rigg Cottage. He hadn't queried the arrangement but just assumed that she didn't care for a more public rendezvous under the eye of Mr Parker or her aunt's many acquaintances.

'What was bothering you? Not Doris Parker's cooking, I hope?'

'No. That's fine. So's she; I like her. She doesn't come at you like dear Phil.'

She nodded. Another shared judgement to bring them closer. He'd guessed that was how she'd feel and though his opinion of the Parkers was precisely as stated, he felt a twinge of guilt at the element of calculation in what he'd said.

So when she asked, 'What then?' he compensated with a dash of unsolicited confession.

'To tell the truth I woke in a cold sweat wondering what the devil I was doing buying your aunt's house.'

He'd expected a very positive reaction to this: fear for her aunt's sake—anger at this hint of masculine dithering—at the very least a demand for reassurance that he hadn't changed his mind.

Instead she nodded once more and said in a matter-of-fact voice, 'Oh yes. The old four AM's. They're dreadful, aren't they. You seem to see everything so clearly, and it's all black, if that's not contradictory.'

'You're speaking from experience?'

'Oh yes,' she said. 'The four AM's and the four PM's too. Doesn't everyone get them, the AM's anyway?'

He shook his head.

'Not me,' he said. 'Last night was the first broken night I've had in years.'

Broken from within, that was. There had been plenty of early risings and sudden alarums. But he could hardly explain this to the woman who was looking at him curiously, and he found he didn't particularly want to press her to reveal the grounds of her own despair at this moment.

'So, where are we going?' he asked brightly.

She responded to his change of mood, saying, 'Well, I knew a Himalayan man wouldn't want to waste his time on pimples, so I thought we'd do Bow Fell via the Crinkles, but to fit it into our limited time allowance I've decided to cheat by starting at the top of Wrynose.'

He nodded as if this made sense to him while he worked it out on his mental imprint of the relevant OS sheets. They had climbed out of Grasmere, passing Rigg Cottage en route, and now they were dropping down again. He glimpsed the blue sheet of Elterwater before they entered its tiny village and left it on the Little Langdale road. Soon they were climbing again and now they were on a steep, serpentine single-track road, with intermittent passing places, and viciously demanding on bottom gear both for ascent and descent. This was Wrynose Pass.

He said, 'This would take us all the way across into Eskdale, right?'

'Right. It's the old drove road, of course. Hard

Knott dropping into Eskdale's even worse, I think.'

'Then I'm glad we're not going that far,' he said firmly.

'Oh I think you should. Halfway up the side of Hard Knott there's a Roman Fort; perhaps you've been there?'

He shook his head.

'It's a place to go on a wild winter's day,' she said. 'Almost a thousand feet up in country that's still wild, so God knows what it was like all those centuries ago; looking out to the west towards a sea which offers only Ireland between you and the limits of habitable creation; thinking of Rome, and Tuscan wine, and the long summer sun, while the sleet blows in your face and you can hear the stones of your castle cracking in the frost during the night watches. You ought to go.'

He looked at her curiously.

'That was ... poetic,' he said. 'I'm not being sarcastic either. But why do you insist I ought to go?'

'No, I don't really,' she answered, faintly embarrassed. 'All I meant was, it must have taken a certain kind of man to survive all *that*.'

'And you think I could be such a man?' he said lightly. 'Should I be flattered?'

'I meant I would be interested in hearing *you* decide whether you could have been such a man,' she said slowly. 'As for whether you should be flattered, that depends on what you feel such a man ought to be.'

'Or had to be,' he said. 'Another test?'

She laughed and said with a hint of bitterness, 'That's what it's all about, isn't it?'

She parked the car by the Three Shires Stone

47

which marked the head of the pass. Their path was clear, the ground firm, the gradients easy, and they walked side by side at a good pace, in a silence which was companionable rather than introspective. The Crinkle Crags, their first destination, at first merely an undulating ridge a couple of miles in the distance, assumed a different aspect as they got near. Instead of a gentle ridge, Jaysmith saw that they did in fact consist of a series of crags, jagged broken buttresses of rock, five in all, each a distinct and separate entity. Their ascent was no more than a pleasant scramble, and moving from one to another was easy enough also. But as Jaysmith enjoyed the exhilaration of the magnificent views, he was aware that this was not a place where he would care to be if the weather closed in and visibility was measured in inches instead of miles. There were precipitous rock faces and narrow steep gullies filled with shattered boulders waiting to crack bones and rip flesh.

They sat on the third Crinkle and drank coffee and looked eastwards. The sun was high in its southern swing and the contours of the fells were picked out in light and shade.

'My God, it's beautiful,' said Jaysmith, almost to his own surprise.

'You sound as if you'd just noticed,' laughed the woman.

'Perhaps I have. I'm still not sure *why* it's beautiful, though.'

'Oh, all kinds of reasons. Space, airiness, sublimity. The sense it gives of something more important than mere human guilts and sorrows.'

She spoke very seriously and her features had slipped back into that ageing watchful look.

48

'Oh is *that* all?' he mocked. 'Like marijuana? It's a long way to walk for a fix.'

It worked. She laughed and lay back, hands clasped behind her head, eyes closed against the light.

'All right. If you want a purely sensuous explanation, I think it's something to do with the way the light shows us all the curves and hollows of the slopes. It's like drapery. Have you never noticed how important that is in painting? As if artists knew that there was some special magic in all that cloth; gowns, dresses, cloaks, curtains, all hanging and trailing in mysterious, fascinating pleats and folds and creases.'

'Not forgetting sheets,' he said. 'And blankets.'

'That is the kind of art you like, is it?' she said. 'That too. And the naked human figures lying on them. It's the same thing, isn't it? Curves and angles and hollows all washed with light.'

She spoke softly, almost dreamily. It sounded almost like an invitation and he leaned over and kissed her.

He knew at once he had been wrong. Her eyes opened wide with shock and her body stiffened as though holding back from some more violent act of repudiation.

'Sorry,' he said, sitting up.

'No need,' she replied, quickly regaining her composure. 'It didn't bother me. Though a respectable gent like you should be careful.'

'Why's that?'

'You may think you can come up here and toy with the milkmaids with impunity. But you're very exposed. There's a hundred places where someone could be lying this very moment, drawing a bead on

49

us.'

His eyes flickered round in such alarm that she laughed and said, 'Hey, I'm joking. You're not going to turn out to be so important that you can't afford to be photographed making a pass on a mountain, are you? A mountain pass!'

It wasn't a very good joke but they both laughed and Jaysmith said, 'No, I'm not that important.'

She regarded him shrewdly, as if doubting him, then said, 'No matter. Aunt Muriel will know all about you when you exchange contracts, won't she? Have you contacted your solicitor yet?'

'Yes,' he lied. 'Actually, he suggests it would be simpler if I got hold of a local man. I don't think he really believes there's much law beyond Hampstead. I think he's probably right, about using a local, I mean. There'll be searches and things, won't there? It'd certainly be more convenient. I wondered if you had any suggestions?'

'Perhaps. But should you be asking me? In a sense, I'm an interested party.'

'I hope so. But as your interest is to ensure that Miss Wilson's sale goes smoothly, you'll be careful to recommend only the best, won't you?'

'Are you always so logical?' she asked.

'Very occasionally I act on impulse. And, as you've just proved, it usually gets me into trouble.'

She was not to be tempted back to that topic. In a swift easy movement she rose and said, 'Time to go. The hard bit lies ahead.'

The hard bit wasn't all that hard, a fairly steep pull up the last five hundred feet of Bow Fell after they had descended from the Crinkles. There they ate their lunch and chatted familiarly enough, but still, despite or perhaps because of the kiss, at a

50

level far removed from the centre of either of them. But it was interesting enough for them to linger overlong and Anya, glancing at her watch, said accusingly, 'You've kept us here too long.'

'I have?'

'You're the official timekeeper, aren't you? Come on. We'll need our running shoes.'

In fact by dint of skirting the western face of the Crinkles as much as possible, they were able to retrace their steps to Three Shires Stone nearly an hour more quickly than they had come. Jaysmith walked a little behind for much of the way, admiring the easy movement of her athletic body as she set a spanking pace. He had no difficulty in keeping up with it, but he shouldn't have cared to try to overtake.

She dropped him in Grasmere after a descent of Wrynose he did not care to remember. When he tried to speak as he got out of the car she said crisply, 'Sorry. I hate being late. I'll be in touch,' and drove off without more ado.

A brush-off? he wondered.

He didn't think so. On the other hand, her reaction to his kiss had not been promising. Perhaps some panic button had been pressed and she was now in full retreat.

He ate his dinner with little appetite and wondered where it was all going to lead. The euphoria of his decision to retire now seemed light years away. *Then* it had seemed to usher in an Indian summer of careless peace; *now* new cares seemed to be pressing in on him from all sides.

'Telephone call for you,' said Doris Parker as she brought his coffee.

The words filled him with alarm. He was

convinced it must be Jacob, so much so that he almost said, 'Jaysmith here,' when he picked up the phone. Fortunately twenty years of caution made him growl, 'Hutton.'

'You don't sound happy,' said Anya. 'I hope I'm not interrupting your dinner.'

'No,' he said, curt with relief. 'I'd finished.'

'Good. I enjoyed our walk today.'

'Me too. Many thanks.'

'Were you serious about wanting me to recommend a solicitor?' she asked.

'Certainly.'

'All right. Eleven o'clock tomorrow morning. Mr Steven Bryant of Bryant & Grose will see you in his office in Keswick. Have you got a pen? I'll give you his address.'

He noted it down with directions.

He began to thank her but she went on, 'Afterwards, would you care to have lunch with me? I should warn you that I will be cooking it.'

'I can't think of anything I'd rather do,' he said.

'No need to be fulsome,' she said. 'Goodbye.'

He realized she hadn't given him directions to her home after he put the receiver down. No matter. Presumably this Mr Steven Bryant would be able to do that, and if not, he was still sure that nothing could stop him finding her.

He took this certainty to bed with him and lay awake for a while, feeling his happiness lapping round his body like the warm waters of an eastern sea. When at last he slipped into sleep, he took his euphoria with him. Soon it developed form and flesh and suddenly it was Anya's body, lean, brown and naked beneath his, and above them the sharp bright stars of the Lakeland sky.

They wrestled and rolled, locked together in an ecstasy of contact which threatened to climax in death. As they rolled, each gaining the ascendancy in turn, Jaysmith saw that the stars were wheeling too, shifting their positions and relationships, till the familiar pattern of the northern sky was quite destroyed and another pattern, richer in background, softer in glow, but just as familiar, took its place.

And he knew without needing to look that the flesh against his was no longer the lean, brown body of Anya Wilson, but had become softer, rounder, a deep honey gold. And now he wanted to look and he rose on his elbows so that he could see the delicately boned face, the huge dark eyes, the uncertain smile, at once shy and inviting. Her arms were still round his neck, but he wanted to see more and, despite her protest, he pushed himself upright, breaking her grip, and looked down on the slight but exquisitely rounded body, laughing in his turn as her hands flew to cover her peach-like breasts and the velvety darkness between her thighs.

'I love you, Nguyet,' he said, letting his tongue relish the strange cadence of the name which was also the Vietnamese word for *moon*.

Then, smiling, he added, 'You are my moon,' but gave the English word the tonal value which turned it into *mun*, which in her language meant carbuncle. It was an old joke between them and she giggled and gave the ritual reply, 'And you are my sun,' turning *sun* into the verb used to describe the decaying of teeth.

He laughed with her, then laughter left her eyes, driven thence by the cloudy onslaught of desire.

53

'Come close, Harry,' she whispered.

Gladly he stooped to her again, but found he could no longer get close. There were strong hands gripping his arms, voices shouting. He could no longer see her, there was a door between them, the door of her apartment. Despite the strength of those trying to hold him back, he burst through that door. And now he saw her again, still naked, still prostrate, but her eyes now wide with terror, blood caking her flared nostrils and more blood smudging the honey gold of her wide splayed thighs.

The room was full of soldiers who glared at him angrily. One of them, a dog-faced man in a colonel's uniform, chattered commands. A rifle butt was driven into his kidneys while a hand dug viciously into his mop of hair and dragged him backwards screaming, 'Nguyet! Nguyet! Nguyet!' as he woke up.

He flung back the blankets and fell out of the bed like a drunken man. He sat on the floor feeling the cool night air trace the runnels of sweat down his naked body. Last night, Jacob. Tonight, Nguyet. Why was he once again so vulnerable after all these years? He rose and went to the window and pulled back the curtain. Above the shadowy bulk of fells was the high northern heaven, pricked with countless stars. He watched it for a long time, defying it to do its planetarium act again and rearrange its crystal spheres into the lower, richer, warmer maze of the stars above Saigon.

Nothing happened. Why should it? Once again, it was only a dream. He closed the curtain and went back to bed.

He was early for his appointment next day. Keswick was a very small town and Anya's directions were precise. The offices of Bryant & Grose, Solicitors were on the second floor of an old house now given over entirely to business and commerce. He thought of killing time with another turn round the block but instead he went in and announced himself.

'Mr Hutton? You're expected,' said the young girl in the outer office. 'Just go right in.'

As he approached the door indicated, it opened and Anya appeared. She stopped on the threshold and smiled at his surprise.

'Hello,' she said. 'So you've decided to be early this morning? And shaven too! That's a good sign. I was just on my way to start your lunch, but I might as well introduce you now you're here. Step inside. I'd like you to meet your new solicitor, Mr Steven Bryant. Oh, by the way, he happens to be my father too!'

She stepped aside as she spoke and started to laugh at the expression on Jaysmith's face.

'Don't look so dismayed,' she said. 'It may be nepotism, but he really is the best solicitor I know. Pappy, I'd like you to meet William J. Hutton. I shall expect my usual commission for the introduction. And I'll see you both in not more than an hour. 'Bye.'

She left and Jaysmith slowly advanced to take the hand proffered by the man behind the desk.

'You'll excuse my daughter, I hope, Mr Hutton,' said Bryant. 'It's so good to see her enjoying a joke, that I can excuse her almost anything.'

'Of course,' said Jaysmith. 'It's of no consequence.'

But it was of more consequence than he had yet had time to apprehend. And he was very glad that Anya had given him some excuse for this expression of amazement, but it had nothing to do with her revelation that the solicitor was her father.

No, that was wrong. It had everything to do with it.

For the last time he had seen the creased leathery features of the man whose hand he now held had been a week earlier, framed in the usually fatal circle of his telescopic sight.

CHAPTER SEVEN

An hour later any faint doubts about the identification had been completely removed.

Jaysmith was sitting in the front garden of the red-tiled house called Naddle Foot. Alongside him, filling the bright air with the pungent smoke of a Caporal, was Steven Bryant. And by turning his head just forty-five degrees, he believed he could actually see the entry hole left in the flower bed by his aberrant bullet. He shifted his chair slightly to remove the temptation to stare and looked instead across the valley to the opposing fellside where he had patiently prepared to kill his host.

'Another sherry?' said Bryant in a voice roughened almost to a growl by a lifetime of chain-smoking.

Jaysmith realized he had emptied his glass unawares.

'No, thanks,' he said. 'One before lunch is enough.'

He studied the other man as he spoke. Distance had made him overestimate his age. The venerable halo of silver hair was belied by his shrewd brown eyes and his ease of movement. Early sixties rather than early seventies, an estimate confirmed in the office when Bryant had said, 'To be quite honest, Mr Hutton, I've more or less given up practising law. There's a book I want to write and I've been devoting more and more time to it over the past ten years, and when I got to sixty, three years ago, I thought, to hell with the law's tediums! I still dabble a bit, however, so Anya has not deceived you entirely. But now that she's played her little trick, to which I was not a party, I assure you, I would recommend you let me pass the actual job of conveyancing over to my partner, Donald Grose. He's very able, much better tempered than I am, and to tell the truth, I don't really fancy getting into any business dealings with old Muriel Wilson. She can be a tiresome old stick.'

Jaysmith could understand why Anya had wanted her father to look him over, if, as he suspected, that was the serious purpose behind her little trick. Beneath this friendly, apparently open approach, he was aware of a keen analytical scrutiny. There was no hint of cross-questioning, but questions were constantly being asked. He guessed that Anya valued her father's judgement highly and did his best to impress the man. But all the time, his concentration was being distracted by his own speculations about the other. He could not be what he seemed, a simple country solicitor. Jaysmith's expensive talents were not turned loose on such prey. But none of his own gentle probings had so far produced even the slightest clue. All he could say was that already he sensed in Bryant a strength of will that might mean ruthlessness, and a dark watchfulness that might mean guilt; but his feeling was vague and might itself be the creation of his own uncertainties.

There was one other possible clue, but this too might just be a creation of his own straining after information. From time to time his sharp linguist's ear felt it detected just the slightest nuance of 'foreignness' in Bryant's speech, vanishing as soon as suspected and probably a simple by-product of his tobacco-growl. There was nothing else to suggest non-English origins, except perhaps the name *Anya*, but that was just the kind of name pretentious middle-class parents might give their daughter anyway.

On the other hand, whatever else Bryant was, he gave little sign of belonging to the pretentious middle class. Beneath his smart clothes and civilized conversation, there was an earthiness and, if Jaysmith was not mistaken, a strong vein of sensuality too, untouched as yet by his age.

The probing questions had ceased as though by mutual agreement during lunch, which was a simple though delicious meal of baked trout and green salad followed by a freshly baked bramble pie, all washed down with a crisp Moselle. Bryant was industrious in topping up Jaysmith's glass, and when it was suggested they return to the garden to drink their coffee, the accompanying brandy balloon was full enough to swim a goldfish.

Still icily sober, Jaysmith decided to let the relaxation Bryant obviously hoped for work for him.

'*Anya*,' he said mellowly as she handed him a cup of coffee. 'That's a lovely name you chose for your daughter, Bryant.'

Glancing at him with surprise, the woman said, 'Less buxom than Annie, certainly. We established that.'

Jaysmith smiled and she smiled back, a shared joke which momentarily excluded her father.

Bryant said abruptly, 'It was my mother's name. Anya Winnika.'

'Polish?' said Jaysmith, trying to make his interest casual. 'Were you born in Poland then?'

Bryant did not look as if he was going to answer, but Anya, as if concerned at any hint of rudeness to their guest, said quickly, 'Pappy was a law student in Warsaw till 1939. He got out when the Nazis invaded.'

'And the Russians,' interrupted Bryant harshly. 'Don't forget the Russians came in from the east at the same time.'

'And your parents, did they get out with you?'

Bryant lit another Caporal from the one he was smoking.

'No,' he said. 'They thought they could sit it out. Why not? How many invasions over the centuries had poor Poland had to sit out! I wasn't any wiser than they were, just younger and more impatient. I followed the provisional government first to France then to England. I found out later that when the Nazis came, they requisitioned our family house for one of their senior officers. As for my parents, they were moved into the ghetto. My mother was Jewish, you see. Not orthodox; far from it; and she had cut herself off completely by marrying a

59

Gentile. It took the Nazis to reunite her with her people. My father went with her of course. He was a gentle man, trusting in human nature almost to the point of foolishness. But they'd have had to shoot him to stop him accompanying mamma. The next time I saw Warsaw it was in ruins. Our house had survived but now there was a Russian general in it. It was a small change, hardly noticeable.'

'And your parents?'

He shrugged massively.

'Who knows? The ghetto uprising of '43; the resistance uprising of '44; in one or the other they died, and so many with them that nowhere in the whole of that ruined city could I find a memory or a trace of their passing. Think of that, Mr Hutton, if you can. Think of that!'

Anya put her hand on her father's arm and Jaysmith sipped his brandy for warmth. The sun still shone, but a chill seemed to have risen in this peaceful valley.

'You speak excellent English,' said Jaysmith with a deliberate banality.

It worked. Bryant coughed a laugh and said, 'And why the hell shouldn't I? I've been speaking it longer than you, Hutton. I learned it first from my grandfather when I was a child. He was an Englishman, you see, sent to look after his firm's affairs in Gdansk—Danzig, it was then—in the 1880s. He never went back. When World War One came, he took his Polish wife's name and moved to Warsaw. And after the Second World War was over and I saw that the Russians had a stronghold on my country, and realized that my life was to be in England, well, I reversed the process and reverted to my true patronym. I really am Steven Bryant,

60

Hutton. Or, more properly, Stefan Bryant. Much more reassuring, isn't it, than something full of 'K's and 'Z's?'

'Reassuring to whom?'

'To solid English burghers looking for someone to do a bit of conveyancing for them,' said Bryant. 'But I'm sorry to have bored you with my family history. In the interests of equity, I will now keep quiet, and you must take your chance of telling us something about the Huttons and their origins.'

He smiled satirically as he spoke and he and Anya settled into near-caricatures of close attentiveness.

A trade-off! thought Jaysmith. He would much rather have relaxed and examined what Bryant had told him, looking for clues to his potentially fatal connection with Jacob.

But he needed all his mental powers now to concentrate on the lies he was about to tell. Glancing at Anya, he was filled with shame, but there seemed to be no choice. But rescue was at hand. Inside the house a voice called, 'Mum? Gramp?'

Anya turned her head, tautening the line from chin through neck in a way which caught at Jaysmith's breath, and called, 'Jimmy! We're out in the garden.'

A moment later a boy of about six ran out onto the terrace. He pulled up short when he saw Jaysmith, then resumed his approach more sedately.

'Jimmy, this is Mr Hutton. Jay, this is my son, Jimmy.'

'Hello,' said the boy. He was small, with his mother's brown eyes but much fairer both of hair

61

and complexion. His expression at the moment was rather solemn and serious, but any suggestion of premature maturity was contradicted by a chocolate stain under his lower lip and a comprehensive graze of the right knee.

'Hello,' said Jaysmith.

He held out his hand. Before the boy could shake it, he turned it over to reveal that there was a fifty-pence piece in the palm. Slowly he made it move across the undulations of his knuckles and back again. Then he tossed it high in the air, caught it with his left hand and immediately offered both hands, fists clenched, to the boy who studied them with that look of calm appraisal Jaysmith knew from his mother.

'What's the problem, Jimmy?' said Bryant after a while.

'Well, I know it's in that one,' said the boy pointing to the left hand. 'Only, it's probably not, as it's a trick, and it'll be in that one.'

'You've got to choose, Jimmy,' said Anya. 'That's what the game is, choosing.'

Her eyes met Jaysmith's for a moment.

'All right,' said the boy with the certainty of defeat. 'That one.'

Slowly Jaysmith opened his left hand to show an empty palm.

'I knew it'd be the other after all,' said Jimmy with resignation.

Jaysmith opened his right hand. It was empty too. Then he shot his left hand forward and apparently plucked the coin from Jimmy's ear. He handed it to the boy who took it dubiously and glanced at his mother.

'Is it mine?' he asked hopefully.

'You'd better ask Mr Hutton.'

'It's certainly not mine,' said Jaysmith. 'Would *you* want a coin that's been kept in someone else's ear.'

The boy laughed joyously and thrust the coin into his pocket.

'Thanks a million!' he cried. 'Mum, what's for tea?'

'Nothing till you've washed your face and I've put some antiseptic on that knee,' said his mother.

She took him firmly by the hand and led him into the house.

'Nice kid,' said Jaysmith. 'He looks fine.'

'Why shouldn't he?' said Bryant.

'An only child without a father, it can be tough. Does he talk about him much?'

'Not to me,' said Bryant. 'Children are resilient, Mr Hutton. A boy needs a man around, that's true. Well, Jimmy's got me, so that's all right.'

He spoke with controlled aggression.

'I'm sure it is,' said Jaysmith. 'How long has it been since his father died?'

'Last December.'

'What was it? Illness? Accident?'

'Climbing accident,' said Bryant shortly. 'But I think my daughter's business ought really to be discussed with my daughter, don't you? Another drop of brandy?'

'No thanks,' said Jaysmith rising. 'It's late. If school's out, it's time I was going. Goodbye, Mr Bryant. Thanks for your help and your hospitality.'

He stretched out his hand. Bryant took it and gave it a perfunctory shake without rising.

'Glad to have you with us,' he said. 'I hope Anya asks you again. Grose will get the conveyance under way.'

He found Anya in the kitchen bathing her son's knee. The boy's face was screwed up in mock agony.

'I must be off,' said Jaysmith. 'It's been a splendid day.'

'Are you coming to Carlisle with us on Saturday?' asked the boy.

Jaysmith raised his eyebrows interrogatively.

'There's a soccer match,' said Anya gloomily. 'He's conned his grandfather and me into taking him as a pre-birthday treat.'

'Birthday?'

'That's the following Saturday. Fortunately Carlisle United are playing down south that day, so he'll have to make do with a party instead.'

'Please come,' urged the boy.

'Well, I'd love to come to the party, if I'm asked, but I can't make the match. I've got to go down to London tomorrow and I may have to stay away a couple of days.'

He thought Anya looked disappointed but it may have been wishful thinking.

'I've been to London,' said Jimmy. 'Granddad Wilson lives there.'

'And Mr Hutton will soon be living up here. He's buying Great-Aunt Muriel's house.'

The boy digested this.

'Is Great-Aunt Muriel dead?' he asked.

'No, of course not! She's just moving down into the village. Jay, if you can hang on till I finish with this monster, I'll see you out.'

Jaysmith said, 'I'll use the bathroom if I may.'

He went upstairs and swiftly checked the landing windows. They were double glazed and fitted with what looked like new security locks. He had already noticed an alarm box high up under the eaves. He opened a bedroom door at random. It proved to be Anya's. The straw handbag she'd been carrying in Keswick was tossed casually onto the bed. He opened it and was amazed at the quantity of bric-à-brac it held. After a little rummaging, he came up with a key ring which he bore off with him into the bathroom. He locked the door and sat on the edge of the bath. Ignoring the car keys, he carefully made prints of the three others in a large cake of soap. It was a process he had seen used in television thrillers but not one he'd ever had occasion to try for himself. Carefully he wrapped the soap in his handkerchief, removed all traces from the keys, flushed the toilet and unlocked the door. Swiftly he made for Anya's bedroom but stopped dead on the threshold.

Anya was standing by the bed in the process of shaking out the contents of her handbag onto the coverlet.

'Hello,' she said, becoming aware of his presence. 'Won't be a sec. I wanted my car keys and as usual they seem to have sunk to the bottom. I keep far too much rubbish in here.'

She resumed her shaking. He stepped into the room, put his hands on her shoulders, and spun her round to face him. He drew her to him and kissed her passionately as he dropped the keys onto the bedspread. It was more successful than his attempt on the Crinkles in that she did not thrust him off but nor did she return the kiss and when he broke off she said calmly, 'Is it the sight of a bed which brings out the brute in you?'

'I'm sorry,' he said. 'I think I just wanted to

assure you that I'd be coming back.'

'Why should I doubt it? After all, you are buying a house up here. Oh, there they are.'

She had turned away from him and seen the keys.

'Am I moving too fast?' he asked gently.

'Not as long as the finance is in order, no,' she said judiciously. 'Aunt Muriel won't want to hang about, you know.'

'You know what I mean.'

'I've only met you three, no, four times,' she replied passionately. 'How on earth should I know if I know what you mean? Or care for that matter?'

She left the room and he followed her down the old creaking staircase. In the hallway he said lightly, 'You're well protected, I see.'

She glanced at him to see if he was being ironical, then followed his gaze to the alarm junction box on the wall behind an old-fashioned coat rack.

'Yes,' she said. 'It's a bit of a nuisance. I keep forgetting.'

Idly he reached up and flicked the box open.

'It looks pretty new.'

'It is. We got burgled a couple of months ago. They didn't take much, but they made a lot of mess and it was rather frightening, being so isolated. So pappy got a firm of security specialists in to tighten things up.'

'Still here, Hutton? Goodbye once more.'

Bryant had come back into the house and was standing in the doorway of what looked like a study or office.

'Mum, can I have my tea now?' demanded Jimmy, appearing at the kitchen door.

Jaysmith looked at the three of them. They appeared as a formidable family group, each splendidly individual perhaps even to the point of wilfulness, but very united too. He guessed that it was going to be hard to get one without the approval of the others.

Soon he might have to decide how much he really wanted that one.

But as he followed Anya out of the shady entrance hall into the ambered warmth of the autumn sunlight, and she turned and offered him her hand with a slightly crooked smile which mocked the formality of the gesture, he knew he had decided already.

CHAPTER EIGHT

He set out for London early on Friday morning while the mists were still grazing the fellsides like the ghosts of old flocks. The pain he felt at leaving all this behind surprised him, but as he'd sat and talked to Bryant the day before, he had known he had to go. Jacob was in London, and only Jacob could tell him why Bryant had been targeted and whether the instruction was still active since the deadline. Further than that, he could not think.

The journey down had a dreamlike quality. He drove with automatic ease, his body at rest in a soundproof cocoon, with soft upholstery, even-temperatured air and gentle music from the stereo cassette. He tried to fix his thoughts on the problems ahead but they kept on drifting back to the quiet joys of the land behind him. Four hours later, when he parked his car and stepped out into the din of Central London, it was like leaving a monastery cell for an iron foundry.

Quickly he made his way to his flat on the west side of Soho. It was twenty years since he had come to live here. The sixties were just beginning to swing. Then, the district's aura of urban picturesque with hints of Bohemian low-life had seemed a perfect match for the times; the old inhibitions were dying and the age of openness, freedom, and guiltless joy was being born. Not that Jaysmith had been very receptive to such optimism then, but now, for the first time, he was aware with more than just his eyes and ears of the squalid side-channels all that flood of high promise had been diverted into.

What had seemed Bohemian was now Babylonian; what had begun as openness was now exhibitionism; the porn merchants had worked out that there was more money in joyless guilt than guiltless joy, and the only freedom celebrated in these littered streets was the one civil liberty that civilized societies never denied their citizens—their right to seek degradation and self-destruction any which way they liked.

His flat occupied the top floor of a building which had once had a Greek restaurant at street level. Now there was an Adult Video shop. He turned into the doorway leading onto the narrow stair which ran up the side of the building. At the foot of the stairs squatted two youths with their arms round each other. One had his head shaved smooth except for a spikey orange-dyed coxcomb; the other had lank black hair and the ten o'clock shadow of an Arafat beard prickling his jowels and

68

jaw. The Coxcomb had his face in a plastic bag, held tight around the neck. He was breathing in with pig-like snorts and when he raised his face, the glue in the bag was running like mucus round his nostrils and lips. Arafat took the bag, while he stared vacantly at Jaysmith. Neither made any attempt to move out of his way.

Holding back his anger, Jaysmith stepped over them and made his way up the stairs. At his door he paused and looked back in case the glue-sniffers had ambitions to become muggers too. All was quiet. He opened his door. It had two deadlocks on it and the windows had internal steel shutters so that the flat was in complete darkness despite the smokey sunshine outside.

He flicked on the light and glanced at the strip of light-sensitive photographic paper which he always placed on the floor near the door immediately before leaving. As he watched, it turned black.

He poured himself a drink and looked round, horrified at what he saw. There was no shortage of comfort—he'd been given a good start, and the money had come pumping in, thick and regular as arterial blood, after that. But what he had constructed was a prison.

He pressed the rewind-and-play button on his answering machine. There was very little on it. Few people had his number, and fewer of those were likely to be making social calls. In fact only one message caught his attention, not really a message at all, but readable as one.

A man's voice exclaimed *Jaysmith!* That was all.

He checked the timing of the call. It had come through less than an hour after he had phoned

Enid to cancel his contract on Bryant.

He listened to the word again.

Jaysmith!

The word was distorted in anger, bitten off short as though there was much else to follow but the speaker had recognized the folly of committing it to an answering machine.

Despite the distortion, despite the brevity, he had no difficulty in recognizing the voice. It was Jacob, no doubt of that. That precise, rather nasal accent was unmistakable, even though the usual drily ironic inflexion had been replaced by something approaching rage. Any emotion which brought Jacob so close to breaking his own security must have been extreme indeed.

The flat had two bedrooms, or rather a bedroom and a boxroom. This last contained a small workbench with a vice and various metal working tools. The kind of repairs and modifications Jaysmith occasionally wanted to make to his equipment were not to be doled out to some jobbing craftsman. Now he carefully unwrapped the soap taken from the bathroom at Naddle Foot and set about producing keys which matched the imprints in the cake.

He worked swiftly and with tremendous concentration and ninety minutes later he was satisfied. Carefully he wrapped up the three keys with a small tungsten file for on-the-spot modification and put the resulting package into his inside pocket.

Now he relaxed and realized he was hungry, not having eaten anything since his breakfast at the Crag Hotel. The freezer held a selection of made-up meals. He selected one at random and put it in the microwave oven. It turned out to be lasagne. He ate most of it, washed down with a half bottle of his best Chablis. Suddenly he felt rather restless and looked at the telephone and thought of ringing Anya in Cumbria. It was a crazy notion, instantly dismissed. He then thought of ringing his Enid number, to let them know he was here. But that would be a mistake too. He had retired. He must not seem to have any desire to make contact. And in any case he guessed that they would know he was back by now and if they wished to contact him, eventually they'd get round to it.

He forced himself to relax, and went through to the bedroom, and lay on his bed, and waited for Jacob.

*   *   *

The first time he ever saw Jacob, he had been lying on his bed.

He swam out of a drug-filled sleep into a world of physical pain and then burst through that into a world of mental and emotional agony, more bitter far, and finally opened his eyes in desperate search of a physical image to blot out the horrors in his mind.

And there was Jacob.

Just a man in a dark double-breasted suit totally unsuitable for the hot, humid climate of South-East Asia, yet there was no sign of discomfort as he sat by the bed, still as a lizard on a wall, his squashed-up face wearing its customary expression of weary puzzlement at the foolishness on display before him.

'You're awake, are you?' he asked. 'Can you

71

move?'

He tried. The pain in his body shifted around a bit but didn't get much worse until he tried to speak. Then he realized that the left side of his face must have been badly cut. A long strip of plaster covered perhaps a dozen stitches.

'Where's Nguyet?' he managed to whisper.

The dark-suited man shrugged.

'I should think she's dead, wouldn't you, Mr Collins?'

'I saw her, she was alive . . .' His voice tailed off as he recalled his last glimpse of that golden body, supine among a forest of dusty boots.

'The civil police say she was a taxi-girl picked up under Madame Nhu's morality laws. The secret police say she was a communist sympathizer fomenting unrest at the university. The Special Force say she was a Buddhist saboteur. They can't all be right, can they? But they all agree that she died resisting arrest, and I'm afraid they can't all be wrong either.'

'It's not true! She can't be dead!'

His voice spiralled high, but not out of conviction. The other did not even argue.

'And you,' he said. 'You'd have been dead too, wouldn't you? If those Americans hadn't happened to come along. What did you think you were doing?'

The tone was one of polite curiosity. He closed his eyes and let the memories come rushing back. Flung out into the street in front of Nguyet's apartment, he had staggered half-demented with rage and terror into the nearest bar. Here he had emptied his wallet in front of the barman and demanded a gun. Saigon, under President Diem's repressive regime, was a city where it was said you could get anything for money. The barman said nothing but removed the money and five minutes later a newspaper-wrapped package was put into his hands. It was not a bar used much by Westerners, but as he left, two Americans came in. They were attached to their Embassy's Cultural and Educational Mission and Jaysmith's British Council teaching contract at the university had brought them in touch. He ignored their greeting and rushed past them, tearing at the newspaper package. Alarmed by his appearance, the Americans followed.

As he arrived back at Nguyet's apartment block, the street door opened and the dog-faced colonel and his entourage came out.

Screaming with hate he had ripped the last of the paper from the package and leapt forward brandishing the ancient revolver it contained. Thrusting the weapon into the colonel's face, he squeezed the trigger. It fell off. A soldier smashed the useless weapon from his hand. Another drove him to the ground with a savage blow to the head. Then they were all at him with rifle butts and boots. Only the arrival of the Americans had saved him from being beaten to death in the street.

'I was going to kill that bastard,' he said with savage hate. 'I still am.'

'Are you? This is the man, I believe, isn't it?'

A photograph was held in front of him. The dog-face of the colonel stared down at him. He nodded, unable to speak.

'Colonel Tai. A very nasty piece of work. Directly answerable to Tran Van Khiem who, as you may know, is Madame Nhu's brother and head

73

of anti-subversion forces. And you're going to kill him, are you? You'll have to be quick, Mr Collins.'

'What do you mean?'

The dark-suited man pointed at an envelope by the bed.

'You're *persona non grata*, Mr Collins. There's a plane ticket in there, valid for this evening's flight only. If you're not on the flight, you will be arrested on a charge of attempted murder, subversion, sabotage, it hardly matters what as you're not likely to survive arrest, are you? I should catch that plane if I were you, even if it means crawling to the airport, naked.'

The superior tone got to him at last.

'Who the hell are you?' he demanded. 'Are you official? From the Embassy? You've got the look of one of those smooth bastards!'

The man laughed drily, apparently genuinely amused by the comment.

'A smooth bastard, am I? Then you'd better call me Jacob, hadn't you, Mr Collins? And am I official? No, I'm so unofficial, I scarcely exist, do I? Come here a moment, will you?'

He went to the window. Laboriously the injured man climbed out of bed and followed. His flat was in a small block on a side street off the Boulevard Charner, one of Saigon's main thoroughfares, choked now as nearly always during the day with cycles, motor-scooters, cars and trucks. The man who called himself Jacob pointed to the intersection.

'At precisely six o'clock this afternoon, Colonel Tai will be going down the boulevard in his jeep. He will be held up there by a slight accident, right at that corner. How far is it? About fifty yards,

74

would you say? An easy shot for a man who was his regimental and university rifle champion, wouldn't you say?'

'How the hell do you know that? Who are you?'

'Nobody. Jacob if you like, but I prefer nobody. What do you think, Mr Collins? Could you pull a trigger? One that wouldn't fall off this time?'

He didn't have to think.

'Oh yes,' he said. 'I could pull a trigger.'

Jacob contemplated him for a moment.

'Yes, I think you could,' he said softly. 'Goodbye, Mr Collins.'

He left so abruptly that there was no time to ask further questions.

An hour later there was a gentle tap at the door.

When he opened it, there was no one there. But against the wall stood a long cardboard box with the name and trademark of a well-known brand of vacuum cleaner on it.

He took it into the flat and opened it.

It contained a Lee-Enfield .303 rifle, old, but beautifully maintained. The magazine was full.

He went to the window and looked out. Fifty yards. From this distance he could not miss. The thought of squeezing the trigger and seeing Tai's head burst open in a shower of blood and brains filled him with such a passion of hate that he had to sit down till the weakness in his legs passed away. He had a bottle of whisky in his case, bought at Heathrow eight months earlier and still unopened.

He opened it now and drank from the bottle. It did him good. He drank again. After a while the drink calmed the wildness in him and his mind began to function again. He knew beyond all doubt he was going to kill Tai, but he now let his thoughts dwell on the mysterious Jacob. Saigon in the autumn of 1963 was awash with rumour. Self-immolation by Buddhist monks; acts of sabotage by God knows who; arrest without trial by Government forces; the sacking of the Saigon pagodas; all these had fuelled the perennial rumour of an imminent anti-Diem coup. Perhaps most significant of all was the withdrawal of American support, signalled in a variety of ways.

Tai's assassination by a Westerner would be just another such signal. That the assassin was English, not American, would mean nothing to the native populace, but it would enable the Americans to claim total innocence. Jacob was probably paying off some debt to the CIA.

But for the full effect of the assassination to be felt it would have to be known that the killer was a Westerner. And there was only one way of advertising that.

He stood at the window and looked out to the intersection. Jacob needed no special plan. Tai would have his usual armed escort. It was only fifty yards to the apartment block's only entrance. If he survived sixty seconds after pulling the trigger, he would be a very lucky man.

No. He corrected himself. A very unlucky man.

He didn't mind dying if that was the price to pay for the colonel's death. His attack at Nguyet's apartment had been suicidal.

But he felt a sudden reluctance to die for the man called Jacob and the mysterious forces behind him.

Despite his aching body, the whisky was making him drowsy. There were still two hours to go and he dare not risk sleep. He pulled on trousers and a

76

shirt and went down into the street.

He strolled aimlessly, ignoring the city's crowded and varied street life which on first arrival had so fascinated him. The beggars, the girls selling flowers, the vendors of books and pictures and ornaments, the street urchins, the workmen in battered felt hats with never-ending, never-removed cigarettes in their lips, the hire-car drivers, the shoe-shine boys, none of these could interest him any more. Only once, when among the steady stream of svelte and graceful Vietnamese women passing in and out of the fashionable shops, he imagined he glimpsed Nguyet, did he show any animation. But even as he pressed forward crying her name, he knew he was wrong.

And he had been wrong even to have loved her.

He had loved his father and he had deserted him.

He had loved his mother and she had died.

He had been willing for the want of any other object to transfer his love to his stepfather, but he had rejected him.

In the Army, at university, he had been popular, active, successful, but he had not made the mistake of allowing anyone too close. When he got the chance to come to this exotic, distant place, there had been no ties at home to make him hesitate.

And here, as if the bitter rules which must guide his life in England did not apply, he had relaxed once more and taken Nguyet into the deepest and most secret places of his soul.

Now she had paid the price.

He stopped so suddenly that other pedestrians bumped into him. But these polite and gentle people showed no irritation or curiosity. He

77

realized he was outside the Hotel de la Paix, one of the city's many monuments to the French colonial dream. Without conscious decision, he went into the crowded lobby and made his way up the stairs to the top floor. Letting his instinct guide him, he turned left and walked to the end of the corridor. There was a bathroom here. He opened the door and went in.

It was a high airy room. A posse of cockroaches scuttled beneath the high-sided cast-iron bath at his entry. Painfully, he clambered up on the side of the bath and, disturbing another huge cockroach on the dusty windowsill, opened the high narrow window.

It gave him a crow's-eye view straight down the boulevard. There, somewhere between three and four hundred yards away, was the intersection where the colonel's jeep would be stopped in just over an hour's time.

He got down off the bath and went to the door. There was a key on the inside. He removed it, went out, and locked the door behind him.

On his way back down the boulevard, he was even less conscious of his surroundings as he carefully paced out the distance. Three hundred and twenty-five yards. Back in his flat, he packed the few belongings he wanted to take with him in a small grip, slipped a small pair of field glasses he used for bird-spotting into his pocket and repacked the rifle in its box.

He arrived back at the hotel at quarter to six. Approaching one of the hire-car drivers he told him he would be leaving for the airport in about fifteen minutes and gave him the grip to look after. It was Nguyet who had taught him this lesson about most of her people. Trust given without hesitation was nearly always repaid in full.

No one paid him any attention as once more he climbed the stairs. Locking the bathroom door behind him, he took out the rifle and adjusted the sights. They had been set at fifty yards and no doubt perfectly zeroed. Jacob was not a man to omit any detail, he guessed.

At five to six, he turned the bath taps on. The ancient geyser made a thoroughly satisfactory din, a series of groans, wheezes, and explosions among which a gun shot would hardly be noticed. Standing on the edge of the bath, he scanned the middle distance with his glasses.

It was perfectly timetabled. At one minute to six he caught his first glimpse of the small convoy of two jeeps moving very fast and scattering the other traffic with much blaring of horns. As they came nearer, he saw that one was crowded with soldiers, guns at the ready.

The other had only one armed soldier sitting next to the driver, and in the back, still and solitary, Colonel Tai.

At the intersection a bent old man pushed an overloaded handcart into the path of an ancient station-wagon which slewed round, blocking the highway. The driver leapt out, shouting abuse at the old man. The jeeps arrived and skidded to a halt.

The trouble was that while there was certainly a clear shot from his apartment in the side street, from the hotel the station-wagon blocked his line of fire. The soldiers were screaming at the driver and the old man with the handcart, who continued their argument, desperately trying to keep things going till the dilatory assassin condescended to fire. Any moment now, the impatient colonel might order his jeep to divert up the side street, taking him safely out of any possible shot.

But the colonel's impatience manifested itself in quite another way. Standing up in his jeep, he too began to shout at the quarrelling men. Three quarters of his head, just enough for identification, were visible above the station-wagon's roof.

He expelled his breath slowly and squeezed the trigger.

The explosion was deafening in the confines of the small room, but he hardly noticed it. All his senses were straining out towards that distant figure. The head snapped back as though flicked by a giant finger, and Tai fell backwards out of sight.

Stepping down, he dipped the rifle into the bathwater, rubbed the stock and butt, then slid it out of sight under the bath. Then, turning off the taps and pulling out the plug, he went to the door and unlocked it.

The corridor was empty. He walked down the stairs, not hurrying, across the foyer and into the street. His driver was waiting with the engine of his ancient Renault ticking over. He got in and the vehicle set off heading in the opposite direction to that in which the colonel's body lay.

He arrived at the airport just in time to check in for his flight. The girl on duty said apologetically over his shoulder to someone behind him, 'Sorry, sir, with this gentleman's arrival, the flight is now full.'

He turned to find himself meeting Jacob's indifferent gaze.

'You thought there'd be a place,' he said with

80

mild accusation.

Jacob shrugged slightly and said, 'Feeling better, are you, Mr Collins?'

'Much better.'

'I'm pleased to hear it. Best hurry. You don't want to miss your plane, do you? Perhaps we'll meet again.'

'No,' he said, 'I never want to see you again. Never.'

He turned away and headed for the departure gate. He didn't look back, neither at the man called Jacob nor at the city of Saigon. He was finished with them both for ever.

*   *   *

He had fallen into a light sleep when a gentle tap at the door aroused him instantly.

When he opened it he found himself looking at the two glue-sniffers from the foot of the stairs. The only difference was that their eyes were no longer blank, but bright and alert.

He stood quite still till their eye-search was over, then the scruffily bearded one called, 'All right, sir.'

A third figure appeared behind them.

'Thank you, Davey,' he said to the bearded man. 'Thank you, Adam. I shouldn't be long.'

The glue-sniffers withdrew, closing the door.

The newcomer nodded casually at Jaysmith.

'Hello, Jay,' he said.

'Hello, Jacob,' said Jaysmith.

CHAPTER NINE

The two men sat and viewed each other like old friends reunited after long separation and uncertain what in their relationship had withered, what remained vital.

Jacob had refused wine, accepted whisky. He raised the glass and sipped it slowly.

He's aged, thought Jaysmith. For many years Jacob had been just an unchanging voice to him. In his mind's eye, he had always stayed as at their first encounter. Now he saw a man in his sixties, fit and active still, but shrunken somehow. The simian puzzlement of that crinkled face had been eroded from great ape to marmoset.

But the mind and the method remained the same.

'You puzzled us, didn't you?' he said with a slight shake of the head. 'What happened up there?'

'I missed.'

Jacob showed no surprise.

'Was the target alerted?'

'No.'

'Of course not, or you'd have said, wouldn't you? What was your range?'

'Twelve fifty.'

'You always liked the long kill, didn't you, Jay? Right from that very first time.'

His voice was gently reminiscing. Old friends finding their way back to the old relationship via shared memories.

'This time I missed.'

'After over twenty perfect hits, you deserve a

miss, don't you?' suggested Jacob. 'You're overreacting a bit, aren't you, Jay?'

'It wasn't the first time. I missed the Chinaman as well,' said Jaysmith.

'Did you? That was a strange miss, wasn't it? Straight through the head.'

'He moved. It was his bad luck, my good. I'd noticed some blurring before, on the Austrian job for instance. I've been to an optician. He gave it a name, says it's unimportant, won't affect any normal use of the eyes. He doesn't know what I do for a living, of course.'

'I'm pleased about that,' said Jacob mildly. 'But if it's so minor, can't it be cured? Or corrected? Or perhaps you should change your style, Jay. Get in closer.'

'Closeness kills,' said Jaysmith coldly. 'Both ways. You want close work, you'll have to get yourself someone else. I'm finished, Jacob. That's my last word.'

'Yes, I can see that,' said Jacob. 'I'm sorry, Jay. You were the best I've known. The very best. I'm sorry to lose you.'

'And I'm sorry I didn't say something after the Chinaman. But this job seemed very urgent. More whisky?'

'Thank you,' said Jacob. 'Yes, it was urgent, wasn't it? But never mind. Win some, lose some, don't we?'

His easy tone was a light year away from the barely controlled anger of the voice on the telephone.

Jaysmith poured the whisky and said casually, 'I wish I could have left you more time.'

'For what?'

'Before the deadline was up. Did you manage to arrange anything else?'

The little monkey face was gloomy.

'No, I'm afraid not.'

'And the deadline was firm, was it? Or can it be resited?'

Jacob shrugged indifferently.

'We'll have to see, shan't we?' he said.

It was not a satisfactory answer. Pushing harder could be dangerous. Jacob was no fool and very hard to read. Jaysmith wasn't deceived by the other's apparent ready acceptance of his reason for quitting. There were plenty of other better reasons, principal among them that he had been bought off, and the first hint of a direct link between himself and Naddle Foot would confirm their worst suspicions.

But he had to push.

'What is he anyway?' he asked idly. 'Political?'

Jacob put down his glass very gently.

'How strange that you should ask,' he murmured.

'Strange?'

'Yes. Your first miss in twenty years, and now your first question, Jay.'

'The one triggers off the other perhaps,' said Jaysmith. 'I've nearly always been able to read in the papers about the targets I've hit. It's not so strange I should feel curious about the one who got away.'

'No? Perhaps not. But I hope retirement isn't going to make you forget our agreement, Jay. You do remember our agreement, don't you?'

'Oh yes,' said Jaysmith softly. 'Like it was yesterday.' He wasn't lying. What was vague in his

84

memory was the period immediately after his return to England from Vietnam. Friendless, jobless and in a near-catatonic state, he had lived in a bedsit in Notting Hill, his days spent aimlessly wandering the streets of London and his nights spent roaming the streets of Saigon. His physical injuries had quickly healed, only the long scar on his left cheek remaining as a permanent memento. But his mind bore wounds which refused even to heal into scars. Day or night, the same images flashed in psychedelic competition across his mind—Nguyet's naked body lying with bloody legs splayed, and Colonel Tai's head jerking back as the bullet struck. Finally his landlady had called in a doctor, and the doctor had called in a psychiatrist, and Harry Collins had found himself sitting in a quiet, dimly lit room, describing all that had happened, all that he felt.

He remembered little of this in detail, except the last few questions.

'Do you regret shooting Colonel Tai?'

'No!'

'Yet you shot him to avenge the girl's death, didn't you?'

'Yes.'

'Did you believe that revenge might bring you peace?'

'Yes.'

'But it hasn't.'

'No.'

'So hitting Colonel Tai was pointless.'

'*No!*'

'What then?'

And now he had stood up and spoken with a quiet intensity more powerful far than any

85

shouting.

'It wasn't enough, that's all. He should have died harder. Or there should have been more. The world is full of them, full of Colonel Tais, murdering, torturing, corrupting, betraying. There are too many, too many, too many!'

The man had given him a tablet. After he took it, he fell asleep. When he awoke he was lying on a bed and once more Jacob was at the bedside.

'What do you want?'

'I was worried about you, wasn't I?'

'Because I didn't get killed, as you expected! Because I might start talking?'

'That's right,' agreed Jacob. 'I did expect you to get killed. But you were cleverer than I realized, weren't you? That was a fine shot, by the way. One of the finest I've known, in the circumstances. You did extremely well.'

'Did I? I survived, that's true. Though I don't know why. And I've talked!'

His voice rose triumphantly.

'Yes, I know. We had to keep an eye on you, of course. Guilt feelings can lead to very embarrassing behaviour, can't they? But there was nothing of guilt in your outpourings, I gather. Just a desire to carry on the good work. Would you like that?'

'Like what?'

'To carry on the good work, of course,' murmured Jacob.

'What do you mean?' he demanded.

And Jacob told him.

'One step at a time, at first,' he concluded. 'You'd never be under pressure from me. We'd supply all necessary equipment, of course. And money.'

'I don't want money.'

86

'You'd have to live,' insisted Jacob. 'You'd have to be comfortable, you'd have to be fit. Think about it.'

He'd thought about it. The idea had occupied his mind to the exclusion of all else, including the streets of Saigon.

Jacob came back.

'Well?'

'I'd need to be sure of this. I'd need to be sure that these—what do you call them?—targets deserve to die as Colonel Tai deserved it. I'd need to know all about them . . .'

'No,' said Jacob simply.

'No?'

'You mustn't know anything more than is necessary to target them,' said Jacob. 'Believe me, that is best. But I'll make an agreement with you. I won't give you any sermon about patriotism or the national interest, but I'll guarantee this. I'll never give you a target who is not as guilty as Tai. And your part of the bargain is that you never ask questions. And never talk, of course. Are we agreed?'

He had nodded and Jacob had shaken his hand.

'One more thing. Harry Collins is dead. We need to start you again from scratch. Think of a name.'

He had replied impatiently. 'Smith. John Smith.'

'It's a little nondescript.'

'All right. Winston Churchill.'

Jacob sighed.

'I prefer John Smith. J. Smith. No, I have it. *Jaysmith*. One word. An English compromise. From now on you may be many people, but to me you are Jaysmith. Jacob and Jaysmith. They march well together, don't you think?'

And so he had been rechristened.

And three months after the christening, from the top of a tall building in Istanbul he had fired the shot which had been his confirmation.

And now it was over.

Or would have been if he hadn't met a slim, dark woman with more sorrow in her eyes than her heart deserved to know.

* * *

'No, retirement doesn't end our agreement, Jay,' repeated Jacob. 'But I will tell you this, as a retirement gift. This man that you missed, I would say that he deserved to die more than any other target I've ever given you.'

He spoke with surprising vehemence.

'That sounds more like a reproach than a gift,' said Jaysmith.

'It was not intended to,' said Jacob, rising.

He held out his hand. It felt dry and cold.

'Good luck, Jay,' he said. 'Take care, won't you?'

'I will.'

One last glance around the room, and Jacob was gone. He had shown no curiosity about Jaysmith's plans. More curiously, he had made no real attempt to probe into his reasons for retiring. At the very least, Jaysmith had expected that his visit to the optician and the man's diagnosis would be carefully checked. Perhaps it had been already, but he doubted it. He'd picked the man at random and made the appointment in person. This could mean that Jacob was certain he had been turned, which was not a healthy state to be in.

There was a tap at the door and he started like a nervous schoolgirl in an empty house.

'Who is it?' he called.

'It's Adam.'

Carefully he opened the door.

The orange-haired glue-sniffer stood there. He wore an earring and light-grey eye make-up. He was probably in his twenties but could have passed for seventeen. His voice was soft and well-educated.

'Jacob sent me back,' he said. 'He forgot to ask the address of your optician.'

Jaysmith took the notepad from the telephone table and scribbled the address. When he handed it over, the youth didn't move but said shyly, 'Davey didn't want me to come back, Mr Jaysmith. He knows how much I've always admired you.'

Jaysmith was taken aback.

'Admired me? You don't know me!'

Adam flushed rather becomingly and said, 'I'm sorry; I meant your record, you know. The way you do things. Always so smooth. Always such long shots. I know how difficult that is. I shoot a bit myself.'

Is this my successor? wondered Jaysmith.

'Save it for the fairground,' he said dismissively.

'It's been a real pleasure meeting you,' said the youth, discomfited.

Jaysmith glowered at him till he closed the door. The young man's apparent adulation had been very disturbing, not so much for its undoubted homosexual dimension (which was no doubt why the bearded Davey objected) but in terms of simple hero-worship. To be a hero because he could, or once could, blow a man's brains out from a mile away was not something he felt proud of.

He went to bed that night wrestling with the

problem of how to interpret what Jacob had said about Bryant. Did his vehemence about the solicitor's deserving to die spring from frustration that the deadline was past and he would now be allowed to live? Or was it a hint that the target-order would be re-activated?

He fell into an uneasy sleep in which inevitably he squatted high on the fellside overlooking Naddle Foot and when he raised the A.R.T. to his eye, the face that sprang towards him was once again Anya's.

He woke up. It was four AM. He got up and began packing. He didn't want to be here and there was nothing more to keep him.

He left by a rear entrance which took him over a couple of walls and down a narrow passage into Greek Street. He saw no sign of Adam with the coxcomb or Davey with the beard; but Jacob would not be short of well-trained watchers if he felt that his lost protégé was still worth watching. When he got to the BMW, he took it on a serpentine route to the south and west out of Central London.

It wasn't till he was completely satisfied there was no tail that he made for the MI and headed north.

It looked lighter up there already.

CHAPTER TEN

At one o'clock on Saturday afternoon he was sitting in the bracken high above the road which ran past Naddle Foot, eating a cheese sandwich. He could see the main gate about five hundred yards away, and his binoculars hung ready round his neck.

At one-thirty there was movement. A car came down the long curving drive. It wasn't Anya's little Fiat but the old Rover that Bryant drove. The gate was closed and the car stopped to let Jimmy out to open it. He was dressed in jeans and a lumberjack's jacket with a blue and white scarf round his neck. Jaysmith moved his binoculars to focus on the car. Bryant was at the wheel with Anya beside him. She was watching her son and saying something to Bryant and laughing at his reply. Jaysmith's throat constricted with pleasure at the sight of her, but another part of his mind was noting that this was the perfect ambusher's situation—a car halted while an obstacle is removed, a stationary target strapped down with a seat belt—and his binocular's focus went slithering wildly up the fellside even though his rationality assured him that Jacob could hardly have got another operative in the field since last night. In any case, the car was now moving. He watched it out of sight, gave it another half-hour to account for an unexpected return to pick up something forgotten, then began to descend.

His first key fitted perfectly, but the second wouldn't turn. He removed it, sprinkled some French chalk on it and inserted it again. A couple of minutes' work with his file smoothed away the impediment and he was in. The third key was the crucial one. This was the one to turn off the burglar alarm during the short period of grace given to the householder after opening the front door. There would be no time for adjustment. If this didn't work first time, there'd be bells clamouring up the valley and probably a demanding buzz sounding in

Keswick police station.

He opened the control box, inserted the key and turned it gently. There was some resistance. He increased the pressure. At last there was a satisfying click.

He waited another whole minute to be quite sure, then he started his search. He had little hope of success for he had no idea what he was looking for, nor what he might do with it if he found it. But in the complete absence of any other plan, it seemed that the most productive thing he could do was to attempt to find out why it was that Bryant had been targeted.

He started with Bryant's study which was downstairs. It was at the same time an old-fashioned study with a leather-topped partner's desk and shelves packed with books of all sizes and ages, and a modern office with an electric typewriter, aluminium filing cabinets and a small photocopier.

He began to search thoroughly and professionally. At the end of an hour he knew that Bryant was writing a history of Poland from its revival as an independent republic under Pilsudski in 1918 to the present day, that he was a methodical and conscientious researcher who left no stone unturned, no fact uncross-indexed, and that his researches had taken him into most major British and European libraries, including those in Poland itself.

But how any of this could have put him on Jacob's target list was not apparent.

He paused, discouraged. Then he recalled his imaginings as he watched Anya and Bryant sitting together in the car, laughing at Jimmy's antics as he opened the gate. He thought of a bullet smashing the windscreen and driving splinters of glass deep into Anya's face and eyes; perhaps even, if his successor was inefficient, or had failing eyesight, the bullet itself burning through her flesh and bone.

He had to know what was going on. Only then could he decide how to handle it. At the moment the only other plan he could think of was to get Anya out of the way and let Jacob get on with having Bryant killed, if he so desired. But, practicalities apart, the implications revolted him.

He returned to his search.

The bedroom was even less helpful than the study, its one potential source of information being inaccessible. This was a wall safe behind a print of a horsemarket by someone called Michalowski. He spun the dial a couple of times, hoping to hit the combination by serendipity. He expected nothing, and was right. Then it occurred to him that a man like Bryant, sharp enough to retain a number in his mind, was probably also sharp enough to know that the passing years could imperceptibly blunt even the sharpest memory. Also modern life had multiplied the number of numbers a man needed to have on instant recall.

An aide-memoire was the answer. He tried to think as Bryant might think. Where better for numbers than among numbers?

He went downstairs to the telephone in the hall. There was a book of addresses and numbers by it. He looked through it hopelessly. Any one of these names could be fictitious. At the back was a list of emergency and tradesmen numbers. Doctor, dentist, water, gas, electricity, police, garage . . .

He paused and went through into the kitchen. He had only been in here once before but his memory had served him well. What was a house without gas doing with a gas board number?

He noted it down and went upstairs. He tried it out in various ways. Backwards proved right. The door clicked open.

His self-congratulation did not last long. The safe contained very little: a British passport and a small bundle of letters. He looked in the passport. Bryant was well travelled, presumably on his research trips. There were several entry stamps for Poland. But there was nothing at all for almost a year.

The letters were in Polish with no address. They were signed *Ota*. Jaysmith's smattering of Polish suggested they were letters from a close friend, perhaps even love letters, but he would need a lot more time and a Polish dictionary to make real sense out of them. They were in envelopes with a single 'S' scrawled on the outside. The only clue to their means of arrival was a larger envelope with Bryant's name and address on it. This was postmarked Manchester. Inside he found a sheet of paper again without any address and a brief scrawl which read *I'll be going again in the autumn. I'll get in touch*. It was signed *Anton*.

He took the letters downstairs and returned to the study. There was paper in the photocopier. He switched it on, then carefully copied the letters. After resetting the counter to zero, he returned to the address book by the telephone. Carefully he went through it. There was only one address in Manchester, and it belonged to someone called Anton Ford. He noted it down, went back upstairs, replaced the letters and shut the safe.

Now he started on the rest of the house. It was distressing to go through Anya's room, but his natural thoroughness demanded it. It surprised him. In design and decor it was very much the room of, say, an eighteen-year-old. Then it occurred to him that it must have been her room till she was married and had probably been left untouched till her return after her widowing.

A photograph of Jimmy in football kit running after a ball in the garden stood on the dressing table, and on the bedside table was another, more formally posed, of the boy standing in front of his grandfather with Bryant's hands on his shoulders. They both looked so broodingly serious that it was impossible to look at the picture and not smile.

Nowhere in sight was there a photograph of anyone who could have been Edward Wilson. Perhaps the memory of his death was still too poignant. Or perhaps after the initial mourning period was over she had bravely resolved not to live with the dead.

That would be most like her, Jaysmith reassured himself as he searched swiftly through her wardrobe and chest of drawers. To his dismay and distaste he found himself tingling with pleasure as his fingers moved across the thin silkiness of her underclothes.

This was adolescent voyeurism, he told himself angrily. He had long passed the age of such hot imaginings as were rising in his brain, as each sight and touch and smell in this room filled him with a sense of her presence.

He closed the last door with an emphatic crash. There was nothing to his present purpose here.

Jimmy's room seemed even less likely to be productive but he glanced around it just the same. It was in a small boy's most desirable state of chaos, with apparently every one of his treasured possessions within sight and reach. Hanging on the wall between the full-sized posters of a footballer and a pop star was the photograph of a man. This had to be Edward Wilson, guessed Jaysmith. It was right that he should be remembered here. A widow could not live in the past, but a boy must not be allowed to forget his father.

He took the picture down and looked at it closely with an as yet unidentifiable emotion. It showed a burly, dark-bearded man in a heavy Norwegian sweater, whip-cord trousers and climbing boots. He was regarding the camera with arrogant impatience as if he felt this was a waste of time. There was something familiar about the face; were those perhaps Jimmy's eyes? He decided it was not a face he liked very much and at the same moment he identified his emotion.

I'm jealous! he told himself in amazement. *Jealous of a dead man!*

He dropped the photograph onto the bed and quickly searched the room. There was, of course, nothing to find. What had he expected? he asked himself sourly. Here or anywhere else? Evidence that Bryant was a Russian agent, or a Nazi war criminal, or head of a gang of terrorists plotting to conquer the world?

His irritation was chopped short by an unwelcome noise. He went out of the room to the landing window which overlooked the front of the house and saw a car coming up the drive. To his relief it wasn't Bryant's brown Rover, which, assuming the football match had run its full length, should not be back for at least an hour, but a bright orange vw Beetle. But his relief soon evaporated as the passenger door opened and the unmistakable figure of Anya got out. She reached into the back of the car and, helped by the woman driver, began to pull out carrier bags and parcels. She and the driver chatted and laughed as she did this. Clearly the early return had nothing sinister in it and Jaysmith concentrated now on his own predicament.

He had to get out fast, but there was the burglar alarm to consider. It was switched off. Anya would notice this as she tried to switch it off on entry. She might imagine that either she or Bryant had forgotten to switch it on as they left, but on the other hand she might remember with absolute certainty that she'd done it. At the least it would be a source of puzzlement, and Jaysmith knew that small and innocent speculations could lead to large and dangerous ones.

He ran swiftly downstairs and reset the alarm then retreated into the dining room as he heard Anya opening the first of the locks. It was only as the key turned in the second that he realized what an idiot he was. He could not exit through the dining room window without setting off the alarm until Anya was actually in the house and had operated the switch in the hall. The dining room overlooked the rear garden, much smaller than the formal terraces at the front where they had sat and drank their coffee two days earlier. At the back there was simply an area of plain lawn bounded by what looked like an impregnable yew hedge. Here was obviously Jimmy's domain. A football lay on the well-worn grass and a game of swing-ball was set up, consisting of a tennis ball on a cord which rotated around a vertical metal pole sunk in the lawn.

The front door opened. He mentally rehearsed the turning off of the alarm, gave a few extra seconds for safety and undid the window catch. There was no blast of noise and he let out a long sigh. It occurred to him that he might do better to try and hide in the house and escape later, but there was no time to weigh up odds. He slid the window up. It was well oiled and made no sound. He stepped out and let the window down. Where now? Left? right? ahead? He tried to work out where Anya would make for on entering the house. To be found skulking about outside was almost as bad as being caught within. Again there was no time. He ran a few steps across the lawn, picked up one of the swing-ball rackets and sent the ball whizzing round the pole with a tremendous blow. Alternating backhand and forehand, he soon got a rapid rhythm going and managed about twenty consecutive hits before he sent the ball too high and the cord got tangled.

'Bravo!' called Anya's voice, accompanied by half a dozen slow handclaps.

He turned. She was at the kitchen window.

'Hello,' he said, going towards her.

'Hello. What on earth are you doing here?'

'Trespassing,' he answered. 'I got finished in London much quicker than I thought, so I drove up this morning. I went for a walk and thought I'd divert here to beg a cup of tea. But then I remembered you'd said you were going to some football match with Jimmy. I thought I'd stroll around the garden for a little while in case you got back. And here you are. I hope you don't mind.'

'Feel free,' she said. 'Step inside. I'll put the kettle on.'

She unlocked the kitchen door and he entered. They smiled uneasily at each other for a moment. He had the feeling that she was not certain whether she was pleased to see him or not.

'Where are Jimmy and your father?' he asked.

'In Carlisle,' she said. 'I decided to skip the match. With pappy to accompany him, Jimmy clearly felt that the presence of a woman might cast slurs on his masculinity. So I met a friend, we did some shopping and she ran me home.'

'My good luck,' said Jaysmith.

'Why so?'

'I might have had to wait another couple of hours to see you.'

She mashed the tea, her sallow face slightly flushed. As she poured it, she said, 'Mr Hutton . . .'

'Jay,' he interrupted.

'Jay. I hope I get this right. Look, you're buying my aunt's house, and that's one thing. You also seem to be . . . interested in me, and that's another thing altogether, distinct and separate. I don't want a . . . confusion.'

She put some sugar before him.

He shook his head and said, 'Of course not. I'm all for clarity. When you suggested your father should act as my solicitor, which of these distinct and separate things were we dealing with? My interest in Rigg Cottage or my interest in you?'

She heaped sugar into her tea and stirred violently.

'That's not quite what I meant,' she started to
99

explain, but he laughed and said, 'No, I know it's not. At least, I hoped it wasn't. I hoped there was a third distinct though not necessarily separate thing. Your interest in me.'

She stared at him blankly. It was not the blankness of incomprehension but of doubt, perhaps even of fear. He guessed what had happened. She had had nearly two whole days to get him in perspective. They had met only the previous Monday. He had exerted pressure. It was in his nature. She had responded, meeting boldness with boldness. There was in her a core of toughness which did not care to feel intimidated. But there was also caution; this was what subjecting him to her father's scrutiny had been all about. And there was also fear. The fox is bold; the fox is wily; the fox is also keen to the scent of danger, quick to flight. She had had two days to think about him. She had believed she had more, till the following week at least. He must have receded in her mind to manageable proportions, to a postponable problem.

Then she had come back alone, unprepared, and there he was in her own back garden. Flight was not possible here, so fear had made her outspoken.

She said, 'I don't know you, Jay. I mean . . .'

'You mean, we only met last Monday. That's true. And I was looking for a house long before I met you, that's true also. You know that. My purchase of Rigg Cottage has nothing to do with you, though it's a very charming vanity.'

He smiled and spoke lightly to remove offence, but she regarded him sombrely and said, 'I've thought a lot about that. I know you were looking for a house before we met. But, looking back, it

100

seemed to me that you weren't looking for—perhaps not even really looking at—Rigg Cottage till after I arrived. Is it vanity? I should like to think so.'

She was as sharp-scented as any fox, he realized. She had sniffed out a not-quite-rightness in him, but, thank God, it wasn't any suspicion of deception in his name and background that bothered her. It was fear of the passion which, on such short acquaintance, could cause a man to purchase a not inexpensive house in its pursuance.

He said, 'I want the house.'

He meant it. He was surprised to find how much he meant it. His sincerity, and perhaps his surprise, reached her too and she looked at him as if in search of an explanation.

He went on, 'London's a slum. I've been everywhere; up here's the only place I've ever wanted to buy a house. Rigg Cottage is the house I want to buy. End of story.'

He finished his tea and stood up.

'There's nothing else up here I want to buy,' he said, stressing the last word slightly. 'I'm not much for possessions. Or possessiveness.'

'Are you going?' she said.

'I'd better. I haven't checked in at the hotel yet. I arranged to keep the room on till my return, but I guess I should give the Parkers some warning that I'll be wanting dinner.'

He wasn't quite certain if he meant this as a hint, but if so, it was ignored.

'Use the phone here before you go if you like,' she said. 'Mrs Parker would probably appreciate as much advance warning as possible.'

'Thanks.'

101

She followed him out into the hall and began to gather together her shopping. There was one long package wrapped round with toy-shop gift paper. It slipped from beneath her arm and Jaysmith caught it.

'Someone's lucky,' he said.

'What? Oh yes. It's Jimmy's birthday next Saturday. I thought this was a good chance to get his present and put it out of sight of prying eyes.'

'What have you got him?' he asked.

'It's a gun,' she said.

He must have allowed something to show on his face which she read as disapproval for she said defensively, 'It fires ping pong balls. There's a target that gets knocked over. One of Jimmy's friends got one and he was full of envy. He's not a greedy child, but I can always tell when he really wants something. I was a bit doubtful, but pappy says that if you're living in the country, you've got to know about guns. You can't pretend they don't exist. It's better to learn to respect them. It seemed to make sense. What do you think?'

'It seems to make sense to me too,' said Jaysmith. 'Here, you go on up. I'll bring this.'

Anya hesitated at the foot of the stairs and Jaysmith said with slight exasperation, 'If you prefer, I'll drop it here and you can come back for it. But believe me, my presence on your landing will hardly compromise your name at all.'

She giggled unexpectedly and said, 'Sorry. Come on.'

In the bedroom she dropped her shopping on the bed.

'There,' she said.

He looked around.

102

'Nice room,' he said.

'Yes,' she said. 'It's a bit shabby now. It needs doing out. It hasn't been done since ... since before my marriage. Six months before, to be precise.'

'As close as that? You were a gayer person then, I think. I use the word properly.'

'Was I?' She frowned and looked around. 'Yes. I suppose I was. Bright colours stopped suiting me after girlhood's flush faded, I suppose. Not to worry. My loss was Oxfam's gain.'

She put the shopping away, hiding the birthday present carefully at the back of her wardrobe.

'Where's your car?' she asked.

'Along the valley a way,' he said vaguely.

'Shall I give you a lift to it?'

'No. These old legs will stagger a little way yet,' he said.

He stepped out of the bedroom and headed for the stairs. It was time to go. Out of the corner of his eye he noticed that he'd left Jimmy's bedroom door ajar as he rushed to check on the arriving car. Had it been ajar when he went into the room? Well, it was hardly something that anyone would notice.

Then it came back to him with all the force of a remembered bêtise that he had left Edward Wilson's photograph lying on the bed.

'Hello,' he said. 'Is this Jimmy's room?'

He stepped inside without waiting for an answer and by the time Anya reached the doorway, he was standing in front of the poster-decorated wall holding the photograph in both hands.

'Jimmy's father?' he said enquiringly.

'Yes, it is,' said Anya. She came into the room

103

and took the picture from him and hung it on the wall. She was very angry, he could tell.

She said in a quietly controlled voice, 'Jimmy, like most small boys, has a highly developed sense of his right to privacy. I try to respect it.'

Was this the real reason for her anger? he wondered. Or was it his sacrilegious temerity in daring to touch the holy image?

'Oh Christ,' he said. 'I'm sorry. I shouldn't have barged in, should I? Privacy wasn't something I knew the meaning of as a child, I'm afraid, though God knows I could have done with it. I suppose it made me insensitive.'

It was merely an attempt to appease her anger, but it emerged with a convincing bitterness. He thought, every time I try to deceive this woman, I find myself telling her the truth by accident!

She slipped out of her anger like a model from a silk gown and said, 'I've no right to lecture you. It was the other way round with me. I suppose it made me oversensitive to invasion.'

'But this *is* Jimmy's room,' he said. 'I shouldn't have barged in.'

'Oh, even if he knew you were in here, you could probably buy his forgiveness with a bag of allsorts. He's crazy for licorice.'

'I'll remember.'

As they went down the stairs he said, 'Sorry if it's painful, but Jimmy's father ... the face looked somehow familiar.'

'Did it?' She was a pace behind him so he could not see her expression. 'He was in the papers occasionally. He was a climber, quite well known some years ago. And when he died, it made a nice little story.'

104

'How was that?'

'Famous mountaineer, Alpine expert, Himalayan expeditionist, falls off hundred-foot cliff in Cumbria and breaks his back; wouldn't you say that was a nice little story?' she asked. 'You probably saw the pictures.'

He stopped and turned and looked up at her.

'I'm sorry,' he said. 'It must have been terrible.'

'It was,' she said. 'Terrible. You haven't made your phone call to Mrs Parker, don't forget. Could you see yourself out?'

'Of course,' he said.

As he dialled the number, she went back up the stairs. He thought she went into Jimmy's room, but he couldn't be sure and when he called goodbye there was no reply. He almost went back upstairs to check she was all right, but he didn't. And as he walked away from the house, he knew he had been afraid he would find her crying.

CHAPTER ELEVEN

He awoke on Sunday to find the weather had broken. Heavy clouds sat sullenly on the tops and by the time he had finished his breakfast, grey vapous had slipped insidiously down the fell slopes and the valley was blind with a thin drenching rain.

It was not a day for the long kill. And a damned uncomfortable one for the short kill too, he assured himself. Bryant should be safe enough today, even if whatever committee or computer made up Jacob's mind still had him pricked down for elimination.

105

He was no nearer any decision on the best course of action. He had studied the letters the previous evening, but had made little progress beyond confirming that on the surface at least they were *billets doux*. This in itself might be reason enough for their method of delivery. Clandestine did not automatically mean subversive; a Polish woman writing to a lover abroad might well resent the risk that her most private thoughts would be subjected to the defiling eye of a censor. Or perhaps it was simply that Ota, whoever she was, did not wholly trust the Polish postal system.

He found himself in an uncharacteristic state of uncertainty. He would have liked a long walk on the high fells to try to clear his mind but in these conditions it was out of the question. He felt an almost irresistible urge to pick up the phone and ring Anya. His mind was filled with an almost comically sentimental picture of the two of them sitting together on a deep soft sofa toasting muffins at a huge log fire while the rain beat at the windows. Where this image came from he did not know. It certainly did not belong to his past. Wet Sunday afternoons in his childhood had been endless wastes of utter boredom. His mother, though long lapsed from her Methodist upbringing, retained sufficient atavistic religiosity to ban nearly all Sunday recreation, and even when he enjoyed the freedom of university life, these remembered glooms still sombred his Sabbaths.

The old boredom was lying ahead now. He knew he couldn't ring Anya, not after yesterday's encounter. Their relationship had developed with rapid promise in his eyes, but to her, after the first quick movement, speed was clearly a threat. Any

106

hint of pressure might send her flying into the forest. Again the dark side of his mind slipped in the thought that the simple solution might be to step aside till Jacob rearranged Bryant's targeting, then step forward to comfort a grief which did not commemorate a rival.

Full of self-contempt, he pushed the thought out of sight. Love that looked for profit in a lover's pain was too despicable to deserve the name.

It occurred to him that in any case a tête-à-tête over muffins this afternoon was out. Anya had told him that she would be taking Jimmy for his Sunday visit to Aunt Muriel's. He suspected Jimmy would not be wildly enthusiastic and smiled at the thought that Sundays still brought their problems even in the most liberal of circles.

The thought that Anya was going to be so close, however, brought him to a determination to get away from the Crag Hotel at least. Until he could get to a Polish dictionary and translate the letters, he only had one possible clue to the nature of Bryant's culpability, and that was the name of his courier, Anton Ford, who lived in Manchester.

He got out his road map and checked. A hundred miles, only a couple of hours' drive. He doubted if anything productive could come out of the trip, but if this weather kept up, anything was better than hanging around the hotel.

By lunchtime the weather was, if anything, getting worse. True daylight had never managed to break through and cars were crawling around with their headlights on. He had a sandwich and a beer in the bar and listened to Parker's cheerfully stoic acceptance of the unremitting drizzle.

In the end he said rather sourly, 'You've got a

hotel, you've got to stay in it. Me, I've got a car. I think I'll try to drive out of it.'

'Won't be long before you've got a house too, Mr Hutton,' chortled Parker. 'What will you do then?'

Sit in front of a log fire and eat muffins, was his unspoken reply.

He waved a hand and went out into the rain.

It was slow driving at first on winding roads in the drizzling rain. But when he hit the motorway he was able to speed up, and eventually as the mountains fell behind so the weather began to improve, at least relatively, and he was able to drive on automatic pilot, his mind wandering aimlessly over the landscape of his life till suddenly distant past and immediate present were united in the shape of an exit sign.

It read, BLACKBURN 7 MILES.

His home town. Where he'd been brought up. Which he'd never returned to after that last conversation with his stepfather twenty-five years ago.

He had made a decision without thought and already the BMW was cutting off the motorway up the sliproad.

Things had changed. He got lost. There were new roads, new buildings. It was like a dream. There were flashes of the familiar, the comfortable, immediately swallowed by the strange and intrusive. The old house was still there, a tiny thirties semi with rounded half-bay windows, with yellowish brick below and greying pebbledash above, the whole topped by buff tiles whose central ridge reminded him now, as then, of a Grecian nose seen on a museum statue. The statue had been naked, he recalled, probably a cast of some

108

well-known Venus. He had stolen a postcard of it and used to stare longingly at those marble breasts in the uncertain privacy of the bedroom he was forced to share with his loutish stepbrother.

That was a really deprived childhood, he told himself. I couldn't even afford real dirty pictures!

It occurred to him that perhaps his stepbrother still lived in the house. Or even his stepfather. He would only be in his seventies, after all.

He had no desire to find out. This had been a mistake. Plunging into the past should only be done in company. It was too dangerous a dive to be undertaken alone. Perhaps one day, in company, with someone to keep an eye on his air-line ... perhaps ...

He put the car into gear and drove on till he found a sign saying MANCHESTER. Soon his past was behind him again.

Manchester he had known too vaguely for the changes to strike him, so oddly it was more familiar than Blackburn. He stopped at an open-all-hours corner shop on his way in and bought a street map. The address he was after proved to be in the southern suburbs, but even in the eighties a wet Northern Sunday afternoon was a street-emptier and he had no difficulty in making his way through the city centre. Eventually he found himself in an expensive-looking suburb, consisting mainly of substantial Edwardian villas each standing foursquare in the middle of its half-acre plot and advertising *brass* as clearly as if the owners had written their incomes on the front gate.

Debtors' retreat, thought Jaysmith, slipping back into the conditioned response of his childhood, and smiling in surprise at the remembered reaction.

109

He found the street he was looking for without difficulty. It was a long crescent, with several 'For Sale' signs on display, including one in the garden of the house next to Anton Ford's. Uncertain before what he might do on arrival, Jaysmith now saw a course of action. He parked the car and walked up the drive of the house with the 'For Sale' sign, taking in the neighbouring house as he did so. There was no sign of life, but a pale green Granada was parked in the drive, and he had a sense of being observed.

He reached the door and rang the bell. After a long while and a second ring, a middle-aged woman answered the summons. She was running to fat, had silver-rinsed hair, looked rather bleary-eyed, and carried a tumblerful of well-iced colourless liquor. She didn't speak but just looked at him.

'I'm sorry to bother you, but I've been looking at a couple of houses in the area and I saw your sign,' said Jaysmith.

'It says appointments only,' said the woman, gesturing at the board and slopping some of the liquid out of her glass.

'I know and I'm sorry, but the agent's office is closed, and I'm only in the district today. However, if it's really inconvenient . . .'

She looked him up and down, and then beyond him to the BMW parked at the gate.

'As long as you don't expect apple-pie order,' she said, turning away.

Taking this as an invitation he followed her into the house. It occurred to him that the last time he had gone through this masquerade, he had ended up buying the place. An expensive habit to get into.

The woman began to show him round. She seemed to be under some strain and the reason for this and the drink was soon made clear as her description of the house gradually became more and more autobiographical. Her name was Wendy Denver. She was selling the house because her husband had died of a heart attack two months before and the house was too big for her and too full of memories and she could go to live with her son in Ireland, only she hated Ireland and her Irish daughter-in-law hated her, so she thought she would buy a flat in the town centre and not lose contact with her friends and neighbours . . .

It was becoming stream-of-consciousness stuff and, as much out of pity for the woman as self-interest, Jaysmith cut in brutally and said, 'Yes, the neighbours. They are important, aren't they? I always like to know about the neighbours when I buy a house. How are they? Easy to get on with?'

The woman considered.

'Well, on this side I don't have much to do with them, not since we had the row about the dog doing its business outside my gate. They've got a gate of their own, I told them . . .'

Her gesture had seemed to indicate the other side to Ford's house and Jaysmith cut in again, 'And the other side?'

But before the woman could answer the door bell rang. Jaysmith could see why she had been so long opening the door to him. She stood stock still as if the source of this strange noise was completely unknown to her and it wasn't till the third ring that she seemed to get her bearings.

'Excuse me,' she said and left the room.

Jaysmith followed her to make sure she reached

111

her destination.

When she opened the door, a couple stood there, she a rather faded woman in a floral smock, he a brawny suntanned man who might have been a docker or a road labourer except that the silk sports shirt straining against his solid chest was by Gucci as were the slacks similarly stressed by his broad thighs; and the three rings on his spatulate fingers together with the embossed gold medallion resting in a nest of gingery hair beneath his open collar must have cost a couple of thousand pounds.

'We thought we'd drop in and see if there was a cup of tea going,' said the woman.

'Come in, come in do. This is handy,' cried Mrs Denver. 'We were just talking about you! Or rather this gentleman here was asking questions about you and I was just about to fill him in!'

She turned back to Jaysmith.

'You wanted to know all about my neighbours, and here are two of the very best you could find anywhere. Anton and Sally Ford from next door, meet Mr . . . ?'

'Wainwright,' said Jaysmith extending his hand. Whether this was good or bad luck, he didn't know. It ought to be good, but there was something unpleasantly speculative about the way Ford regarded him as he shook his hand.

'We didn't know you had any appointments to view arranged for this afternoon,' said the faded woman.

'Didn't have. Mr Wainwright was just passing,' said Mrs Denver indifferently.

Jaysmith relaxed a little. This could be the simple explanation of the man's scrutiny. Good neighbours, and knowing that this vulnerable

112

woman had had no viewing appointments made for that day, they had come over to make sure he wasn't the local Raffles.

'If you moved here, Mr Wainwright, you'd be the luckiest man in the world to have neighbours like these. What I'd have done without them . . .'

She had begun with a perfect control which made its sudden loss all the more disturbing. Suddenly everything seemed to go, speech, movement, awareness. She simply stood before them, puppet-slack, with tears streaming down her face. Sally Ford put her arm around her and led her unresisting out of the entrance hall into the lounge, closing the door behind her.

Jaysmith shook his head.

'I'm sorry,' he said. 'I didn't realize . . .'

'You're not much acquainted with grief then, Mr Wainwright?'

The biblical turn of phrase rang oddly. The man's voice matched his clothes rather than his physique. It was light, well educated, with just a distant hint of accent, the voice of a pre-mumble-film romantic hero, or romantic rogue.

'Enough. I meant, I didn't realize how close to the edge she was.'

'Bereavement can be a wasting disease if it gets a hold,' said Ford, moving easily from a scriptural to a medical idiom. 'The broken heart is not a clinical reality, but the *eroded* heart, now that's something else. Grief wears away the will to live. Which other properties are you interested in?'

'Properties of grief, you mean?' said Jaysmith, puzzled.

Ford smiled. He had two gold-filled teeth.

'You said you were looking at other properties in

the area. I wondered if you'd been visiting anyone else in our crescent. There are plenty for sale.'

'No, not in this crescent. A bit further south, in fact, closer to the airport. Nothing I saw took my fancy, so I just drove around and thought I'd try pot luck here. I'm sorry I picked on Mrs Denver. What's she asking, by the way? We hadn't got onto prices.'

His attempt at diversion seemed to work. Ford mentioned a figure, then went on to sing the virtues of the house and the district.

'And you needn't worry about the airport. It's twenty minutes at the most, fifteen if you're late.'

'You sound expert. Do you use it a lot?'

'All the time. Domestic flights, the Continent. It's very handy. Hang on a moment.'

He gently opened the lounge door and stepped inside. A few moments later he emerged and said, 'I don't think Mrs Denver's going to be fit to resume her sales-talk for some time. The drink doesn't help. They think it perks them up, but alcohol's basically a depressant. Look, I've got to pop across to my place. Why don't you come with me, and anything more I can tell you about the area, I'll be happy to. Basically the houses are the same too. You could even look around our shack if you liked.'

It was so precisely the kind of invitation Jaysmith had been desperately seeking a means of eliciting that he was taken aback, as if his mind had been read.

'That would be fine,' he said.

*   *   *

114

Ford's house was decorated and furnished in an expensive modern style which Jaysmith did not care for. This surprised him. Or rather, it wasn't the judgement that surprised him but the fact that he was making it. After two decades of almost total indifference to the style of his surroundings, he was suddenly developing a critical taste. There was in the lounge a huge artificial log fire with real gas flames but it was not, he decided, looking at the modern sculpture lines of the pure white armchairs, a room to toast muffins in.

Ford had unlocked a cabinet and taken out a flat black leather case from which he removed a small bottle.

'I'll just take these over to Wendy,' he said. 'Make yourself at home. Have a look around if you like.'

He went out whistling 'A Wandering Minstrel I' from the *Mikado*. This was getting to be too good to be true. Jaysmith went over to the black case which was still lying open. It was full of pill bottles, capsules, ampoules, all neatly stored in separate compartments. He looked in the cabinet from which Ford had removed the case, but there was nothing there. Indeed the rest of the lounge promised little, so he went out into the entrance hall and after trying a couple of doors found a small room used as an office.

Quickly he went through the drawers of the stainless steel desk. The mystery of the black case was solved. The man's business notepaper revealed he was the sales head of a large drug retailing company. His desk diary showed he was a busy man, travelling all over Europe. There had been three visits to Poland in the last twelve months.

And three letters had been received by Bryant from Ota. But this was just confirmation of facts already known. It didn't open up new avenues.

A filing cabinet contained nothing but business files. There was a wall safe but this was locked, and though he tried the same approach that had worked at Naddle Foot, Ford's telephone book contained nothing that looked like a hidden number. He checked that Bryant's number was in it, then he heard the noise of Ford's cheerful whistling returning.

Quickly he glanced around the office to make sure he had left no sign of his presence and returned to the lounge.

Ford looked in a moment later, said, 'All right? With you in a sec. Pour yourself a drink,' then ran lightly up the stairs.

When he returned, Jaysmith was sipping a gin and tonic.

'I think I'll have a little one too,' he said. 'Nothing like an alcoholic depressant for picking you up, as long as you're not suffering from anything serious, that is.'

'How is Mrs Denver?'

'Fine. I've given her something that'll see her right.'

Suddenly he smiled and the gold teeth flashed again.

'By the way, in case you're wondering, I do have an MD. Not practising, but fully qualified. Couldn't stand the hours. No, I went into research with a drug company at first, but that was a bit of a dead end, I decided, unless you had real flair which I didn't. But I discovered I could sell things; and medical people are much more likely to buy from

116

someone in the sacred circle, so to speak, than unqualified outsiders, so I went onward and upward. Now I work as hard and as long as most GPS, so perhaps I wasn't so clever after all. Another drink? Look, try some of this stuff. Plum brandy. It's really smooth. Best thing to come out of Poland, though perhaps it's a bit disloyal of me to say so.'

'How disloyal?' asked Jaysmith, refusing the brandy.

'My parents were Polish,' he explained. 'My father was a doctor. He didn't like the way things were going and decided to get his family out in 1938. I wasn't born then but I was six months on the way. Three months later I entered the world in London.'

He talked easily, readily, with hardly any prompting. It was curiously like listening to Bryant's account of his escape from Poland, except for one essential difference. Bryant's tone had been harsh and tragic; with Ford, Jaysmith had a faint sense much of the time of being gently mocked.

The Ford family, consisting of the parents, an elder brother and sister, and Anton himself, settled down in England with varying senses of permanency.

'My mother was very ill after I was born. I was a very late child. My brother was thirteen years older than I, and my sister seven. Mother was in her forties when she had me. She recovered, but I guess that she'd had enough trial and tribulation in her life by the time the war ended. My brother had joined the army when he was eighteen you see, and got killed during the Normandy landings. So mother wanted no more change. She wanted to stay quietly in England; there was rationing, of course, and all kinds of shortage and deprivation, but she knew that here there would be no secret police, no occupying army.

'Father on the other hand always planned to go back. They argued and argued. Finally they had to agree to differ. And in 1948, father went back. My sister Urszula, who was sixteen by then and old enough to make her own choice, went with him. She thought the sun shone out of his stethoscope and had managed to grow steadily more Polish despite her ten years in England. Me, I was bilingual, but I was British. And I wasn't going to leave mother. To tell the truth, at ten years old, father scared the hell out of me, and I wasn't crazy about my bossy sister either.'

He laughed ruefully.

'But I'm long over that. My parents are both dead, but I go to Poland on business sometimes and I visit Urszula when I can. She's got five kids and two grandchildren. Good Catholic! I'm both a bad Catholic and also we never hit it lucky with kids, so it's nice to have a ready-made family at a safe distance. And they all seem to like their rich capitalist uncle!'

They talked on for another quarter of an hour; for the most part Ford talked, Jaysmith listened.

'Did you change your name?' he asked. 'Or anglicize it?'

'No. Ford was the family name. Like the film director. Aleksander, the Pole, I mean, not John, the Yankee. That made it handy. No Ws and Zs and Ys to puzzle the natives!'

Another echo of Bryant, but not significant, except that it hinted the two men had sat together

118

at some time, and talked about their residual Polishness, and perhaps laughed at English xenophobia.

'If you don't mind me saying so, you still have a very faint accent of some kind,' said Jaysmith.

Ford groaned.

'When I was in my teens, some girl told me it was sexy, so I started exaggerating it, and since then I've never got rid of it altogether!'

The two men laughed. Sally Ford came into the room and said, 'You two seem to be enjoying yourselves.'

'Just men's talk,' said Ford. 'How is she?'

'She'll be fine. She's gone to sleep now. I'll pop back later.'

Jaysmith had risen at the woman's entrance and now Ford joined him.

'Mr Wainwright,' he said, 'if there's anything else I can tell you or show you before you go, just say the word.'

It was a dismissal; it was also a mockery; but how or why, Jaysmith could not work out.

'No thanks,' he said. 'You've been most kind and helpful. I hope we meet again.'

'Now that you've found out what kind of neighbours you'd have, I hope so too.'

They shook hands and Jaysmith left.

Driving back through Manchester, he tried to analyse what he'd found out and it came to very little. The simple explanation was that Ford, a friend of Bryant's whose business took him to Poland from time to time, acted as a courier between Bryant and his girlfriend, Ota, bringing her love letters out and presumably taking Bryant's in. There need be nothing sinister in that. But somewhere in it he was convinced must lie the reason for Bryant's targeting.

He tried to concentrate on the problem but found his mind wouldn't stay there. He found himself thinking not of Ford and Bryant, but of Wendy Denver, of the emptiness of her gaze, the tightly clutched glass, the sudden tears. Did every death push a survivor to the edge of the void? He tried to take his mind back to Saigon and Nguyet but found that it was all far beyond his conscious mind now, a receding dream. What rose vividly before him was Wendy Denver's expression, and when he tried to push into the past, he could get no further than Anya Wilson holding her husband's photograph and staring blankly at the disappeared face.

The drink had given him the start of a headache and he decided to stop for a coffee. He lingered over it, curiously reluctant to return to Grasmere with so little achieved. Realizing he was going to have to hurry to be back in time for dinner, which on a Sunday was between seven and eight he decided to have a snack in the service station cafeteria. All he wanted was the necessary fuel; he had very little real appetite.

The foul weather he had left with the mountains was waiting for him with the mountains once more. He did the last few miles at a careful crawl and reached the Crag just before nine. Parking as close to the door as possible, he dashed in through the clinging rain.

Phil Parker looked out of the bar.

'Mr Hutton, glad to see you back. No weather for driving, this.'

'You've said it.'

120

'There's been a lot of accidents. Young couple turned their car over on Dunmail Raise. And then old Miss Wilson's niece from Rigg Cottage . . .'

Jaysmith, his face composed to token regret at Parker's catalogue of disasters, felt his heart constrict with violent, oxygen-hungry fear.

'Anya, Anya Wilson, you mean?' he cried. 'Has there been an accident?'

'Yes, I'm afraid so. Young Mrs Wilson came down here to see you in fact. Some message from her aunt about the house. She wrote you a note. Then the phone rang. It was old Miss Wilson. They'd just rung from Windermere Hospital. There'd been an accident . . .'

'It wasn't Anya then? It wasn't Mrs Wilson in the accident?' interrupted Jaysmith, his relief almost as physically painful as his terror.

'No, I was telling you. She was here,' said Parker looking at him curiously. 'It's her father, Mr Bryant. His car evidently came off the road coming down into Ambleside from Kirkstone Pass. He's been seriously hurt, I gather. It sounds very very bad.'

CHAPTER TWELVE

Parker's human relish at passing on bad news disappeared completely as he saw that Jaysmith was not the disinterested auditor he had expected. He insisted on pouring him a large Scotch and then gave what details he had as succinctly as possible.

Anya had arrived at the hotel with Jimmy at about five forty-five. On finding Jaysmith was out, she had sat down to write a note and Doris Parker had made her a cup of tea. Then the phone call had come.

The Parkers had clearly been marvellous and Jaysmith forgave the garrulous Phil all the minor tediums he had from time to time subjected his guest to. Anya had been almost completely overthrown by the news and Doris Parker had taken control. She had organized Phil to take Jimmy back up to Rigg Cottage while she herself had driven Anya to the hospital.

Doris Parker joined them at this point in the story.

'I had to leave her at the hospital,' she explained guiltily. 'I didn't want to, but she was so much more herself by the time we got there. They said Mr Bryant was very poorly, but not in danger. I wouldn't have left her if he'd been in danger, but the girls don't come in tonight and I couldn't leave Phil to do the dinner by himself.'

'She knows my limitations,' said her husband almost proudly.

'But I'm on my way back now. Phil, keep the coffee going, will you? And if things get quiet, you might make a start setting the breakfast tables.'

'Will do,' said Parker. 'How long do you expect to be, darling?'

Before Doris could reply, Jaysmith spoke.

'I'll go,' he said.

They looked at him in surprise and he felt the need for explanation.

'I know Mr Bryant,' he said. 'He's acting for me in my house purchase. And the weather's really foul out there, Mrs Parker. You've done enough, I reckon. You've got your hands full here.'

122

Doris Parker gave it a moment's thought, then nodded as if two and two had finally made four. Jaysmith guessed that Anya's attempt to avoid the keen-eyed gaze of the village vigilantes on their few meetings had not been totally successful.

'All right,' she said. 'If that's what you want, Mr Hutton.'

'Tell me how to get to the hospital,' he said.

She gave him brief, clear directions. As he turned to head out into the night again, Parker said, 'Don't forget your note.'

He picked it up from the table beneath the key hooks. It was addressed to J. Hutton, Esq.

He read it in the car.

Dear Jay,

Aunt Muriel's solicitor seems to think you'll be sending a surveyor to look at the house before completing your purchase. Aunt Muriel on the other hand can't for the life of her see why you'd want to waste your money on a surveyor. The house has stood for a hundred and fifty years and will easily see you out (I quote!). Could you give her a ring or call to let her know what's what?

It was signed simply *Anya.*

No suggestion of a future meeting; on the other hand, she had come to the hotel when she might just as easily have telephoned.

He sent the BMW cutting through the tangles of rain.

He saw her as soon as he entered the hospital, standing in a telephone booth. As he approached, she replaced the receiver, turned and saw him.

123

'Hello,' she said.

She looked pale and strained, but far from the point of collapse.

'How is he?'

'He's all right,' she said, rubbing her forehead with the back of her hand as if to clear her thoughts. 'He's broken an arm, cracked a couple of ribs, put his knee out of joint, torn several muscles and got himself spattered with various cuts and contusions. But all the nasty other things they've been looking for, like fractured skull and internal bleeding, they just haven't found. They seemed almost disappointed.'

She tried a laugh. It didn't come out very well.

'You've seen him?'

'Briefly. He recognized me. There's a lot of shock, naturally. He'll be in for a few days. *They* say a week, perhaps more, but they don't know pappy.'

'I'm so glad,' he said. 'So very very glad.'

He spoke with such intensity of feeling that she opened her eyes wide as though really registering his presence for the first time. Then they blurred with tears.

'Thank you, Jay, thank you.'

Her gratitude filled Jaysmith with guilt. All his real concern was for her, not Bryant. In fact the thought had crept into his mind as he drove there that the solicitor's accidental death would be the best solution for everyone.

Everyone, that is, except the most important person concerned. There was no way he could permit anything to happen which would reawaken the pain he had seen in her eyes.

'Come on,' he said. 'I'll take you home.'

'Yes please,' she said. 'I've just rung Aunt

124

Muriel. Jimmy's fast asleep, so I'll leave him there tonight. I was going to ring Doris Parker . . .'

'She knows I'm here,' said Jaysmith. 'Come on.'

They drove in silence. Anya sat away from him, leaning her head against the window and seeming to sleep. But he felt a closeness, a warmth, between them which he was reluctant to break when they arrived at the gates of Naddle Foot. She awoke as he got back into the car after opening them.

'I'm sorry,' she said. 'I haven't been very companionable.'

'If it's company I want, I'll join the YHA,' he said lightly.

She opened the front door and went in, switching off the burglar alarm in a conditioned reflex. He followed. The house felt big and cold and empty.

She said, 'Perhaps I should have stayed at Aunt Muriel's too.'

He said, rather sententiously, 'It's minds that are lonely, not places.'

'Perhaps,' she said. 'But at least you can warm yourself against people, can't you?'

'Are you hungry?' he said. 'I can manage to scramble a few eggs.'

She didn't contradict this assumption of command but shook her head and said, 'No, I'm not hungry. I'm tired. At least my body's tired but my mind won't stop running.'

'I'll make you a drink,' he said.

'Brandy,' she said. 'Thanks.'

'What I had in mind was cocoa.'

She smiled wanly but genuinely.

'You have cocoa,' she said. 'I'll have brandy.'

He compromised and made two mugs of cocoa

125

liberally laced with cognac. She drank it greedily.

'We were both right,' she said.

He wanted to ask about the accident, but didn't care to, without some hint from her that she was ready to talk about it. She yawned widely several times.

He said, 'It's time for bed, I think.'

She nodded but didn't move.

'My car,' she said. 'It's still at the hotel.'

'Yes. It's all right. I'll fetch you in the morning.'

She yawned again but still didn't move.

He rose and gently pulled her out of the chair.

'Bed,' he said emphatically.

He led her unresisting up the stairs, opened her door and switched the light on.

'It's a long way for you to drive, there, and back again in the morning,' she said.

'I could stay,' he suggested.

'Yes. If you like,' she said.

He kissed her gently on the forehead and said, 'I'll use Jimmy's room, shall I? I'm sure he won't mind.'

'No. He won't mind,' she said.

He paused in the dooway and regarded her for a moment. She stood at the foot of the bed, as still and as slack as Wendy Denver after her collapse, like a puppet resting on its strings. An easy target. All the time in the world to check the range, take aim, and fire.

'Go to bed,' he said harshly. 'Quickly. I'll see you in the morning. Goodnight.'

He went along to Jimmy's room. Before getting into bed he studied the photograph of Edward Wilson and remembered yet again that other empty lonely house in Manchester with its lost and baffled occupant roaming round in vain search for some surviving shard of her broken happiness.

He fell asleep and dreamt of Saigon, but not of Nguyet, or Tai, or Jacob. In fact the city was totally empty except for himself, wandering its streets, vainly searching for someone to love, or someone to kill, he didn't know which.

*   *   *

The next morning he awoke at eight fifteen to the smell of frying bacon. Quickly he got up, washed, shaved with a borrowed razor, dressed and descended to the kitchen.

'Good morning,' said Anya. 'You have the gift of perfect timing.'

She was no puppet this morning, but a bright-eyed, alert young fox in her heather-mix sweater and russet slacks. She placed a plateful of bacon, egg and mushrooms on the table before him.

'He's doing all right,' he stated rather than asked.

'It shows, does it?' she said, smiling. 'Yes, he's doing all right. I rang half an hour ago. Early for us but the middle of the day for a hospital, of course! They said he was awake, hungry, and causing trouble. Then they remembered to say that medically he was as well as could be expected.'

She filled another plate and sat opposite him.

'That's great,' said Jaysmith. 'What time's visiting?'

'Ten thirty. So if you can drop me at the hotel car park . . .'

'I'll take you to the hospital,' he said. 'That is, if you don't mind me going along.'

127

She considered.

'No, I don't mind,' she said.

She chewed on a mouthful of bacon and went on casually, 'You missed a golden opportunity last night, you know.'

'Did I?'

'Yes. I was there for the taking, you must have seen it. Any way you wanted. It would almost have been a kindness.'

She was looking at him very seriously.

He said, 'A kindness to you last night, perhaps. But a cruelty to me this morning. Would I be eating fresh mushrooms if you'd found my head on your pillow when you woke up?'

She didn't respond to his smile but said, 'I'm suspicious of chivalry in a man who shows no sign of being fond of horses.'

'Not chivalry but self-interest,' he said. 'I like to take a long view.'

'Yes. I see. Long-term gains rather than a quick killing?' she said. 'That makes sense. Come on then. We'd better hurry. We're picking up Jimmy first. I rang Aunt Muriel too.'

'Jimmy? What about school?'

'I'll let them know he's taking the morning off,' she said firmly. 'I want him to see for himself that his grandfather's all right. Otherwise . . .'

'Yes?'

'Well, he's got this idea that people go into hospitals to die. You just never see them again. Ever since his father died. Will you clear up in here while I ring the school?' On their way to Grasmere, he felt able to bring up the question of the accident.

'I don't know much. He went off the road

128

coming down from Kirkstone Pass towards Ambleside. You'll know it, I expect.'

'Yes,' he said. He'd used it when returning from Dockray to Grasmere. It was a steep descent, one in four at its worst, and a winding road, but nothing compared with Wrynose, say. He cast his mind back. There were solid drystone walls on either side he recalled, no fences to smash through with deep drops behind.

But of course he was thinking of it in bright sunshine.

'The locals call that stretch "the Struggle",' said Anya. 'Up there the mist and rain had cut visibility almost to nil. He must have missed a bend. He smashed through a gate into a field and turned over. He was lucky to be found.'

'Who found him?'

'A local man, a farmer I think. I must look him out and thank him.'

'There was no other vehicle involved?'

'Not as far as I know. I wasn't really taking things in, you understand. What the hell was he doing on that road in those conditions anyway?'

Jaysmith thought of the road. If you didn't turn off to Dockray, it ran via Patterdale the full length of Ullswater to Penrith.

He said, 'Perhaps he'd been to Penrith.'

'Perhaps. But from Naddle Foot it'd be much quicker and easier to go by the main Keswick to Penrith road,' she said in a dissatisfied voice.

The roads were still very wet and Jaysmith drove with care. At least the rain had stopped and there was promise of sunshine above the low ceiling of mist. When they reached Rigg Cottage, Jimmy came running out to greet his mother. Leaving

129

them together by the car, Jaysmith joined old Miss Wilson in the doorway.

'Good morning,' he said.

'Morning,' she replied, regarding him grimly. 'No need to look so proprietorial, young man.'

'Was I? I'm sorry. Though it shouldn't be long now,' he said, glancing up at the old house.

'I wasn't meaning the cottage,' she said. 'You spent last night at Naddle Foot, I gather.'

'Yes, I did,' he said.

'How old are you, Mr Hutton?'

'Forty-three,' he said.

She snorted significantly.

'You feel it's a dangerous age for a man?' he asked politely.

'They're all dangerous ages,' she said. 'What I want to know is . . .'

She paused as Jimmy came running across to them followed by his mother.

'Hello, Mr Hutton,' said the boy. 'Mum says you'll show me that magic trick with the coin again.'

'Yes, I will, Jimmy, I promise. I'm sorry, Miss Wilson, you were saying you wanted to know something.'

The old woman looked at her niece and said, 'What I want to know is, are you sending a surveyor to look round my house or not?'

'Would you mind?' he said, very serious.

'If you mean, do I think the old place is going to fall down, the answer's no,' said Miss Wilson. 'But there was nothing in our agreement about subject to survey, that's what I told that half-witted solicitor of mine. So if you want the place surveyed, I should prefer you do it in your time, when the house is yours, rather than waste mine when I've got better things to be doing!'

Behind the old woman's shoulder, Anya made a mockingly wry face at Jaysmith. He scratched his nose and looked at the ground, then went and kicked one of the posts holding up the porch, and pressed his ear to the woodwork. His reward was a wide rejuvenating grin from Anya.

'All right,' he said.

'All right, what?' demanded Miss Wilson.

'I'm ready to complete. The money should be available today. When can you be out?'

For a moment she sucked in her cheeks and glared at him frostily, then gradually relaxed and smiled.

'You're a bit of a joker, aren't you, Mr Hutton? I'd not have thought it when we first met. I could be out a week on Friday but I won't be, because if you move on a Friday and things go wrong, which they always do, there's no hope of getting hold of a tradesman over the weekend. So it'll be a fortnight today if that suits.'

'Fine,' said Jaysmith, offering his hand.

They shook and the old woman said to Anya, 'I'm glad that's definite. I had that brother of mine on the phone last night and I nearly told him, but I wanted to be definite.'

'You think he won't be pleased?' said Anya.

'He will not but he'll just have to lump it. Hadn't you better be off? Here, I put a jar of rum butter out for your father.'

She stepped into the hallway and returned a moment later with a large jar topped with a round of greaseproof paper held on with an elastic band.

'Thank you,' said Anya. 'He'll enjoy that.'

131

'Tell him to keep it hid from those nurses,' she said severely. 'I'll be down myself to see him when he gets home. I'll not go to a hospital again, not till they carry me.'

'No, auntie,' said Anya, kissing her cheek.

'And you'll set things in motion, young man,' said Miss Wilson to Jaysmith as he got into the car.

'Yes,' he said. 'I'm just off to see my solicitor.'

CHAPTER THIRTEEN

As they approached the hospital Jimmy, who had been chattering excitedly for most of the journey, fell silent, answering his mother's cheerful questions with monosyllables. Getting out of the car, he grasped Anya's hand tightly and when Jaysmith said that he would wait for a while before joining them at Bryant's bedside, the boy looked up at him with the accusing eyes of the betrayed.

A nurse came down the corridor which led to the ward, accompanied by two uniformed policemen.

She recognized Anya and stopped, saying to the policemen, 'This is Mr Bryant's daughter.'

'Is he all right? What's happened?' asked Anya anxiously while Jimmy clung tightly to her leg as well as her hand.

'He's fine,' said the nurse reassuringly. 'And in excellent voice. He's been insisting on seeing the police ever since he woke up this morning.'

'We'd have wanted a statement in any case,' said one of the men, a big, raw-boned youngster with an engaging smile. 'But your dad seems to reckon he was run off the road by some idiot overtaking him down the Struggle. He seems to think we should have road-blocks out, and Scotland Yard in, looking for him.'

'I daresay you'd be a little upset if you'd been put in a hospital bed by some maniac's carelessness,' snapped Anya. 'Come on, Jimmy.'

She walked away. The young constable looked after her admiringly.

'Could it be true?' asked Jaysmith.

'Could be, but it'd really need a maniac to overtake on that road in those conditions. Excuse me, but who are you, sir?'

'Just a friend of the family,' said Jaysmith. 'Who was it who found Mr Bryant, by the way? I know his daughter wants to thank him.'

The officer checked his notebook.

'It was a Mr Blackett, of Nab Farm, Ambleside. It was lucky he came along. The car was upside down with Mr Bryant hanging in his seat belt unconscious.'

'Did Mr Blackett say anything about another car?'

'Not that I know of. Now if you'll excuse us, sir. Come on, Bob. Time we were off.'

Jaysmith waited another ten minutes, then went into the ward. Bryant was sitting up in bed. With his head bandaged, his face flecked with small dressings and his arm in plaster, he looked almost a caricature of a hospital patient. But his eyes were alert and he greeted the newcomer with a pleasing energy.

'Mr Hutton, I've been hearing about your kindness. Thank you. Good of you to come.'

Anya was sitting by his side, holding his hand, and Jaysmith was pleased to see Jimmy wandering

133

around the ward, looking with wide-eyed curiosity at the many strange and wonderful sights it contained.

'It's good to see you like this,' said Jaysmith. 'I gather it was a close call.'

'Very close. You'd think I'd know after all my years in the legal game just how obtuse the police can be, but I can't get them to show any interest at all in the lunatic who did this!'

'Lunatic?'

'Yes. I was crawling along, hardly able to see more than a couple of yards . . .'

Anya interrupted him with the tartness of relief at finding him in such a lively state.

'Crawling? You've never crawled in that car of yours in your life! And you must've been moving pretty fast to smash through a five-barred gate!'

Bryant replied grimly, 'Lucky it was there. The alternative was a five-foot wall. Oh all right, I had got up a bit of speed, but that was this idiot's fault. He'd been following behind me for half a mile at a steady pace, then suddenly he started crowding me. Last thing you want in those conditions is someone up your exhaust, so naturally I speeded up a bit. I'd just begun to realize how fast he'd got me going when suddenly he was overtaking and cutting back inside on a bend. That's when I went through the gate and flipped over. Madman!'

'What was it?' asked Jaysmith. 'Car? Van? Truck?'

'Car, I think,' said Bryant slowly. 'It's all a bit mixed up still. But I'll get it all sorted once I'm out of this place and can get a bit of peace.'

'You'll stay here till you're fit to move!' commanded Anya. 'Jimmy!'

She rose and went down the ward to where Jimmy had got into conversation with a man bandaged like a mummy, whose grapes he was eating with gusto.

'She was wise to bring the boy,' said Bryant. 'He'd developed a real phobia of these places. I don't much care for them myself.'

Jaysmith reached into his pocket and produced a small labelless bottle wrapped in a paper bag.

'I gather you're not damaged internally,' he said. 'This might help you survive your stay.'

Bryant opened the bottle, sniffed and said, 'Hutton, you can visit me as often as you like.'

'Don't be too grateful. It's your own Scotch. I filled it from your decanter this morning.'

'Yes,' said Bryant. 'Anya was saying you'd stayed the night.'

'It seemed best. In the circumstances.'

'Yes, it probably was. In the circumstances. I suggested you might be persuaded to stay a few more nights till I came home. She did not seem enthusiastic.'

Jaysmith was taken aback as much by the suggestion as by Anya's response. Bryant was observing him closely and it came to him that the solicitor was once again probing. The suggestion had been made to Anya to test her response, and the information passed to him so that his reaction could be noted and analysed also.

He smiled and said, 'Last night was an emergency. Help's welcome from any source in an emergency, even from a stranger.'

'I don't think of you as a stranger, Hutton,' said Bryant. 'Somehow I feel I've known you better and longer than just a couple of meetings. That's odd,

135

isn't it?'

The return of Anya and Jimmy ended this line of conversation, much to his relief, and for the rest of the visit talk centred on Bryant's and his daughter's widely differing estimates of his discharge date. An elderly doctor trailing crowds of nurses arrived with the end-of-visiting bell and smiled benevolently when invited to umpire.

'Don't want to miss the next fell-race, do we?' he said. 'Well, we'll see. We'll see. Let's have a look at you now.'

They took their leave. Jimmy kissed his grandfather and went running off to say goodbye to his mummy-wrapped friend who clearly fascinated him. Anya went in pursuit. As Jaysmith waited, he glanced back at Bryant's bed. A curtain had been pulled, but not all the way round. The sheet was drawn back to his knees and his pyjama jacket was opened so that the doctor could examine the considerable bruising on his chest, but it was not this that caught Jaysmith's eye. It was an extensive area of scar tissue down his left side. There was a matching area down the other side which presumably joined up with the left round his back, and in this were four little hollows, as though a child had pushed its fingers into plasticine.

At some point in his life, Bryant had been badly beaten up and shot, though not necessarily in that order.

Anya was ushering Jimmy out of the door. Jaysmith stored this new information up in his mind and went after them.

The visit had clearly done both mother and boy a lot of good. From fear the boy had moved to proprietorial curiosity and it required a firm hand

136

to keep him from peering through every door they passed. Anya smiled at Jaysmith, sharing her double relief, but at the exit she stopped and said, 'Damn! I wanted to find out about the man who found him. I wonder who I should ask.'

'How about me?' said Jaysmith. 'Mr Blackett. Nab Farm. Ambleside.'

She looked so amazed he laughed out loud.

'I asked that policeman you were rude to. I thought you'd want to know.'

'You're a pretty clever fellow, aren't you?' she said thoughtfully. 'You don't miss much.'

'A lot,' he said. 'I think I've missed a lot.'

In the car she said, 'Would you mind if we stopped off in Ambleside? I'd like to thank Mr Blackett personally.'

'Surely. Do you know where the farm is?'

'We can ask. Or it'll be marked on the Ordnance Survey map, probably.'

'In there,' he said, indicating the glove compartment.

She opened it and pulled out the selection of maps it contained.

'My,' she said after a while. 'You are thorough, aren't you?'

He glanced across to see what she meant and saw with a shock that she was holding the OS sheet NY 32 which Jacob had sent him. Naddle Foot was ringed in red and five black lines radiated from it, his possible lines of fire. Retirement had quickly made him careless.

He said, 'I'm one of nature's doodlers.'

'You surprise me. But it's a very orderly kind of doodle and that fits, I suppose.'

She refolded the sheet and rummaged around

till she found the map with 'Ambleside and district' on it.

'Here we are,' she said. 'Nab Farm. Follow my directions.'

'My pleasure,' he said.

Blackett turned out to be a burly, blunt and busy farmer. His reply to Anya's thanks was, 'I weren't going to leave him, were I?'

Jaysmith said, 'Mr Bryant seems to think he was forced off the road by another vehicle overtaking him.'

'Is that so?'

'You didn't see another vehicle?'

'I could hardly see a thing,' he said. 'It was that bad. I got to that bend and saw the gate was broke and there was some lights in the field, so I stopped to have a look.'

'How long after the accident was this, do you reckon?'

He thought then said, 'Not long. Engine were still hot.'

'And you didn't see another car? Or hear anything?'

There was another pause for thought, then he said, 'There might've been something. Another engine somewhere when I stopped mine and got out. But sound travels funny in them conditions. Now, I'm glad your dad's all right, missus, but I've got to get back to work.'

He turned and stumped away.

'One of nature's charmers,' said Jaysmith as they got back into the car.

'He'll get my vote whenever he wants it,' said Anya fiercely. 'What do I care about charm? He saved pappy's life, didn't he?'

'Yes. I think he probably did.'

'You seem very interested in pappy's story about this other car,' said Anya.

'I thought it worth checking.'

'Why?' she asked.

'I don't know. Because your father was so certain, perhaps. If there were another car, the driver needs to be brought to book, don't you think?'

'You're into retribution now, are you?' she said.

'I suppose I am. You're not?'

'I'll stick with gratitude,' she said. 'For the time being. In any case, I don't see how it can be quite like pappy said. Concussion can do queer things.'

'True. But what makes you think your father's got it wrong?'

'Well, if there was a road hog belting down the Struggle, how come he didn't overtake Mr Blackett first? I mean, if he was travelling so fast, while pappy and Blackett were crawling along, well, it's a narrow twisting road with no turn-offs, so he can't have been between them, can he? It doesn't make sense.'

She had a sharp mind, he acknowledged again. She marshalled the facts as efficiently and neatly as he himself did. The difference lay in the conditioning of their two minds. Her conclusion was that if the third car had not sped past Blackett also, it didn't exist. His conclusion was very different.

If the third car had not passed Blackett, it was because it too was crawling along, a little way behind Bryant, content to keep at the safe snail's pace till the right moment came. Then the sudden acceleration, the near contact, the violent change

139

of direction, the crash.

But at that speed, even dropping off the road like that and turning over, Bryant was likely to survive. So the third car would stop, its driver get out to make sure. And distantly he would hear Blackett's vehicle grinding along, see his lights approaching.

There was no guarantee that his conclusion was sounder than Anya's, but he did not need guarantees. He had seen last night what the threat of her father's death had done to her and he now acknowledged formally what he had recognized then.

It didn't matter what Bryant was, or had been, or what he deserved. For Anya's sake, Jaysmith could not allow him to be killed.

CHAPTER FOURTEEN

At the hotel car park Anya refused his invitation to have a drink and got straight into her Fiat.

'This young man's got to have his lunch, then get to school,' she said.

'Do I have to go, mum?' the boy demanded. 'Couldn't I go back tomorrow instead? Mr Hutton hasn't shown me his magic trick yet.'

'I'm sorry,' said Jaysmith. He took a fifty pence piece out of his pocket and rolled it round his knuckles. The boy watched in fascination.

'My father wanted you to stay at the house a bit longer,' said Anya.

'He said so.'

'I told him no.'

He didn't say anything and his silence seemed to provoke her.

'Look, I stay by myself when he goes away; there's never been any of this helpless little woman stuff before.'

'Does he go away often?'

'Yes, quite often,' she said firmly, then corrected herself as though feeling she was overreacting. 'Not quite so often as he used to, not since I came back to live with him. But I made it clear that I didn't expect him to alter his life just to fit me back in.'

'Does he ever go back to Poland?' he asked idly.

'Why do you ask?' she said sharply.

'Just making conversation, to extend the pleasure of your company,' he said, smiling. 'I remember he said he went back at the end of the war and I wondered if he'd ever made any other visits, that's all. It's not important.'

She frowned. When she looked serious, she made a perfect third for the photograph of Jimmy and his grandfather that she had in her bedroom.

'You must have misunderstood,' she said. 'He didn't go back at the end of the war. He was there already when the war ended.'

'Good Lord. You mean he was an agent?'

'Something like that. He doesn't talk about it; if you mention it, he'll only joke that it didn't last long enough for the glue on his false moustache to dry. His version is that he got shot when they arrested him and he spent the rest of the war in hospital, recovering just in time for the peace.'

'And you believe that?'

'I believe he doesn't want to distress me, Jay,' she said. 'But I'm neither illiterate nor stupid. Wherever he was, it was a million miles away from

141

the crisp comfort of Windermere Hospital. Look, we must dash. Jimmy, into the car, *now!* I'll be in touch.'

'You mean it?'

'Yes.'

Their gazes locked and he nodded. Last night and this morning had eased them closer together, fractionally but discernibly. The fox was at the edge of the trees almost ready to step into the moonlit glade.

'*Jimmy!* I won't tell you again.'

It was the still-moving coin which was petrifying the boy.

'Hop-lah!' cried Jaysmith flicking it high into the air, catching it in his right hand, showing the empty palm to the wide-eyed boy, then with his left plucking it out of the youngster's ear and presenting it to him with a flourish.

'Thanks a million,' said Jimmy, running round the car and climbing into the passenger seat.

'You can't afford to keep this up,' said Anya, switching on the engine.

'I can't afford not to,' said Jaysmith.

That afternoon he drove into Carlisle, forty miles away. It was the nearest town of any size, and he wanted a reference library with a Polish dictionary in it, and also the chance to use it with minimum risk of being observed by any of the Grasmere vigilantes. The library was situated in a pleasant old sandstone building between the attractively small cathedral and the sullenly squat castle. This was, he realized, the furthest north he'd ever been in the UK.

This was frontier country. Here for centuries a line had been drawn, across which the English and

142

before them the Romans had defended their heartlands against the Scots. He recalled Anya's suggestion that she sensed in him the kind of make-up which would have maintained its stoic vigil on the barren heights of Hard Knott Castle. Was she right? Perhaps. But nowadays the frontiers were different. They ran through cities and villages, streets and houses; they split nations and parties and families and even single human minds; and the conflict was bitterer and more deadly than it had ever been before.

He settled to his task.

It didn't take him long to realize he was wasting his time. These were what he had guessed, love letters. They began with the equivalent of *darling*, ended with expressions of love and longing. In between, so far as he could make out, lay nothing but what one would expect to find in such letters— descriptions of domestic events, gossip about mutual friends, all infused with a passionate desire to be sharing these things at first hand instead of in a letter.

It was of course possible that there was a code here, but it would need a cypher expert fluent in Polish to spot it. He was neither. He put the letters back in his pocket, returned the dictionary to the shelves and went to the service desk.

Yes, they kept copies of all the Cumbrian newspapers. He was vague about dates and got a supply of weeklies covering October to December of the previous year. He found what he was looking for in the last edition before Christmas.

TRAGIC DEATH OF WELL-KNOWN LOCAL CLIMBER

143

There was no reason to be looking at this, except that a careful man studied all aspects of possible opposition before starting an operation. There was something ghoulish about treating a dead man as a rival, but his presence was still powerful. Part of Anya was striving to let go, but another part seemed to be desperately clinging on.

The facts of Wilson's death were simple enough. He had been climbing Pillar Rock when he fell. He had been alone and had sustained severe back and head injuries. It had been well over twenty-four hours before he was found and he had died in the West Cumberland Hospital without regaining consciousness.

Jaysmith rose and went back to the library shelves. There was no shortage of books on the Lake District and on mountaineering. Pillar Rock, he discovered, was a crag on the eastern face of Pillar Fell, overlooking Ennerdale. Remote, steep and dangerous, it provided rock-climbers with ascents ranging from 'Difficult' to 'Very Severe'.

Jaysmith returned to the paper, slightly puzzled why, on what was evidently such a famous and, in climbing terms, popular crag, Wilson's fall should have gone unnoticed. It also seemed rather odd to him to be climbing alone.

The inquest report answered the first point. Weather conditions, it seemed, had been atrocious. Sleet and snow lashed by near gale-force winds; none but the hardiest climbers had ventured out in such conditions, and only to destinations less remote than Pillar Rock. The coroner animadverted sternly on the foolhardiness of the inexperienced and ill-equipped treading the fells at this time of year, using the tragic death of Edward

Wilson to show how even the most skilful, experienced and expert of climbers could become vulnerable in such terrible conditions. Verdict was death by misadventure.

On the same page and of much greater length than the inquest report was an obituary appreciation, which provided the answer to Jaysmith's second mental query.

Even making allowances for local pride in a favourite son, Wilson came across as a formidable figure. Educated at Granton, a Scottish public school working on Outward Bound principles, and Trinity Hall, Cambridge, where he read law, he had eschewed the brilliant career forecast for him and opted for a Lakeland solicitor's life in preference to the Inns of Court. The only thing which could draw him away from his beloved Cumbrian mountains was the challenge of other greater mountains. He had taken part in numerous expeditions, including the joint Anglo-Australian Himalayan venture of 1974. In 1976 he had married Anya Bryant, daughter of a fellow solicitor and there was one son, James, born the following year. He had been widely expected to be selected for the multinational attempt on Everest in 1978, but while climbing in the Alps in the winter of 1977, he had been taken ill and had nearly died before his companions got him to hospital where it was discovered he was suffering from diabetes mellitus. Though this disease for the purposes of normal everyday living is easily controllable via diet and insulin injections, it had virtually disqualified him thereafter from any major expedition. This had been a great loss to the world of climbing and a great tragedy to Wilson who had reacted by cutting

145

himself off more and more from his old mountaineering circles and becoming very much a loner in his Lakeland climbs. The irony that this should have eventually contributed to his death was rather ghoulishly underlined, and the piece ended with a purple passage about his spirit on the mountains which would not have been out of place in *Wuthering Heights*.

Checking further, Jaysmith discovered Wilson had even made a couple of the nationals, which could have explained the familiarity of that brooding, bearded face. Jaysmith studied it thoughtfully. It was a potent spirit to exorcise. Somehow Wilson, dead, seemed to retain all the strengths and capacities of the living; while he, Jaysmith, could only offer a life as undefinable as a phantom's existence, and a talent as unrevealable as the face of God.

He drove slowly back to Grasmere, stopping en route in Keswick to call at Bryant's office and make an appointment to see his partner, Donald Grose, the following morning. His purchase of Rigg Cottage must still go ahead despite all these alarums, and there were many details to sort out. Also, he was hopeful that Grose might be able to add some useful shading to the picture he was drawing of Bryant and perhaps even of Edward Wilson. No; not *hopeful*, he corrected himself. He could feel he was getting nowhere, and now he was ready to clutch at any straws at all.

* * *

In the event Grose proved rather more substantial than a straw in several ways. He was a confusion of men. His round face and plump body seemed to promise a placid temperament and measured speech. Instead he was full of nervous energy, unable to find a pen without taking a turn around his office, opening and slamming half a dozen drawers, all the while talking rapidly in a Northumbrian counter-tenor.

He had been to visit Bryant in hospital the previous night and his natural garrulity plus his understanding that Jaysmith was a family friend inclined him to talk freely.

'He looked well—I said, how're you going on, Steve? and he said, I'll be better when I'm going out which won't be long, and I believe him—he's remarkable but he's his own worst enemy—he'll be out too early and coming home to get under Annie's feet. I told him this and I said I'd rather rape a gorilla with gripes, and I certainly didn't want to see him round the office this side of Martinmas—but it's like talking to a lady magistrate with a hair appointment—her mind's made up and it'll not be changed even if it means hanging you for parking—will you sign here, and here, and here, Mr Hutton?'

He signed and said, 'I understood Bryant to say he rarely came into the office anyway.'

'Rarely? No, not rarely. A year or so back and it was maybe getting towards rarely but this last year he's been finding himself plenty to do in here—not that I object—we ought to have been training up a new man for a good while now, and without Steve, rare or not, I'd be hard pushed—that's the way to lose business—they're sharp-eyed these Cumbrians and if they think they're not getting one hundred and fifty per cent attention, they're off in a flash.'

'But he's not old,' said Jaysmith. 'Early sixties isn't old these days. I'm surprised that he started to act semi-retired so early, a man like him.'

'Semi-retired?' Grose laughed. 'You're joking—no, he was working as hard as ever—you must know about this book he's writing on Polish history—well, he doesn't do things by halves does he?—well, he flung himself into it heart and soul a few years ago—lots of research trips to Poland, that sort of thing—he discussed it with me first, of course, and I said, go ahead, I can hold the fort—and in any case it seemed likely that . . .'

He paused. Jaysmith thought, he's reached a point beyond which even my misconstrued status as a friend of the family doesn't entitle me to go without a ticket.

He made a guess and said knowledgeably, 'Yes, it did seem to make sense that Edward would have eventually joined the business as a partner.'

Grose nodded.

'That looked as if it would be the way of it to most people,' he said. 'But Steve's a hard man to please.'

'You mean he didn't like Edward?' said Jaysmith.

'No, I don't mean that,' said Grose, slightly offended. 'He's not the kind to discuss his daughter's business with other people, you should know that. But he did once say to me that when we took someone new into the business, it'd not be someone who couldn't give it any more time than he himself could!'

'Oh, you mean all this climbing?'

'That's it,' said Grose. 'Now, let's talk about money, shall we?'

*   *   *

He left the solicitor's office with no significant new information but a picture was forming. Anya had married. Bryant, left alone, had launched himself into his Polish project. It was during these years that the period of his frequent visits to Poland had begun, visits during which he had either resumed or begun an affair with the woman called Ota. Then, going by the entry stamps on Bryant's passport, the visits had stopped about a year ago and they had since kept in contact by letter. This was the time in which Anya, recently widowed, had returned to Naddle Foot. So the simple explanation was that Bryant had felt reluctant to leave his grieving daughter alone for any significant length of time.

But visits even to Poland need not be long. Perhaps there was another dimension. Perhaps Bryant, finding himself responsible not only for a grieving daughter but also a much-loved grandson, did not feel he had the right to put himself in danger.

Yet something had put him in danger despite, or could it be because of, his efforts.

It did not surprise Jaysmith. His own experience was teaching him the hard way how hard it was to retire from danger. It was harder to shake off than a spurned lover.

If you did not go looking for it, it came looking for you.

CHAPTER FIFTEEN

Two days later against all medical advice and filial pleading Bryant discharged himself from hospital.

Jaysmith had not visited him again. There was a faint chance that Jacob had a man watching the hospital, though in Jaysmith's eyes this would have been stupid and unnecessary. There was also a faint chance that Jacob's man didn't exist. Perhaps Bryant *was* concussed and imagining things. Or perhaps another slightly faster crawler had indeed grown impatient and gone past him on the Struggle, quite unaware of the accident happening in his wake.

In either case, he felt Bryant was as safe in hospital as he could be, outside a top-security jail.

Jaysmith did get involved in the homecoming, however. He had rung Anya each evening, ostensibly to ask how her father was, but really to check on her own well-being. She seemed to welcome the calls and it was usually Jaysmith who, reluctant to seem importunate, broke them short. He made no attempt to suggest a meeting, but passed his days walking the high fells in the still-persisting rain which gave him physical horizons to match the brume of his mind. The near view was quite clear—he had to protect Bryant, if protection were needed—but beyond that, it was all a confusion, shifting and deceptive. On the Wednesday night when he rang, Anya told him that Bryant was coming out in the morning, though the hospital would have preferred him to stay till the weekend at least.

'But he's very strong willed,' she finished. 'The doctor said he couldn't spare an ambulance and I said I certainly wasn't going to fetch him, and he announced that he would walk, if necessary.'

'But you *are* going to fetch him?' said Jaysmith.

'I learned early not to call pappy's bluffs,' said Anya.

'Want any help?'

She paused.

'Well, the only compromise we got out of him is that he said he'd use a wheelchair till he's told he can start exercising his leg. Getting in and out of the Fiat's not going to be easy . . .'

'What time shall I pick you up?' he asked.

'No, it's all right, I'll meet you there and save you the double journey.'

'Nonsense,' he said. 'That'd mean I'd have to drive him back unchaperoned. He'd probably hijack the car and make me head for the nearest pub.'

She laughed and said, 'All right.'

Beneath her exasperation with her father, he sensed a deep relief at having him home, and this was confirmed as he drove her to the hospital the following day. She was full of life and chatter and around her throat she wore a scarlet and golden scarf, the first truly gay colours he had seen her wearing. The weather too looked as if it was doing its best for the occasion. The cloud had risen above all but the highest peaks, its greyness now more inclined to white than black, and in one place it was positively threadbare to the light where the sun was trying to rub its way through.

Bryant greeted his presence without surprise and accepted what assistance was necessary with a good

151

grace, and with no signs of any over-macho assertion of independence. It wasn't till he got back to Naddle Foot and discovered that Anya had made up a bed for him in his study on the ground floor that he showed any signs of exasperation.

'I am a temporary invalid, not a permanent cripple,' he said to Anya. 'I have not broken out of that penitentiary in order to rest uneasily on any put-you-up. I desire the comforts of my own house which include my own bed.'

'Well that's fine if that's all you want,' retorted Anya. 'But I also presume you'll expect to enjoy the comforts of your garden and your study and your dining room too. In other words you'll be wanting to be downstairs as much as upstairs and you're in no fit state to manage those stairs.'

'I'll fall down if necessary.'

'But you can't fall up,' said Anya. 'And I'm just a weak woman, remember? I'll nurse you if I have to, but I'm not in the business of giving piggy-backs.'

Jaysmith listened to this exchange with considerable amusement. The strong will was clearly firmly printed in the genes.

'You're right, my dear,' said Bryant, suddenly and unconvincingly humble. 'I can't expect you to bear my weight, physically or metaphorically. I'm sorry.'

Anya looked triumphant, but suspicious. She was right to be.

'What we need is a man's strength around the place,' continued Bryant. 'Mr Hutton, it must be costing you a fortune staying at that hotel. Why not come and spend a few days here till Rigg Cottage is yours? No strings, but if you happen to be around when I need a shoulder to lean on, that would be a kindness to a poor, sick man.'

He spoke with a heavy irony directed at his daughter. But there was more to it than that. Jaysmith felt himself once again closely observed, and Anya too, by those still sharp eyes beneath their grizzled brows. Bryant was still probing their relationship, trying to understand what it meant and where it might lead.

If he finds out, I hope he'll tell me, thought Jaysmith sardonically.

He said, 'Look, hadn't you two better talk privately? I mean, done like this, it's very difficult for Anya to say she doesn't want me here . . .'

Father and daughter replied almost simultaneously.

'No, it's not,' declared Anya.

'It's my house,' growled Bryant.

They glared at each other, a glare diffusing gradually into the glow of an amused, exasperated affection which was exclusive enough to make Jaysmith feel a pang of jealousy.

Anya said, 'Jay, I can't imagine why you would want to be within a hundred miles of the world's worst invalid, but if you *can* bear the prospect for a few days, then please stay. It would be a great help and might even bring a little ease to undeserved suffering and stoically borne pain. I refer of course to myself.'

It was the right note. Bryant smiled almost triumphantly as if he had prepared the way for this, or had some theory confirmed by it.

He said, 'That's settled then. Let's have a drink to seal the contract.'

To unseal the contract would be a better phrase, thought Jaysmith.

And wondered why it was that so often with both these two he felt as if he had spoken his thoughts out loud.

*   *   *

The move was made that same afternoon. Parker, scenting a romance, accepted his guest's sudden departure with an almost Pandar-like joviality, insisting that Jaysmith take a bottle of champagne to speed the invalid's recovery. His wife, on the other hand, frowned a little and took an almost formal farewell. Jaysmith guessed that, while her hopes for Anya's happiness did not altogether exclude the involvement of a well-to-do middle-aged man, the speed at which things seemed to be progressing gave her pause. It was clear that she did not know Bryant very well, if at all, otherwise her common sense would have seen that his perceptive care was more than likely to compensate for Anya's vulnerability.

Yet she's right, thought Jaysmith, they're all right to be suspicious. I am a deceiver. The sensitive nose must be able to smell it on me. What confuses them is the unguessable nature of the deceit.

And it confused himself also. He was in a trap from which there was no escaping. Even the route of altruistic chivalry was not open to him. If he simply vanished, any pain he caused Anya was likely very soon to be subsumed by the greater pain of losing her father, perhaps having him killed before her eyes, perhaps even being endangered herself by the nature of his killing.

If he stayed, as he knew he must, he could offer some defence, but for how long? And what would

154

be Jacob's response when he discovered, as *he* must, Jaysmith's involvement? What could he believe but that Jaysmith had been bought off by a higher bidder?

Even the fox in a snare had the alternative of gnawing off his own foot to escape. The nearest he could get to such amputation might be complete confession to Bryant and Anya, but what would that change? Very little, it seemed to him; but as he drove back to Naddle Foot, his mind dark with these heavy thoughts, it began to feel like the only way out.

He arrived at the house just as Jimmy got back from school. The boy was delighted to see him and when he heard that Jaysmith was staying for a few days, he said with the uncomplicated approval of the young, 'Smashing! You'll be here for my birthday!' and dragged him off to play table tennis in the stone-flagged basement.

Anya rescued him half an hour later so that he could go up to his room and unpack.

'We eat early in the evening, six at the latest. That way we can all sit down together at table and have a bit of evening left over before Jimmy goes off to bed. It's a child-centred house, and that includes pappy!'

It was forecastable that the boy would use Jaysmith's presence to delay his bedtime and it was after nine before he found himself sitting in front of a gently crackling and sighing log fire with Bryant and his daughter. Here at last was the opportunity for confession. But he knew without debate that tonight at least this was an impossible option. What would it change? he asked himself that afternoon. Then the self-questioning had felt

155

like an evasion. Now he knew at least part of the answer. It would change this evening with its atmosphere of quiet content. Seated at the table, enjoying a plain meal washed down with a jug of beer, listening to Jimmy's chatter of school life and the amiable bickering between father and daughter about whether Bryant needed help to cut up his meat, Jaysmith had felt himself seduced by happiness. And now, deep in an old armchair, with Anya straining her eyes to read the local newspaper by the fire's glow and Bryant half-asleep, listening to the record of Ashkenazy playing Chopin waltzes which had been his choice, Jaysmith felt . . . he did not know what. Definitions might seem sentimental. Or clichéd. Or pretentious. A half-remembered and never understood phrase from his sixth-form days came to him . . . *the holiness of the heart's affections* . . . here for a while, for these moments at least, it made sense. Tomorrow was soon enough for death and danger. Tomorrow.

CHAPTER SIXTEEN

He awoke the next morning feeling more rested than he'd done in years. His bedroom was small and simple with white painted walls and pine furniture. The morning sun was pouring through the thin cotton curtains and bursting against the white emulsion and pale wood in a haze of warm gold. He stretched and yawned and smiled and for a moment it felt good to be alive.

Then he remembered.

He got out of bed and went to the window. It

overlooked the terraced garden to the front of the house. He had slept well. The sun had already cleared the ridge of the eastern fells and was drawing smoky curls of mist through the bracken and up the gullies. There were still plenty of clouds in the sky but now they ranged over broad acres of blue. The improvement in the weather was continuing; and with it, the improvement of conditions for a marksman.

He got out his binoculars and began to scan the distant fellside. There, not much over a fortnight ago, he had sat and plotted death for the man who now lay under his protection only a few yards away. He thought he glimpsed a movement on the fell and slowly quartered the area with his glasses. There it was again. A grazing sheep. He watched it for a while. It showed no sign of alarm or disturbance and he moved on.

'What is it? A hawk?'

Startled, he spun round. Anya was in the doorway with a cup and saucer in her hand. She smiled at his alarm.

'I wouldn't have thought you were the nervous type,' she said.

'You move very quietly,' he said. 'Like a fox.'

'What does that make you?' she mocked. 'A chicken?'

She was in an ebullient mood this morning. The weather was not the only area where an improvement had been maintained. She was wearing blue jeans and a blue-checked shirt, and she looked about eighteen.

She said, 'I took pappy his breakfast and I thought you might like a cup of tea also, particularly as Jimmy is threatening to pay a call before he goes off to school.'

'We're always at home to a friend,' he said.

She put the cup of tea on the bedside table and he sat down on the bed to drink it. A minute or two later the door was opened cautiously and Jimmy's uncertain face peered round the jamb.

'Hello,' he said.

'Hello. Are you going to bring the rest of you in, or did your head just come up by itself.'

Grinning broadly, the boy entered.

'Mum says if I want you at my party tomorrow, I should ask you properly.'

'She's quite right, but I was coming whether I was asked or not. Only, if I hadn't been asked, I was going to ruin it by putting fireworks in the jelly. That way, everyone gets a bit.'

Jimmy's eyes opened wide in delight. Clearly he felt that far from ruining things, such an explosion would set the seal on his celebration. One thought led to another.

'Were you in the war, Mr Hutton?' he asked.

'Why do you ask?' said Jaysmith.

'That mark on your face,' said the boy, looking in fascination at the long scar down his left cheek. 'In one of my comics there's a man with a scar like that and he got it from a bomb in the war.'

'Sorry. With me it's simpler. I cut myself shaving.'

The youngster's face registered keen disappointment. Anya's voice called from below, 'Jimmy! Hurry up or you'll miss the bus!'

'Better go,' he said. 'See you later, Mr Hutton!'

'My friends call me Jay,' said Jaysmith.

'See you later, Jay!' yelled the boy as he galloped down the stairs.

Jaysmith got washed and dressed and descended to the kitchen. Anya was drinking coffee and reading a newspaper.

'I didn't give you any choice last time,' she said. 'I just assumed that big macho you must be a bacon-and-egg man. For all I know you're really a muesli freak.'

'I like the occasional fry-up,' he said. 'But most of the time it's fruit juice, toast, and lots of strong coffee. How's your father?'

'Fully recovered except for my female fussiness. At least that's the game he's playing. He's determined he's not going to stay in bed.'

'In that case,' said Jaysmith, 'I'd better start earning my keep.'

'Stay where you are and have your breakfast,' she ordered. 'He knows it's only a game. He's not going to break his neck trying to get downstairs by himself, I assure you.'

'If you're sure,' said Jaysmith. He drank some fresh orange juice. 'How long is it since your mother died?'

'Oh, a long time,' she said vaguely. 'I was thirteen.'

'Not all that long,' he said, smiling. 'Did he ever think of remarrying?'

She considered the question.

'He took mum's death hard,' she said. 'It was a tumour, and she was a long time dying. I blamed him in a way, I suppose. We were at loggerheads for a long time after that. I expect I was ripe for the mid-teen rebellion anyway and mum's death just exacerbated matters. What I'm saying is that for a long time after that I'd no real idea of, or interest in, what was going on in his mind. Eventually we

159

drifted back together. At least it was drift in my case, though I suspect in his it was a carefully charted voyage to the rescue of a vessel in distress. He's cool, he's patient, and he's perceptive. He also loves me very dearly.'

She broke off and Jaysmith glanced sharply at her, but saw that it was the silence of self-contemplation, not imminent tears.

'At eighteen, my school career ended and I was waiting for the "A" level results which, it was anticipated, would be good enough to let me take up my provisional university place. I was going to read law! He must have thought that he'd got me firmly in tow and that the harbour was in sight. Then one day he came home and I calmly told him everything had changed. I was going to be married. It never crossed my mind that there could be any objection, or indeed that his feelings came into the matter in any way. It's amazing to think what a self-centred little bitch I must have seemed. Seemed? *Was!*'

She laughed, half in embarrassment.

'How did I get onto this subject?' she asked.

'I asked if your father ever considered remarrying?'

'That's right. And I was trying to explain that in those first five years, he devoted himself to me, though I didn't really notice it. And when I told him I was getting married, I suspect he came near to exploding. At the time I think that could have destroyed everything between us. So in the end he shut up and paid up. I got married. And he really got down to researching his book. He spent a lot of time away, in Poland in particular. Edward, my husband, and I had a house in Borrowdale, so it

160

was easy enough to see him when he was home. We came much closer together after I was married, particularly after Jimmy was born; and I got the feeling that he'd met someone over there he'd grown very fond of. We've never spoken directly of it, but I have an impression that she won't leave Poland and he finds it hard to contemplate going back there to live. He really hates the communists, you know. And his home is here, his life . . .'

'And you. And Jimmy,' suggested Jaysmith. 'Does he still see her?'

'No. What I mean is, he hasn't been back to Poland, not since . . . since Edward died, and Jimmy and I came back here to live. I asked him about it. I was worried in case it had something to do with our being here but he said it hadn't and he'd be going back as soon as his book research needed it.'

She sounded doubtful as well she might. A man did not give up seeing his lover just because his daughter and grandson were living with him. What he might give up was danger; what he might want to avoid was piling another tragedy onto his already battered and bleeding child.

He finished his breakfast and went up to Bryant's bedroom, where he found his host fully dressed.

'Morning,' said Bryant. 'How did you sleep?'

'Loggedly. And you?'

'I would have liked to toss and turn but when that proved impossible, I went to sleep instead. Is your strong right shoulder available?'

'Yours to command.'

He helped the injured man downstairs and into the lounge. Anya appeared and looked critically at her father.

'You look awful,' she said.

'A breath of fresh air will soon put the roses back in my cheeks,' said Bryant. 'I'll take coffee outside in the sunshine.'

Jaysmith was alarmed but Anya said firmly, 'No, you won't. It's still damp out there and the wind's chilly. Dr Menzies is coming to see you this afternoon and we'll let him decide on what you can or can't do.'

Bryant looked disgusted but did not object. Jaysmith said, 'I thought I'd go into Keswick and do a bit of shopping if that's OK.'

They both looked surprised.

'Now see what you've done,' said Anya to her father. 'Jay, you're a guest, not a male nurse, no matter what this poseur may have said. You must feel completely free to come and go.'

'Of course,' said Jaysmith. 'I thought, afterwards, I might go for a bit of a walk, so don't bother about me for lunch.'

'Lucky devil on a day like this,' said Bryant. 'Anya, why don't you go too? I'll promise not to do any gymnastics while you're away.'

Jaysmith looked at her apprehensively. Much as he desired her company, today there were several reasons against it. He did not know whether he was relieved or disappointed when she said, 'I'd better not. I've got a lot of baking to do for tomorrow's junket.'

She added as she saw Jaysmith to his car, 'I would have liked to come, but really, I want to be around when the doctor comes. I don't trust pappy even to let him in!'

He smiled and touched her arm lightly.

'I'll see you later,' he said.

His shopping did not take long and soon he was driving back into St-John's-in-the-Vale. He drove slowly the whole length of the valley; there were no cars parked in view till he approached the junction with the main Keswick-Ambleside road where the great Castle Rock of Triermain lowered to the east. Here a car park with access to a picnic area was quite full. Any one of them could belong to Jacob's man.

He turned and drove back along the road. It was probably a useless precaution, but he wanted to leave his own car out of sight if possible. He had noticed in his earlier researches of the terrain that there were several disused quarries below the eastern line of fells. A rutted and greened-over track led obliquely off the road towards one of them. A sign, sun-peeled to illegibility, probably forbade entry, and a rusty iron pole wedged across the track between two rotting posts reinforced the prohibition. It required little effort to drop it to the ground and he sent the powerful BMW up the steeply curving track till he was hidden from the road by a long spoil-heap of loose shale.

It was a bleak and dismal place. The shattered fellside seemed to lean out in a series of huge rectangular slabs of rock, tiered above an artificial amphitheatre of which the other walls were long steep wedges of waste. It was possible to imagine some bitter contest taking place there for the vile entertainment of some warped and troglodyte race.

Jaysmith shuddered. The place chilled him disproportionately as though it spoke to him of something in his own existence.

Quickly he put on his boots and anorak, raising

163

the hood less for protection against the gusting wind than as a bar to identification. He wanted to be just another fellwalker if he came within range of a pair of field glasses.

A fence ran at a crazy angle up the fellside along the edge of the quarry, presumably to inhibit sheep from grazing themselves into danger. He climbed alongside it. A couple of hundred feet up, a broad ledge of rock jutted out over the amphitheatre. He paused here and looked northwards up the valley. Naddle Foot was just visible at, he estimated, about fourteen hundred metres. He brought his binoculars up. It was an oblique view of the house, partially blocked by trees. The front porch was visible and the gravelled drive, but most of the garden was completely shielded. Distance, angle and screening made it a useless line of fire and he had not even considered it on the map.

He climbed higher till finally he was on the grassy slopes of the fell top. It was a steep and unsafe scramble, not one which any ordinary fellwalker would be tempted to undertake. Now he walked along the path which took him above Wanthwaite Crags. He had amused Anya and her father the previous night by pronouncing the name as written. *Wanthet*, Anya had told him. *Can't have you talking like a bloody foreigner*, Bryant had added. From time to time he paused and used his binoculars, trying to give the impression of a man fascinated by the flight of various birds whose identity he was generally totally ignorant of. As usual, Clough Head seemed untroubled by human company that day. He paid special attention to the gill which he had chosen for his own hide. The recent rains had increased the volume of water pouring down, but there was no other visible change, no fag ends, matchsticks or boot prints; nothing to suggest any other visitor had descended there.

Satisfied at last he settled down on a rock near the summit and suddenly, with what was almost a shock of guilt, he became aware of the view. On his previous visits here, as on all his jobs, his sensitivity to the surrounding terrain had been purely practical. It had to conceal him, and help him make good his escape; he had to work out its likely effect on wind and atmospheric conditions; it was simply a factor in a computer program which contained as its essentials the target's death and his own survival.

Now for the first time he saw with an unblinkered eye. He turned his head to the north and let his gaze travel up the shattered face of Blencathra. Slowly he turned his head and there, central amid a swell of lesser peaks, was the green head of Skiddaw. Slowly he turned, till his gaze moved through west and into the southern sector. And here what a turbulent sea of fells met his view. Stretching into a distance of probably fifteen miles on the map, but an infinity on the mind, they crowded the skyline with a beauty at once superb and intimate. With luck he would walk on them all, yet in essence they would always remain beyond his or any man's reach.

With a sigh whose meaning he did not altogether comprehend, he dropped his gaze into the valley below and with his glasses brought Naddle Foot leaping into view.

The terraced garden was empty. Either Anya's will or the uncertain weather had kept Bryant indoors. But he would not remain indoors for ever.

He let his glasses slide up the face of the building. The windows stared blankly back, revealing little of what was inside. Only twice had he essayed a window-shot, both times successfully; but it was not something he cared for. The window of his own bedroom was open as he had left it, and here he did glimpse a movement within. Only a narrow sector of the room was visible and he had to hold his focus there for a whole minute before he was sure. It was Anya, presumably making his bed. As if to confirm her presence, she now came to the window and stood in plain view. She was holding his pyjama jacket, he saw, and neatly folding it. As he watched she raised it to her cheek as if testing its temperature and at the same moment raised her eyes so that she seemed to be looking directly at him.

He let the glasses fall and the house was miniaturized instantly, a token artefact to show off the surge of the fell against which it nestled. On his maps it was marked as High Rigg but locally it took its name from Naddle Beck, paralleling St John's Beck on the western side. Hence the name of Bryant's house, he had also learned last night, situated at the foot of Naddle Fell. It was a more appropriately homely name for the fell which, though rugged enough, at not much over a thousand feet hardly merited the epithet 'High'. It struck him that this was not a bad place to live, this pleasant little valley with the heights in view and your own friendly fell to lift you well above the level of bustling humanity whenever you felt like a short stroll.

No, not a bad place to live, nor a bad place to

die, either. The fancy occurred to him suddenly that really *he* was the target and down there in Naddle Foot, which he had once thought to threaten and claimed now to protect, they were drawing a bead on him and just waiting for a clear shot to make the kill.

Well, at least today he was sure no one was taking a shot from up here. And it would have to be from up here, unless Jacob got hold of a rank amateur. High Rigg itself offered very little cover, was a popular area for casual strollers who'd been visiting the curious little church of St John's which gave the valley its name, and allowed a clear line only into the rear garden of the house which Jimmy alone seemed to use.

The only possible hide in the valley itself was a ruined barn alongside a small stand of trees where the ground began to rise from the beck to the fell. The upper storey of the barn gave sufficient elevation to look into both the front and the rear gardens of the house at a range of about seven hundred metres. But again it was a sideshot, though the short distance made it feasible. Escape was across open pastureland, however, and what really put it out of the question was a 'For Sale' notice where the track joined the road. His house-hunting cover had served him well, permitting him to check out the barn openly. But it meant that others, either attracted by the sign or sent by the estate agent, might come bumping along the farm track at any time. Not that the 'property' attracted many viewers. *Ripe for the conversion* was the come-on phrase. But the shell of the barn, which under local planning restrictions would provide the property limits, was small, there were no services laid on, and the asking price was exorbitant.

Nevertheless any risk of interruption was unacceptable.

Now he scanned the old building with his glasses. Others might accept risks he wouldn't take. There was no sign of life except for a magpie which came floating down in a flutter of black and white to settle on the barn. He watched it for a moment. It showed no alarm.

Satisfied, he swung back to the house. Anya had vanished from the window. He searched other windows for her without success. He willed her to reappear. So, it occurred to him, he had often willed targets to appear when their dilatoriness was distorting a carefully planned schedule.

Angrily he put the thought out of his mind, but it had already tainted the clear air between his lofty vantage point and the lovely old house. Friendly no longer, its walls and windows now seemed to mock him, blank as a human brow and human eyes behind which unreadable thoughts pulsed their dangerous secrets.

CHAPTER SEVENTEEN

'Hello,' said Anya. 'Had a good day?'

She looked deliciously domestic, with a flowery apron round her waist and a floury smear on her cheek, standing in the kitchen surrounded by the birthday baking whose sweet smell filled the air.

'Fine. Sorry I'm late.'

'Late?' She sounded surprised. 'Late for what? Dinner will be an hour at least.'

168

He found himself rather hurt not to have been missed.

'Where did you walk?' she asked.

He answered vaguely. His precise route wouldn't have made much sense to a seasoned fellwalker like Anya.

'How's the patient?' he asked.

'Dr Menzies was pleased with him, but they're old allies, those two. I'll wait to see what they say when he goes back to the hospital on Monday for his check-up. Pappy seemed a bit down at lunch, but Jimmy's with him now and that should dispel the gloom. A six-year-old on the eve of his seventh birthday's got enough joy to spread out over half the world.'

'And enough food too by the look of it! Want an impartial sampler?' said Jaysmith, reaching his hand out to a trayful of lemon curd tarts and withdrawing it rapidly as Anya cracked it hard with a wooden spoon.

'Jesus!' he said, blowing on his knuckles.

'Sorry,' she said, looking abashed. 'Pure instinctive reaction, I'm afraid. Pappy and Jimmy have both got fighter's knuckles.'

'I can believe it. If this is what joining the family means, I may not apply for admission.'

She went very still, and he was angry with himself for having so unpreparedly come close to what in the old days was called a declaration. Putting aside all question as to whether he had a right to, this was certainly not the time or occasion for it. But there was no way of going back.

'Jay,' said Anya in a suddenly strained voice. 'What is it that you want from me?'

The lounge door burst open and Jimmy erupted.

169

'Jay!' he yelled. 'We played football today and I scored three goals. Come and play football and I'll show you. Are you any good? I bet you are. Come and play, please!'

Jaysmith held Anya's gaze till the strain began to dissolve.

'To be going on with,' he said, 'a lemon curd tart will do nicely.'

'Help yourself,' she said.

'Mum, can I have one?' demanded Jimmy.

'You can have half of mine,' said Jaysmith. 'Your mum's conceded quite enough for one afternoon. Never push your luck, son. Now I reckon I can spare ten minutes before I get cleaned up to see an action replay of your three goals. With your mother's permission, of course.'

'Granted,' said Anya. 'But not a second more.'

'Agreed,' said Jaysmith. 'But not a second less either. I'm a man for full measure.'

Chewing his half of the tart and with Jimmy's hand firmly clamped around three fingers of his, he let himself be pulled into the garden.

*   *   *

At dinner that night, Jimmy's bubbling anticipation of his birthday joys set the mood. It wasn't till Anya had persuaded him that sleep was the most rapid route to the promised land and led him off to bed that Bryant showed any sign of the depression of mood his daughter had mentioned.

Nursing his balloon of plum brandy, he said abruptly, 'I rang Donald Grose this afternoon, just to check on things at the office. He said everything's going ahead full steam on your job.'

'Yes. It's remarkable how fast the law can move when it has to,' said Jaysmith, gently mocking.

'You'll be living at Rigg Cottage alone, I gather,' said Bryant.

Jaysmith was beginning to understand what had happened. Dr Menzies during his visit had expressed a natural curiosity in the stranger who had somehow installed himself at Naddle Foot. This outsider view had brought it home to Bryant just how little he actually knew about his guest. It might even be that he was feeling guilty. It couldn't have escaped him that Jaysmith's concern for the Bryant family was focused on Anya. Perhaps it had crossed his mind that the best solution to the problem of his own visits to Poland would be for Anya to be safely settled in a good second marriage.

And suddenly the doctor's remarks had brought it home that this man he had invited into his home and by implication his life was indeed a stranger.

First thing had been to check that at least he was irrevocably committed to the purchase of Rigg Cottage. And now he would want to fill the blanks in. He could either try subtlety or go for the direct approach. Jaysmith guessed the latter.

'Yes, I'll be alone,' he said. 'I'll need to get someone to "do" for me, I suppose.'

'No wife and family waiting to descend on you then?'

Jaysmith smiled to himself at his good guess.

'Not even an aged parent,' he said.

'It's a largish place for one, even if they do call it a cottage,' said Bryant.

'Miss Wilson lived there by herself quite happily,' replied Jaysmith. 'Except when her nephew was with her. He did grow up there, didn't he?'

'Why do you ask?'

'I was wondering about the associations the place might have for Anya.'

That was returning directness with directness!

Bryant was silent for a while as though considering his next move in a game of chess.

Finally he said, 'Yes, Edward spent a lot of his childhood there. James, his father, is some kind of civil servant, Trade and Industry I think it is. When he was widowed it must have seemed to make sense to let the boy be brought up here rather than in some London flat.'

'You don't sound as if it made sense to you.'

'Don't I? Perhaps I believe a boy needs a man. Muriel Wilson's a decent enough old stick but *old's* the operative word. She's about twelve years older than her brother and absolutely rigid. She knows nothing outside Grasmere. Nothing! Mind you, I don't blame *her*. Soon as the boy was old enough he was off to boarding school and, when his father could manage him, he would spend at least part of the holidays in London.'

'You sound as though you feel his father neglected him.'

'And you sound as if you think you've got a pretty sharp ear for nuances, Hutton!' snapped Bryant. 'Perhaps I do think his father neglected him. It wouldn't have been my way. But perhaps my way left something to be desired too. Anyway, I saw his father shedding tears at the funeral, and that's something I shan't forget. Begetting children is man's greatest act of creation, Hutton, but after that it sometimes seems like destruction all the
172

way!'

For a moment he was uncharacteristically agitated but before Jaysmith could speak the door opened and Anya came in.

'What a pleasant picture!' she said. 'The old men sitting round the camp fire reminiscing about their wild youth. Are we back in Poland, pappy? Or is it Jay's turn?'

There was a faintly aggressive note in her voice and Jaysmith wondered if she had overheard something of their conversation.

Bryant smiled at his daughter and said, 'No, we're not back in Poland, dear. But yes, I do think it's Jay's turn.'

They both looked at him expectantly, Anya settling onto the corner of the broad wooden fender which ran round the grate.

He said, 'My wild youth wasn't all that wild.'

'Nevertheless,' said Anya. 'Do tell.'

He launched on a light-hearted account of his upbringing in Blackburn. They listened attentively, but they rarely smiled and he realized after a while that his attempts at light-heartedness weren't covering up the cracks in his story and that his teenage unhappiness was seeping through.

'I never went back to the house,' he concluded, deciding to bring things to a rapid end. 'My stepfather packed up my few things and sent them on to me. I went straight up to university after National Service and stayed there during the vacations. I got myself a variety of jobs to tide me over, and at the end of three years I got my degree and lived happily ever after.'

He smiled and stretched and yawned to show that the narrative was finished.

173

'Is the house still there?' asked Anya.

'Oh, yes,' he said unthinkingly.

'How do you know if you've never been back?' said Bryant.

'I've seen it,' he said sharply. 'I meant I've never been back inside.'

'Ignore him,' said Anya. 'He always thought he should have been a barrister. What happened next, Jay? After you got your degree?'

'Oh, jobs,' he said vaguely. 'You know, the usual progression. Office boy, filing clerk, managing director.'

'And now retirement at forty,' said Bryant.

'Forty-three,' corrected Jaysmith. 'Don't forget the three. After forty, every year counts twice, so they say. Mind you, under ten, every year counts a hundred times, and in anticipation of a long hard day tomorrow, I think I'll retire early. Unless my services as beast of burden are required.'

Anya smiled and said, 'No, that's OK. I'll drag the poor old crock upstairs. Goodnight, Jay. Sleep well.'

He left. It was a retreat, of course, but after those painful recollections of his teenage years, he did not want to be forced into the glib lies necessary to chart the period of his maturity. He paused at the door a moment and glanced back. Bryant's chair was turned to the fire and its high wings almost completely concealed its occupant. But Anya was leaning forward, profiled by the flames, and the sight of her narrow intense face and long thin body filled him with such a rage of desire that he felt his whole person burning, and with the door closed behind him, he had to lean against the hall wall for a while till he recovered.

He fell asleep quickly but was soon disturbed by such terrible dreams of sexual violence involving both Nguyet and Anya that he awoke. The third time this happened he rose and brought himself to a climax with his hand and after this he slept, though so shallowly that the first glimmer of dawn brought him awake once more.

* * *

Jimmy's birthday was a perfect autumn day. There was very little wind. The sun's heat drew the morning mists up into a sky of cornflower blue and set the colours of woodland and fellside hotly glowing. The recent storms were now only a memory, recorded in fillets of creamy white marking the distant descent of mountain streams, and by the music of their falling waters.

It was excellent shooting weather.

Jaysmith got washed and dressed. As he came out of his bedroom a figure with a levelled gun leapt out of ambush on the landing. Instinctively he flung himself sideways, hitting the floor with a tremendous crash and rolling away in a vain attempt at evasion. The finger was already on the trigger, and he could only lie helpless and watch as a stream of ping pong balls hit him on the chest.

'Jimmy! I told you! You must never fire at people!' cried Anya coming out of her room.

'I wasn't going to, honest,' protested the boy. 'But Jay started playing and I couldn't help it, could I, Jay?'

Jaysmith sat up and leaned back against the wall.

'No,' he agreed. 'You couldn't help it. But your mother's right, Jimmy. You mustn't fire at people.'

'Are you all right?' enquired Anya, coming towards him. He reached up his hand. She took it and began to pull. For a second he resisted. He knew—they both knew—that if the boy had not been there, he would have drawn her down to join him.

'I'm fine,' he said, rising in an easy movement.

'You look a bit shook up to me,' she said, examining him closely. It was true. He could feel in himself a slight nervous reaction to the incident.

He said, 'I'm not used to holding hands with pretty girls.'

She drew her hand away sharply and said, 'You mean you're too old to be flinging yourself around like an all-in wrestler.'

Jimmy who had been recovering his ping pong balls said impatiently, 'Come and see my presents, Jay.'

'All right,' said Jaysmith. 'But hold on. I almost forgot.'

He went back into his bedroom and returned with a gaily wrapped parcel, which Jimmy with youthful impatience and despite his mother's protests ripped open immediately. It contained a large box of licorice allsorts and a pack of trick playing cards. Jaysmith had been tempted to buy something much more expensively impressive, but had decided that such ostentation from a newcomer to the family circle would be at best vulgar, at worst distasteful. He was rewarded now with Jimmy's unbounded enthusiasm and Anya's approving smile.

The new presents were added to the horde already strewn across Jimmy's bed. They included a highly colourful children's encyclopaedia from

Bryant and, most impressive of all, a complex of video games from his paternal grandfather. Anya saw Jaysmith studying this and said as if in explanation, 'Grandpa Wilson would have liked to be here himself.'

Jaysmith had to show Jimmy how to use the trick cards and it was only Anya's force of will and a solemn promise that he would join the boy in some target practice later that got him into the kitchen for breakfast.

'Jay, could you do me a favour?' asked Anya as he drank his fourth cup of coffee.

He looked at her quizzically and said, 'Perhaps.'

'That's a little short of enthusiastic,' she said.

He said, 'I'm not a man who makes commitments lightly.'

'It's only a form of speech,' she said in irritation. 'I mean, even if you say yes, and then find you can't, it's not a breach-of-promise case, you know.'

He didn't speak but regarded her with such unconcealed affectionate amusement that she flushed and said, 'All I wanted to ask was if you could pick up Aunt Muriel this afternoon and bring her to the party. Pappy can't, of course, and I'm going to be rather busy . . .'

'It'll be a pleasure,' he said.

The telephone rang in the hallway. Anya went out, closing the door behind her. After a few moments he heard her running lightly upstairs, presumably to tell her father to take the call on his extension. On her return to the kitchen she poured herself a cup of coffee and offered Jaysmith a refill.

'No,' he said. 'I'm fully awake now, I reckon. What's the drill this afternoon?'

'It will be something between *The Lord of the*

Rings and *The Lord of the Flies*,' she said. 'Hobbit appetites modulating to atavistic savagery. Between two and three, a dozen or more delighted mums and dads will dump their rapacious offspring here and drive rapidly away to enjoy a few hours of peace.'

'Mixed offspring?'

'Oh no,' she said, shocked. 'When you're seven, it's very *infra dig* to let a mere girl anywhere near your party.'

'You sound very expert,' he laughed. 'Of course, you must have a few of these do's under your belt.'

She shook her head and said, 'In fact, not. Edward didn't much care to have our house in Borrowdale "infested", as he put it. We used to take Jimmy to Rigg Cottage more often than not and Aunt Muriel would run a little celebration there.'

This was practically the first time she'd referred to her husband so openly. He knew instinctively he must not treat it as an opening.

He said, 'And now Aunt Muriel comes here. Is she the only adult help?'

'Yes,' she said. 'And I don't want to overtax her, of course. I was relying rather heavily on pappy to help organize games and things . . .'

She let her voice tail off and he stared at her until she flushed once more and looked away.

He laughed out loud and said, 'You're learning. That's a much better way to ask for a favour. I'll be delighted.'

'Thanks a million,' she said, catching Jimmy's tone and inflexion perfectly. He laughed again, stood up, leaned forward and kissed her lightly on the cheek.

'I'll go and see if your father's ready to descend,' he said.

As he made for the stairs he noticed that Anya had forgotten to replace the hall telephone on the hook after she had told her father to take the call. As he passed he heard a tinny voice emerging from it. He paused in mid-stride and glanced towards the kitchen. He could hear the sound of dishes being washed. He picked up the telephone, put his hand over the mouthpiece and pressed the receiver to his ear.

Bryant's voice said, without enthusiasm, 'You'll be in touch then.'

And the other voice, the one that had attracted Jaysmith's attention, replied without warmth, 'You can bank on it, can't you? Take good care of yourself, Stefan. Goodbye.'

The line went dead. Gently Jaysmith replaced the instrument on its rest. For a moment in the kitchen he had inhabited a world in which the only peril was that his passionate longing for Anya would trap him into a wrong move, but now he was back in a world much shorter of profit and delight but much more crowded with fatal hazard.

The voice on the phone had been unmistakably Jacob's.

CHAPTER EIGHTEEN

Miss Wilson opened the door before he could ring when he arrived at Rigg Cottage. Despite the gentle warmth of the autumn sun she wore a thick tweed coat and a fur hat.

179

'No use you coming in just to come out again,' she said, stepping over the threshold and firmly closing the door behind her. A few more days and it would be *his* front door, thought Jaysmith, not without amazement. He helped her into the car. She made herself comfortable and looked around critically.

'Fancy motor,' she commented. 'Foreign, I daresay.'

'So is Anya's,' he replied defensively.

'Yes,' she said. 'But it'll have cost next to nothing compared with this.'

He took the point. To buy foreign by way of economy was sensible; by way of luxury was unpatriotic.

'I bought it abroad,' he said. 'Cheap.'

'Cheap!' she echoed disbelievingly. He negotiated the hill down into Grasmere. The village was full of visitors lured out by a sunny autumn Saturday. There was no shortage of locals either, and these with their Cumbrian eye for the out-of-the-way, almost to a man and certainly to a woman, spotted Miss Wilson in the BMW and waved their greetings. It was like a royal progress, thought Jaysmith.

'You've got your feet under the table then,' said Miss Wilson out of the blue.

'Sorry?'

She did not deign to elaborate, forcing him by her silence to admit he understood her meaning perfectly.

'I'm glad to be of help to Anya,' he said.

'She's a good girl,' said the old woman. In what sense 'good' was intended was not clear.

'I think so too. A good woman,' said Jaysmith.

180

'Yes,' she agreed. 'A good woman. She married a bit too early, I sometimes think.'

He did not reply and this time it was his silence that seemed to force her to carry on.

'Edward wasn't always an easy man,' she said. 'From a boy, he wasn't easy. I should know. I had the bringing up of him.'

This was the first hint of criticism of the man who, though dead, he still, absurdly, thought of as his rival, and he felt rising in him a greed to hear more.

Controlling his voice to conceal his eagerness he asked casually, 'In what way, not easy?'

'He could be moody,' she said. Then, family solidarity suddenly making itself felt, she added sharply, 'But we can all be moody, can't we? And he was a grand lad in a lot of ways. Not afraid of hard work. A heart like a lion.'

Like a lion. He thought of that face he had only seen in photographs, with its heavy mane of dark hair and almost sullen gaze. Yes, there had been something leonine about it. Still was; a recumbent form guarding the approaches to the cave.

Christ! he thought. This is becoming positively Freudian.

A blare of horns brought him back to awareness of his driving. He had turned north on the main Windermere–Keswick road and was second in a line of cars behind a slow-moving farm-truck piled high with bales of hay. Traffic was heavy in the opposite direction and overtaking was only possible intermittently and one at a time. But a metallic-gold mini, impatient of waiting its turn, had started queue-jumping, nipping into the stopping space between cars to avoid the oncoming traffic and causing much irritation in both directions. He took the final stage from two cars behind the BMW to beyond the hay-truck in a single swoop. Jaysmith saw him as he flashed by, a young man with a shock of ash-blond hair, sun-goggles and a cigarette drooping from his lips. He felt a sudden pang of envy for that youthful impatience, that certainty that there was only one speed possible, and that was headlong. It was life's irony that by the time you decide that such speed might not be necessary, the advancing years were already making it so.

'He's in a hurry,' said Miss Wilson. 'He'll be lucky to get there in one piece. Youngsters!'

The widening of the road as it climbed up Dunmail Raise permitted Jaysmith to overtake the hay-truck without problem, but he found himself opening up the BMW almost as an assertion of his right to be included in the old woman's condemned grouping. Miss Wilson, however, clearly had no objection to speed when it was combined with comfort and gave every sign of enjoying the experience. Indeed, as they made their way along the winding road through St-John's-in-the-Vale, she remarked with some satisfaction, 'There. It didn't do him much good, did it?' as they overtook the golden mini which had pulled off the road ahead.

'Aye, and he looks the type for that too,' said the old woman scornfully.

'For what?' enquired Jaysmith.

'For spending money on a broken-down barn and doing it up, isn't that what they call it? Places where there's been nowt but rats and cow-dung for centuries! They must have more money than sense!'

Jaysmith realized, glancing in his mirror, that the

182

mini had indeed stopped at the mouth of the track leading to the old barn that was for sale.

'I looked at that,' he said provocatively.

Unabashed, Miss Wilson said, 'Aye, but you're not a smooth-faced lad, are you? You settled for a real house. And a real bargain, I might add!'

A few minutes later, they reached the gateway to Naddle Foot and had to wait to let a couple of cars come down the long drive, doubtless fresh from dropping Jimmy's guests though it was barely two o'clock.

Anya greeted them with relief.

'There's quite a lot here already,' she said. 'Parents apologetic but some urgent appointment is taking them to the far end of the country, and they know I won't mind little Fred turning up a mite early, will I?'

'And do you?' asked Jaysmith.

'Not really,' she said with a wide smile. 'Jimmy would have burst if we'd had to wait much longer for his party to begin. They're all out in the back now, raising hell. Aunt Muriel, come and say hello to pappy before I toss you to the lions.'

They found Bryant sitting in the lounge looking out of the french window which opened onto the rear garden where Jimmy and three other boys were playing a wild game of football. Such energy, such youth. He glanced at the other occupants of the room. Bryant and Muriel Wilson were greeting each other with a wary courtesy from which Anya obviously derived some wry amusement. She looked so young and fresh. He found himself wondering where exactly she placed him in the gamut of animal youth to prickly age being played before her.

183

'I'm well enough,' Bryant was saying in response to a formal enquiry after his health. 'What of you? All ready for your move? What's that brother of yours think about it?'

'He can think what he likes,' Miss Wilson replied with spirit. 'It's me own house. There's no family entail or owt of that. And if he wanted it to stay in the family he should have come up here to live and run me up and down that hill in his motor car!'

'You *have* told him you're moving haven't you, auntie?' asked Anya.

'Last Sunday he rang. I told him then. I was able to tell him about your accident too,' she said to Bryant, reducing his misfortune to a trifle compared with the sale of Rigg Cottage. 'What were you thinking of, man? Speeding down the Struggle on a night like that?'

Her effort to redirect the conversation was instantly successful.

'I was not speeding,' snapped Bryant. 'Unfortunately some idiot in a Dinky-car was. I was forced off the road!'

'Hmm,' said Miss Wilson, conveying a volume of scepticism. 'Now where's that nephew of mine? Doesn't he want his present?'

'Jimmy!' called Anya. 'Aunt Muriel's here.'

The boy came running in, flushed from his exertions.

'Hello,' he said, halting before the old woman.

'Is that all I get?' she said sternly.

'Sorry,' he said, and gave her a swift kiss. Jaysmith guessed that his fondness for his great-aunt was laced with just a little fear. She now handed over a box-shaped parcel wrapped in a bright striped paper which looked as if it had been

184

used before.

'Don't tear it,' she instructed as Jimmy began the assault which was his normal method of unwrapping gifts. The paper came off to reveal an old cardboard box which bore a legend announcing it contained a dozen cans of baked beans. But there was nothing old or edible about its contents now which turned out to be a radio-controlled police car.

Jimmy's delight was unbounded.

'That's smashing,' he yelled. 'Thanks a million!'

Giving his great-aunt a now uninhibited kiss he rushed out to show off his new treasure to his friends.

'You shouldn't have, Aunt Muriel,' protested Anya. 'It's far too expensive.'

'Nonsense,' said the old woman, gathering up the wrapping paper and smoothing it out. 'He might as well have it now as when I'm gone. And there'll be a tidy bit of cash to have, especially when Mr Hutton here gets round to paying his debts.'

The imputation that he was dragging his feet in closing a deal which had been processed at something like ten times the normal speed made Jaysmith stare. Anya walked past him and nudged him sharply in the side. He saw that she was having difficulty holding back her amusement, and suddenly he was too.

'Come and enjoy the sunshine, auntie,' said Anya. 'It'll get nippy later on.'

Pulling her coat around her to indicate that perhaps it was nippy already, the old woman followed the young into the garden, where Jimmy was demonstrating the manoeuvrability of his

185

police car to his admiring friends.

'They've come a long way since Dinkies,' said Bryant. 'With one quarter of the technology they use for making toys now, we'd have won the war in half the time.'

'Dinkies,' said Jaysmith slowly.

'Yes. Surely you remember Dinky-cars? Not part of my own childhood, of course, but Anya went through a phase of collecting them. She was always tomboyish! Little metal models of real cars, very well made. I think the firm went out of business. The recession, electronics. The usual tale. Tragic.'

'Yes,' said Jaysmith. 'Tragic. But you mentioned them earlier too. You said when you had your crash, you were overtaken by some idiot in a Dinky-car. Why did you say that?'

'It's called a figure of speech,' said Bryant ironically. 'I thought *I* was supposed to be the bloody foreigner.'

'You mean it was a small car . . .'

'It was a mini, bright yellow I think. I've never liked them, buzzing around like a fart in a bottle, they seem to do something to their drivers . . .'

'You mean, you've remembered? You never mentioned it to me!'

'Should I have done?' said Bryant, puzzled. 'You were out, I think. It was yesterday; it suddenly came back. I rang the police. They didn't seem very interested. Not half as much as you, certainly!'

He was regarding Jaysmith with open speculation. The ringing of the front door bell postponed the need for explanation, however. Gratefully he excused himself and went to answer the summons. It was another young guest, the first of a steady stream which kept him occupied for the

186

next twenty minutes, directing them through the house to the rear garden where Anya was organizing a series of energy-sapping games in the hope of rendering them all quiescent by teatime.

When the last car drew away he went to the BMW and got his field glasses. Running lightly up the stairs, he entered Jimmy's room which looked out to the south from the side of the house. Careful not to disturb the curtain, he positioned himself so that he could see the winding road and followed it back. The end of the track where the yellow mini had stopped was not within sight, he discovered. He turned his attention to the ruined barn. It stood blank and still in the sunlight. There was no sign of any human presence. But what did he expect to see? he asked himself. A nest of FN MAG 7.62s bristling in the broken walls?

A sudden cry of pain and anger made him start. But it was only an occupational sound-effect of whatever riot was going on in the back garden. Surely, he thought, even if Bryant did limp out into the open and present a target, surely no one was going to risk a shot when he was surrounded by highly excited, wildly active children?

He realized he was putting the argument to himself on emotional grounds and checked himself firmly. As a professional, how would he react? He was relieved to find the professional objections were as strong as the emotional ones. The boys by their violent movements might distract the target himself into a sudden movement. Or they might simply run into the line of fire. He would certainly decide they presented an unacceptable level of risk.

But he was Jaysmith. He wouldn't be situated anywhere as unsuitable as that barn in the first

187

place. He tried to reassure himself that Jacob would never send a mere apprentice to do such a job, but that effort to run Bryant off the Struggle had not been very professional.

Probably there was no connection whatever between the golden mini he had seen on the road through the valley and the yellow mini Bryant thought he remembered on the Kirkstone Struggle. But the thought of some nervous newcomer pumping bullets into a garden which contained Anya and Jimmy and Miss Wilson and fourteen happy young boys, as well as Bryant himself, was not one he could live with a moment longer than necessary.

He went down the stairs, moving swiftly past the lounge door—fearful of being spotted and summoned—out to the BMW once more. The rifle in the concealed compartment was no use to him. Running around with an assembled M21 would rapidly draw attention to himself, and besides, it was hardly a close-quarter weapon. Instead he sought out his only other armament, a broad-bladed, razor-edged Bowie knife in a metal sheath. Slipping it into his waist band, he strolled back to the house. If he was under observation, he didn't want to alert suspicion.

He exited via the door from the kitchen into the garage, which was on the north side of the house, and keeping the bulk of the building between himself and the distant barn, he strode out across the neighbouring fields till he hit the curving beck. The banks were too shallow to give the kind of concealment he would have liked, but it was the best cover he could find on the open valley pastures. Anyone working in the fields, or strolling along High Rigg, would be able to see him quite plainly. Perhaps he would look like an eccentric ichthyologist in pursuit of some rare stickleback! In any case, all that mattered was that his approach should go unobserved by any watcher in the barn.

From time to time, particularly when the course of the beck was in direct line with the barn, he advanced through the shallow water to gain as much depth of concealment as possible. Though St John's Beck was at this point more than halfway on its winding journey to join the Glenderamackin at Threlkeld Bridge and with it form the Greta which curves round Keswick, it still held the chill of the shaded length of Thirlmere whence it sprang. Jaysmith hardly noticed it, however; he had endured greater discomforts in lesser cause. And when the channel reached its nearest point to the barn, he actually dropped down on all fours and half crawled, half floated till he was beyond the ruined building.

Now he climbed up the bank. If there was a watcher in the barn, his attention would be all on the house. Unless, of course, he'd spotted Jaysmith's approach, in which case, it didn't matter. He looked down the track which ran across fields to the road. There was no sign of the mini where it had been parked earlier. He felt the beginnings of relief. Perhaps its presence was innocent and coincidental after all. But thoroughness required that he check out the barn anyway. And after a few seconds of still cautious approach, he felt his relief loose its always tenuous grip on his doubting mind.

In the stand of trees on the high side of the barn, he could now glimpse the metallic sheen of gold.

It took him another fifteen minutes to reach the

189

trees, and then he lay there, his chest resting against the rough bark of an alder, simply looking at the car for another ten.

There was no sign of the driver, either here or in the barn which was some twenty yards away. He had to go forward. There was always the chance of interruption from some local farmer or prospective purchaser, and he needed to know the truth without interruption. There was, of course, also the chance that the mini was quite innocent, the property of some keen bird-watcher, or local historian, or country rambler . . . he halted the list of possibilities. Looking for innocent explanations was a new weakness. He had survived hitherto on the assumption of guilt.

He went forward to the car.

The doors weren't locked. Ready for a quick getaway. He opened the driver's door very quietly and peered in. The mini was fitted with every refinement, ergonomic and mechanical. It was the 1275 GT version, and from the look of the dashboard, the owner was bent on closing the gap between GT and Grand Prix.

He tried the glove compartment. It fell open at his touch. He jerked back with a small gasp of shock as tresses of ash-blond hair slithered out over his hand.

It was a wig. He draped it over his fist, combing out the locks with the fingers of his other hand and trying to envisage the young profile he had glimpsed briefly as the mini overtook him. What was under the wig? What was it necessary to conceal? Brown hair? Red? Black? A crew cut perhaps, or something even closer, in the modern idiom.

Then he saw it clearly. A gleaming razored skull with its arrogant, absurd coxcomb of bright orange spikes.

Adam. Protean Adam, moving from glue-sniffing punk to trained operative to homosexual hero-worshipper in the brief period of their recent acquaintance. And now here he was again, Adam the watcher, Adam who knew him, and must have seen him, and whose respect and admiration might even have made him guess at Jaysmith's next move.

It was time to get away from the mini.

He straightened up and gently closed the door. The click it made still seemed too loud for this still autumn air, but it didn't matter anyway. Some instinct, which he had been refining for twenty years, told him he was not alone a long but useless second before he heard the voice, full of respect but full of urgency also.

'Please put your hands on top of the car, Mr Jaysmith. And please don't make any sudden movement, I beg of you.'

Slowly Jaysmith put his hands on top of the mini. And slowly he turned his head.

CHAPTER NINETEEN

The young man was standing about twenty feet away. He wore a green and brown camouflage jacket with a matching hat. There were leaves on his shoulders and mud stains on his knees. He must have been lying there in some shallow fold of ground, completely unmoving, for God knows how long. It was a talent to be respected. As was the

191

pistol he held in his hand.

It was a Heckler and Koch P9, which meant that it delivered 9mm Parabellum bullets at a muzzle velocity of 11,180 feet per second. Jaysmith's mind automatically recalled the technical information. It also registered that it was levelled with a very professional steadiness at the centre of his chest.

'I saw you at the house,' said Adam accusingly, touching with his free hand the field glasses which hung round his neck. 'I saw you go out to the car twice. You went back inside the second time and then after a while, I could see the young woman was getting worried about something. She kept on looking towards the house, then she went inside and when she came out, she shook her head at the old lady. And I began to wonder. I didn't know what it meant, but I tried to work out what you'd do if you got suspicious I was here. I've spent a lot of time thinking about the ways you do things, Mr Jaysmith. So I came down from the barn and hid.

'And I was right.'

He didn't sound happy at his rightness. In fact there was an expression not much short of distress on his face and suddenly it struck Jaysmith that the young man was genuinely upset.

'You didn't know I was at the house till you saw me then?' he said.

'No,' said the young man with an overtone of pain. 'I didn't.'

He doesn't want to believe I've turned traitor, thought Jaysmith. But he can't see any other explanation.

'What happens now?' he asked.

'I'm thinking about it,' said Adam.

'The longer you stand there thinking, the more

192

chance there is of someone strolling along and wondering what strange game we're playing.'

'Yes,' said Adam. But he didn't glance nervously round.

'I appreciate your problem,' pursued Jaysmith. 'What you would really like is to get me locked up, or tied up, or any way rendered *hors de combat* while you contact Jacob and let him know what's happened and find out what you should do next. But you're rather worried in case I jump you. Right?'

'That's about it,' admitted Adam. 'All I can think of is getting close enough to hit you over the head and that might be dangerous.'

'Yes, it might,' agreed Jaysmith. 'Always keep as much distance between yourself and a target as you reasonably can.'

'I see that,' said Adam. 'But it wasn't quite what I meant. Dangerous for *you*, being hit over the head, that's what I was trying to say.'

Jaysmith laughed.

'Well, if that's how you feel, and I certainly don't mean you any harm, the problem's solved. Look, let's just sit down and talk around things. I'm not even armed!'

He stretched wide his arms to prove the point. Adam took a step back but still kept the HK P9 levelled. There was a noise somewhere over to their left.

'Someone's coming!' whispered Jaysmith urgently. 'For Christ's sake, put that thing away!'

The gun vanished inside the combat jacket, but the hand went with it and remained out of sight. Jaysmith walked round the car, looking at it admiringly.

'Nice little job,' he said. 'Though I bet it's heavy on the petrol for its size.'

Joining in the game, Adam said, 'Not really. It depends how you drive, I suppose.'

'I've seen how you drive,' said Jaysmith. 'You passed me this afternoon, didn't you know that?'

'No,' admitted the young man. 'I didn't notice. But I wasn't looking, was I?'

'No excuse!'

The noise came again, the crackling underfoot of twigs and dry leaves, accompanied almost simultaneously by a long *baa*.

'Christ! It's only a sheep!' laughed Jaysmith.

This time the young man turned his head. The sheep peered at them through the trees as though trying to work out whether whatever it was that had brought these strange long creatures to stand in this unpromising spot might make an excursion from the surrounding pastures worthwhile. It was a comic sight and Adam laughed till he felt the knife blade at his throat.

'Pull the gun out slowly,' said Jaysmith.

Nervously the young man began to withdraw his hand at too fast a speed. The fine-edged blade nicked his skin.

'Slowly,' said Jaysmith.

The gun crept into view.

'Drop it.'

It fell to the brown and fibrous earth.

'Now walk backwards with me. Good. Far enough. Now sit down, hands clasped beneath your bum. Excellent.'

Adam sat in the required position and Jaysmith took four quick paces forward and scooped up the gun.

194

'Now let's take a walk. On your feet, but keep your hands clasped behind you. Like the Duke of Edinburgh. Now let's get under cover, shall we?'

He urged Adam before him into the barn. Its dark interior was musty with animal odours. A shaft of light almost church-like in its angle and effect fell through a hole in the roof. A rickety ladder led up to the hayloft.

'Up we go,' said Jaysmith. 'And if you're thinking, here's my chance, just remember that a bullet up the arsehole is not only undignified, it's extremely painful.'

He kept a safe distance behind the other, ordering him to sit down on his hands once more before he himself emerged onto the loft floor. Then he approached the seated man whose eyes widened in fear as suddenly the Bowie knife snaked out towards his throat. With a deft flick, Jaysmith cut the strap which held the field glasses and caught them as they fell into Adam's lap.

He moved towards the loading window which faced south towards Naddle Foot.

'I have excellent peripheral vision,' he said. 'Don't stir, not even if you find you're sitting on a rat's nest.'

He trained the glasses on the house.

It was, as he knew, a very poor line of fire with the trees which bordered the garden permitting only intermittent visibility. The children were still playing in the back garden. There was no sign of Muriel Wilson or of Bryant, but he could see Anya who was clearly supervising some team game. The young voices raised in competitive excitement carried quite clearly in the still air. Anya's face, flushed with exertion and youthful with sharing her son's happiness, seemed almost incandescent in the golden heat of the autumn sun. He felt like an envious voyeur. Or one of those pale helpless ghosts called up out of Erebus to comfort some emissary from the world of living men, but unable to speak till they have tasted fresh blood.

So rapt was he that, peripheral vision or not, he might have been susceptible to a sudden attack. Instead, Adam interrupted his reverie with speech.

'Mr Jaysmith, look, what *are* you doing in that house? Does Jacob know you're there?'

He still sounded puzzled and anxious, but that could be part of an act. A learner he might be, but he had already displayed some talent for the game.

'Don't muck me about, son,' said Jaysmith wearily. 'If Jacob knew I was there, he'd have told you, wouldn't he? Let's concentrate on you. What the hell are *you* doing here?'

'I'm just observing,' said Adam, convincingly ingenuous. 'Jacob told me to keep an eye on the house, that's all.'

'Balls,' said Jaysmith. 'Running Bryant off the road, that was keeping an eye on him, was it? No, sonny. You've been given my job, haven't you? Well, I shouldn't plan a long-term career in it, if I were you.'

He spoke with deliberate scorn and was secretly amused to see the youngster flush. If his hero-worship was genuine, this was probably the best route to provoke information out of him.

'What do you mean?' asked Adam.

'Just look at this! A lousy line of fire, a position open to approach by local farmers or casual strollers, your car parked next door where anyone can spot it. Not to mention the fact that you're

196

leaving more traces of your presence than a bull in a china shop.'

He indicated several cigarette ends and a crushed-up lager can on the floor.

'I'd have cleared up before I left,' protested Adam in the tone of a student whose seminar paper has been unjustly attacked by his tutor. 'But do go on. It's very interesting.'

He was not being sarcastic. Oh Christ, thought Jaysmith. The poor bastard really wants to become another me, God help him!

'I'm not here to give you tips of the trade,' he said wearily. 'How on earth did you get into this business anyway?'

'I got friendly with Dave three or four years ago,' said Adam artlessly. 'He was working for Jacob and when he wanted me to move in with him, I had to have security clearance. I knew something odd was going on, so one night in bed I asked him, and he told me, and then he got me the job so it would be safe for me to know, if you follow.'

'You know,' said Jaysmith, 'I find it hard to believe in you, Adam. Jacob's no fool. He's not going to send anyone wet behind the ears out on a job like this.'

'That's rather cruel,' protested the boy, flushing. 'Anyway, Jacob just sent me to observe.'

'Observe? Oh yes. And like I say, I suppose you were just *observing* when you ran Bryant off the road last Sunday?'

Again that rather becoming flush.

'Yes, that's how it started,' said Adam. 'Jacob wanted Dave to come up last Saturday after he'd seen you on the Friday night, remember? But on Saturday morning Dave went down with flu—he's very susceptible—and I was told to go instead, just to observe. I got up on Saturday night and put up at a truly *awful* hotel in Keswick. Everywhere decent was booked up, you see. And on Sunday I started watching. It was a really dreadful day, wasn't it? It was so dull too, just sitting there in the drizzle, watching. I began to feel quite nostalgic for your stairs and that awful bag of glue.'

'Get on with it!' growled Jaysmith.

'Well, in the afternoon, first the woman left with the child. Then Bryant appeared. I followed him. He went along the main Penrith road and then turned off through a place called Dockray and down to Patterdale village. Patterdale's at the foot of Ullswater . . .'

'I know where it is,' snapped Jaysmith. 'What did he do there?'

'He went into a house.'

'Whose house?'

'I don't know! He was in there a couple of hours or so. When he came out he didn't go back the way he'd come but set out up Kirkstone Pass and down the other side into Ambleside. The visibility was absolutely dreadful. I was crawling along behind him when suddenly I got this brilliant idea. Do you mind if I smoke?'

'If you can get a cigarette out and light it without moving your hands, go ahead,' said Jaysmith.

Adam nodded admiringly as if he had expected no more.

'I thought here was the perfect chance to get rid of Bryant with no questions asked, and do myself a bit of good in Jacob's eyes too. So I accelerated past him and forced him through the wall. Unfortunately before I could check he was dead, I saw this other vehicle approaching, so I got out quick. I still expected him to be dead. I rang Jacob and left a message telling him what had happened. When he rang back, he was furious. He'd found out Bryant was still alive and he wasn't happy!'

He shook his head ruefully.

'What happened then?'

'I was told to get back down to London. I said, what about the observation? and he asked me if I was going to dress up as a nurse. He can be very sarcastic. But I must admit I was happy to be back in town and Dave was much better. Then on Thursday night Jacob said Bryant was out of hospital and I was to get back up here and start observing again. The nearest place I could find a decent hotel was Windermere. And when I got up this morning I found that my petrol pump had gone kaput. Getting things done in this wilderness on a Saturday morning is almost impossible, but I managed it somehow though it took ages.'

'Which was why you were carving up the traffic to get here to do your job this afternoon,' said Jaysmith.

'That's right. But just observing. Jacob was very insistent on that. And almost the first thing I observed was you. Please, Mr Jaysmith, what *are* you up to?'

Jaysmith almost smiled at the note of pleading.

'That's for Jacob's ears alone,' he said. 'But if it's any comfort to you, I'm not in the employ of an enemy power or anything like that. I mean no one any harm. Now let's go and find a telephone, shall we? I think the time has come for me and Jacob to talk.'

He could see no alternative. It had to happen

sometime. His only real hope had been that Bryant was no longer targeted, but that was clearly a vain hope now, and eventually more efficient operatives than Adam would be despatched to complete the job. He would have liked a little more time to see if he could find out anything more, but his encounter with Adam had brought things to a head. He could hardly hold the boy captive for any significant length of time. He had neither the means nor indeed the inclination. This was between Jacob and himself. He had no desire to complicate matters further by using violence against any of Jacob's operatives unless absolutely forced to it.

'Now that we've established that neither of us wants to harm the other, please may I have a cigarette?' said Adam.

'So you can harm yourself?' said Jaysmith. 'I've been doing you a favour. But go ahead.'

Adam smiled and slowly produced a gold cigarette case and matching lighter. He really was an extremely attractive young man, thought Jaysmith. It must have been a great disappointment to a lot of impressionable girls to discover his lack of interest in them.

Jaysmith went down the ladder first and waited for the boy to follow. Outside the barn he tucked the HK P9 into his waistband under his shirt. He judged the danger of conflict was now past, but he was still careful to maintain a safe distance between them.

As Adam reached the golden mini, he took a last drag at his cigarette and flicked it away. It landed in some dry bracken.

'Whoops, sorry,' he said. 'Mustn't set the place on fire, must I?'

And he stooped to retrieve the glowing butt.

This totally natural hiatus in his progress brought Jaysmith close up behind. Again he had a split second's foreknowledge of what was going to happen, too little to forestall it, but enough to slightly alleviate its effect.

As Adam, half-crouched, swung his elbow back into Jaysmith's crutch, the older man was already flinching away. It meant he took the blow in the groin rather than in the testicles. The result was agony, but not total immobilization, and through the pain he could still feel amazement at the youngster's decision to attack. He fell heavily on his side and tried to roll away from the follow-up, but Adam was young and lithe and hit him with his full body weight while his hands attempted to gouge the eyes.

The boy was serious, thought Jaysmith, shaking his head violently to keep the grasping fingers out of his eye-sockets. One strayed into his mouth and he sank his teeth into it with all the strength of his jaw. Adam shrieked as the teeth met bone and drove his other fist hard against Jaysmith's neck. He gasped and the finger slipped from his mouth, leaving the taste of blood behind. He managed to roll over onto his left side and grasp the gun in his waistband. Adam rose up slightly and struck at his wrist, numbing it halfway up to the elbow. The gun was halfway loose, and now the young man grabbed for it and pulled it free. Jaysmith sought his intention in his face. All he could see there was death. Given a few moments to reflect, to discuss, to consider, the youth might well see reason. But those few moments were not in Jaysmith's gift.

Adam pulled himself up so that he was kneeling

201

astride Jaysmith and could get a clear shot at his head. Rolling onto his back, Jaysmith lifted his useless right hand to cover his face.

'No!' he cried. It came out like a plea for mercy. An older adversary might have known that men like Jaysmith did not ask for mercy, might have recognized that it was merely a stratagem of delay. But Adam was a young man and for a moment he hesitated. Perhaps the moment would have stretched long enough for reason to assert itself. Perhaps not. And it was not Jaysmith's sole risk to take. His left hand found the haft of his Bowie knife and as Adam teetered on the edge of decision, the pre-emptive blade sliced up through his belly, beneath his rib-cage and into the madly working muscle of his uncertain heart. For the few seconds that life continued his face twisted into a mask of almost comic betrayal, or revelation, of death, and the ruptured heart's final spasm jetted sufficient blood over Jaysmith's hand and along his arm to make articulate a whole battlefield of spirits.

CHAPTER TWENTY

He sat on the ground for a long time, looking at the body by his side. This was the closest he had ever been to one of his killings. He knew now why he always went for the long kill.

At last, recognizing the stupidity of delay, he rose and lifted the body and carried it to the car. The young man was very light. His jungle hat had slipped off in the fight and the comb of orange hair, crushed flat beneath the wig, flopped pathetically over the skull, bald and as vulnerable as a baby's.

The boot of a mini proved to be no place to stow a body. It occurred to Jaysmith's mind, eager for distracting rationalities, that there was even less room than might have been expected. The reason was not far to seek. As in his own car there was a false panel which removed to reveal a hidden compartment. Adam was a loyal consumer. It contained a Heckler and Koch 33K rifle, not perhaps the weapon for the long kill, but accurate and deadly over the ranges from here to the house.

So much for Adam's claim that he was a mere observer. Jacob did not issue weapons like this just in case his operatives fancied bagging a few pigeons. It made Jaysmith feel a little better, but not much.

There was a map too, the same OS sheet he had received when given the job. A heavy line had been drawn from the rear garden of Naddle Foot to Adam's observation point. There was a fainter line running from the front of the house across the valley and ending at a point on the fellside not far from where he'd built his own hide. There was some writing above it, almost indecipherable. He studied it a moment before it made sense.

J's line!

He could almost hear the admiration in the young man's voice.

'You fucking idiot!' he said out loud. 'What did you think this was? The Wild West? Kill the fastest draw and you get his reputation? Oh you fool!'

Finally, after taking out the spare wheel, he got the body in. He removed the bloodstained sweater he was wearing, used it to clean up his hands which were caked with drying blood, and tossed the garment into the boot with the body. His feet and the lower part of his trousers were still wet from the beck but fortunately the dark material did not show up the dampness very much. Despite the autumn sunshine, the air was chill among the trees beneath their lattice of branches and he found he was shivering.

He did a last check round, then got into the car and sent it steadily down the track and onto the road. He drove the half-dozen miles to Keswick as fast as he could without breaking any limits and when he reached the town, he put the car into the large and crowded car park behind the main street. He realized he had no money with him. Fortunately Adam had tossed an elegant suede jacket onto the back seat and in this he found a well-filled wallet and a plentiful supply of silver. He purchased the maximum ticket from a machine and stuck it on the windscreen. Then he walked swiftly away from the car and went in search of a public phone box.

In the booth he hesitated. Twenty minutes ago he had been determined to contact Jacob and lay his cards on the table. But twenty minutes ago Adam had been alive and well. Now the case was altered. He needed more time to think. With Adam's death he had bought time, though he didn't know how much.

He looked up 'Taxis' in the directory and five minutes later he was on his way back to Naddle Foot. He glanced at his watch and was amazed to see that barely an hour had passed since he had left the house.

Barely an hour for him, but a lifetime for Adam.

He had hoped to enter the house unobserved but he was out of luck.

'And where have you been, young man?' demanded Miss Wilson.

She was standing in the doorway of the dining room. Behind her he could see a table loaded with the kind of indelicacies which appealed to small boys. Before he could answer Anya appeared.

'Oh, you're back,' she said indifferently. 'Auntie, is everything ready?'

'There's enough to feed an army in there,' retorted the old lady. 'Bread and butter and jelly, that'd have been quite enough.'

'I'm sorry,' said Jaysmith. 'I got . . . called away. What can I do to help?'

'Very little now,' retorted Anya frostily. 'I've had to organize all the games, so Aunt Muriel's had to do all the work in here. Now it's all ready. You've timed your return perfectly.'

'Don't be daft,' said Miss Wilson. 'Never cut off your nose to spite your face. Sit him at the table and put him in charge and you'll see he'll earn his keep.'

'Oh, all right,' said Anya. 'Think you can manage *that*?'

'I think so. I'll just have a quick clean-up first.'

She studied him critically and said, 'Yes, you look a bit, if not dishevelled, then not exactly *shevelled*. Where's your sweater?'

'I must have left it somewhere,' he said. 'I got a bit warm. I won't be a minute.'

He ran upstairs away from her curiosity which, while preferable to, was also more dangerous than her frostiness.

When he descended a little while later, the boys were already gathering at the table where they were subjected to a close examination by Miss Wilson who dispatched eighty per cent of them into the kitchen to make themselves decent under the hot tap.

'Here's Jay!' yelled a very excited Jimmy. 'Where've you been, Jay? We've been playing with my gun and I told them you got ten out of ten and they wouldn't believe me. You did though, didn't you, Jay? You must be the best shot in the world!'

They'd had a practice session with the ping pong gun after breakfast when Jaysmith discovered that up to about six yards it was fairly accurate. Jimmy had been hugely impressed.

Jaysmith took his place at the table and soon discovered that Miss Wilson had not been exaggerating. Anya's scheme to wear them out before tea had failed miserably. Team rivalries excited by their outdoor games continued and disputes broke out which were usually settled either by missiles above, or wrestling bouts beneath, the table. His penance was extended to the post-prandial period when Anya announced that Uncle Jay had kindly agreed to entertain them with a few tricks. In revenge, after doing a couple of coin and card tricks, he contrived a Yuri Geller-type bending of a couple of teaspoons and soon had the whole group energetically but quietly assaulting the household cutlery.

'I'll make you pay for replacements,' said Anya.

'No more than I deserve,' he said.

'What did happen to you? Stage fright?'

'No. It was silly. Someone turned up out of the blue. It was business. They must have found out at

206

Parker's hotel that I was staying here. I didn't want to clutter up the house with my own affairs, not today, so I suggested we drove into Keswick and sorted things out over a drink. Sorry. I should have told you I was going.'

'No need. You're your own boss. Was it OK?'

'What?'

'The business.'

She looked at him with a clear deceit-challenging gaze he found very disconcerting.

'So-so,' he said.

'Not a disaster then? He just got the sweater, not the shirt off your back?'

'That's about it. No need to worry about Aunt Muriel's money if that's what's bothering you.'

She shook her head.

'No, that's not what's bothering me,' she said. 'Oh Andrew!'

A plump red-faced boy who was a local farmer's son was proudly displaying a trifle ladle which had clearly been bent into horseshoe shape by main force. Jaysmith slipped away and went in search of Bryant.

He found him dozing in his study with a whisky glass by his side and an open book threatening to slip off his lap. Jaysmith picked it up and the movement woke the sleeping man.

'Hello,' he said. 'You're back. I heard you'd defected. Would you like to join me in a drink, or is it too early for you?'

'I've just presided over the tea party,' said Jaysmith.

'Then it's probably too late, but have one all the same.'

Jaysmith poured himself a generous measure

and topped up Bryant's glass.

He nodded at the book he had saved from the floor. It was in Polish.

'Interesting?'

'Economic analysis,' said Bryant. 'More essential than interesting.'

'Essential to what?'

'My own book. Not that I'll ever finish it.'

'That sounds a trifle pessimistic.'

'Realistic,' laughed Bryant. 'I set myself an impossible task, you see. There doesn't seem much point in attempting the possible, somehow. As old age approaches you begin to understand the dangers of actually *completing* anything. That moment of relaxation, the inevitable anti-climax, the sense even of disappointment, these make up the *nunc dimittis* syndrome. Better, if you want to live long that is, to attempt the impossible.'

'Which, in your case, is?'

'To try to explain Poland. To tell the truth, despite what I say, I thought when I started I had a chance of success. I had a good viewpoint, it seemed, a firm platform. Of, but not in, Poland. An insider looking from the outside. But I soon discovered that such a condition does not exist in nature. Also I discovered that, as in autobiography, I suspect, the material to be dealt with increases as a cube of the time spent on dealing with it. Fortunately these discoveries coincided with my realization that ripeness, far from being all, is merely the name we give to the first stage of decay.'

Jaysmith smiled and drank his whisky and wondered how much Bryant had downed before he fell asleep.

'How do you see things now?' he asked.

'Solidarity? All that?'

'I'm still a long way from reaching Solidarity in my analysis,' said Bryant, suddenly guarded.

'But you must have thought about it. Are you a Roman Catholic, by the way?'

Bryant shook his head.

'Was. Lapsed. Or should I say prolapsed.'

'Sorry?'

'I mean, it still hurts sometimes. They sink the hooks deep and you never really get away altogether.'

'Anya?'

'Oh no,' he laughed. 'I married a good C of E girl which, as you know, covers everything from atheist to agnostic. Anya was brought up to think, not to believe. At least that was my intention. Sometimes, I regret, she does not act very logically.'

Am I being talked at? wondered Jaysmith.

He said, 'I know how disorientating bereavement can be, how long the effects can last. Too long, if you let them.'

Twenty years, he told himself bitterly. And here felt a pang of self-disgust as he thought of Adam. God knows what grief that boy's death would cause. Parents; friends; Dave. Grief spreading out like an oil slick from a wrecked ship. And here he was, probably with the youngster's blood still forensically traceable on his hands, talking platitudes and playing the considerate suitor.

Bryant's response seemed to fit his thoughts rather than his words. He barked a humourless laugh and said, 'Is that so? Do I take it you are making, or wish to make, what in the old days was called a declaration?'

'Not till I'm sure that Anya can consider it

209

logically,' said Jaysmith.

It seemed a decent thing to say, a trifle pompous perhaps, but in a solid, old-fashioned kind of way and none the worse for that. Again Bryant's response surprised him.

'I hadn't taken you for a fool, man,' he said.

'Look,' said Jaysmith, impatient in return. 'Are you saying I shouldn't say anything to Anya? Or that I should? Or what?'

'For God's sake, why do you insist in making this a scene out of a Victorian novel?' demanded Bryant. 'You're old enough to make your own decisions! What the devil do they have to do with me?'

'I thought you might have some concern for matters affecting Anya's happiness,' said Jaysmith, rising. 'Thanks for the drink. I'd better get back to the celebration.'

As he reached the door, Bryant spoke.

'Mr Hutton,' he said. 'Let us not part on a misunderstanding. In matters of Anya's happiness, I count it my right and my duty to take an absolute interest.'

He spoke without undue emphasis but to Jaysmith who had had some experience in these matters the words sounded very like a threat.

Half an hour later the first parent arrived to collect her offspring and another thirty minutes after that the last guest departed. Jaysmith went out into the garden to help Jimmy collect the scattered apparatus of play.

'Enjoy your party?' he asked the boy who had at last come close to exhausting all his vast reserves of physical and mental energy.

'Yes, thanks, it was great,' said Jimmy, yawning.

210

'Have another go with my gun, Jay.'

'We'd better get the clearing up done first, I think.'

'Please!'

'All right.'

He picked up the toy, aimed it at the bull's-eye target about twenty feet away and hit it five times in a row pretty near the centre. It wasn't bad shooting in the circumstances.

Ironic applause came from the french window.

'You must have a kitchen sink full of gold fish in plastic bags,' said Anya. 'Jay, would you mind running Aunt Muriel back to Grasmere now? She's pretty well tuckered out, I think, and if she stays any longer, she'll just insist on helping with the washing up.'

'Which I will escape if I take her home?' said Jaysmith. 'It's a deal.'

The old lady made only a token objection to being ferried home, and in the car she sank back with an audible sigh into the soft upholstery and said, 'I've had a grand time but it'll be good to get back to me own fireside.'

'I don't doubt it,' said Jaysmith. 'You won't miss it not being your own fireside too much, will you?'

'When I move out, you mean? Well, I'm bound to, I expect. It's human nature to get attached to what you've known a long time. But don't you fret, I'll be snug as a bug down in the village. Betty Craik's cottage always had a grand fire to sit by. And it doesn't smoke when the wind's in the east either.'

At Rigg Cottage he saw her into the living room just to check that all was well.

'Thanks for fetching and carrying me,' she said.

'My pleasure.'

'Not much pleasure in lugging an old parcel like me around, I doubt!' she said. 'You like young Jimmy, don't you, Mr Hutton? I mean, really like him?'

'Well yes, I do,' said Jaysmith. 'Very much. He's a fine boy.'

'That's good. I thought you did, but there's no harm in being sure; and asking right out's the only way I know of finding out right.'

'Why did you want to find out right?' enquired Jaysmith.

She regarded him steadily with her ageless brown eyes.

'It doesn't take a blind man to see what you feel about Annie,' she said. 'And there's some might think it a clever move to make much of the son to get on the right side of the mother.'

'And an even cleverer one to get on the right side of the aunt too,' smiled Jaysmith.

'There you would be wasting your time,' she said peremptorily. 'I doubt if I've much influence over Annie. She's a grand lass, but she's not one to share things, not with me, anyway. With that father of hers, maybe. But she's only kin to me by marriage and that makes a difference. Or it ought to. Not that I've ever had much success in understanding even my own flesh and blood!'

'Edward, you mean?'

'Edward, aye. I had the bringing up of him like I had the bringing up for a dozen years of his father before him. Strange how there can be barriers even the same blood can't run through.'

'Edward was . . . difficult?'

The eyes suddenly blazed with defensive anger.

212

'He was a good nephew to me. A son almost,' she said angrily.

Here was a grief he'd forgotten about, so anxious was he to understand the depth and duration of Anya's sorrow.

He said, 'I'm sorry. I didn't mean to offend. It's just that I don't want to offend Anya . . . Annie . . . either, by treading too close.'

'You don't look much to me like a man frightened to act, Mr Hutton,' said the old lady. 'Not at all. I'll say goodbye now. Watch how you drive though. It's a dangerous road that.'

*   *   *

That night, Jimmy tried to extend his birthday as long as possible, but sheer fatigue defeated him in the end.

'Goodnight Gramp. Goodnight Jay,' he said wearily as his mother led him from the room. 'Thanks a million.'

The three adults ate a snack supper in the lounge and watched a film on television. It was a second-rate film, but no one seemed in the mood for conversation and in fact Bryant was dozing off before the end. Awoken by the swell of music which signalled the happy ending, he announced that he was ready for his bed also.

'And then there were two,' said Jaysmith, re-entering the lounge after helping Bryant up the stairs.

'One soon,' said Anya, yawning. 'Fancy a nightcap?'

'Yes, please.'

She poured him his customary whisky and water

213

without further enquiry. Such domestic assumption was both pleasant and problematical. It implied a closeness, but it also implied a role.

'I'm sorry if I sounded a bit testy this afternoon,' she said.

'You had every right to.'

'Not to treat you like the paid help, I didn't,' she said.

'I hoped I was being treated like a friend who'd let you down,' he answered.

She had finished her whisky very quickly and looked at the glass as if surprised to find it empty. She rose and poured herself another. She seemed restless and nervy.

She said, 'Jimmy was asking me if we'd still be able to pay visits to Rigg Cottage after Aunt Muriel had moved out and you'd moved in.'

'What did you tell him?'

'I said I thought you might tolerate him for a couple of minutes a month.'

'I'd be delighted. And flattered.'

'Don't be too flattered. There's a conker tree in the garden which he considers to be his own property.'

'I see. And what about you? Would you still visit the cottage also?'

'I suppose so. I'd have to bring him, wouldn't I?'

He smiled ruefully.

'I see that again I'm not to be flattered.'

'No, I'm sorry, I didn't mean to sound rude . . .'

Now she sounded flustered. He took a deep breath, rose, and went towards her. She pretended to think he too wanted another drink and held the decanter before her like a buttress.

He said, 'No, that's not what I want. Anya, listen,

214

I'm sorry if this is too soon but . . .'

She interrupted him, saying, 'Pappy says he thinks you're getting interested in me.'

He was taken aback.

'You needed your father to tell you that?' he said.

'No! Of course not,' she retorted with a flash of spirit.

'Well then,' he said. 'Anya, I was talking to your father this afternoon and he said I sounded like a scene from a Victorian novel. I think he was right. The thing is, I'm not sure how to sound like a scene from a modern novel. Should I be flip? Or outrageously direct? Or use sign language? Or what? The trouble is that they don't write the lines I want to use any more. Such as, *I know it's too soon, but at least tell me I can hope*, that sort of thing.'

'Jay, for Christ's sake, what are you trying to say?'

He was standing only the decanter's width away.

He said, 'How about, I know it's too soon, but at least tell me I can hope?'

She turned away from him which seemed a perfect invitation to grasp her round the waist but she twisted out of his hold without turning to face him.

'Let's get one thing out of the way,' she said in an unpromisingly harsh voice. 'This "too soon" business.'

'Yes?' he prompted.

'Understand me, this isn't a promise, or a commitment, or even a postponement. It's merely to clear up what's becoming a tiresome assumption on your part and an oblique deception on mine.

215

Edward died almost a year ago . . .'

She paused. He didn't speak. She turned now to face him.

'But I am not still mourning his death,' she went on. 'In fact, I don't think I have ever mourned it. I was *glad* my husband died; not wholly, and not solely, but certainly beyond all contradiction *glad*. And I've remained glad ever since, Mr Hutton. And while sometimes I can't deny that I've felt very guilty at feeling so glad, what I am definitely not is a grief-stricken widow!'

She banged the decanter down, finished her second drink and said, 'Now I think I'll go to bed too, if you'll excuse me. You'll put the lights out and see the fire's safe, won't you?'

'Yes,' he said. 'I'll see the fire's safe.'

As if taking her words literally, he sat for nearly two hours after she had left, watching the burning log decay through a series of slow crumbles and sudden collapses, of blue-green fire jets and chiffon-like flames which floated around the wood without seeming to touch it, until all that remained was a level bed of dark-grey embers fretted with gold.

This he stirred once with the poker, then went to bed.

CHAPTER TWENTY-ONE

When he awoke the next morning Jaysmith lay for a while, expecting the despairing weight of his predicament to come crashing through the flimsy barrier of residual slumber. Instead he found

216

himself listening to the fluted dissonance of competitive birdsong outside his window and finding pleasure in separating the melodic snatches to their individual sources.

The *chook chook*—that was surely a blackbird; the many-throated but still gentle twittering song must come from the family of house-martins he had noticed in the eaves; that rapid repetition of notes belonged to a song thrush, and, more distant but a constant background noise, came the unmistakable cawing of the rooks in the tall beeches near the road.

Another sound joined them, the gentle creak of his bedroom door. Slowly it opened. There was no one there. Then with a yell which might have been learned from a raiding Apache, Jimmy erupted into the room and flung himself onto the bed.

A mock-battle of considerable ferocity was interrupted by the appearance of Anya.

'Jimmy,' she said. 'Out!'

'No!' he protested. 'Me and Jay are having a game, aren't we, Jay?'

'Well, I'm not sure about you,' said Jaysmith gingerly, feeling his nose which had received a kick from the boy's flailing heels.

'Go on, Jimmy,' urged his mother sternly.

The boy didn't say anything but didn't move either, his lower lip out-jutting stubbornly.

Jaysmith put his hand on the mop of unruly hair and said, 'On your way, Tarzan. I'll be down to whup you at target practice shortly.'

'Will you? Great!' cried Jimmy and rushed from the room with a Tarzan yodel.

'Ah, the power of masculine command,' said Anya with heavy irony.

'The trick's novelty,' said Jaysmith. 'When he gets used to me he'll soon stop taking notice.'

'Oh you're planning to be around long enough to get used to?' she said. 'In that case, I'd better make sure breakfast is to your taste. Ten minutes?'

'Nine,' he said.

As he hastily shaved he studied his face in the glass and with genuine bewilderment asked, 'Who *are* you? *What* are you?'

Yesterday he'd killed a man and yet this morning he searched himself for remorse, for grief, for pity, and he searched in vain.

Eventually Adam would be missed. Jacob would investigate, replacements would arrive, Jaysmith's involvement could not long remain hidden. After that, what? He had no plan; the most likely scenario would be for himself to be targeted alongside Bryant. Yet he found in himself no fear of that future, no desperate searching after an escape from it.

The truth was, he realized with amazement, he was hooked on happiness! Anya's words to him the previous night had given him a shot of hope which had knocked his immune system quite out of balance. Grief, remorse, pity, fear—for the moment there was no room for these. It wasn't that they were absent, just that they were not wanted on this particular voyage.

Soon enough they would have to be unpacked. Soon enough. He went down to breakfast.

Halfway through the morning he drove into Keswick to pick up a selection of newspapers for the household. Jimmy went with him. Jaysmith avoided the main car park where he'd left Adam's mini but after they had got the papers and Jimmy

218

had been provided with a huge chocolate ice-cream cone, he felt sufficiently secure among the already considerable press of tourists to stroll within sight of the car park. The yellow mini was still there. It could mean they'd already found it but left it *in situ* in the hope that someone would return to it.

As he returned to the BMW, he checked back a couple of times to see if there was any sign of a tail but spotted nothing. Not that they would need to follow him. With the boy by his side, they would know that Naddle Foot was where he'd be.

He felt uneasy at the thought of Anya and Jimmy being exposed to whatever threat hung over Bryant, and now himself, and, though he was eager to find some time alone with Anya to press on down the avenues she had opened up the previous night, he was as much relieved as disappointed when after lunch she told Jimmy to get ready for their Sunday visit to Great-Aunt Muriel in Grasmere.

'Do we have to go?' protested Jimmy. 'I only saw her yesterday.'

'That was special,' said Anya firmly. 'We always go to Grasmere on Sundays.'

'And the old girl expects her pound of familial flesh,' interposed Bryant sardonically.

Anya shot him a reproving glare and ushered Jimmy out of the room.

'What about you?' said Bryant. 'Are you joining this dutiful expedition to Rigg Cottage?'

'Hardly,' said Jaysmith, surprised. 'I'm not invited, for a start.'

'No. But the place is almost yours, isn't it?' said Bryant, surprisingly illogical for a lawyer. 'And you seem to like the old bird.'

219

'So I do,' said Jaysmith. 'Nevertheless. You don't seem to be all that fond of her, though, or do I misinterpret?'

'You must remember I'm not English,' said Bryant. 'It's only the English who find wilful and eccentric middle-class old ladies endearing. Were she a peasant, it might be different. A Pole can like an old peasant. But there are no peasants in England which is why your class system is so divisive. True equality and real democracy are only possible when you have a firm peasant base. Failing that, as they worked out in modern America and ancient Greece, slaves will do at a pinch.'

'Is that why, after the Russians had freed their serfs, they took over the Poles to fill the gap?' suggested Jaysmith, smiling.

Bryant responded with a glare.

'If I didn't need a helping hand to come downstairs, I'd throw you out of my house,' he said. 'What *are* you going to do this afternoon?'

'Keep you company, if you like.'

'I don't like,' said Bryant firmly. 'I shall read myself to sleep with the papers and I do not want to be disturbed by any more of your witty conversation.'

He was clearly determined not to be nurse-maided, and it occurred to Jaysmith that any nurse-maiding might well be best done from a distance. The problem of what to do in the long term had still to be faced. It had been his firm intention immediately before Adam's death to arrange an interview with Jacob, but now the young man's body lay between them, rendering any deal much more difficult, if not impossible. But something had to be done. Meanwhile the short-term essential was

220

to keep Bryant alive.

'In that case, I think I'll go for a walk,' said Jaysmith. 'A few hours on the fells will do me a world of good.'

He asked Anya to give him a lift along the road as far as the King's Head at Thirlspot.

'I thought I might take a look at Helvellyn,' he said.

Anya was surprised.

'It'll be like Blackpool up there on a fine Sunday,' she said. 'Much better to go mid-week a bit later on. And I can show you a more interesting route. Helvellyn ought to be special.'

He smiled to himself at her underlying possessiveness both of the mountain and, he hoped, himself.

'All right,' he said, glancing at his map. 'I'll content myself with Raise and walk north via all these Dodds—Stybarrow, Watson's and Great—and come down into the Vale off Clough Head. How does that sound?'

'Lonely,' she said with genuine envy.

In fact he had just as little intention of following this route as he'd had of climbing Helvellyn. Leaving the house with Anya and Jimmy in the car might lull any watcher and it was his intention to check the vantage points overlooking Naddle Foot once more. Curiously, lying to Anya about her precious mountains distressed him more than anything else had done that day.

He kissed her on the cheek as he got out of the car and ruffled a rebellious Jimmy's hair.

'*Please*, mum!' pleaded the boy. 'Can't we go with Jay just a *little* way?'

For answer Anya rolled her eyes, and

221

accelerated away into the main road traffic.

Jaysmith watched the car out of sight and then turned and started walking back along the road. A mile on, the minor road leading back into St-John's-in-the-Vale forked off to the right, but he kept on going a little way till he had crossed Smaithwaite Bridge where he left the road and began to climb the wooded slope of the southern shoulder of High Rigg. He saw no one at this end of the fell but as he came in view of the summit, he glimpsed several figures. A quick glance through his field glasses reassured him that they were merely a group of tourists, ill-equipped by the look of them for any real walking, but attracted by the prospect of a good if lowly viewpoint after an easy scramble up from the Church of St-John's-in-the-Vale. He settled down and began to scan the fells on the other side of the valley. Satisfied finally that, unless someone had camouflage skills better even than his own, they were clear, he dropped his sights to the valley, looked for parked cars as much as for movement. There was nothing suspicious. The old barn appeared empty, the stand of trees where he had had his fateful meeting with Adam showed no glint of any foreign colour through their sun-ochred foliage.

Turning his attention to Naddle Foot itself, his view of the rear and side showed no sign of life. There was always a chance that Bryant had decided to do his snoozing in a deck chair in the front garden, of course, and Jaysmith began to drop down the eastern slopes so that he could check. He followed a winding sheep trod, enjoying the walk and the air like any rambler. But when he finally glanced towards Naddle Foot again, his pleasure died in his heart.

He could not see the facade of the house yet, but he could see the driveway in front of it, and parked there was a strange car, a dark-blue Escort.

It might mean nothing. There must be many local people who were likely to drop in at Naddle Foot on social calls.

Yet the thought that his own obsession with the long kill had made him leave Bryant alone and unguarded against anyone who cared to walk into the house filled Jaysmith with such guilt at his own stupidity that already as he began to scramble down the fellside he was more than half convinced he was too late. The direct descent was surprisingly steep and several times he stumbled and almost fell till he took a grip of himself and slowed to a pace commensurate with safety.

At last he reached the road and could break into a steady jog. As he turned into the gate of the house he removed the small rucksack from his shoulders, placed the field glasses in it and took out the only other object it contained, the HK P9 he had taken from Adam the previous day.

This he tucked into his waist band under his sweater. The rucksack he tossed under a decaying hydrangea bush.

On reaching the house, he ignored the front door but made his way along the side by the garage and round the back. Here he could see that the french window opening into the lounge stood open. Crouching below the level of the kitchen windowsill, he headed for the open door, his hand on the butt of his gun. When he reached it he halted, pressed close against the old red bricks of the wall which still retained the warmth of the morning sun. Inside the room he heard a movement. And now there was a noise, a man groaning, a long-drawn shuddering cry of scarcely conscious pain.

Jaysmith brought out the pistol, checked the safety was off, and stepped into the doorway.

Bryant was lying back in a deep armchair, his head thrown back, his eyes closed. His plastered leg rested on a foot stool, the other was splayed wide from it. Between his knees knelt a woman. She was naked to the waist and the fall of her shining blonde hair screened her face and her activity, but another long bubbling sigh, not of pain but of pleasure, from Bryant's lips left no doubt as to what it was.

Jaysmith stood petrified for a moment, his mind playing with the absurd thought that perhaps this was Jacob's new method of execution. After the long kill, the little death.

Then Bryant stiffened and convulsed, crying out loud in his native Polish, and his eyes opened wide.

Jaysmith stepped back quickly, uncertain if he'd been seen, if indeed the ecstasy of his orgasm permitted Bryant to see. He went back down the drive and recovered his rucksack and put the gun away. Then he walked along the road a little way and sat by the beck and let himself think about Anya.

There was no denying that what he had just seen had roused his desire, that desire which had been there since the first moment he laid eyes on the girl. It was a desire which had rapidly and irresistibly developed in the direction of obsession. But what he had felt this morning had moved beyond the obsessive, had somehow been purged of all the darkness and heaviness associated with that dead-ended and despairing intensity of feeling. Happiness and lightness had been there, the kind of hope, almost *expectation* of joy that he had not known since he was a young man. Since Saigon.

But desire was still part of it, with all its dark undertows. To have her as his love-partner in the widest terms of space and time and activity was what he longed for, somehow to claw out of this mess a future for himself with Anya and Jimmy and, God willing, Bryant.

But the purely physical imperative was still there, in his veins, urging him beyond consequence or despair simply to have her, and to let one mindless moment of white-out ecstasy pay for all the empty blackness beyond.

He stood up, suddenly as weary as if he had just passed a night of demanding passion, and glanced at his watch.

An hour had passed. Time enough, he told himself cynically, and returned to the house. The car was still there.

Anya had supplied him with a front door key and he entered noisily, calling out, 'Hello the house! I'm back!'

'In here,' Bryant called from the lounge.

He went in. Bryant was still in the same chair, looking very relaxed and smoking the inevitable Caporal. The woman, middle-aged, handsome in a heavy Germanic kind of way, was sitting on the sofa, fully clothed, sipping a glass of sherry.

'Hello, Hutton,' growled Bryant. 'Maggie, this is Jay Hutton, our house-guest. Mrs Orbison, an old friend, come to visit the sick.'

'How do you do?' said Jaysmith.

225

The woman smiled up at him, finished her drink and rose.

'I must be off, Steve,' she said. 'It's good to see you recovering so quickly. But take care. Don't overtire yourself. Give me a ring if you'd like a little company any time. Bye.'

She kissed Bryant briefly on the cheek, said, 'Nice to have met you, Mr Hutton,' and left.

'I hope I haven't driven your friend away,' said Jaysmith, dropping onto the sofa.

'Cut the small talk, Hutton,' said Bryant curtly. 'I saw you at the lounge window an hour ago.'

'Ah.'

'Maggie Orbison and I have known each other a long time. She's a nice woman. She was a client of mine years ago.'

'And now you're a client of hers.'

'Don't be smart,' said Bryant wearily. 'We are mutually helpful, that's all. I usually see her on Sunday afternoons . . .'

'In Patterdale?' guessed Jaysmith.

Bryant looked surprised then nodded. 'You're right. That's where I'd been last week when this happened. I go most Sundays when Anya takes Jimmy off to Muriel's for tea. Maggie was worried when she heard about the accident. She just called round to check on me.'

'And found all well, I daresay,' said Jaysmith. 'No need to explain.'

'I'm not explaining,' snapped Bryant. 'I'm telling you. And now I'm asking you not to say anything to Anya.'

'Really?' said Jaysmith in surprise. 'Why not? She's an adult woman. She can hardly believe you're a monk.'

226

'No. But she knows I am in . . . I have a strong commitment elsewhere. There are reasons why things are difficult in that area, reasons of distance and . . . other reasons.'

He spoke with bitter longing and Jaysmith knew he was speaking of Ota, the woman in Poland who had written the letters he kept in his safe. But Bryant was not about to make a full confession of his love life.

'I'm sure she would understand,' insisted Jaysmith.

'You're an expert on my daughter suddenly?' said Bryant. 'Well let me tell you, it is my experience that women on the whole only pretend to understand such little arrangements as mine with Maggie Orbison whom, incidentally, Anya doesn't like. At the very least she'd be . . . disappointed. And I don't care to disappoint her. You see, Hutton, Anya has inherited from God knows where an almost feudal notion of loyalty.'

He laughed rather sourly.

'A notion which extends to her memory of her dead husband?' said Jaysmith.

The laugh stopped.

'Meaning?' said Bryant softly.

'Anya put me right on a couple of things last night,' said Jaysmith. 'No details, but she just made it plain that her memories of married life, her attitudes to her husband's death were . . . ambiguous. I'd like to know more but I don't want to risk causing pain by an over-robust probing. Anything you can tell me, anything which might help me to help . . . And you needn't worry. You'll find me as discreet about this as you will about Mrs Orbison.'

227

He smiled to show that the implication of blackmail was merely a joke. Bryant did not smile back but he clearly discounted the implication for he asked, 'Why should I tell you anything?'

'Because, perhaps, you did not care for your son-in-law much. No, no one's said anything. It's just my guess that this is at the root of the antagonism between you and Miss Wilson. A clash of blood loyalties.'

'You're a sharp bastard for an out-of-work salesman,' mocked Bryant, running his fingers through his halo of grey hair. 'But even if you're right, it's still hardly reason enough for me to lay out my daughter's business before a stranger, is it?'

'I love her,' said Jaysmith flatly.

'*Love!* You've only known her a couple of weeks!' came the sceptical reply.

'Nevertheless.'

'And how does she feel about you?'

'It takes sharper eyes and greater wit than I've got to know that,' said Jaysmith. 'What do you think?'

'I think nothing. But if she put you right about Edward, that must mean something,' mused Bryant. He came to a decision. 'All right, Hutton, I'll tell you what I can without breaking Anya's confidence. In other words, I'll tell you what I know from observation and report, but nothing that Anya herself has told me. That's up to her to decide. So. Edward Wilson. I never liked the man from the start, but I am old enough to recognize bias. My daughter was eighteen, just finishing school, with a university place open for her in a good law faculty. I had high hopes for her, not just selfish hopes either. It was *her* future that seemed

228

bright; it was *her* future that seemed in danger when she fell in love with Wilson. She was adamant that she was going to be married. She'd always had a mind of her own, but suddenly I didn't know her. Nothing I could say swayed her in the least. And of course she was of age. The worst I could do would have been to cut her off without a penny in the good old Victorian tradition. I thought of threatening it, so you can see how troubled I was! But in the event, I swayed with the wind and walked her up the aisle and gave her away. I might as well have sold her into slavery. At least I'd have got a price!'

He spoke with such bitterness that Jaysmith was filled with a retrospective alarm.

'For God's sake, what happened?' he demanded.

'I told you, I'm not breaking any confidences,' said Bryant. 'In any case, I'm sure I got from Anya only what little her desperate need for expression forced past that overdeveloped sense of loyalty I mentioned before. But what I saw with my own eyes I'll tell you. I saw a happy, laughing, open and confident child on the threshold of life gradually turn into a taciturn, reserved, and introspective woman. She was a girl of such brightness, Hutton! Bright in thought, speech, movement, dress. And now there was none of this. It was early spring to late autumn with no summer between.'

'But the boy—she must have had him very quickly. That must have helped?'

'In the first year,' said Bryant. 'And I suppose he helped from the point of view of company and occupation. But in real terms Jimmy's birth just bound her to Wilson even more, at first because she had a double loyalty now, to husband and her

229

child's father; later, because Wilson made it clear that if she went, he would do everything in his power to make certain Jimmy stayed.'

'*If she went?* Then she was contemplating leaving him?'

'It came to that. That's when she spoke to me openly for the first time. Not that I hadn't tried to speak to her. I was away a lot in the early years of her marriage and perhaps didn't pay enough attention to what was going on.'

'Away in Poland?'

'That's right.'

And, of course, thought Jaysmith, once he became aware of Anya's problems, any thought of making a new life in Poland with Ota must have been put aside completely. The poor bastard probably even felt that his absence had been a kind of culpable neglect!

'You still haven't told me much about Edward Wilson,' said Jaysmith.

'He is not a man I care to talk about,' said Bryant. 'But I can see you will have to know. He was a strange, solitary man, not unpersonable, not without charm. I don't know how much his upbringing affected him, but I tend myself to believe that what we are is written in our genes.'

'His aunt brought him up, I gather?'

Bryant nodded. 'Yes, but I doubt if she was the major influence. His life was divided between Grasmere, boarding school—some god-forsaken hole in Scotland where I've no doubt that beating and buggery figured large in the curriculum—and visits to his doting father in London.'

'You don't like the father either?'

'I met him at the wedding and I met him at the

230

christening and I met him at the funeral. He struck me as a solitary like his son, who'd put what few emotional resources he had into the relationship. That was peculiar. He clearly thought that this odd upbringing was the very best he could have done for Edward. And any guilt he may have felt was assuaged by lavishing the best of everything on the boy when he saw him once or twice a year in London. No I didn't care for the man. I think he would like to treat Jimmy in the same way if he could, but there's no chance of that. To get back to Edward, you know he was a climber of some eminence?'

Jaysmith smiled at the choice of phrase, but Bryant did not notice.

'That was his means of self-expression. Completely typical. I've done some rock climbing myself. It's a solitary, self-absorbed pursuit, even in a team. You're pinned against a bare face, moving fingers and feet by slow inches, seeking the minute purchase which will hold you safe for a little longer. Yet it is not the desire for safety that holds you there; it is not hope of achievement which edges you upward by skill and will; no, what you fight against is what you *want*; it is the prolonging of pleasure by the delay of orgasm; what motivates the climber is the knowledge that at any moment, by chance or by desire, he may abandon this snail-like creeping, and push off from this sheet of cold unresponsive rock, and *fly*!'

Bryant spoke with a violence of passion which made Jaysmith stare in surprise.

He said softly, 'I think perhaps you understood your son-in-law very well.'

'Perhaps,' said Bryant, recovering his
231

composure. 'Perhaps I understood his father too. We were both left with a child to bring up. I brought mine up differently. I too thought I'd done well enough by her, better certainly than James Wilson. Yet they both ended up, these children of ours, in a cold, lonely farmhouse halfway up a fellside in Borrowdale.'

'Wilson ended up at the foot of Pillar Rock with a broken back,' said Jaysmith.

'You know that, do you? Yes, of course you would. You strike me as a very thorough man, Mr Hutton. Then you almost certainly know about his illness too. His physical illness, I mean.'

'I know he was a diabetic.'

'That's right. For most sufferers these days it is merely a long-term inconvenience. But for Edward it struck at the most important area of his life which was not, I assure you, either his family or his profession. It meant the end of his career as an expeditionist. It removed from him the only good reason he ever saw for working with and relating to other people, for considering their needs and judgement.'

'But it didn't stop him climbing?'

'Oh no. It just meant that it was too risky to take him on long and arduous expeditions. In domestic and European terms, it needn't have made any difference at all. But Edward Wilson wasn't a man to accept a secondary role. His response was to throw it all up. Not the climbing, of course. That was a drug as important to him as insulin. But he severed all connections with official mountaineering bodies; he turned his back completely on the climbing fraternity and he became what I think he'd always been, except

232

through necessity: an utter loner. He'd meet old acquaintances on the fells and walk right past them without a glance, let alone a word. There were reports of him doing incredibly difficult climbs, that is to say, climbs made incredibly difficult by his choice of route, his indifference to conditions and, of course, by his being alone.'

'The coroner didn't refer to this,' said Jaysmith.

'I was right. You *are* thorough, aren't you, Hutton? Of course he didn't. *De mortuis* and all that. But everyone at the inquest knew that no other climber in the country would have been out alone in those conditions doing what he did.'

'I see,' said Jaysmith slowly. 'But it's still odd he wasn't found for two days.'

'Odd?' said Bryant sharply as if scenting a reproof. 'Not at all. No one was looking for him, so why should he be found? Anya was visiting me here. It wasn't till I took her back to the farmhouse that we realized Wilson was missing. She still feels guilty about that, of course. It's natural. But time will cure that, I know. It's been a slow change these past months, but she's coming out of it. Much more quickly in these last few weeks. That may be something to do with you, but don't flatter yourself overmuch. Any personable man showing an interest might have helped her process, particularly when he appears mature, middle-aged, safe.'

'That's how you see me, is it?' said Jaysmith, smiling.

'No,' said Bryant seriously. 'I don't believe it's how *I* see you at all. But at least I can talk to you. And this is what I want to say. Anya's vulnerable, Hutton. Don't be tempted to take advantage.'

The note of threat was undisguised.

233

'I can't promise,' said Jaysmith and laughed out loud as Bryant sat upright and glowered at him.

'I mean, I can't promise not to be tempted. As a lapsed Catholic, you should know that temptation is almost necessary to a pure soul. But I shall do all within my power not to take advantage! Will that do you?'

'As a lawyer, I'd prefer something a little more binding,' grunted Bryant. 'But I suppose I'll have to make do with what I can get. How do you like Jimmy, by the way?'

First Miss Wilson, now Bryant! The question was clearly of the essence, and Bryant the lawyer would probably require a more detailed answer than the old lady.

'I haven't had much to do with small boys, not since I was one,' he said slowly. 'But from our acquaintance so far, I like him a great deal. He seems lively, affectionate, full of fun and with a lot of natural charm. On the other hand, I've no doubt he can be noisy, over-boisterous, stubborn, and reluctant to eat his crusts.'

He spoke lightly but Bryant's response was sombre.

'You should have seen him a year ago, Hutton,' he said. 'You wouldn't have known him. It's been as though he's rushed to catch up with all the boyish things he'd been missing.'

He shook his head at some inner vision, then shook it again more violently as if to clear that vision away.

'And now,' he cried, 'to you! In the space of one hour, you've seen me in an extremely, embarrassingly intimate position and I've poured out my private thoughts to you. Fair's fair, Hutton.

234

Now it's your turn. We managed to drag something about your childhood out of you the other night. But now it's time for serious talking. First, finance. How're you fixed for money? What are your prospects?'

There was a kind of heavy jocularity about the questions, but Jaysmith did not doubt they were serious.

'I'm comfortably off,' he said. 'Fairly rich, I suppose, by most people's standards. I have enough put away to see my time out, unless I miraculously survive to be a hundred and fifty. At the moment I'm jobless, an independent businessman who has given up his business . . .'

'Why?' rapped Bryant. 'And what business?'

Jaysmith was prepared for this; his cover stories were always well researched; in the past they had had to convince much more doubting and much more dangerous auditors than an anxious father.

Bryant interrupted him before he'd got to the end of his authenticating detail and said, 'And your personal circumstances, what about them?'

'If you're still wondering whether I have a wife and family hiding in the bushes, the answer's still no,' retorted Jaysmith. 'Neither present nor past. I have never been married, nor do I have any emotional entanglements. Nor am I homosexual.'

'You do function physically, I take it?' said Bryant sardonically.

'Adequately; though whether I could make it with my shoulder out of joint and my leg in plaster, I've not yet had to discover.'

Bryant smiled widely and said, 'This tea's cold. There's a bottle of Islay malt in the sideboard. Why don't you fetch it and a couple of glasses?'

'Are we celebrating something?'

'Do we have anything to celebrate?'

'Hope,' said Jaysmith.

'Yes. Perhaps you're right. *Nadzieja!*'

'What's that?'

'Hope in Polish. That's where my hope really lies, you see, Hutton. I've been thinking things out. There's a woman there, that other commitment I mentioned before. Whatever time remains to me I'd like to spend with her. And my book, I'm never going to finish it here. England's been good to me, but my stay here has been an interruption merely, a respite.'

'Forty years? A bloody long respite!' said Jaysmith.

'Not really. How old are you, Hutton? Forty plus? Think back. I bet you blinked your eyes when you were in your early twenties, and here you are now. Blink them again and you'll be as old as me. No, time's a much overrated element, Hutton, much overrated. We imagine that, to use legal terminology, it is of the essence. It never is. We are of the essence, Hutton, you and me. To blink or not to blink, that is the question!'

'You'd go back to Poland? To live?' asked Jaysmith.

'I'd think about it, if once I was happy that Anya and Jimmy were in good hands,' said Bryant.

Jaysmith raised his glass.

'*Nadzieja!*' he said.

The two men drank together.

CHAPTER TWENTY-TWO

That Sunday evening was one of the happiest Jaysmith had ever passed. The new understanding between Bryant and himself seemed to fold itself round Naddle Foot like one of those isolating and insulating autumn mists which cuts off the outside world, shifting its intrusive shapes and sounds to a separate dimension. Within, there was warmth and ease and a sense of safe and comfortable domesticity which made luxuries and excitements seem a tinsel toy.

Anya and Jimmy had returned from Grasmere after a pleasant visit, but not without relief at being home. They dined late, to let Aunt Muriel's tea settle, and Jimmy inveigled Jaysmith into playing at the video game his other grandfather had bought him for his birthday. It was a complex and obviously highly expensive piece of equipment and Jimmy was delighted with it. The speed of Jaysmith's reactions made it necessary for him to hold back considerably to make a match of it. Anya observed this and smiled her thanks.

The boy would have played all night, but Anya said, 'We're eating soon, Jimmy, and you've still got some of your thank-you letters to write. Have you written to Granddad Wilson yet?'

'Don't need to,' said Jimmy. 'I can thank him when he comes, can't I?'

Bryant said without enthusiasm, 'He's coming up, is he?'

Anya glanced at Jaysmith apologetically and said, 'Aunt Muriel said he wanted to come up before the house-sale went through. He doesn't really approve, I gather.'

'Well if he's got any ideas about stopping it, he's out of luck,' said Bryant gleefully. 'Contracts have been exchanged, finance is all tied up, not all the wheeling-dealing of Whitehall can stop Rigg Cottage becoming Jay's next week.'

'Perhaps he just wants a last look at the place before it passes away from the family,' said Anya.

'If it does,' murmured Bryant slyly.

'Sorry, pappy?'

But to Jaysmith's relief Bryant did not repeat his comment.

They had a casual meal, washed down with cider and beer. Afterwards Jimmy persuaded his mother to let him play one more game. Jaysmith let the boy run away into an almost impregnable position, then, with a devastating burst which excited at the same time his young opponent's admiration and his fear of being overtaken, he drew level before dropping behind again in the dying moments.

After Anya had put her son to bed, she said to Jaysmith, 'You'll have to be careful not to let him always win.'

'Oh it won't be always,' said Jaysmith. 'Eventually we'll play off level, and then when I'm old and decrepit it'll be his turn to let *me* win.'

She didn't look at him but said as she poked the fire, 'You seem to be assuming a long future for your games.'

'Why not?' said Jaysmith, affecting surprise. 'We're going to be practically neighbours, aren't we? And you did say you'd bring Jimmy to visit *me* in Rigg Cottage every Sunday, didn't you?'

Bryant, who had been apparently dozing over his

paper, snorted derisively and said, 'I rather fancy a nightcap. Who'll join me?'

'I will,' said Anya promptly. 'Especially as I see the Islay's been opened. You two must have been in a very jolly way with yourselves this afternoon.'

'Just a celebration of youth and hope,' said Bryant.

They sat at their ease before the crackling log fire and drank their golden whisky and talked in a pleasant, undemanding, desultory manner for another hour. The room was lit only by a single standard lamp and the fire's shifting glow. The whisky and the warmth made them all drowsy, but beneath his drowsiness Jaysmith felt the stretching, waking shape of strong desire whenever his eyes dwelt on Anya's relaxed and outstretched body. At one moment their gazes met and she looked away abruptly enough to make him hope that she too was troubled by this restless visitor.

Bryant at last announced that he was for his bed. Jaysmith rose to help him and was told that he was now feeling able to negotiate the stairs unaided.

'A man of ingenuity can overcome mere physical disadvantages, wouldn't you say?' he asked.

'True, but you've had a tiring and demanding day,' said Jaysmith. 'At least let me bring up the rear to catch you if you fall.'

This compromise agreed, Jaysmith and Bryant slowly processed up the stairs.

When he came down again, Jaysmith found Anya kneeling before the fire with her arms outstretched as though embracing the heat.

'You'll ruin your skin,' he said.

'Perhaps. But you wouldn't like a cold-hearted woman, would you?'

He knelt beside her, feeling awkward.

'Is that an invitation?' he asked, putting his arm around her waist.

'Is this an offer?' she replied.

He turned her body towards him and kissed her. It was not an easy or elegant manoeuvre from this position and after a few seconds she disengaged and pushed him away. For one chillingly detumescing moment he thought she was going to resume her seat and their previous domestically comfortable but definitely non-passionate relationship. Instead she pulled a couple of cushions off the sofa, dropped them on the rug in front of the fire and lay back on them. She looked more like a gymnast about to engage in some trimming exercise—with her body perfectly straight, legs close together, arms by her side, features relaxed, eyes closed, breathing steady— than a woman hot with desire. But when he crouched over her and kissed her again and ran his hands over the small firm breasts beneath the fine woollen sweater, he felt a convulsion run like a tidal bore the whole length of her body, and then her thin arms were round his neck, drawing him down with a strength which surprised him. She kissed him, she ran her tongue over his face into his mouth, his eyes, his nostrils, she wrapped her limbs around him as if intent on fusing their bodies together beyond all hope of separation, she had clearly loosed her hold entirely on the intellectual and conventional universe and was conscious of nothing but the burning agonizing demands of her raw and exposed nerve endings.

Jaysmith's response was almost as absolute, except that while his passion took him far beyond

240

considerations of place or person or morality, he was unable by his mortal and masculine nature to transcend the constraints of time. Their hands were inside each other's clothes, but the very violence of their embrace was an obstacle even to the minimum degree of nakedness necessary for its consummation, and Jaysmith felt himself within a caress, a touch, a warm breath of explosion. Forcing his mind away from the lithe, pulsating body beneath him to memories of the coldest and most physically agonizing experiences of his life—a dawn in Sweden when his target came late and a blizzard came early; a night in the Vosges when a landslip cut him off from his car—he prorogued his orgasm while he dragged the clinging jeans down over her narrow buttocks. Even his steely will could not hold out much longer and once the impeding garment had passed over her knees, he delayed no more. He thrust straight into the liquid heat of her vulva and did not need to thrust again. As he convulsed, he felt her enfolding, squeezing, rubbing with desperate need against his soon-to-vanish hardness. Then she cried out and pressed her wide gaping mouth against his neck to stifle her cry as she came also.

Afterwards she lay quietly in his arms for perhaps fifteen minutes, then she began to cry. He listened to her sobs and pressed her closer still and felt them racking her body long after she had controlled their noise.

'I'm sorry,' she said. 'I'm sorry.'

'Why?' he asked gently. 'I mean, why did you cry?'

'Shame, I think. Something like that.'

'Shame? Because of us?'

'No! Because it wasn't us, perhaps. It was *it*, not us. There was no room for identity in there, was there?'

'Perhaps not. But there's identity now.'

'Yes. That's what I mean. You, me. Before, it was just *it*. That's how it was with Edward in the beginning. Shit! I swore that if ever you and I came to this, I wasn't going to talk about Edward. Not now, not so soon. And now listen to me!'

'So you foresaw it might come to this?' said Jaysmith, glad of a chance to lighten the exchange.

'The first time you looked at me, I saw it *could* come to this,' she said seriously. 'If you think you've a poker face, disillusion yourself.'

'Love isn't poker,' said Jaysmith. 'You work by admission, confession even, not bluff. You were confessing about Edward. Don't back off. If we continue, we'll get back here some time. Best to carry on now.'

'Are you right? Perhaps you are,' she said softly. 'I'm not sure, but I'll pretend you are. Edward. In the beginning there was a girl; just out of school, on the brink of university, with all the ignorant self-assurance of a bright and pretty creature who knows she's pretty and knows she's bright and never doubts that the whole world loves her. Then I met Edward and one night he touched me and something like this happened and suddenly it didn't matter if the whole world hated me as long as I had Edward. *It* was me and Edward, you see. No others; we alone. And now I've experienced *it* again. With you. You're the only other man, ever. And now it occurs to me that perhaps *it* is independent, just waiting to be summoned up by any man. An intermittent nymphomania; a mere physical
242

syndrome masquerading as an emotional need!'

'And that was why you wept?'

'I wept at the thought that if this were so, perhaps *it* conned me into conning Edward into marrying me.'

They lay quietly for a while, deep in their separate yet parallel thoughts.

'You want to feel guilty about him, don't you?' said Jaysmith. 'Well, perhaps you ought to. Tell me about the things you made him do.'

'I'm sorry?'

'If you *are* guilty, then presumably you accept responsibility for his oddities of behaviour, isn't that the point of all this? So, tell me what it was you made him do.'

She rose on one elbow. He'd never succeeded in getting her sweater off and it was rolled up over her tiny breasts which hung like pale apples beneath the bough of rolled-up wool. Seeing his gaze, she pulled the garment down in a movement more automatic than censorious.

'It was after he found out about his diabetes that he changed,' she said slowly. 'After he found out that he wasn't going to be eligible for any more expeditions.'

'Hardly your fault,' said Jaysmith.

'I was all he had afterwards,' she said fiercely. 'I should have been able to offer . . . something.'

'You were all he had because he chose that you should be, surely?' said Jaysmith. 'Didn't he establish you in some out-of-the-way farmhouse before he found out about his illness? He obviously foresaw another twenty years of shooting off to the Himalayas or wherever, but it never crossed his mind that his wife might like to be living

243

somewhere a little less isolated while he was away.'

'You seem to know a lot for a man who knows nothing,' she said suspiciously. 'Have you been pumping pappy?'

'Only in a general way,' said Jaysmith. 'He told me nothing you ever told him, believe me. But I persuaded him I was entitled to know something.'

'On what grounds?'

'On these grounds,' said Jaysmith, patting the hearth-rug. 'I rest my case.'

She responded to his smile, albeit wanly.

'I didn't mind the farmhouse,' she resumed. 'I helped choose it, after all. I've never minded isolation. And I had a car. The Lake District's not a large area. And to be alone with your husband never seems such a terrible prospect to a newly wedded wife, does it? But things did change, in all kinds of ways. I had Jimmy, and right from the start, I found Edward's attitude . . . disturbing. He was very proud of Jimmy, I could tell that, but very resentful of anyone else having much to do with him. At the same time, right from the start almost, he was talking about sending him away to school, just like it happened to him. Almost as soon as he could walk, Edward was wanting to take him out on the fells. I put my foot down. Besides it being absurd for someone so young to be walking very far at all, I was already getting worried about the kind of expeditions Edward was making by himself. He used to tell me about some of them at first, but when I protested about the danger he was putting himself in, almost wilfully it seemed, he stopped telling me. Another failure, you see.'

'You're a real sin-eater, aren't you?' observed Jaysmith. 'And what was his reaction when you got

244

between him and Jimmy?'

She didn't reply, but folded her legs up to her chin and rested her forehead on her knees. Her jeans were still round her ankles but she didn't seem to be aware.

'So he hit you,' said Jaysmith. 'Often?'

'I didn't say anything about him hitting me!' she protested. 'I didn't even imply it.'

'No? Of course, what you implied was that you *made* him hit you! Did you force him to violence often?'

She did not react to his sarcasm but said, 'He wasn't really a violent man. I just think that something had happened in his mind. He needed sharp contact with physical reality to convince him of his own existence. I'd sometimes come across him outside the house, just clinging onto a tree, or pressing his head hard against a drystone wall, as if he was desperate for lines of delimitation.'

'I believe Wordsworth in his youth had something of the same trouble,' said Jaysmith. 'But he stopped short of beating up women.'

'He didn't beat me up!' she said fiercely. 'He struck me, on occasion. Not many occasions, and never more than one blow.'

'Moderation in all things! But you got to the point of wanting to leave him, despite his moderate behaviour?'

'Did pappy tell you that?'

'He told me you were staying here when your husband had his fatal fall.'

'That's true,' said Anya. 'But I doubt if I would have left him. It never became absolutely unbearable, though perhaps all that that shows is how much human beings can bear. I suggested a

245

separation once; that at least had the effect of making him break the customary silence. He told me simply and categorically that as far as he was concerned, there'd be neither separation nor divorce, and assured me that if I ever acted unilaterally, he would ensure by legal or, if necessary, by illegal means that Jimmy stayed with him. That was when I confided in pappy. He was furious. He tried talking to Edward but got nowhere. He even tried talking to Edward's father but that wasn't very productive either. Pappy was all for my leaving Edward forthwith, but I wouldn't. I went back home; things blew over I suppose. Not that I noticed. I was just surviving with as little pain as possible. What had to be, had to be.'

'I can't imagine your father falling back on philosophy,' said Jaysmith.

'He seemed, if not reconciled, at least quiescent. I regretted having said anything to him, so I did my best to undo the damage by pretending things had improved. I suppose that helped. In the middle of last December, pappy announced he was giving a party the Saturday before Christmas and asked me to help with the preparation and to be hostess. He invited Edward to the party, of course; but Edward of course refused. But he said I could go and help, or at least he didn't say I couldn't. Pappy came to pick us up on the Friday, just to be sure, I suppose. I took Jimmy with me. Edward didn't care for that, but I told him straight that I wasn't leaving the boy in the farmhouse.'

'I suppose he suspected you might be going to bolt?' said Jaysmith.

'He asked me that. I told him I wasn't. He trusted me.'

'All the same, it might have been a good opportunity. What did your father say?'

'He asked the same question as soon as we got back here. I just told him nothing had changed, I wasn't running and I wasn't risking losing Jimmy. He didn't persist. I think he just hoped that my pleasure in being at Naddle Foot again and meeting old friends might be so great that I'd refuse to give it up. It almost worked too. I loved the feeling of being busy preparing for the party, and it was all a tremendous success. But come Sunday, after I'd cleared up and we had lunch, I said it was time I was going back. Thank God I did. I couldn't have lived with myself if I'd made up my mind to leave Edward and then found out later what had happened!'

'You seem to have accepted pretty full responsibility as it is,' remarked Jaysmith. 'But come on, don't stop now. All or nothing.'

'It was mid-afternoon when we reached the farm, but the weather was so foul it was dark already. There were no lights on, no fires. It was clear to me at a glance that the place had been empty for twenty-four hours at least. I looked for Edward's climbing gear. When I saw it was gone, we called out the mountain rescue. They set out that evening but with the weather like it was, there wasn't much hope of finding him then, and it was Monday morning before they spotted him. He was deep in coma by then and he died within hours of getting to hospital. His back was broken too, so it was probably for the best. A day in a wheelchair would have driven him insane, let alone a lifetime. They were kind at the inquest. They called it misadventure. But I knew better.'

'Why? What did you know?'

She stared at him, her rich brown eyes filled once more with that intense feeling he had first mistaken for grief but now knew as guilt.

'He'd been looking for death every time he went out on those solo climbs,' she stated flatly. 'Looking for it, challenging it. But so far, despite all the dangers, his skill had always won. This time he stacked the odds against him to the point of impossibility. He didn't go into a coma because he was lying out there among the rocks without insulin. He fell among the rocks because he went into a coma. I know. I checked the ampoules later. I always kept a close eye on them because I knew he tended to be slap-happy in his use of them. He hated that sense of dependency, you see. He deliberately didn't inject himself before he went out on the Saturday.'

'But you can't be certain it was deliberate,' protested Jaysmith. 'You say he was slap-happy about taking the stuff? Perhaps he just forgot.'

'That would be bad enough,' she said. 'But I'm sure it was deliberate.'

'Why? Because that makes you feel more guilty?' said Jaysmith angrily. 'I don't see that you have a damn thing to feel guilty about, even if it was deliberate.'

As if explaining something to a slow child, she said very clearly, 'All the time I was feeling sorry for myself and moaning on to pappy that I was getting near the end of my tether, Edward, quietly and without much fuss, reached the end of his. There was only one person close enough to notice and that was me.'

248

A hundred refuting arguments rose in Jay's mind, but he voiced none of them. Anya's feelings were not to be dissipated by logic. The mere act of articulating them had probably done much to help, but the process could not be advanced by mere persuasion.

'I'm glad the bastard's dead!' he said with a vehemence which surprised himself as much as Anya.

'What do you mean?'

'If he wasn't dead, I'd have to kill him,' he stated with simple force. 'I want you, Anya.'

'It was my firm impression you'd just had me,' she said.

'I want more than that,' he said. 'I want everything about you and I want it on a permanent basis. Believe me, a mere husband would have been no obstacle!'

He spoke with an intensity that clearly impressed her, even though she could hardly begin to guess at the real and dark truth behind his retrospective threat.

'Look, Jay,' she said, attempting lightness. 'There's no need for all this, you know. All this talk of futures and permanency, I mean. OK. *It* was very good. If you want to slip off now and remember me from time to time as the best fuck in Cumbria, that'll be all right, believe me.'

He must have looked shocked at her unexpected coarseness, for she laughed out loud.

'You see,' she said. 'You're going off me already.'

'No,' he said. 'Good try, but it won't work. Nothing will work, you'll find that out eventually.'

'We'll see,' she said, rising. 'I'll make us a pot of coffee, I think.'

She stooped to grasp her jeans and pull them up. He stared up at the long slim legs and the curve of the boyish buttocks and he reached out and grasped her wrist.

'No,' he said.

'No?'

'It took me too much hard effort to get those things where they are,' he said. 'I'm not letting you pull them up until it's absolutely necessary.'

'And when will that be?'

He drew her down towards him once more.

'We'll have to see,' he said.

This time after he entered her, he paused, and looked down at her once more flushed and eager face, and said softly, 'You are Anya Wilson.'

But this assertion of identity was turned against him like a knife when she smiled up at him and murmured, 'And you are Jay Hutton.'

This time his orgasm felt like an act of betrayal as well as an act of love.

CHAPTER TWENTY-THREE

Next morning he was awoken by the rattle of wind in the old sash window of his bedroom. Summer had gone again. The sky was a shifting patchwork of greys, and round the beeches in the garden swirls of bright leaves were dancing a mournful morris. He stood by the window and watched them and felt his thoughts scatter around his mind as drily and as pointlessly.

Last night it had been different. They had not shared a bed. Anya did not trust his assertion that he could wake up at any time he ordained, and she feared an early visit from Jimmy. But they had lain on the hearth till the logs crumbled to fluffy ashes. No promises were asked and none were spoken, but promises had been made in every touch and breath and silence, promises which he now knew he'd had no right to make. Last night, everything had seemed possible. He could tell her the truth, and she would listen, amazed, as Desdemona had listened to Othello, interrupting now and then with gasps of vicarious terror at his perils and sighs of vicarious suffering at his pains. Or he could keep silent and become Jay Hutton permanently. What was identity? A stamp on a passport. Harry Collins, that boy he had been in Saigon, was a stranger, totally alien now except in this turbulence of the heart.

Either way, confessing or silent, he had felt utterly confident of waking this morning and finding that the tooth-fairy had visited him in the night and left a solution under his pillow.

Now he stood and watched the death-dance of the leaves and knew that there was only one solution, or rather only one faint hope of solution. Adam's death had in reality changed nothing. He had to talk to Jacob.

He should have done this much earlier, of course. But there had been uncertainties then which he had allowed to dull his judgement. He had let himself hope that Bryant's death would cease to be necessary; and he had even flattered himself that his own expertise could protect the man. Now he knew that the target directive remained unchanged, and he admitted that in the long run, no single man, however expert, could protect that target against Jacob's forces.

So now he must parley, must attempt to persuade Jacob to abort. Why the hell was Bryant targeted anyway? What was the man supposed to have done? He was a simple country solicitor, half retired; what *could* he have done? There must have been a mistake . . .

With a groan he acknowledged the pathetic futility of this line of thought. At least to himself he must be completely honest. The best he could reasonably hope for from a discussion with Jacob was a reassurance, in acknowledgement of his own long, loyal and efficient service, that Anya and the boy would in no way be endangered by the removal of Bryant.

And Adam's body lay between him and even that basic assurance.

He suddenly found himself wishing with an irresistible and passionate intensity that Bryant's crash on Kirkstone Pass had been fatal. It would have passed as an accident and even the question mark above it in his own mind would soon have faded with the passage of time.

'Are you hoping to impress a passing milkmaid or something?'

He turned. Anya, fully clothed, had come unheard into his room and was smiling at him, genuinely amused to find him standing naked at the window. She showed no sign whatsoever of embarrassment and he loved her for it. Once she had given herself, there was clearly no retreat to a position of pseudo-modesty. She had caressed just about every part of his body with every part of hers and was not going to step back from that intimacy now.

He likewise resisted the impulse to reach for his

252

bathrobe or, even more absurdly, cover himself with his hand. Instead he went towards her and, pulling her close, kissed her fiercely.

'Good morning,' she gasped.

'Good morning.'

'Jimmy's gone to school. I stopped him from disturbing you—I thought you might need your rest—but pappy's rattling around the bathroom now, and despite his new agility when climbing upstairs I'd still prefer to have you ready to catch him as he comes down. He's got to go back to the hospital this morning for a check-up and I'd like him to show some sign of improvement.'

'All right,' he said. 'It's a pity though.'

She broke loose, stepped back and glanced down at the inevitable result of their passionate embrace.

'You may still have time if you hurry,' she said. 'For a cold shower, I mean.'

Laughing, she evaded his grab and went out.

Breakfast despite Jaysmith's inner sombreness was a gay meal. Anya was alight with a happiness which shone out in her simplest movements and most everyday speech. Bryant observed, guessed the cause, and showed his own pleasure in a kind of sly avuncularity, full of verbal winks and nudges which might have amused Jaysmith in another place, another time. He felt it necessary to volunteer to take Bryant for his hospital appointment but was relieved when Anya firmly insisted that she was taking him, even though this meant squeezing him into the Fiat.

'I want to hear what they've got to say for myself,' she said. 'Otherwise I'll just get a load of nonsense. Come on, pappy. We'd better be on our way. We don't want to be late.'

'Don't we? It's a pity those quacks never return the compliment,' grumbled Bryant. 'Jay, be warned. You see what a fat tyrant lurks beneath that skinny exterior. Anya, why don't you let Jay drive us there in his nice comfortable car? That way you can have your cake and eat it.'

Anya glanced at Jaysmith who said, 'Well, to tell the truth, I'd rather thought I'd go into Keswick and do some shopping. Also I ought to call in to check one or two things with Mr Grose.'

They both looked disappointed and after he had helped Bryant into the Fiat, Anya walked back to the front door with him.

'Jay, I hope pappy's not bothering you,' she said.

'No. Why should he be?'

'He's got sharp eyes,' she said, 'and he's obviously guessed about us. All this unsubtle innuendo can be a bit wearing. It's not really his style somehow. I think it must be some atavistic Polish family thing! I'm sorry.'

'Honestly, it doesn't bother me. If it means he approves, I'm delighted.'

'There is something to approve of, isn't there, Jay?' she asked, holding his gaze with her own clear unblinking eyes.

'You'd better believe it,' he said.

*　　*　　*

After they'd gone, he went out to the BMW. He could have telephoned from the house now it was empty, but somehow he felt uneasy at the thought of dialling that number on Anya's phone. Besides, he had another reason for wanting to visit Keswick. He wanted to check on Adam.

By contrast with the tourist bustle of the previous morning, the cold, wind-funnelled streets were almost empty this morning. There were still quite a lot of cars in the main car park, but the yellow mini was not among them.

He went into the Royal Oak Hotel on the main street and sat in the lounge and ordered a pot of coffee. While it was coming he went to the public telephone and dialled the London number.

There was no ringing tone, only a single high-pitched note.

He tried again. The same, so he dialled the operator and asked him to try. After a few moments the man said, 'I'm afraid that number is out of service, sir. If you'll tell me who you're trying to ring, I'll check if there's another number listed for them.'

'That's OK,' said Jaysmith and replaced the receiver.

He returned to his table and sat down, ignoring the coffee which the waiter placed before him. When he finally got round to pouring himself a cup, he found it had gone quite cold.

As he drove back to Naddle Foot he was still assessing the implications of the cancelled number. Normal procedure when a key operative retired? Coincidence? Or was it a deliberate cutting of his line of communication with Jacob? This last would mean they knew of his involvement. If they knew that and were not interested in making contact, then the obvious decision must have been taken—to target him also.

Why not? His protection of Bryant, his killing of Adam, could mean only one thing in their eyes—that he had gone over to the side of Bryant's

255

masters, whoever they were.

He pulled into the side of the road and watched the traffic go by. There was no suspicious slowing of any vehicle or turning of heads as they passed. Why should there be? There was no need to tail him; if they knew of his existence, they knew he was staying at Naddle Foot.

He started the car again and drove on.

As he travelled up the drive to the house, all looked still, but his perception was refined by suspicion and in the rear-view mirror as he parked before the front door, he thought he saw a shift in the light-catching planes of a huge hollybush at the edge of the garden. He got out of the car, ran lightly up the steps, opened the front door and stepped inside. Pausing only to switch off the alarm system, he went straight through the kitchen and out of the rear door. His hand was on the HK P9 inside the windcheater he was wearing.

This is getting to be a habit, he thought, as he crouched low along the back of the house. He doubted this time if he'd find anything as interesting as therapeutic fellatio going on. Probably the shifting of leaves was caused merely by a couple of blackbirds foraging for berries.

But as he entered the line of shrubbery which ran alongside the house and began to make his way towards the front garden with great stealth, he saw he had been wrong. Through the screen of leaves and branches ahead he could make out a more solid area, vague at first, but now, like the significant shades in a colour-blindness test, emerging to form the shape of a man.

Drawing the gun, Jaysmith advanced. Despite all his efforts at silence, the dead leaves of autumn

256

betrayed him as the live leaves of the evergreen had betrayed the watcher. Alerted by the telltale rustle, the man turned, saw him, and turned to run.

'Stop!' yelled Jaysmith, bringing the gun up to the two-handed aim position.

Whether the fugitive would have surrendered, or whether he himself would have opened fire, he didn't find out. The man's foot skidded on the dew-glossed grass and he crashed down onto his knees, flinging his hands forward to prevent himself from measuring his length on the lawn.

'Hold it there!' commanded Jaysmith. 'Don't move a muscle!'

His choice of phrase was rather clichéd, he had to admit. But he was surprised at its effect, or rather lack of it.

The man, who was wearing an expensive dark-grey Crombie and a matching Homburg which had slipped over his forehead as he fell, stood up, adjusting his hat and brushing at his knees.

'For heaven's sake, Mr Wainwright,' he said wearily, 'neither of us is going to harm the other, so why not put that thing away?'

Jaysmith found himself looking into the face of the man he had met once before and knew as Anton Ford.

CHAPTER TWENTY-FOUR

Anton Ford's attitude puzzled Jaysmith but he did not let himself be lulled by it. With the barrel of the gun firmly pressed against the top of Ford's spine, he ran his free hand over, then under, the grey coat but found no weapon.

'Right, let's go inside,' he said.

'I'll be glad to. This damp grass isn't doing my shoes any good.'

The shoes, which looked custom-made, had been designed for elegance rather than athletics and were showing the strain. As at their first encounter, Jaysmith was surprised by the contrast between the uncompromising physicality of the man's appearance and the fashionable expensiveness of his clothing. The contrast was further stressed inside the house when, without waiting for instruction, Ford removed his overcoat to reveal a dark-blue mohair suit on which some expert tailor had lavished his considerable skills to minimize the inelegant brawn it had to cover. They were in the lounge and, tossing his coat over the back of the sofa, Ford sat down and examined his knees.

'Grass stains,' he said. 'That's meths, isn't it? But I'd better not meddle. You only make things worse when you meddle, don't you? I'll let the dry cleaner sort it out.'

Jaysmith had put the gun away, but left the safety off. He now sat down also, a safe distance away, and said, 'What are you doing here, Mr Ford?'

He kept his voice harsh and aggressive, the tone of an interrogator who knows most of the answers and will not shy away from any degree of persuasion to get the rest. But in truth he was bewildered. Ford's clothing and lack of armament did not chime with his being here as one of Jacob's firm. And what was it the man had called him—Wainwright? That was the name he'd given when he first met the man in Manchester, true. But why was he using it now?

'I suppose I *could* say I was looking for a house to buy,' said Ford, his weathered boxer's face creasing momentarily into a smile. 'But that's never very convincing, is it?'

He seemed perfectly at his ease, but Jaysmith's sharp eyes caught the fingers of his right hand plucking rhythmically at the gold identity bracelet round his left wrist and this sign of underlying nervousness reassured him.

'What are you doing here?' he repeated.

The mask dropped suddenly; it was after all no more effective a cover of Ford's real state of mind than all this expensive tailoring was of his brawny physique.

'What the hell do you imagine I'm doing here?' he demanded. 'I had to find out for myself, didn't I? I mean, I can't believe it, that's the top and bottom of it. I know that someone's said that about every traitor ever unmasked, but the fact remains, it's true, and I can't, not till he tells me himself!'

Jaysmith kept his face a blank as his mind raced to fit together the implications of this.

'I don't see why it should be such a trouble to you,' he said sceptically.

'You don't see?' growled Ford, his skin flushing a pinkish red which clashed unpleasantly with his carefully coiffured ginger hair. 'What the hell sort of man are you? It's me who's going to have to tell Ota, isn't it?'

'Ota?' said Jaysmith. 'And why should that bother you?'

Ford looked both angry and amazed.

'Why should it bother me?' he demanded. 'You

mean it wouldn't bother you to have to tell your own sister that the man she's in love with has sold out everything she ever believed in?'

His sister! He cast his mind back to the mini-biog Ford had so readily offered him on their first encounter. His elder sister (Urszula, wasn't it?) had gone back to Poland with his father, married, had five children, was widowed. And Urszula was Ota! No wonder Ford had been ready to bear messages for her and probably to her as well.

Yet there had to be more.

He said cautiously, 'Doesn't the evidence speak for itself?'

'Evidence? You mean Tusar's arrest? That was always on the cards. The man was a drunk. Every UBEK agent in Krakow must have heard him shooting his mouth off about the government at some time or other. As for Lomnicki . . .'

He paused. Jaysmith prompted him, saying in a sneering voice, 'Yes, go on. And how did they know enough to arrest Lomnicki?'

He knew he'd made a mistake instantly. Ford looked at him in puzzlement.

'Arrest? Why do you say *arrest* when you know they shot him down in cold blood?'

Jaysmith tried to carry it off by assuming an expression of cynical superiority implying a closer acquaintance with the facts than the other could hope for, but Ford was not impressed.

Half rising, he demanded, 'Who the hell are you, Wainwright?'

'Sit down!' commanded Jaysmith, producing the pistol again. Slowly Ford subsided before the weapon. Jaysmith thought of using its threat to force everything he could from the man, but a new

260

degree of hardness in that bruiser's face suggested that this might not work, or at best would require a very long and ultimately bloody session.

With a sigh he eased the gun back into his pocket.

'ok,' he said. 'You're right. I don't understand half of what you're telling me. But I'd be very grateful if you'd explain. What about a whisky? I'm sure Stefan wouldn't object.'

He rose and went to get the drink.

The ease with which he found the bottle and the glasses seemed to relax Ford even more than the disappearance of the gun, but there was still suspicion in his voice as he said, 'If you're not one of Jacob's men, who are you? You're not with the others, are you?'

His voice rose in alarm.

Jaysmith handed him a glass of whisky and smiled.

'Hardly,' he said. 'If I were UBEK or KGB, I'd know all about Lomnicki, wouldn't I? No, I'm a friend of Bryant's. Sorry, let me correct that. I'm a friend of Anya's. A close friend.'

'Of Stefan's daughter?'

'That's right. You know her?'

'I have never met her,' said Ford, frowning. 'I have only been here a couple of times before and then she was married and living elsewhere.'

'Didn't Bryant talk about her?'

'Very little. To tell the truth, he talked little about himself in England when we met.'

'Yet you feel you know him well enough to be convinced he is innocent.'

Ford's face darkened. 'I know my sister, Mr Wainwright, if that is your name.'

Jaysmith ignored this and said, 'Mr Ford, let me put my cards on the table. I'm in love with Anya. By chance I discovered that her father was in danger and that it seemed to have something to do with his visits to Poland. I got your name and address from the covering note with some letters you forwarded. I was, I still am, eager to protect Bryant, for his daughter's sake more than his own, I freely admit. Please will you tell me what you can to help me help him. I am no one's man, but I am not without influence.'

It was the best he could do by way of reassurance, but Ford's face was still stony with suspicion. He didn't want to have to resort to the threat of the gun again and he added urgently, 'Look, Ford, I know enough already about you. I know you're a courier, I know that you work for Jacob ...'

'Jacob? Who works for Jacob? Not me. I've never met him in my life, though I've heard enough about the bastard!'

He spoke with indignation as though working for Jacob was as low as a man could sink. Curiously hurt, Jaysmith found himself for a brief moment tempted to contradict, but that would have been stupid and pointless and re-aroused Ford's suspicions. As it was, he managed to do this by saying, 'But Bryant deals direct with Jacob. They were talking together on the phone here.'

'Were they? That surprises me. He must be in real trouble then. But how the hell do you know what Jacob's voice sounds like?'

'I heard Bryant use the name, that's all,' lied Jaysmith. 'And it was what this man Jacob was saying that made me realize Bryant was

262

threatened.'

This flimsy piece of extemporization proved surprisingly successful at convincing Ford, or perhaps it was simply that the man, despite his tough appearance, was frightened enough to grasp at any ally. The tension left his body and he held out his glass for more whisky.

Jaysmith poured and said casually, 'So. You're a courier, are you? Nothing more?'

'You know that too?'

'I guessed it.'

Ford smiled wanly and said, 'So much for secret service! All right. That's what I am, from time to time, from place to place. And Stefan, he's even less. That's what makes all this business so stupid!'

The floodgates were now open and he spoke freely. He had been recruited via another Polish expatriate in the early seventies whose attention had been attracted by Ford's strong anti-communist attitudes plus the ready access his job as a drug company salesman gave him to Eastern Europe.

'I carry things, that's all. What I carry, I often do not know. What's it matter? I'm told it will help in the anti-Russian struggle, and that's quite enough for me.'

He spoke rather defiantly and seemed surprised at Jaysmith's sympathetic nod.

'I understand,' he said. 'We've all had to take things on trust.'

The only difference being that what he had taken on trust was more than twenty lives.

'How did you meet Bryant?' he asked.

'I didn't. Urszula did.'

'Urszula who is Ota.'

263

'That was a childish name. Her second name's Dorota, and Ota was the best she could manage. When she got older, she insisted on being called Urszula. That's when I got worried, when I went to visit her and met this stranger she allowed to call her Ota!'

'How had they met?'

'She works in the university library in Krakow. Stefan had permission to use its facilities for research into some book he's writing. It was a common interest, the identity of Poland or some such thing.'

'You say you got worried. Why?'

'It's a neurotic country, Poland,' said Ford gloomily. 'You suspect everything. The thing was Ota—Urszula—was getting more and more involved with the protest movement.'

'You mean Solidarity?'

'That's its public side. There are plenty of other more secret and subversive dimensions. I won't deny there was a selfish side to my concern. If Urszula drew UBEK's attention to herself, they were certainly going to be interested in her young brother with the British passport too. So when I saw how friendly she and this Stefan Bryant were becoming I passed his name on to my London control and suggested they should check.'

'And the result?'

'The good news was that he was absolutely clear. The bad news was that he'd actually done some undercover work with the SOE during the war and someone got the bright idea of recruiting him to the courier service. So all I'd managed to do to protect my sister was to get the man she was involved with into the same dangerous game as

264

myself.'

'Hardly your fault,' said Jaysmith. 'He'd have to agree to be recruited.'

Ford smiled and said, 'You don't know Urszula. Stefan's a man of strong character, but he's met his match there. Her own commitment is so total that there's no way a man could love her and remain apolitical. I think he was probably sympathetic to the cause to start with. After Urszula finished with him, he'd be totally conditioned and ripe for official recruitment in the great anti-communist struggle!'

'And how much actual responsibility did— does—Bryant have?'

'As little as me,' shrugged Ford. 'Less. He works purely into Poland while I'm much more general. A mere message carrier, or at the most, the occasional parcel.'

'Then how does it come about that a mere messenger can be targeted as a traitor responsible for the betrayal and deaths of important people?' mused Jaysmith.

'It's just not possible!' proclaimed Ford. 'I refuse to believe it!'

His vehemence surprised Jaysmith. Nothing that had been said indicated a particularly close relationship with Bryant, certainly not one productive of such defensive indignation.

Then it hit him.

'It's Urszula you're bothered about, isn't it?' he said. 'The only real access to information that he would have must be Urszula. In fact, his only known contact with Poland during the past year has been via these letters you brought back for him from Urszula . . . !'

'There was nothing in them. Nothing!' protested Ford. 'I read them. I told Urszula I must be able to read them, to make sure I knew they contained nothing incriminating, in case I was checked and they were discovered. They are love letters, nothing more, nothing less!'

He looked ready to explode and Jaysmith hastily poured him some more whisky.

'Who told you what was happening?' he asked.

'A friend in London. He works at the control bureau. He visited me yesterday on another matter to do with my next visit to Poland. During the conversation he suggested I would be wise not to try to see Bryant before I left . . .'

'Were you planning to?' demanded Jaysmith.

'I rang him up yesterday morning,' said Ford. 'To ask if he had any letters he wished me to take to Urszula. He has not seen her for nearly a year, you know. I think it is because he did not wish to leave his daughter after she was widowed. Even at a low level, it is a risky business being a courier, and he felt he could not take such a risk till he was happy that Anya was recovered.'

'And did he have a letter?'

'Yes. Also he told me about this accident. I was most distressed. I said I would come to see him next weekend before I went so that I could pick up the letter and be able to give Urszula a first-hand report on how he looked.'

'And yesterday afternoon you were warned off,' mused Jaysmith. He'd been right not to trust the telephones in Naddle Foot. They must be bugged. 'What did your friend say?' he asked.

'Very little at first. He tried to give the impression it was just a routine check-up. But I

266

remembered the other one then and I got angry and told him I would go to see Stefan anyway, and then he told me how serious it was. I couldn't believe it. I lay awake all night thinking about it. I *know* my sister could not be involved in such a thing; I was almost as certain of Stefan too. I had to speak to him, and I daren't use the phone.'

So he too had worked it out, thought Jaysmith approvingly.

'So you drove up to see him.'

He didn't mean to sound accusing, but so it must have emerged.

'What else could I do?' protested Ford. 'I parked a long way down the road in case anyone was watching. And I pulled this absurd old hat I never wear any more over my brow and wrapped my scarf round my face to prevent recognition.'

'Bravo,' mocked Jaysmith gently. 'And when you heard my car approaching, you hid. Bravo again.'

'I am not a secret agent like in the thrillers, Mr Wainwright,' said Ford, not without dignity. 'The risks I take are a smuggler's risks, knowing when to smile at customs officials, when to be indignant. I carry no weapons, have no expertise in kung-fu, would probably have a heart attack if I had to run a hundred yards. Of course I bloody well hid!'

He spoke with convincing force, but for all that Jaysmith did not feel he would care to come within receiving distance of a blow from those burly arms.

He said, 'Just now when you said that your London friend tried to give the impression it was just a routine security check on Bryant, you remembered the other one. What other one?'

'About six months ago, they ran a check on Stefan. It happens to all of us from time to time.

Security clearance can't be forever, can it? Usually it's just a simple simultaneous check: that is, they question the subject and his associates at the same time and cross-reference their stories.' He laughed without much humour and said, 'That's what I thought you were doing when we first met, Mr Wainwright. I didn't like the sound of those questions about the neighbours you'd been asking poor Wendy Denver. Then I left you in my house alone. I have a security camera hidden in my study, Mr Wainwright. I checked when I came back and there you were, rummaging around. I nearly challenged you there and then!'

'Instead, you decided to take the piss by telling me the story of your life!'

'It amused me to bore you by making you hear harmless details I was sure you would have in your file already,' said Ford bitterly.

'Tell me about this check on Bryant,' said Jaysmith.

'At the time it seemed straightforward enough. Two men called on me at my office. They were quite open. They showed me their credentials. I checked them and they were in order. It was just a routine check on Bryant, they said.'

'And was it just routine?' enquired Jaysmith.

Ford frowned and said, 'It was very thorough, but that's not unusual. They started by asking about Stefan's relationship with my sister.'

'Did that surprise you?'

Ford shrugged.

'It's their business to know such things, but I knew that Stefan and Urszula had kept their affair very quiet from the start. It was in their natures. And once Stefan began to work as a courier, they

268

had double reason to keep a low profile. But like I say, it's hard to keep anything from the Service. What did bother me was that they knew about the letters.'

'The ones you brought for him? Why should that worry you?'

'Only selfishly,' said Ford. 'At least, *then* my worry was merely selfish. Technically I should have mentioned in my reports that I was carrying letters between the two of them, but it was a private matter, a family matter, so I hadn't bothered. Now they knew.'

'How?'

'God knows.'

'And were you reprimanded?'

'Obliquely. It was suggested that I ought now to be completely open. It was the kind of suggestion that hinted they knew many other things already, and if I didn't mention them all, this would be taken very unkindly. They were just a pair of youngsters, but, by Christ, they frightened me! I was glad to see the back of them. This is what I remembered when my London friend started flannelling about a routine check. It struck me that two checks in such a short space meant trouble, and suddenly it was quite clear that the last one had been anything but routine. But I suppose I was so relieved that I didn't get into hot water myself that I just took it at face value.'

'They didn't seem too bothered about the letters, then?'

'No. In fact they told me specifically it was OK if I went on carrying them.'

'And did you?'

'Oh yes. Well, I've only been back once since

then and I took a letter from Stefan and brought one back from Urszula. I read it, as always. I may have skipped through the others, but this one I read very carefully, believe me. I'm no fool, Mr Wainwright, and those fellows had frightened me, routine or not. There was nothing in it, I swear. Nothing! All this is some ghastly error. It has to be!'

He is hopelessly biased, of course, thought Jaysmith. Like me. I'm hopelessly biased too.

He glanced at his watch. Time was passing, too much time. If the house was being watched, then they would know he was here with Ford, or at least with *someone* if Ford's elementary disguise tactic had worked. Would they make a move? Perhaps. The sooner Ford got safely away, the better. There was no reason for him to get tangled up in this. Also there was the possibility if they delayed much longer that Anya and Bryant would return. Ford's presence and its explanation would only cause more complication and things were complicated enough already.

But there were still things he wanted to ask.

'These two men, what were they like?'

'Like? Well, youngish. One was very blond, a good-looking young chap in a pop-starish kind of way. The other wasn't quite so young, long black hair, one of those ten o'clock shadow beards, nose a bit twisted as though someone had broken it for him.'

'Did they have names?'

'Yes, though I doubt if they were their real names. The blond called himself Mr Adam and the other one was Mr Davey.'

Adam and Davey. No simple security vetters

these, but Jacob's men. And now Adam was a decomposing corpse in whatever grave Jacob set aside for his deceased operatives.

And Davey, where was he?

He glanced towards the window, and the hunched-up fells looked indifferently back.

'What did they ask about Bryant?' he pursued.

'They just made me go over every contact I'd had with him back for almost a year,' said Ford.

'Anything in particular? Was there anything in particular that interested them?'

'Just one thing,' said Ford slowly. 'About six months earlier, that is a year ago from now, Stefan got in touch. He was going to Poland a short while after. That was his last visit as it turned out. He hasn't been back since, hence the need for these letters. He asked if there was anything for him to carry. I checked and there wasn't. Then he asked if I could do something for him in my capacity as a drug salesman. Someone over there in Krakow had asked for it specially as a personal favour. Well, with shortages like there are, it was understandable, and I said yes.'

'What was it?' interrupted Jaysmith.

'It was one of my firm's packs of insulin capsules,' said Ford. 'Adam and Davey didn't seem all that interested in this. I had to mention it, of course. For all I knew, Stefan had told them already, or was telling someone else a hundred miles away. But, as I explained, there was no danger. Even if Polish customs spotted them, all that Stefan had to do was say he was a diabetic. *What's that?*'

Jaysmith had heard the sound a moment earlier but he had been so riveted by what Ford was telling

271

him that he had ignored it. But with Ford on his feet now, alarm brutalizing his boxer's face, the conversation was obviously at an end.

'It's a car,' he said. 'It sounds like Anya's Fiat.'

He went to a window overlooking the front of the house. The Fiat was coming up the drive.

Ford had relaxed when he realized it was only the Bryants returning but Jaysmith, bustling round the room, replacing the whisky bottle and concealing the glasses, said, 'Don't sit down. You'd better be on your way.'

'What for?' demanded the other in surprise.

Jaysmith frowned. The only answer was that he himself had a dozen reasons for not wanting Ford and Bryant to talk just now. But none of them felt good enough to persuade the man to flight. Nor would the gun help. The time for threats was past. Besides, Ford would know he was not about to use it with the Bryants on the doorstep.

'Trust me,' he said. 'It's better this way. For Stefan and Anya, I mean. I'll get in touch in a day or two and put you in the picture, I promise.'

Ford hesitated. Jaysmith remembered that it was brotherly love and loyalty which had brought him here rather than deep friendship for Bryant.

'There is no way your sister can be involved in any of this, believe me,' he said slowly. 'Jacob's seen the letters. He'll have had them analysed upside-down and sideways. Urszula's completely clear.'

Even as he infused the lie with sincerity, he realized he was probably telling at least part of the truth. Hadn't Anya said there'd been a burglary a few months earlier as a result of which they'd got the alarm system fitted? It must have been Jacob's men, already looking for evidence of Bryant's treachery. And like Jaysmith himself, all they had found had been the letters which they'd photographed for closer study. It was discovery of the relationship between Urszula and Bryant that had sent Adam and Davey to interrogate Ford. But at what point, and for what reason, had suspicion of Bryant hardened into certainty and his name gone on the target list? And why not just arrest him and squeeze everything he knew out of him?

Unless of course it was all part of some great bluff and Bryant's killing was to appear someone else's responsibility.

These thoughts flickered through his mind in a mere second, the same second which brought Ford to a decision.

'Forty-eight hours,' he said. 'Ring me at home.'

He thrust a printed address card at Jaysmith.

'Forty-eight hours. If I don't hear from you, I'll talk to Stefan.'

Jaysmith said, 'Agreed.'

They heard the front door open and Anya's voice calling, 'Jay! We're back.'

'In here,' called Jaysmith.

The domestic familiarity of greeting and response seemed finally to convince Ford. He nodded, either in confirmation or farewell, picked up his coat, pulled the homburg over his brow, and went through the french windows into the garden.

The lounge door opened. Anya came in. Jaysmith went towards her to make sure she was delayed sufficiently for Ford to get quite clear, but she came into his arms with a movement so natural that he felt a surge of shame at his own duplicity.

CHAPTER TWENTY-FIVE

That night Anya came openly to his room, only insisting that her alarm clock be set for six AM so that she could be back in her own bed before Jimmy awoke.

The news she had brought from the hospital had been good. Bryant was mending well, there were no complications, the prognosis was a full recovery in a matter of months. Bryant himself claimed that this was merely confirmation of what he had been saying all along, but even he was visibly lightened by the news. As for Anya, her delight was manifest in her every word and movement during the evening, and the promise of pleasure she gave him whenever their eyes met or hands brushed was paid in triple measure from the moment the bedroom door closed. They shared roles, each in turn accepting the mastery and driving the other to the limits of ecstasy; and it was almost as if they exchanged bodies too, for Jaysmith at times felt himself a willing victim in the grip of Anya's undeniable power and strength, yet when she sensed that finally his long stamina was failing, she relaxed instantly and, curling up against him, seemed to shrink to a kitten's weight and softness, and he folded her tenderly to him, fearful lest he should crush her.

They slept. Soon he dreamt the old dream, or a combination of many old dreams, labyrinthing from the heat of Saigon through many countries, many deaths, to a high place in the Cumbrian fells where he raised his gun sight to his eye and saw

Anya magnified in that lethal circle.

He awoke. She was lying across him, her arms spread wide, her legs coiled round his splayed right leg, like a wrestler who has his opponent pinned in a fall. Yet she felt no weight at all.

He lay in the darkness and recalled their mutual pleasure. If news of her father's expected progress towards recovery could bring her to such a pitch of joy, into what depths of pain and despair would his death plunge her? The previous evening he had responded so readily to Anya's joyous mood that he had once more been able to push the agony of decision out of his mind. But the point of no return was close. Ford's visit the previous day had told him as much as he was likely to find out about Bryant's 'crime'. He had to act on what he knew now, and the alternatives were few and unattractive.

'Are you awake?' she said.

'Yes.'

'What are you thinking of?'

'The future.'

'Our future?'

'Is there another?'

She laughed and gripped him tightly.

'You'll take care of me, and Jimmy, and pappy, won't you Jay?' she whispered. It was only marginally a question.

'What makes you say that?' he asked, uneasy at the way she had intersected his own thought.

'Nothing. Pure selfishness. Pappy's been taking care of me for a long time now, and recently I've been taking care of him, and we've both been taking care of Jimmy, and suddenly, you're here, and I feel as if we can all relax at last and somehow,

275

with no effort at all, you'll take care of everything! Like I say, pure selfishness. Ignore it!'

The anguish her words caused him must have made itself felt in some tensing of the body for she pushed herself up off him slightly and said, 'Am I too heavy?'

He pulled her back down and said, 'No. A feather, you're no more than a feather.'

'Yes,' she said, pressing against him. 'You're right. Hold me close. Tonight I feel so light that a cold draught from the fells could easily blow me away.'

Again her choice of words cut across his heart like angina, but this time he gave no sign and after a while he heard her breath slip into the shallow rhythms of sleep, but sleep did not return to him that night and when the alarm began to shrill at six o'clock, his hand had muffled it in a moment. But she was awake already, and stretching sensuously, letting her hands run the whole length of his body.

'Oh Christ,' she said. 'I'm so happy.'

Then she slipped out of his arms and bed, picked up her discarded wrap from the floor and pulled it with coquettish slowness around her shoulders, laughing at his expression.

'There'll come a time when you'd prefer a cup of tea and the morning paper!' she said. 'See you at breakfast.'

After the door had closed behind her, he rose and went and stood by the window. The sky was blue, but pale as a marsh forget-me-not fast fading in the summer's drought. That drought was long past here, and the wind which was taking shape in the beeches and scouring the colour from the sky would before long be summoning clouds to glut the

276

streams once more. For the present though the fell tops were clear. He raised his eyes to them and felt a surge of longing, almost sexual in its intensity, to be up there, to be walking with the wind on his face and his mind clear of all past guilt and future care.

He had fallen in love with more than a woman, he told himself, wonderingly. He had fallen in love with a landscape too. The two were linked in a way he did not attempt to analyse further than saying that the woman he wanted was here, and the place he wanted to be with that woman was here also.

He turned from the window and sat on the bed. Looking out on the fells was about as helpful to a logical assessment of the courses open to him as looking down at Anya's naked body would have been.

The courses were few and unattractive. He could either concentrate on getting Bryant out of harm's way or persuading Jacob to de-target him. To get Bryant out of the way would mean revealing himself to the man. Hitherto he had shied away from this because it would have almost certainly meant revealing himself to Anya also, for, however Bryant might feel about entrusting his own safety to the hands of a self-confessed professional assassin, he was certainly not going to trust his daughter's future to those same polluted hands.

But now things had changed. Anton Ford had done more than give the background of why Bryant should be a security target. He had incidentally and unconsciously dropped into Jaysmith's lap a weapon to make the solicitor malleable and keep him silent. And yet it was a weapon that Jaysmith felt the strongest revulsion against using.

He had not consciously and logically worked his

way to his conclusions but his subconscious must have been burrowing away all night for now they rose clear and unmistakable to the surface of his mind.

Anya had revealed to him two nights earlier her guilty certainty that Edward Wilson had deliberately missed his insulin injection before going out on the fells that fatal Saturday.

Now there was another explanation, neither accident nor suicide.

Stefan Bryant a few weeks before Edward Wilson's death had obtained a pack of insulin ampoules from Anton Ford.

Suppose he had doctored them so that their contents were diluted or completely useless.

Suppose, driven by rage at Anya's unhappiness, guilt at his own imagined neglect at letting it happen, and despair at her inability to break out of it, he had substituted this dud pack for a real one when he collected Anya to host his Christmas party.

Did Bryant have it in him to be so ruthless? It was Jaysmith's reading of the man that he did. His wartime experience proved he had the nerve and the stomach for it, if the cause were right. And how much righter a cause can a man have than his child's happiness?

Besides it was an ambiguously indirect form of killing, fatalistic almost. Wilson may not have gone climbing. He may have collapsed in company or near a telephone. He may have been found in time.

These variables were just the kind of tackle men use to shift a heavy weight of direct responsibility. Even when the corpse lies at the other end of a straight line of fire, a man can easily find mental pulleys to help him take the strain. Patriotism; justice; or when all else fails, simple distance will sometimes do the trick.

For not the first time recently it came to Jaysmith that his own preference for the long kill was not simply a factor of his physical safety, but, even more important, of his mental stability.

He shrugged the introspective mood away. The dark of night was the place for such thoughts. Here in bright morning he must concern himself with practicalities and action.

If Bryant had set out to kill his son-in-law, then the threat of having this revealed to Anya would make him completely malleable. The fact, if it were fact, was simply a weapon. Ethical judgements were not apt for this situation, nor, Jaysmith admitted bitterly, from this source.

Yet he did not want to use the weapon and he knew the reason why. At the moment all he had was the strongest suspicion. Confront Bryant, and he guessed that the man might readily acknowledge his guilt. And the prospect of having the weight of this knowledge added to all the other heavy secrets he kept hidden from Anya was more than he could bear.

No; it would be a last resort. His mind was made up. Somehow or other he would contact Jacob and ask for a parley.

But he would not go empty handed to the conference table.

He had a writing case with him. He took out some sheets of paper and spent the next half-hour covering them with his small, neat handwriting. By the time he'd finished, there were sounds of life in the house: taps running, Anya's voice urging Jimmy

279

to haste, the boy's footsteps, sluggish at first, but soon accelerating to their normal breakneck pace.

On his way downstairs, Jaysmith looked in on Bryant. He was sitting up in bed with a hardly touched breakfast tray pushed to one side and a cigarette between bloodless lips. The trip to the hospital for his check-up seemed to have produced a reaction at odds with the up-beat prognosis. He complained of feeling tired and certainly looked rather pale and drawn. As he looked down at him, Jaysmith wondered again about his guilt with regard to the Polish betrayals. Did his new suspicions about Wilson's death make this alleged treachery more or less probable? In point of ruthlessness, more; but not in point of motive. Not unless a threat to Urszula had been the lever to treachery. That did make some kind of sense. If so, this man had enough on his mind and his conscience to make a Tartar haggard.

'Are you measuring me for my coffin?' growled Bryant.

'Sorry?'

'You're studying me with a very professional eye,' said the older man sourly.

'Was I? I was thinking of something else. By the way, can I use your copier? I noticed you had one in your study.'

'Did you? Quite the lynx-eyed detective, aren't you? Well, what you didn't notice was that since Friday when Anya used it to run some things off for Jimmy's party, it's not been working. You want to watch that girl, Hutton. What she touches often seems to fall apart.'

'Does it? She must have had her hands on your temper this morning then,' said Jaysmith with a smile. 'Is there a photocopying shop in Keswick, do you know?'

'No idea,' grunted Bryant and then, as if to make amends for his surliness, added, 'But there's a machine in my office. Use that if you like.'

'That's kind of you. I will,' said Jaysmith. 'Are you finished with your tray? You've hardly touched it.'

'Yes, I'm finished. And one nagging nurse in the house is quite enough, Hutton.'

'Sorry,' said Jaysmith, picking up the tray. 'I'd better go and get my breakfast, I think. Any message for your office?'

'No. But you can get me some cigarettes in town. I'm running low and Anya will just accidentally forget. Caporals!'

'I know, I know,' called Jaysmith as he descended the stairs.

*   *   *

He left for Keswick straight after breakfast. It had been a comfortably domestic meal with the pair of them very much at ease with one another.

'We're like an old married couple,' he said as she accompanied him to the door. 'Little wife seeing hard-working hubby off to the City.'

He accompanied his remark with a satirical peck on the cheek, but she fastened her arms round his neck and forced her mouth against his so hard that he tasted blood when they broke apart.

'You did that like it was the last time,' he said. 'Much harder, and it might have been.'

She didn't respond to his smile but said seriously, 'There's something about you, Jay, which

281

makes every time feel like the last time. You're not going to run out on me, are you?'

'Jilt you, you mean?' he said, still aiming at lightness. 'You can always do me for breach-of-promise!'

'Seriously, Jay,' she said steadily. 'This is for real, isn't it? We're going to last.'

'It's for real,' he said. 'Whatever happens, never doubt that, my love. I haven't loved anyone for twenty years. She was the first and she died. Now there's you. You're the last, Anya. After you, no one, nothing. This is for ever.'

He kissed her again passionately. Suddenly he too felt her sense of finality, as if it had been contagious. But it was absurd. He was only going to Keswick.

'See you later,' he said, smiling. And left.

CHAPTER TWENTY-SIX

Jaysmith did not drive direct to the solicitor's office. There was something else he had to do first and it was best to do it as quickly as possible before the tourists got on the move.

He skirted Keswick on the road which took him down towards Derwentwater and then turned south on the road into Borrowdale. After a couple of miles he turned left and began to climb, crossing the picturesque hump of Ashness Bridge on the narrow road to Watendlath and turning off into the trees which began to crowd both sides half a mile further along. The wind was here already, using the branches as its vocal chords to sing and sough its growing strength, but there were no other cars yet and no sign of anyone on foot.

He opened the boot, unclipped the false bottom and took out the rucksack which contained the M21. It took him longer than usual to assemble it, a matter of seconds only, but he felt the difference, then he found the target he was looking for, the rotten trunk of a fallen tree resting against a grassy bank. He began to pump shots into the decaying wood. The Sionics noise suppressor and the tree-loud wind combined to dissipate the sound of the shots, but he was still aware of the risk he was taking. But the time had come for risks.

It took just a few seconds, then he began to dig into the bank with the short-handled spade he had brought from the car.

Ten minutes later he was crossing Ashness Bridge once more on his descent to the lakeside road. He parked in Keswick not far from where he'd left Adam's mini. On his way to the solicitors' office he stopped at a stationer's, and bought several small padded envelopes and a couple of large ones.

Donald Grose was not in, but the pretty young secretary smiled at him and said, 'There you are, Mr Hutton. Mr Bryant phoned to say you'd be coming in to use the copier.'

And probably thus told Jacob too. Not that it mattered. By the time the message got to London and its significance was analysed, even if they guessed at the truth, it would be far too late. And in any case Jacob would know soon enough.

The copying did not take long. With the girl's permission, he then went into Bryant's little-used office and prepared his packages, filling them and printing the address neatly on in black ink. Finally he put half the small packages in one of the large padded envelopes, and the rest in the other. As he finished, the door opened and Donald Grose looked in.

'Hello there,' he said. 'How's the invalid?'

'Cantankerous,' said Jaysmith. The telephone rang in the outer office and a moment later the girl appeared.

'It's Miss Wilson for you, Mr Hutton. I'll put it through here, shall I?'

'Do that,' said Grose. 'I'm not sure if I like this direct contact between client and customer. I don't see how I can charge you for it!'

Why do lawyers joke about extorting money? wondered Jaysmith. It's like doctors joking about killing patients!

He waited till Grose had closed the door and lifted the phone.

'Mr Hutton?' said Miss Wilson's unmistakable voice. 'I rang you at Naddle Foot and Annie said I'd catch you here. It's about furniture. I've worked out what I can fit into Betty Craik's old house, but there's a lot less space there and I don't want to end up cluttered like a junk shop. There's a couple of pieces I want Annie to have, and my brother wants one or two things, but that still leaves quite a lot of stuff I can't take with me, large items mainly. There's the kitchen dresser, for instance, and a big chest of drawers in me bedroom. I thought I'd give you first refusal before going to the trouble of getting them shifted to a saleroom. Are you interested?'

She was as abrupt and direct as ever.

'Yes,' said Jaysmith, knowing he was really

saying yes to a dream of normality, yes to the hope of a settled future.

'Well, I'll not be contacting the saleroom till this afternoon,' she said. 'I'll be here all morning.'

The phone went dead. Jaysmith smiled admiringly. The art of the hard sell was far older than modern marketing!

He jiggled the rest till he got a dialling tone. From his wallet he took Anton Ford's card and dialled the number. He intended telling Ford that he had decided to confront Jacob. If the man could contribute anything else in support of his contention of Bryant's innocence, this was his chance. Also, if he were agreeable, he could provide Jaysmith with a London link via his control to Jacob. The man might not care to have his own involvement thus publicized, but Jaysmith doubted if his amateurish efforts at concealment had not been easily penetrated already.

The phone was answered by a woman.

'Mrs Ford?'

'Yes.'

'Could I speak to your husband please.'

'I'm afraid he's not at home.'

'Could you tell me where I might be able to get hold of him? At his office perhaps?'

'No, I'm sorry, he won't be there today either.'

Something in her voice made Jaysmith probe a little further.

'I'm a business acquaintance of his, Mrs Ford,' he said. 'He assured me he'd be at home if I phoned this morning.'

'I think he expected to be,' she said. 'But he rang last night to say he'd been detained and would be spending the night away.'

'I see. Did he mention the hotel? Perhaps I can contact him there.'

'No, he didn't. He didn't give any details.' Suddenly the anxiety came through unmistakably in her tone as its cause was expressed in her words.

'Who shall I say called?' Mrs Ford asked.

'Smith,' he said unimaginatively. 'Mr Smith. Goodbye.'

He rang off. He was filled with a cold foreboding. Perhaps Ford had decided to stay in Cumbria of his own volition in order to keep an eye on Naddle Foot, but Jaysmith doubted it. What need then to be so unforthcoming to his wife? Again Jaysmith assured himself that Ford could not be at risk of physical harm. But if Jacob's men had picked him up, they must be very close and probably close also to action.

He looked in frustration at the pair of bulky envelopes he held in his hand. Threats were useless unless their object knew he was being threatened. He picked up the phone again and tried the old London number. All that sounded was the unobtainable tone.

And then he laughed out loud and said, 'Idiot!'

There was an obvious and direct line to Jacob under his nose.

He dialled Naddle Foot.

Anya answered.

'Hi,' he said. 'Listen. Aunt Muriel got through to me. There's some furniture she thinks I might like to buy only I've got to look at it this morning.'

'Typical,' said Anya. 'But it's probably too good a chance to miss. Mind you, it won't be cheap. Some of her stuff's aeons old.'

'I gather that I'm being offered what's left over

286

after she's taken her share, and the family vultures, to wit, brother James and yourself, have picked over the rest, so I'm not anticipating any genuine Chippendale. But I'd like to look, so I'd better excuse myself for lunch and hope to get back this afternoon.'

'I'll do my best to survive,' she said lightly.

'You do that. Oh, by the way, I seem to have mislaid my billfold. I think I may have left it on the dressing table in my bedroom. Could you check for me?'

'Hang on.'

He waited till he heard her footsteps running lightly up the stairs, then he said harshly, 'Tell Jacob I want to talk. Tell him, any action before we talk and he'll regret it. He'd better believe it! Tell him I'll be in the bar at the Crag Hotel in Grasmere between twelve-thirty and one. He can ring me there. Tell him to ask for Mr Hutton.'

He heard Anya's footsteps returning.

'Jay? Sorry, it's not there,' she said anxiously.

'It's OK,' he laughed. 'I've found it. It had slipped down the lining in my jacket somehow. There must be a tear.'

'You need looking after,' she answered.

'Oh yes. I do,' he said. 'I really do.'

CHAPTER TWENTY-SEVEN

As he drove through Grasmere, the threat of deterioration in the weather was fast being realized. The sun still shone in the eastern sky, but its wash of cornflower blue was now smeared by high trails of cloud and over the western fells a creeping barrage of heavy mist was inexorably advancing. The lake's surface was like an unhealthy grey skin, wrinkled by the chilling wind which at every gasp stripped the remaining leaves from the trees to regild the woodland paths and top up drifts already deep enough to cover half a dozen babes-in-the-wood.

Or one dead drugs salesman.

It was a stupid, morbid thought, he told himself fiercely. There was no reason why any harm should have come to Ford. Or should come to Bryant now. He had posted his packages in Keswick before leaving. At the very least they should give him a breathing space, and in such a space, surely an accommodation could be reached?

But it wouldn't be easy. Under threat, Jacob might stay his hand, but it would take more than mere threat to persuade him to reverse the target directive. How much actual power did Jacob himself wield? He realized he had very little idea. What he couldn't believe was that Jacob would have targeted Bryant on the flimsy evidence that he himself had now had a chance to consider. Look at the facts. Bryant hadn't been anywhere near Poland for a year; his only communication (correction: the only communication he knew of) had been with Urszula via Anton Ford. There might, of course, be some subtle code in those letters, but he found it hard to believe. Why on earth should Urszula send information to him in this way? It was a thousand miles away from the whispered indiscretions of a post-coital bed. The use of codes implied something deliberate, something premeditated. It must mean, to be blunt,

288

that Urszula was a traitor also. And if that were the case, why this circuitous route for the passage of information when all she had to do was make a simple direct contact with an UBEK agent in Krakow?

No, it made no sense. It seemed much more likely that someone had blundered and, like many blunders in political and private life alike, the easiest way of concealing it had been to carry it through.

'*Sic probo*,' he proclaimed aloud, but even as he spoke he knew he had proven nothing. God knew what as yet unrevealed and far weightier evidence of Bryant's guilt Jacob had at his disposal. And no one knew better than himself just how ruthlessly Bryant was capable of acting if he thought that those he loved were being threatened. Thank God Jacob could have no suspicion of that, at least!

His recent optimism was vanishing as rapidly as the sky. It was the pathetic fallacy at work in reverse. His mind was adjusting to the falling leaves and the dismal lake. What was the point of parleying with Jacob? He had nothing but a threat that might be regarded as feeble, and logic fragile as a bridge of snow. Proving a negative was never easy, not unless you had a positive to balance it out. And what did he have to offer? Nothing!

Filled with frustration, he took a corner far too quickly, drifted into the centre of the road, and found himself on a collision course with an oncoming truck. Both drivers hit their brakes and put their vehicles into gentle skids. They ended up as close as they possibly could without actually hitting and Jaysmith found himself looking at the bonnet of the other vehicle at point-blank distance.

The truck driver wound down his window and began to swear. But Jaysmith ignored him. All he could see was the name of the other vehicle's manufacturer, large in his eyes like a message from heaven.

Ford.

He mouthed an apology and slowly drove on, letting his mind do the speeding now.

Ford!

If Bryant was pressurable by threats to Urszula, then so was Ford.

If Urszula was going to talk freely of her work with Solidarity to Bryant, then why not to Ford?

And who was it that had still been visiting Poland, still seeing Urszula, while Bryant was self-denyingly in England, guiding his daughter out of the despair into which first her marriage, then her widowing, had plunged her?

Ford. Ford whose concern for Bryant might seem exaggerated unless you saw it as a reaction to what must have been a devastating onslaught of guilt as he realized that the sister he was protecting by his acts of treachery was indirectly going to have her life destroyed by them. And where was Ford now? So frightened, perhaps, by his certainty that he himself was going to be discovered after his encounter with Jaysmith yesterday that he had decided to make a run for it?

Or better still, already in the hands of Jacob's interrogators who were at last beginning to put two and two together.

It made such sense that he could not see how he had missed it till now, but he was glad he had, for that made it more believable that Jacob and his men had missed it too!

Buoyant once more, he turned into the driveway of Rigg Cottage and, stepping out of his car, stretched his arms and turned his face upwards as though the watery glow in the greying east were the full hot orb of the Mediterranean sun.

'It's a bit late to be looking for broken tiles,' said Miss Wilson sharply from the entrance porch. 'Come you in, before I catch my death.'

He entered and felt at once that sense of comfortable home-coming he had experienced from the start of his acquaintance with the building. Naddle Foot was more spacious, its gardens more elegant, its architecture more distinguished; but Rigg Cottage was a house for living in. At least that was his feeling. But how strong would its associations with her late husband be to Anya? he wondered once more.

Despite her businesslike approach, the old lady did not ignore the social niceties and there was a pot of tea to be drunk and some freshly baked shortbread to be eaten before the sales inspection began. During this interval she questioned him about Bryant's health, receiving the news of the hospital's optimistic prognosis with mild scepticism.

'Well, they're not going to tell him he's dying, are they? Especially as I daresay he's private; no National Health for that one!'

'I wouldn't know about that,' said Jaysmith, whose own vagueness of official identity made him by need as well as for speed a private patient on the rare occasions he consulted a doctor.

'Me, I've stayed National Health,' declared Miss Wilson. 'Me brother's always said I should take out some of this insurance, but I never have, and as I've never ailed more than a cold in the head or a bit of belly ache after someone else's bad cooking these fifty years and more, I must have saved meself a pretty penny.'

She spoke with triumphal emphasis. Jaysmith nodded his approval and drank some more tea. Then the tour began.

The old lady had been meticulous in her preparation for her imminent move. Every article was labelled. Those she was taking with her all had her new address on them plus the room into which they were to go. Of the rest, some pieces were labelled *James*, and *Annie*, and the remainder had blank labels attached. Miss Wilson also provided a check sheet on which the saleroom valuer had indicated his estimate of the likely fetching price of each item.

'It'll be low,' she averred. 'They'll not raise a body's expectations, and likely they'll have some of their own contacts looking to buy up cheap to sell dear. But we'll take it as read, seeing as you've got your feet under the family table, so to speak.'

She said this too neutrally for Jaysmith to be able to gauge an attitude.

His task was easy. He had no furniture of his own and everything in Rigg Cottage looked so much in place that he found himself agreeing to take practically all that was on offer. Miss Wilson ticked off the list and carefully wrote *To Stay* on the blank labels in a still strong, round hand. In the room which had been occupied by Edward Wilson in his youth, he noted that the mountaineering pictures had James Wilson's name on them.

As though to a spoken question, the old lady said, 'I thought they'd bring a bit too much back to Annie, and James is keen to have them. He'll see

292

they get to young Jimmy in the end.'

It was, he thought, a worthwhile acknowledgement of his right to know.

Returning downstairs he said, 'Will you get your solicitor to send me a bill?'

'Don't be daft,' she said. 'I'm not giving him owt else to charge me for. You add it up now and give me a cheque.'

Smiling, he did so.

She folded up the cheque without looking at it and said, 'Will you stay and have a bite of lunch? I got an extra chop, but then James said he wouldn't be in.'

'Your brother's here, is he?'

'I told him he'd best get up quick if he wanted to see the place before it was sold,' said Miss Wilson. 'So, you'll stay then?'

Jaysmith glanced at his watch. It was twenty-twenty.

'I'm sorry,' he said. 'I'd love to but . . .'

'No? Well, no doubt you're a busy man,' she said reproachfully.

He rose to leave and she accompanied him to the front door, then she said, 'Hold on a minute. If you're not staying, I won't waste the chops. I'll come down into the village with you, bank this cheque and call in at my new house. I've got one or two things to do there, and Betty Blacklock next door'll be having some Scotch broth as it's Tuesday and she always makes plenty, even if it does turn out a bit thin.'

She was ready in a minute, leaving her front door key under a stone in the porch, 'in case James comes back,' she announced. Jaysmith wondered if he would ever reach such a level of simple trust in

293

his fellow men when he owned the house. He doubted it.

He dropped her outside the bank.

'You going far?' she said through the car window.

'I thought I'd call in at the Crag and say hello to Mr Parker. Then I'm meeting a friend,' he added hastily in case she should be offended at the thought that he simply preferred a bar-snack to her chop. 'If I see you later, perhaps I can give you a lift back up the hill.'

'No need,' she retorted. 'I'm not quite broken down yet and I reckon I can manage the haul a couple more times. Good day to you!'

It was just on twelve-thirty when he reached the Crag. Doris Parker was busy in the dining room organizing lunch while Phil was in the almost empty bar.

'Mr Hutton!' he said. 'It's good to see you. What'll it be?'

'Whisky, please. How are things?'

'Still pretty busy, thank God. Not in here, but there's a party having lunch. I've got to take these drinks through. If anyone comes in, tell 'em to ring.'

'OK,' said Jaysmith. 'By the way, I'm expecting a telephone call, so if it rings, don't rush. I'll yell if it's not for me.'

'Fair enough,' said Parker and left.

The bar was empty except for a young couple by the fire. After a while they got up and headed for the dining room and Jay took their place by the welcome flames. You probably needed a fire up here even in the middle of summer. He didn't mind the thought of that. There was something sacramental about the business of laying, lighting and enjoying a fire. It sealed a bond between a man and the place he was in. He stretched out his hands and warmed the whisky glass, then slowly drank the golden liquid as if he were drinking the flames themselves. It was a moment of pure tranquillity unsullied by plans or fears or even thought itself.

Then a voice spoke behind him.

'Mr Hutton, isn't it? I thought I recognized you. I'll join you, if I may.'

He looked up, disproportionately aghast. He had not expected this but it was more than a surprise. It felt like an intrusion into the very private places of his soul.

Before him stood Jacob.

CHAPTER TWENTY-EIGHT

To the casual eye, Jacob was a faintly comic rather than a menacing figure. He was dressed very much as an elderly lover of the Lakes might be expected to dress. He wore an ancient dog-tooth tweed jacket with leather patched elbows, a pair of balding and baggy corduroy trousers, and on his head was a shapeless inverted sauce-boat, also of tweed, which may once have been a deerstalker.

Yet Jaysmith felt menaced.

'Sit down,' he said. 'I'll get you a drink.'

'Not yet. Later perhaps,' said Jacob, sitting. 'It's a little early still for me, isn't it? You looked a bit startled, Jay. Why was that?'

'I didn't expect to see you in person,' said Jaysmith.

295

'No, I don't suppose you did. But you can't trust phones, can you, Jay? I was close enough to get here myself, and I wanted very much to see you face to face, Jay. I don't think I'm going to believe what you tell me, not unless I hear it from your own lips. What are you playing at, Jay? Tell me. I'd very much like to know.'

He sounded genuinely anxious rather than angry, though Jaysmith acknowledged he had a right to be both. Yet he was determined he was not going to be put on the defensive.

'I've got reason to believe you've made a mistake in targeting Bryant,' he said flatly. 'I think you've got the wrong man.'

'The wrong man?' echoed Jacob. 'It's not impossible of course. Mistakes do happen, don't they? I take it Adam was a mistake.'

'I'm sorry about Adam,' said Jaysmith, edged off track by the need for self-justification. 'It wasn't my idea. He seemed to need to push for it.'

'Suicide, was it?' The irony was mild.

'A desire to prove something,' said Jaysmith.

'And prove something he did, didn't he?' murmured the older man. 'He was a great admirer of yours, perhaps you knew that?'

'I don't get much fan mail,' said Jaysmith, tiring of these obliquities. 'Now, tell me about Bryant.'

'Oh no. First you must tell me why you want to know, mustn't you? Turn about; and you first, you do see that? It's the only way, unless you're planning to slip a knife between my ribs too, though that would hardly be a solution to your problem, would it?'

'Depends on what my problem is, doesn't it?'

'Indeed it does. Yes, I'm curious, Jay, I admit it.

At first I thought you must have been turned, didn't I? But by what? Money? Perhaps. Conviction? Not likely. In any case, if you'd simply been turned, then you'd simply have warned Bryant and he could have taken off, couldn't he? So do tell, what's it really all about?'

His monkey-like features were crushed up into an expression of almost comic bafflement.

Jaysmith went through the motions of draining his almost empty glass before he spoke.

'All right,' he said. 'I have become ... involved with the Bryant family. It has become important to me that they are not harmed.'

He didn't care for the note of defiance in his voice, like a schoolboy standing up to a strict and feared teacher.

As if to confirm the relationship, Jacob was frowning at him magisterially.

'Involved?' He savoured the word. 'Involved with the Bryant family? As far as I recall, there are only two others. A grandson. And a daughter.'

Jaysmith said, 'I met the daughter.'

He stared unblinkingly at the old man, as if defying him to raise his eyebrows, or smile, or register by any means that he found the situation amusingly absurd. Jacob returned the gaze seriously and said, 'And did your meeting with the daughter pre-date your decision to abort this target?'

'No!' said Jaysmith, feeling ludicrously offended. 'What I told you was the truth. I missed. It was my eyesight. You must have checked with my optician.'

'Indeed,' said Jacob. 'So, you decide to withdraw, to retire, and *then* you meet this woman, is that it?'

Jaysmith nodded.

'And then you discover Bryant is her father. And then, naturally, you start to feel you cannot stand by and let him be killed, do I read you correctly?'

He nodded again. Jacob frowned again.

'You knew this when we met in London,' he stated. 'I remember thinking then you were curiously curious about Bryant, but I put it down to the nostalgia of retirement. Why did you not speak out openly then as you're doing now?'

'I hoped time was of the essence, that with the target deadline passed, the job would be aborted,' said Jaysmith.

'Yes, that makes sense. But it's not all, is it?'

'No,' said Jaysmith with a sigh. 'Of course it's not. I wanted if possible to avoid the . . .'

He sought for a word.

'Contamination,' suggested Jacob softly, almost sympathetically.

'Contamination,' accepted Jaysmith. 'Yes; the contamination of telling you.'

'And what was it you feared would be contaminated? Your desire for this woman?'

'I love her,' said Jaysmith assertively. Then he repeated much more quietly as if for his own benefit, 'I love her.'

There was a silence after this, deep enough, it felt, to last forever, and certainly deep enough to make Jaysmith start like a nervous horse when Phil Parker's voice said, 'Anything you require, gents, while I'm here?'

He had re-entered the bar and was opening a bottle of wine.

Jaysmith said, 'I'll have another Scotch. A large one.'

He ought to keep a clear head, but he needed a drink. He glanced enquiringly at Jacob who said, 'A half a bitter would be nice, wouldn't it?'

Parker poured the drinks. Jaysmith collected them and paid and the hotel owner left the bar with the wine.

Jaysmith resumed his seat and took a long pull at his Scotch, but Jacob just stared thoughtfully at his beer.

'You love her,' he said finally. 'And you'd like to marry her. She's a widow, is she not? Of how long standing?'

'Ten months.'

'Not very long. And there's a child. You'd like to marry her, but what of the child? Dump him on Bryant, perhaps? Is that why you want to keep him alive?'

There was a note of scorn in his voice which stung Jaysmith.

'Don't be offensive!' he rasped. 'I love the boy too, but even if I didn't, I wouldn't expect a woman like Anya to agree to being separated from him more than the length of a honeymoon.'

'*Honeymoon!*' said Jacob, his squashed-up face almost straightening out in amazement. 'You're a man of unsuspected fantasy, Jay. Marriage! Honeymoon! Aren't you forgetting something, Jay? Aren't you forgetting what you are? What makes you think that after a career like yours, you're fit for any close human relationship, let alone something so impossibly intimate as marriage? Have you told this woman about yourself? *Will* you tell her about yourself? What do you imagine she will say, Jay, when you tell her about the men you've killed? What do you imagine she will say?'

299

The savagery of the attack reduced Jaysmith to silence for a moment. He felt great anger, and also the beginnings of despair as one part of his mind acknowledged the justice of what Jacob had said. Yet he knew that the road of introspective analysis was a dangerous diversion at this time and place.

'That's between me and her,' he said harshly. 'But one thing's certain. Feeling for her the way I do, I can't stand by and see her father killed.'

After his outburst, Jacob had immediately relapsed into his customary mask of puzzled enquiry.

'Of course not,' he said softly. 'And the purpose of this meeting is to persuade me and my masters to change our minds, is it?'

'To persuade *you*, Jacob,' said Jaysmith wearily. 'I'm sure you are quite capable of taking care of your masters, whoever they are. Listen to me, Jacob. I know it sounds absurd, the way you put it. But I'm not just asking a favour; and I'm not just offering a threat, though I've got a threat to offer, believe me. But what I genuinely believe is that you've got the wrong man!'

'You said that before,' said Jacob. 'Then you asked me to tell you why Bryant was targeted. If you don't know why, then you can't know he's the wrong man, can you?'

'I think I do know why,' said Jaysmith. 'But I'd like to hear it from the horse's mouth.'

At last Jacob reached for his glass, raised it and slowly sipped the bitter.

'The beer's different up here, isn't it?' he said. 'It's earthier somehow. More straightforwardly *beery*. I'm not sure if I prefer it. But some things should be plain and straightforward, shouldn't they? Perhaps our relationship is one of those things. I've no right to tell you anything about Bryant, and you've no right to ask. Incidentally it's odd, isn't it? You didn't need to know anything about him when you set out to kill, only that he was guilty and a foreigner! It's only since you've decided to save his life that you've become curious. Still, despite all this, I'm going to tell you as much as I can.'

He paused as if to consider and approve his own assertion, then resumed.

'Bryant is intermittently and in a small way one of our Iron Curtain couriers. He had got himself established as a regular visitor to Poland before we started using him and though that doesn't make him perfectly safe, it increases his chance of success. Anyway, he's not really very important, one of a dozen like him. Unfortunately he has got himself into a relationship with someone who *is* important, a Polish woman who's a fairly key figure in subversive circles in the Krakow district. UBEK, their secret police who are KGB trained and eager to outshine their masters, have discovered the situation and used it rather nicely, I think. Because the woman loves Bryant, she talks freely to him; and because Bryant loves the woman he talks freely to UBEK. Now isn't that a nice economic bit of organization!'

'But this is crazy!' interrupted Jaysmith. 'Even if it's true, it doesn't justify him as a target. He can be stopped, simply by arresting him! Or used, by feeding him false information! Why kill him, for God's sake?'

'I think you underestimate the damage he has caused,' said Jacob gravely. 'People have died and

301

disappeared because of Bryant. Not just Solidarity people either. What he has told UBEK together with what they suspect already has pointed them towards some of our own people. One was killed just recently. They tried to make it look accidental. There's an unwritten rule which says you don't kill agents. Politicians, generals, public figures of importance, they're all fair game, but not agents. That's why Bryant has to go, and go with a bang, so to speak. It's an unambiguous statement that we know what's been going on, that we know what happened to our man was not an accident, and that it had better stop here if they don't want a general escalation.'

'And for this you'll kill him? As a gesture?'

Jaysmith sucked at the melted ice which was all that remained of his second Scotch. He desperately wanted another one, but there was no time.

Jacob said, 'Don't sound so horrified, Jay. Retirement doesn't rub out the last twenty years, you know.'

He didn't rise to the gibe, but said, 'I still think you've got the wrong man.'

'Do you now? But then who is the right one? I presume you have a candidate?'

'Anton Ford,' he said. It was curious but now he came to state the man's name, this too felt like a betrayal. He'd only met the man twice, he found that he quite liked him, and now it seemed to him that his accusation was based on little more than a flimsy web of circumstantial evidence, interpreted with extreme bias.

Nor was Jacob impressed.

'Anton Ford, is it?' he said. 'Well, it would have to be, wouldn't it? Who else do you know to put on

302

your short list, Jay? But go on. Explain your thinking.'

He argued his case as best he could. Oddly, though it sounded weaker on Ford's guilt than he'd hoped, it sounded stronger on Bryant's innocence than he'd expected.

'So you've got to admit there's a reasonable doubt,' he concluded. 'Ford's just as strong a candidate as Bryant. Stronger, I'd say. As I say, Bryant's only been in contact with Urszula by mail for a good year now, so how the hell can he be responsible for anything that's happened recently?'

'As you know, Jay, we're not in the reasonable doubt business,' said Jacob. 'That's for lawyers. As for Bryant's communications with Poland, there have been other channels.'

The bar door opened and a group of people came in, but Jaysmith ignored them.

'What the hell do you mean, other channels?' he demanded, his voice rising so that heads turned his way.

Jacob said disapprovingly, 'Please, Jay, we don't want to look like a pair of quarrelling queens, do we? What you've told me about Ford has made me think, I must admit. We've got him of course. We picked him up on his way from Naddle Foot yesterday. He's quite close. That's why I came up here, actually, to have a chat to him. Your own little invitation just fell quite fortunately, and I diverted here as soon as I heard about it. So why don't we go and see Ford together? I'm not unsympathetic to your dilemma, believe me. If I can be even half persuaded, well, a gesture which kills the wrong man would have them laughing from here to the Urals, and I don't care to be

303

laughed at. Will you join me? Clearly we mustn't go on talking here. Bored British holidaymakers are the best eavesdroppers in the world.'

It was said most naturally and Jaysmith's instinctive reaction was to rise and accompany the other without question.

Instead he shook his head.

'First, there's something you should know,' he said. 'Just to make sure that I don't end up staying with Ford.'

'Ah yes. The threat. I'd really begun to believe it was simply that you would use your own talents to remove anyone who tried to remove Bryant. Like poor Adam. But it's more than that, is it?'

From his pocket Jaysmith took one of the sheets he had photocopied that morning. He passed it over.

Jacob read it without changing expression.

'Very impressive,' he said. 'I'd forgotten some of these. And I see we have an anniversary too. Many happy returns. With a *curriculum vitae* like this one you could easily get a job in South America, I should think. Mind you, they would probably want to take up your references. After all, anyone could compile such a list and claim to have carried out all these assassinations under the auspices of any government he cared to nominate.'

'I'm not applying for a job, Jacob,' said Jaysmith.' 'I've arranged for a copy of this *curriculum vitae*, confession, call it what you will, to be sent to the authorities in every country concerned and to newspapers also. As for references, that was easy. One thing I've always left behind me is a single bullet. Accompanying each of these sheets will be a bullet fired this morning from

304

my M21. I've used that rifle on more than half of my kills. A simple forensic check will confirm the bullets are from the same weapon. The earlier ones will just have to take it on trust, or cross check with a friendly country later on the list. I think this should cause a lot more embarrassment than your masters would be able to tolerate, don't you?'

'Perhaps,' said Jacob, showing little concern. 'And when does this get sent out?'

'Oh, in a couple of days, unless my distributor hears from me in a very specific way.'

'Very ingenious,' approved Jacob, returning the sheet. 'But totally unnecessary. Shall we go now?'

He led the way out of the bar. Outside the air was gloomy despite the earliness of the hour. The sun was buried deep beneath a turbulent sea of cloud.

'Is it far?' asked Jaysmith as they reached the BMW.

'Not far. Pointless taking two cars, I think. Will you drive?'

'I don't mind,' said Jaysmith, unlocking the passenger door and letting Jacob in.

As he walked round to the driver's door, a voice called to him.

He turned. Approaching with a look of angry determination on her face was Miss Wilson. In her hand she clutched a piece of paper which she waved in his face.

'I've just stood an age in a queue in that bank and when I got to the counter they wouldn't accept your cheque,' she said wrathfully.

'I'm sorry, but why not?'

'Well, look at it! You've put the wrong date. It's not 1963, is it? You're twenty years out.'

305

He examined the cheque. She was right.

He said, 'I'm sorry, I don't know what I was thinking of,' as he altered and initialled it.

But he knew very well what he had been thinking of. That date was carved on his mind like many other dates. He had written it only this morning on the sheet which he had just shown to Jacob.

Twenty years before, on this day in 1963, he had shot Colonel Tai.

He returned the cheque to Miss Wilson whose attention seemed to have been diverted. She had spotted Jacob in the front seat of the car and was looking at him with puzzlement. He opened the door and got out, glancing towards a black Metro parked along by the exit from the car park. Its door opened. A man got out and began walking rapidly towards them. He wore an anorak with the hood up and his head was bowed against the wind but there was something familiar about him. Jaysmith, however, found his attention diverted by a puzzling turn in Miss Wilson's conversation.

'So this is where you got to,' she said accusingly. 'And what are you up to, I wonder?'

She was not, he realized, addressing him.

'Just a friendly chat, isn't that right, Mr Hutton,' replied Jacob.

Full of bewildered suspicion, Jaysmith rasped, 'What's going on, Jacob?'

'Jacob!' exclaimed Miss Wilson. 'Well, I've not heard anyone call him that since our father died. Muriel, he'd say, you're a rough tough lass and if you'd been a lad, I should have called you Esau. But as for this other smooth young thing, I just about got him right. James; which they used to call *Jacobus*; my second born, Jacob, the smooth man!'

306

The man from the Metro was close now, his familiarity confirmed. Under the monklike hood was the beard-shadowed face of Davey, Adam's glue-sniffing companion and lover. His right hand in his anorak pocket was bulkier than a hand ought to be. But Jaysmith had no mental capacity to spare for such minor matters as this.

'What the hell's going on?' he repeated.

Jacob smiled at him and said, 'You are, of course, already acquainted with my dear old sister, aren't you, Mr Hutton?'

'Of course he is,' said Miss Wilson contemptuously. 'He's buying my house, isn't he? And he knows just whose house he is buying, James; and he knows it's nowt to do with you. Nowt at all. I don't know what he's been saying to you, but it's mine to sell, and the deal's settled.'

Jaysmith was too dumbfounded by this turn of events to do more than nod, but this seemed to satisfy the old lady.

'Right then,' she said. 'Now I'll be off and see if they'll take this cheque this time. But I'm not standing in a queue again. I made that clear. I know where he's at, I said, and I'll be back when I get this sorted, but I'll not stand in any queue again!'

She turned on her heel and stumped away.

Davey was standing close behind Jaysmith now and he felt an unmistakable hardness against his spine but his mind was still racing too fast for him to concern himself with the trivia of here and now.

'I hope you haven't changed your mind,' said James Wilson. 'But just in case you have, let Davey here persuade you to change it back.'

'No need for Davey,' said Jaysmith. 'No need at

307

all. You and I have a lot of talking to do, Mr Wilson.'

He got into the car. Jacob nodded at Davey who with some reluctance retreated towards the Metro.

'Let's go,' said Jacob, resuming his seat and slamming the door.

CHAPTER TWENTY-NINE

He drove slowly and with great care out of Grasmere. There was deep in his mind a turbulence of question, revelation, doubt and accusation, but he felt no desperate need to uncap the well and relieve the pressure. It was as if his will had been suspended and his own sense of personality reduced to a dancing atom in the inconceivable unity of the heavy fells and the roaring wind and the surging sky.

He asked and received no directions. Jacob, as he must still think of him, seemed as little inclined to speech as he was, but sat staring gloomily out of the window as though understanding but not approving the desolate scene. Occasionally the wind would tear open a gap in the cloud and a pillar of sunlight would tremble momentarily on a peak or in a valley before collapsing under the weight of the sky. One such pillar lasted longer than the other, focusing like a spotlight beam on the dramatic bulk of the Castle Rock of Triermain, and this brought Jaysmith to his first awareness that he had driven nearly ten miles in this trancelike state and was now heading into St-John's-in-the-Vale on the road which would take him back to Naddle Foot.

The realization was enough to break the paralysing spell. Naddle Foot was no place he wanted to be in the company of the man by his side. And not just Jacob. A glance in the rear-view mirror confirmed what he had already subconsciously known, that the black Metro was matching the BMW's pace a couple of hundred yards behind.

Things were falling into place in his mind which made a long, intimate conversation with Jacob very desirable. But a conversation without witnesses. Probably when he revealed to Jacob what he now guessed, the other man wouldn't want witnesses either. But he wasn't about to consult him.

He slammed down the accelerator of the BMW. The car surged forward and in a few seconds on the twisting road was out of sight of the Metro. It was probably possible simply to outrun the smaller car, though there was no guarantee what kind of engine might be hidden beneath its bonnet. In any case, Jaysmith did not fancy a high-speed car chase along this narrow road. But he kept his foot hard down till ahead on the right he saw the angled track which led up to the disused quarry he had visited four days earlier. He had replaced the rusty iron bar which blocked the entry, but knew it rested lightly on rotten posts.

Swinging the wheel hard over, he went through it with hardly any loss of speed, racing up the steep track, rounded the bend at the top and, to ensure minimum visibility from the road, sent the car grinding up the steep bank of waste which bounded the amphitheatre of the quarry till the engine stalled.

He pulled the handbrake on and in the ensuing silence they heard the roar of the Metro's engine as it screamed by below them along the road.

Jacob did not speak but peered forward with mild curiosity at the ravaged face of the fell. He appeared quite unmoved by the sudden violence of Jaysmith's driving.

'Now that's what I call a view,' he said finally.

It was difficult to tell if he was being ironic.

'Let's talk,' said Jaysmith harshly.

'Yes.'

'About Bryant.'

'If you like.'

'Yes, I bloody well like! Bryant's no spy, no traitor, is he?'

'There is some evidence, wouldn't you say?' said Jacob judiciously.

'Of course there's evidence! When you decided you wanted him killed and that I should do your dirty work for you, of course you made sure there was evidence! Even *you* are answerable to someone!'

'Yes, I am, aren't I? And to experts too.'

'Then you must have made a bloody good job of it. How far did you go, Jacob? Did you just grab at opportunity or did you actually provide the bodies too?'

Jacob's eyes opened a little wide in a faint parody of surprise.

'You mean, did I betray my own people just to point a finger at Bryant? Come on, Jay, that's a bit much, isn't it? Why on earth should I do a thing like that?'

'Because you're totally unbalanced,' said Jaysmith contemptuously. 'I'd like to believe that it was your precious son's death that tipped you over, but by all accounts he was such a nutter himself, he must have got it from somewhere!'

This made contact. Jacob turned a little pale and rubbed the back of his neck as though attacked by a sudden pain. But his voice remained as controlled and unconcerned as ever as he replied.

'Why do you say all this, Jay?' he asked. 'What do you think I have done?'

'I think,' said Jaysmith slowly, 'that when your boy, Edward, died, you were devastated. Perhaps it was something you knew of him, or something he'd said, or something Bryant said, or perhaps it was simply good old parental pride that made you dissatisfied. Perhaps it was the hint of suicide . . .'

'Not that,' interrupted Jacob swiftly. 'Not Edward. He was strong, positive; he loved the dangers of climbing, he told me that; he found them exhilarating, and he loved pushing himself to the limit; but he wouldn't slacken the odds in that way. In the end he might have fallen to his death, that was always on the cards; but not off a piffling rock face in the Lake District; not because he'd decided not to take his injection!'

'No? What did you imagine had happened then?' demanded Jaysmith.

'This is your show, isn't it?' replied the other. 'You tell me what I imagined.'

'I'm not sure if you imagined anything. Or perhaps you imagined everything. You must have had some idea of the kind of man he was, some idea of the kind of hell Anya had to live through. So you decided to take a closer look at her father, at Bryant. You had the home burgled, didn't you? Your boys really turned it over. It was a happy

311

chance that Bryant had done some courier work for the department. That gave you an excuse. Information received. Perhaps already a little evidence planted. But you found nothing except the letters from Ford's sister. Was that the first you knew of the affair? God, they must have been discreet! And Ford was acting as an intermediary, so you sent your boys to talk to him. What were they looking for? Anything? Nothing? Something damaging to Bryant, simply because you didn't much like Bryant? But they came up with gold. They came up with the business of the insulin capsules, didn't they? And suddenly Bryant wasn't just a pain in the arse, a man you didn't like, the guardian of and father-substitute for your grandson and namesake, young Jimmy. He was a murderer! Edward's killer! You must have wanted to kill him with your own hands then. But that's not your way, is it, Jacob? You've always been a setter-on, a man of stratagem rather than a man of action. You targeted him. You put him at the end of my gun.'

'And that was an error, wasn't it?' murmured Jacob.

'You don't deny it then? None of it?' cried Jaysmith.

'How strange. I think you'd really prefer it if I denied it all, wouldn't you? Why? Because it would make you less of a tool? But that's all you've ever been, Jay. At first I had hopes of you, high hopes. After Jacob, Jaysmith. A nice line of succession. But soon I saw what you were. A simple craftsman with no potential for partnership! A weapon, a hit-man, nothing more.'

'Nothing more,' echoed Jaysmith. 'You may be right. But that didn't entitle you to use me as a

312

private executioner, Jacob! That didn't entitle you to turn me into a simple murderer!'

Jacob laughed, a metallic grating sound, as if old, long-disused cogs were being forced into movement.

'There's your weakness,' he said. 'All these years you've acted the hard emotionless executioner, but always you needed reasons. Or not even reasons, just reassurances. You had to be convinced that everyone you killed deserved his death as much as poor old Tai! Not that he deserved it all that much. He was only doing his job, wasn't he? And that little yellow girl of yours, Nguyet, wasn't it? She really was a communist subversive, wasn't she? Didn't she ever tell you that? Or did she too work out that what her naive young Englishman wanted was reassurance, not truth!'

Jaysmith felt rage surging up from his belly to his brain. Only the sense that Jacob was deliberately provoking him in an effort to direct his own mind from his own actions and reactions enabled him to keep control.

'All right,' he said quietly. 'Perhaps I did need that reassurance about my targets. That makes it all the worse to have pointed me at Bryant.'

'You fool!' said Jacob contemptuously. 'In your simplistic terms, half the men you've killed have probably been twice as innocent as Bryant! At least I condemned him for a crime; most of the others died for the sake of a policy!'

Suddenly the rain came, lashing the windows on the breath of a wind which shook the car. Down the distant fell slopes, the summer-browned grass seemed to run in panic from the line of mist that the violent blasts were driving into the valley.

313

Closer, the shattered quarry face met this latest assault with the indifference of old pain. Then the rain was cascading down the windscreen and the desolate world outside the car was reduced to a damp nothing.

So, thought Jaysmith dully. Now I know. I am Faustus, after all. My soul sold for twenty years of emptiness, of ignorance, of simple misuse. No profit or delight. A simple public hangman.

'Come now, Jay,' said Jacob with something approaching glee. 'Don't take it to heart. Remember what Eichmann said in his glass box. You were only following orders!'

There was no conscious reaction, just a distant cry of rage and despair in a voice he recognized as his own. Then his hands were at Jacob's throat. The older man's strength of resistance was surprising but it could not have sufficed, and his face was flushing a streaky purple when the door was dragged open and Davey slammed his pistol barrel hard against the side of Jaysmith's head.

He fell back in his seat with the tacky hotness of blood oozing down his neck and over his collar. The muzzle of Davey's gun was boring into his jaw line. He looked up into the man's face and to his dull surprise saw there a physical longing to squeeze the trigger.

It was Jacob who prevented or at least prorogued this.

Massaging his throat, he croaked, 'You took your time, didn't you?'

'I had to turn round,' growled Davey. 'Shall we get on with it?'

'Soon. Get in the back, will you?'

The bearded man slipped into the back seat.

Rain was streaming off his bulky anorak and Jaysmith found himself thinking of the mess it would make on the upholstery. It was interesting how the mind found its escape routes from horrific reality. He should know, better than most. Bloodstains, of course, would be far worse than water.

Gingerly he raised his hand to his head. Behind him Davey moved menacingly.

'It's all right,' said Jacob, some of his old calm returning with his old voice. 'Jay, you're bleeding.'

'Just a bit. There's a first-aid kit in the glove compartment.'

'Be my guest,' said Jacob.

Jaysmith slowly reached forward across the man in the passenger seat. With luck, Jacob's body would screen him just long enough to get hold of Adam's gun and blow a hole in Davey before the bearded man had time to do the same to him. With luck.

Taking a deep breath, he opened the glove compartment door.

He could have saved himself the anxiety. The HK P9 was gone.

No one spoke. He took the compact first-aid box out, opened it, removed a lint pad and a small antiseptic spray, sprayed the pad, put the aerosol back in the box, and closed and replaced it as he pressed the pad to the back of his head.

'That's better,' he said. 'Don't want to die of blood poisoning. Jacob, I'm sorry. It was stupid to lose my temper like that.'

'You wouldn't be trying to humour me, would you?' said Jacob, still gently massaging his neck.

'I'm trying to find the least damaging route through all this for everyone,' snapped Jaysmith.

315

'And what do you suggest?'

'Go ahead. Kill Bryant. I know you don't want to harm Anya and the boy. That's why I had the time limit, wasn't it? They were staying with you till the Sunday! So, kill Bryant, but make it look like natural causes for the girl's sake, for your grandson's sake.'

This clearly took Jacob by surprise, as it was intended to.

'Kill Bryant but make it look natural? You know, Jay, you almost sound like the man I once hoped you'd be! It's well suggested, well argued. But what about you?'

Jaysmith shrugged. It was painful. He wanted to say that his own fate didn't matter but doubted if such altruism would impress the other.

So he said, 'I'll do what I should have done in the first place. Slip quietly out of view. Of course, you might have some other ideas, but don't forget my little bundle of *billets doux*.'

Jacob relapsed into a reverie, his fingers steepled together under his chin, his monkey face, whose features Jaysmith now knew he had half recognized behind the beard in the photos of Edward Wilson, completely still. The rain had stopped as suddenly as it had started as the wind which had brought it now drove the clouds further east, dragging a train of light blue sky behind them. The change was almost springlike in its violence, and not much more trustworthy than spring.

Jacob roused himself.

'Looks a bit brighter now, Davey,' he said. 'I think I'll go on to the house. You'll look after Mr Jaysmith, will you?'

'My pleasure.'

316

'Jacob,' said Jaysmith in alarm. 'What are you going to do?'

'Now you mustn't worry,' reassured the older man. 'I'm just going to pay a call on my daughter-in-law and her father, what's wrong with that? Perfectly natural, isn't it!'

He opened the door and stepped out of the car, then turned and stooped to address Jaysmith once more.

'You got most things right,' he said approvingly. 'Except about yourself. I don't like the sound of your *billets doux* as you call them. In fact I didn't like the sound of them from the moment my listener heard Bryant ring his office to say that you were to have the freedom of the copying machine. So I had a word with Davey here. Show him, Davey.'

The bearded man reached into the capacious side pocket of his waterproof and pulled out a package. It had been opened. He handed it to Jacob who looked at the address.

'A bank manager in Brighton!' he exclaimed. 'What is it, Jay? A small account for emergencies? *Please dispatch the enclosed by airmail where appropriate on the first day of October and debit my account.* Signed *Henry Collins.* Jay, we didn't know about this, honestly. How clever of you! In Brighton. And using your own name. I am right, aren't I? It's been so long. It is your own name, isn't it? That's the cleverness of it, hiding behind your real name. Don't look so shocked. I know we like to think the Royal Mail is sacrosanct, but nothing is out of our reach, you know that now, don't you, Jay? And don't worry, by the way; Davey got both packages, didn't you, Davey? Including

317

the fail-safe one addressed to your bank manager in Switzerland.'

'What are you going to do?' said Jaysmith dully.

'What I said. Go down to the house. Talk a little. Jimmy will still be at school, so we can have a really good adult talk. There's another thing you didn't get quite right, Jay. Yes, I was suspicious; yes, I sent a team in to go over Bryant's house. But it wasn't Bryant I wanted investigated; it was my precious daughter-in-law! Finding those letters and what they led to was just a stroke of luck. Bryant arranged everything, that much is clear, but she connived; she'd driven poor Edward halfway to despair with her insensitive, carping stupidity! She's just as guilty as Bryant, more guilty in my eyes. That's why I decided he should go first, so she could feel the pain of loss she had never felt when Edward died!'

'First?' Jaysmith seized upon the crucial word. 'First?'

'Oh yes. She had her chance to survive. I wouldn't willingly deprive Jimmy of a mother, you see. But after Edward's death she refused my offer of a home and protection, and settled with her murdering father. Even then, even when I knew what the pair of them had done, I gave her another chance. I asked her again when she and the boy visited me a few weeks ago. She was adamant. She was almost insolent. I offered everything, comfort, money, the best of education for Jimmy. I'm entitled to a close involvement, don't you agree, Jay? After what I've lost. Don't you agree?'

'Yes, yes, I agree,' cried Jaysmith aghast. 'But you won't do anything against her now, will you? Listen, once her father's dead, she'll need someone

318

to turn to. It'll be natural for her to turn to you . . .'

'That's what I thought before,' said Jacob softly. 'If you'd done your job properly, Jay, I'd have been with her when the news arrived. I'd have seen her pain, I might have profited from her grief. But you botched the job, didn't you? And now things have moved on. Now she's got to know everything; what her father did; who I am; and who you are too, Jay. That's part of it also. She's got to suffer! Ten months in his grave, not even a year, ten little months and what's this grieving widow doing? Fornicating with a stranger, fornicating with a hapless, rootless, middle-aged killer, the first man to push his body at her. God, she must have been desperate!'

He opened the passenger door and got out, then stooped to address Jaysmith further.

'Really desperate,' he said softly. 'It wouldn't surprise me if she started looking at that goatish father of hers with speculative eyes. I mean, tucked away together in that nice isolated house, it wouldn't surprise me if from time to time . . .'

There was no chance of getting anywhere near the throat this time. Indeed his outstretched hands hadn't even made contact with the tweed jacket before Davey's gun had ploughed a new furrow along his skull and he collapsed across the passenger seat, crying out in rage and pain.

'You're useless, you know that, Jay?' said Jacob with contempt. 'You're going to die, of course. Davey here will take care of that. And Bryant will die, and my daughter-in-law too. In that order. Fortunately I'll be around to take care of Jimmy. He'll be all right, believe me. I'll see to that. He'll have the best, the very best of everything. So don't

319

take it too badly, Jay. You'd have had to go anyway, even with none of this. A weak man in retirement gets to thinking, gets to worrying about his life. And his after-life. We don't like deathbed confessions, Jay, so if necessary we anticipate the deathbed. And you were a likely candidate. I'll tell you why. I checked up with your optician. And he confirmed that you'd been to see him about your sight. He agreed with you, of course; at his prices, he's not going to fall out with his patients. But what he told me was that there was no physical reason whatsoever for the trouble you were having with your right eye. No reason whatever! It's your mind that's getting things out of focus, Jay. Just your mind. I suspect you may find something comfortable in that. If you do, then good luck to you. And goodbye, Jay. Goodbye.'

He slammed the door and walked away, nimble for his age on the steep and shaley slope. Soon he disappeared round the turn and a moment later Jaysmith heard the Metro's engine burst into life then slowly fade away as the car reversed down to the road.

Davey's gun pressed hard against his neck.

'And now, sunshine,' said the bearded man, 'there's only you and me.'

CHAPTER THIRTY

Jaysmith sat up slowly and turned to face his captor. The bearded man regarded him without expression but there was nothing inexpressive about the way he held his gun. It was a SIG-Sauer

320

P230 automatic, of combined Swiss-German manufacture, beautifully made, very accurate, and as little likely to jam as any weapon on the market. Jaysmith's only immediate consolation was that whatever fate was planned for him probably did not involve having him found with a bullet in his brain.

He said thickly because the taste of pain was still in his mouth, 'What's the plan, Davey?'

The bearded man stared blankly at him. Jaysmith guessed that he was working out which would be more distressing to his prisoner, knowledge or ignorance.

He opted for knowledge.

Davey said, 'Jacob's going to take care of them at the house. He'll use the Heckler Koch, the one you took from Adam. It's plastered with your prints, isn't it? They said you were clever, Jaysmith. That wasn't so fucking clever. There'll be other signs too, all adding up to you fancying a slice of the lady, the lady objecting, daddy intervening, you going berserk. You'll be missing, natch. The mysterious third person, the stranger in the house. Crazy with guilt, you've driven like a lunatic up into the hills. Somewhere up there, in the mist, on a narrow twisting road, you'll have an accident. Or perhaps it will be suicide. Either way, this thing will turn over and over, breaking your neck. Perhaps there'll be a fire too. How's that grab you, Mr Jaysmith?'

'It's crazy!' said Jaysmith. 'What's worse is that it's personal. For Christ's sake, Davey, what are you getting yourself into? You heard Jacob. You know this has nothing to do with his job, with *your* job. It's unofficial! It's private! You'll be crazy to get involved!'

321

The words suddenly felt prophetic as he realized there was something indisputably unbalanced about the way the man was looking at him. Nor was the overtight control of his voice as he replied reassuring.

He said slowly, 'You're right, Mr Jaysmith. It is private. It is personal. You remember Adam?'

Jaysmith knew what was coming now.

'Yes,' he said sadly. 'I remember Adam.'

'He was my friend,' said Davey. 'He was my very good friend. You mother-fucking bastard! We were married! Do you understand that? Married!'

His voice had cracked into a harsh high scream and the gun was rammed deep into Jaysmith's throat and he could see that the man needed only the flimsiest of excuses to pull the trigger.

He kept perfectly still and perfectly quiet, refusing to meet the glaring, accusing eyes, hardly breathing even. Gradually Davey relaxed.

'I'm sorry,' said Jaysmith. 'I didn't . . . realize.'

The gun jabbed at him but, thank God, more in emphasis now than threat.

'You didn't *realize*? What does that mean? That you knew we were screwing together, but didn't realize that a pair of perverted puffs could actually love each other, and feel pain and loss and grief? Is that what you mean? And tell me this, Jaysmith, if you had realized, what fucking difference would it have made?'

'No difference,' said Jaysmith quietly. 'I told him all I wanted was to come in with him and make contact with Jacob. But he had to try for me. It was his choice. You knew him, you were close to him. You must be able to tell if that'd be the way he'd have played it.'

322

'Oh yes. That'd be the way,' said Davey. 'That was Adam. But don't start thinking that makes a difference, Mr fucking Jaysmith. No difference! No difference whatso-fucking-ever! I loved him and you killed him and I don't give a shit what's in this for Jacob. I'd get down on my knees and I'd stick my head up his arse for the chance to kill you, you know that, Mr Jaysmith? Up to my bottom lip!'

There were tears in the man's eyes. It might have been touching if Jaysmith had been in the mood to be touched; it should have been frightening if Jaysmith had not moved far beyond the significance of fear.

'So what happens now?' he asked.

'I'm going to lock you in the boot of this car,' said Davey in a matter-of-fact tone. 'That's how Adam ended up, wasn't it? Packed in the boot of his car. Not a nice big comfortable boot like yours, but folded and twisted and crushed, like a sack of garbage!'

The matter-of-factness was going. Hastily Jaysmith said, 'And then, what then?'

'Don't you listen, man? Like I said, drive you somewhere nice and high and lonely, and I put you back in the front seat, and I see you over the edge. Then I'll scramble down and make sure you're dead.'

'Just like Adam should've done with Bryant,' said Jaysmith.

'No! He made it up as he went along. That was his trouble, Adam. He was always acting on impulse, playing it off the top of his skull. In bed, that was fine, Christ yes, that was bloody marvellous. But out on a job, you follow instructions to the letter. He never really grasped that, poor love. And it killed him.'

'But you follow instructions? And I presume Jacob wants me alive when the car goes over?'

'Oh yes,' said Davey. 'But don't get any ideas, sunshine. He's given me carte blanche to deal with you any which way I like, as long as the marks gell with a car smash. And if they don't, like I say, I can always burn them off, can't I? So out you get and walk slowly round to the boot.'

Davey got out of the car and kept the automatic trained unwaveringly on Jaysmith as he followed suit.

'You'll need the keys,' said Jaysmith, taking them from the ignition. 'Catch.'

He threw them a yard to the right of Davey. They skittered past him down the slope. The man's eyes did not even flicker towards them as he retreated, perfectly balanced despite the steep and uneven track, to a point a couple of yards behind the car.

'You pathetic old man,' he said. 'Come forward slowly and pick 'em up.'

Jaysmith obeyed, his own footwork much more unsure as he felt the full effect of the blows.

'Now open the boot.'

As Jaysmith inserted the key in the lock, he knew that his last chance was approaching fast. Davey would not want him in the boot, alive and literally kicking as they drove to the chosen accident site. And to knock him unconscious he would have to come close.

But the bearded man was taking no chances.

'Now climb in,' he ordered from his safe shooting distance. 'And lie down.'

Jaysmith looked at the boot floor. Beneath that

324

false panel was his rucksack, especially constructed to carry the stripped-down M21. Even if he remained conscious, was there any chance that he could get it out and assemble it and have it ready to fire when Davey reopened the lid?

He doubted it. The boot was roomy, but it would need someone as double-jointed as Houdini to unfasten and raise the panel while lying on it.

'Get in!' yelled Davey angrily. 'Or I swear I'll finish this here and now!'

'I'm getting! I'm getting!'

He climbed in, moving awkwardly as an old, tired man might be expected to. It was a piece of play-acting that came easy.

'Now crouch down, on all fours. Hold it there!'

He rested still. He would have to lie flat before the lid could be closed, but now he guessed Davey's intention.

To render him quiescent for the next half-hour or so, he was just going to come close enough to bring the boot lid crashing down on his head.

Davey was out of his line of vision. He strained his ears through the gusting wind to hear the sound of his approach. There would be a moment when he would raise both arms to bring the lid down with maximum force. Just a moment. A second too soon and the SIG-Sauer would still be aimed; a second too late and his head would be cracked open by the solid metal.

A stone rattled close behind. He counted two seconds, daren't wait another.

He swung his right hand up over his left shoulder. In it he held the small antiseptic aerosol which he had palmed as he pretended to replace it in the first-aid box. Now the sleight of hand which had so delighted Jimmy was all that stood between him and the warping of the boy's life forever. He only had a fractional moment's touch to tell him he had the nozzle pointed the right way and there was no chance for a sighting aim.

He squeezed the nozzle and held it down for a long long burst before twisting round to see what had happened.

He had been lucky. The squirt of antiseptic spray had taken Davey full in the left eye. The bearded man screamed in shock and pain, but he was still able to see Jaysmith scrambling awkwardly towards him and to bring the gun in his upraised hand crashing down on his head.

Now it was Jaysmith's turn to ignore pain and attack. The steepness of the slope and the height of the boot meant that gravity compensated in part for the rubberiness of his limbs. He fell upon Davey in the literal sense, taking another blow to the skull which robbed him of almost all his power to grapple with the man. The best he could do was press close and involve him in a tangle of limbs which would at least inhibit use of the gun. Meanwhile his fingers scrabbled in the earth, muddied by the recent deluge, seeking for a stick, a stone, anything which could be used as a weapon.

All he got was a handful of splintered shale which crumbled in his grasp. At the same time, the younger man's strength was taking control. Jaysmith felt himself thrown off his opponent's body like a dozing cat flicked off a favourite chair. He fell on his back and tried to scrabble his way back up the slope to take refuge beneath the car. Not that it would have been any refuge if Davey had decided to use the gun. But now, either out of care for Jacob's command or his own vengeful lust to inflict maximum pain, he chose not to fire. Instead, scrambling to his feet, he offered to help Jaysmith's progress uphill by swinging his fell boot into the recumbent man's crotch.

Jaysmith twisted away from the blow, managing to absorb some of its force on his inner thigh instead of his genitals, but the pain still seared his body like a red-hot file being twisted in his guts from his groin to his heart. His pain and terror almost took him to the doubtful sanctuary of the boot, but now Davey was standing right over him, using the gun as a club once more, smashing down at his skull and face. He felt his nose go and suspected that the blow which loosened several of his teeth must also have cracked his jaw. Dully he thought that there was no way that these injuries were going to look as if they'd been received in a car crash, but the thought brought no consolation. Davey must know he'd passed that point also. Now he had put Jacob's plan quite out of his mind and was striking for the sheer pleasure of it.

The gun barrel caught him on the right temple, splitting it open and sending a blinding gash of blood into his eye. He cried out, a bubbling, whimpering cry of despair trailing off into a complete silence as his body went slack. His head twisted to one side and was still, and no breath seeped out with the blood and mucus oozing from his gaping mouth.

Davey hesitated, the gun poised for another blow.

'You bastard!' he cried. 'Don't die yet. You bastard!'

The feeble flick of Jaysmith's right wrist, the

327

ponderous kick of his left leg, should have been as meaningless as the last spasms of any dying man. But the flick sent the handful of shale into Davey's eyes, and the kick caught him where the ulnar nerve stretches tautly over the elbow, sending an electric shock of pain running up his forearm till it passed out of the irresistibly splayed fingers of his hand.

The gun fell, hit a stone and, instead of sliding away down the slope, bounced up and under the boot. Davey could have finished his opponent merely by dropping to his knees on his belly. Instead he dived sideways to retrieve the gun.

It was at best a brief respite. Somehow Jaysmith was upright and staggering up the slope, his feet slithering wildly in the crumbly shale. His idea was simply to keep the car between Davey and himself. But it was like running knee-deep in water and he had only got as far as the driver's door when the bearded man got the gun, rolled a couple of feet downhill to give himself a clear shot, and fired.

Jaysmith felt the bullet hit him in the back. Oddly its immediate effect was almost anaesthetic, but he could run no more. He fell sideways through the open door of the car across the driver's seat. His outstretched right hand rested on the handbrake. With an instant reaction that had nothing to do with thought and a strength that had nothing to do with muscles he pressed the release button.

Instantly the twenty-five hundredweight of metal began to move backwards down the steep track, dragging him with it. He concentrated so much on trailing his legs safely out of the reach of the front wheels that he scarcely registered the long high-pitched shriek which coincided with a momentary interruption of the steady acceleration. Then almost instantly there was a grinding of metal on stone, a slight change of angle and suddenly acceleration had stopped altogether.

Slowly he slid off the seat till he was lying on the ground. He looked around for Davey and found him, with a shock of terror, less than twelve inches away, his open eyes staring with uncomprehending dismay into Jaysmith's face.

'Oh you bastard,' he said. 'Oh you tricky murdering bastard.'

His body from the waist down was beneath the car. The offside rear wheel had passed completely over his body, mounting at the hip, and cracking his lower vertebrae en route. The offside front wheel had followed much the same route except that the car had come to a halt at the apex of its climb and the bearded man's body was now pinned firmly beneath it.

The pistol had fallen from his nerveless hand and lay just out of reach. Jaysmith rose, using the car door as a support. He looked down at the pistol and then kicked it down the track. The success of this movement gave him confidence to try a few staggering paces, still leaning against the car, towards the boot. What he was after were the car keys, still in the boot-lock. But when he reached the back of the car, he realized that his effort was vain. The grinding metal noise he'd heard had been the bottom of the car scraping along a broad flat stone. The onside wheel had then left the track and settled in a marshy ditch bringing the vehicle's whole weight to settle on the stone. With full strength and some assistance he might have

329

contrived to get it free, but in his present state, there was no hope.

He let his mind consider his present state for a moment and then redirected it into more profitable fields. Once he let himself be fully aware of his injuries, he guessed his body would just pack up. He concentrated instead on Naddle Foot.

He had no choice. One alternative was to go back to the road and hope that a car would stop and pick him up and take him along to the house. But cars might be few and far between on a day like this, and English drivers had become as wary as their American and European counterparts of picking up unsavoury-looking hitch-hikers. Alternatively, he could try to walk to Naddle Foot. It was less than a mile as the bullet flies, but nearer a mile and a half on the winding road, ten minutes jog for a fit man, twenty minutes walk for a strong rambler, but three quarters of an hour of agony for a man with a bullet in his back.

The agony he could bear, but the time was too long. And losing blood at the rate he must be doing, he doubted if in any case he could keep going for that time.

It came as little surprise to discover that during these moments of mental debate, his will had already decided, and his fingers were unscrewing the nuts which held the false boot bottom.

The panel slipped out easily. Lifting up the rucksack was more of a problem, but he managed it and it wasn't till he hefted it on to his shoulders and screamed aloud with the pain that he remembered he'd been shot in the back.

There was another echoing scream close to. It was composed of pain and pleading and anger and it came from Davey.

'Help me,' he pleaded. 'You murdering mother-fucking bastard, help me!'

Jaysmith stopped and looked down at the trapped man. He was pinned facing downhill and there was no way he could twist round to look up the track. Satisfied of this, Jaysmith retrieved the automatic and put it within reach of Davey's hand.

He didn't speak but stepped over the body and set off uphill. After he'd covered a slow dozen yards he heard a shot but he didn't look back.

There was pain in his back, or rather a complex scattering of pains across the whole of his body. He couldn't ignore them so he concentrated on drawing them all together till he had a network of pain so tight that no telltale pain-free area remained to occupy his mind with useless energy-sapping longing. He was climbing alongside the steep line of fencing which protected the grazing sheep from the yawning quarry. Last time he had climbed up here, a million years ago it seemed, it had taken him at most five minutes. Now he felt that hours had passed and still he seemed no nearer that jut of rock which would bring Naddle Foot distantly into view, always providing of course that the rain did not return, or the mist descend, or the blindness which seemed to be affecting his right eye pass over to his left.

No physical reason for his eye trouble, wasn't that what Jacob had said? When had he said it? Years ago, surely? But no, scarcely more than twenty minutes! It seemed impossible. No physical reason. What then? Something deep inside, some repressed distaste, self-disgust, something which slowly turned away from his vile trade, his dreadful mystery? He did not understand these things and it was too late to start wrestling with them now. A man was what he did, not what he wished he had done.

Much more significant had been Jacob's amazement, genuine amazement cutting through all his own unbalanced obsessive hatred, at the thought that Jaysmith could even contemplate a straightforward relationship with Anya. He'd been right, of course. It was a dream, a fantasy, an obsession even more lunatic than Jacob's own. And yet her father had killed; and would knowledge of that make her love him the less?

He didn't know, but he knew how much pain the knowledge would cause her. He thought of all the pain her mad father-in-law was planning to pour down on her, perhaps had already started pouring. The pain of knowledge that her father had murdered her husband; the pain of discovering that the man she thought she was falling in love with had been a hired killer sent to murder her father; and then the agony of her father's death before her eyes. That was what Jacob in his craziness planned.

And finally with the moment of her own death fast approaching, the greatest agony of all perhaps, the realization that what Jacob planned was to claim Jimmy for his own and to set about moulding him in the image of his dead father!

These thoughts had carried him high up the fellside and almost to the craggy vantage point from which he would be able to look up the valley towards Naddle Foot. He must have lost a lot of blood, his body felt drained of strength almost to the point where the pain no longer existed. That was a bonus, he must take that as a bonus. Just a

332

few yards more. Dragging in huge breaths of cold air that rasped the exposed nerves of his broken teeth, he gained the ledge.

He could have wept with disappointment. Somehow, despite his previous visit to this spot, despite his awareness of distance and angle, his mind had been deluding itself that the house would be almost at his feet, visible in every detail. His gaze strayed directly down, dragged there by the dreadful attraction of the dismal amphitheatre of barren rock. Looking backwards a little, he could see the BMW with the dead man's torso sprouting from its side.

Angrily he forced himself to look upward and forward, finding the line of St John's Beck and following its twists until, incredibly hazy, impossibly distant, he discovered the monopoly-chip red roof he had become so familiar with those few short weeks ago.

He sat down and with nerveless fingers scrabbled at the buckles and straps of his rucksack. At last he got it open and pulled out the A.R.T. Raising it to his right eye, he discovered he could see nothing at all. He'd forgotten about his eye. Had it been damaged in the fight? Gingerly he touched it. It was caked with a solid patch of blood. He began to pick at it and it came away easily. He recalled that it was in fact the cut on his temple which had released the flow.

Absurdly cheered by this discovery, he cleaned the scabbed blood away and picked up the sight once more.

Naddle Foot leapt across the valley towards him. But from a marksman's viewpoint, the magnification only revealed difficulties. It was distant and it was a side view, obliquely angled to the front of the house and partially obscured by trees. But he could see the front porch. And before it, partially masked to his view by a rowan tree at the edge of the garden, was the black Metro.

A cry of despair rose in his blood-tainted throat. But what had he expected? Jacob was in there. Perhaps even now it was too late. Perhaps whatever he did, it was too late. What had he hoped to do anyway? His will had concentrated all its force on bringing him to this point which was the closest contact he could hope to gain with the house. So, what now? What was there to do?

There was only one thing he could do, and that was give what warning he could. He must pump bullets at random through the side windows, against the porch, taking a chance on hitting those within, and hoping that Jacob would be thrown off balance when he realized what was happening. Off balance? That's where he was already! How would Jacob react when he realized that Jaysmith was out there, alive and apparently functioning normally?

There was no way of predicting, but when there was only one choice, there was no point in debating it.

He tried to force his mind to an estimate of the range and flexed his fingers in preparation for the assembly of the M21. But the sky seemed to be darkening, and Naddle Foot even through the scope was fading into the surrounding fields, and his pain-wracked, blood-starved body was being summoned to meet some last mocking challenge in that dismal amphitheatre below.

Then suddenly everything snapped back into sharp-edged focus. Out of the porchway of Naddle

Foot stumbled Anya. She fell on one knee at the foot of the two steps down to the drive, recovered and dashed towards the parked car.

After her came Jacob, moving fast for a man of his age. In his hand was Adam's Heckler Koch. He caught Anya by the car, seized her, spun her round to face him and pressed the pistol against her breast.

They were partially obscured by the rowan, its branches heavy with the blood-pearls of its fruit. But Jaysmith knew from his glimpse of Anya's ravaged face what must have taken place, what her desperate lips were saying.

Jacob had carried out his plan. Bryant was dead. What resistance could a man in a wheelchair offer? And Anya, seeing her father dead, had turned her thoughts wholly towards her living son, soon to return home from school, and set off running to try to reach him.

And now Jacob had her, was doubtless telling her the rest of his plans, describing how he proposed to bring up Jimmy, and making sure that she understood that any hope she had of rescue from Jaysmith was vain. A killer, a long-distant assassin; perhaps in his sadistic lust for revenge, Jacob was even implying that all of Jaysmith's relations with her had been a mere masquerade.

There was no time for further speculation, in any sense. He put down the ranging telescope and sent his fingers diving into the rucksack in search of the disassembled rifle. Out it came, piece by dull metallic piece. In full health and without the pressure of the most urgent need of his life, he was able to assemble it in under twenty seconds. But now his fingers were clammy with fear and fatigue, his muscles found it hard to obey the screaming commands of his will, and the familiar shapes and contours of the weapon seemed strange and awkward. All the time he desperately wanted to stop and pick up the scope and look once more to see what was happening so far below. But to look was to waste precious seconds which might be of the essence. He forced thought out of his mind and let his instincts deal with the familiar sequence. Install bolt assembly and operating rod; engage connector lock; install and engage connector assembly; install custom-made shoulder stock to main stock; install stock with butt-plate assembly; install firing mechanism; install A.R.T.; install magazine.

It was done. He hadn't bothered with the noise suppressor. What did noise mean to him any more? He raised the M21 to his shoulder and squinted down the scope, cold with fear that Jacob would already have forced Anya back into the house.

They were still in view, but just. They had reached the top of the steps with Jacob thrusting Anya ahead of him through the doorway. Obviously he didn't want to shoot her outside. His plans required that she die inside, with her clothes ripped off perhaps to give the impression of sexual assault.

And Anya was aware of this reluctance, for she was struggling still, desperate not to be pushed back into the house where she had to die.

It was tempting to take an instant snap shot at Jacob's back, but that would accomplish nothing. With Bryant dead, he was going to kill Anya now no matter what he guessed about the situation with Davey at the car. This had to be sure shot, a shot to the head, a long kill.

There was wind to take into account, gusting hard, perhaps up to forty miles an hour. And the light was failing again as this same wind brought up the next wave of cloud over the western fells. And the distance was different here from his original stand, perhaps another two hundred yards of carry.

Carefully he made his checks and adjustments. Anya and Jacob might disappear at any moment, but that must not affect his judgement any more than the growing insistence of the destructive pain in his back.

And now he was ready. All those years of pseudo-life to be reclaimed by a single shot. Anya was out of sight in the porch now and all that was visible of Jacob was a fraction of his back. Another second and he would be out of sight.

But Jaysmith waited. In him was no more fear; just a calm assurance that all he must do was wait for the moment.

And now it came.

Anya must have turned in one last desperate effort to escape and pushed Jacob away from her. He staggered back, the gun came up in his hand, he had decided the hallway would do for his killing.

Jaysmith let out a shallow breath and squeezed the trigger.

For a moment which stopped all things like a hair-crack in time, he thought that he had once more missed.

Jacob did not stagger or twist or indicate by any violence of movement that he had been hit. On the contrary he seemed to stand quite still. Then, though it was quite impossible, it seemed to Jaysmith that he saw the back of Jacob's head collapse slowly inwards, and now the man crumpled to the ground as straight as the demands of gravity on human physiognomy could take him.

It had been the perfect head-shot, the perfect long kill.

Slowly Anya advanced out of the porch. The clouds had not yet quite obscured the westering sun and she did not stop her advance till she was out of the shadow of the house and stood in the sun's sallow radiance. And now she slowly raised her face to the fellside on which Jaysmith was sitting.

He looked into that dear, dear face, quartered by the cross-hairs of his scope. Jacob had told her about him. She knew he was up there, looking down at her. Her face was grave and pensive.

She's wondering what I really am, he thought. She's wondering how all this has come to pass, how it can possibly end. She's on her own with Jimmy now. What will she do? Where will she go? Will she turn in on herself once more? Will she run like a wild fox for the cover of the high hills and crouch in her earth, fearful now beyond taming of the world of men?

Be strong, he urged her. Be curious. Stay with the police as they track me back through all those wasted years, milestoned in marble slabs, till at last they reach Harry Collins, 23, who still blushed in company; rather fancied himself as a tennis player; wrote fair Romantic poetry; enjoyed very hot curries, Hollywood musicals and historical fiction; wept with joy at his first inhalation of the sounds and the scents of the Orient; and loved a woman till her loss meant more to him than the sum total of everything else in his existence.

Find him, he urged. Find him and understand.

His strength was failing fast, draining out through the hole in his back, and the rifle was growing unbearably heavy in his hands. But still he held it steady, still he kept her fixed in his unwavering sight.

She was his last and best target. It was life and hope he was firing at her and he dared not doubt his aim.

So they remained, looking at each other across the peaceful valley, till the wind drove the curtain of cloud full across the sun and her face was shaded, and darkness drifted across his face too. The rifle slipped from his hands and fell like a challenge into the dismal amphitheatre below. A sheep grazing on the safe side of the steep fence looked up in alarm, but after a moment it decided there was nothing to fear from either the length of metal which had caused the noise or the still figure slumped on the ledge above. It began to rain. The sheep scrambled nimbly down the fellside in search of shelter.

Soon nothing stirred except the falling rain.